LANGBOURNE'S

Empire

LANGBOURNE'S Empire

ALAN P. LANDAU

In loving memory of my wife of 24 years, a beautiful lady in every way.

Karen Deborah Landau.

1964 – 2009

CHAPTER ONE

February 1894 - KoBulawayo

I T HAD BEEN eighteen hard days of riding from Mafeking, but the new settlement of KoBulawayo was finally in sight. The four BSAC soldiers, together with Morris Langbourne, sat taller in their saddles as the anticipation of the end of the long trek filled them with excitement. Even the horses seemed to know they were at the end of the journey as they had a spring in their step. For the soldiers it was a stiff whisky, some laughter surrounded by their comrades, and a hot meal that filled their thoughts. Morris, on the other hand, had his mind locked on a freshly baked short-bread slice over a hot brew of coffee and an intense planning meeting with his brother David in order to rebuild their devastated business. Morris was desperate to start trading again, so much so, that he felt as if he was about to explode with impatience and the journey's end could not have come soon enough for him. Only days earlier, Morris' 18th birthday had just slipped past, unnoticed by anyone, since dates meant nothing in the African bush. All that mattered was putting the monotonous and lengthy journey behind them so the future could be tackled in earnest.

As the five horsemen rode through the ghostly remnants of

KoBulawayo it felt very eerie. The old settlement had been abandoned some three months earlier and all that remained were the skeletons of some mud-and-pole shelters, some broken wooden boxes, and other debris that could not be used in the new settlement. The absence of any sounds of men, of wagon wheels grinding the earth, or the occasional bark of a dog was most peculiar, and it gave Morris goose bumps. It looked as if the old camp was a graveyard. Almost immediately after learning of his army's resounding defeat at the hands of the British South Africa Company, King Lobengula had burnt his village to the ground and fled the Royal Court, less than a mile to the east of the old settlement. Although the king's army, or impi, had consisted of tens of thousands of soldiers, armed with Martini-Henry rifles and countless more spearmen, the British had the Maxim machine gun, a weapon that had never been tested in Africa before, but it had proved to be extremely lethal. As a result, the 20,000-odd Matabele soldiers stood very little chance against the 700 BSAC troopers. After the confrontation had come to an end, the final count was over 4,000 Matabele dead, as against only four BSAC soldiers. News of this massive victory had travelled quickly to the Imperial nations and Matabeleland had come to be regarded as safe and well protected by the British troops. Together with rumours of large deposits of gold in the area, it was believed the country would boom, and Morris wanted to be ready to capitalise on this.

Barely five minutes later, the men entered the area of the new KoBulawayo settlement and were in awe at what they saw. It was a hive of activity: new mud and thatch buildings were being erected everywhere; men walked with a purpose in their stride, while the womenfolk in their long-flowing skirts and tight-fitting lace or floral blouses were working just as hard as, if not harder than the menfolk. Streets were now well defined; simple street signs had been erected; and wooden lamp posts on the street corners supported some rusty oil lamps on bent and crooked nails. Wagons loaded with timber, thatching grass, and mounds of earth were traversing the simple dirt roads that had been laid out in very wide, perfectly straight lines.

The contrast with what the settlement had looked like less than two months ago when the men had seen it last, was quite unbelievable, so much so that they pulled their horses to a stop and simply sat and took in the scene.

"Well, I never…!" their leader trailed off as he watched a buggy of men round a corner and head off into the distance.

"Look," said Morris, pointing to a building not far off, "some of those buildings will be permanent. They're using bricks and mortar."

"You're right," another soldier agreed. "They must be allowed to use bricks now. Where do you think they are getting them from?"

"That must be the BSAC camp over there," said another of the soldiers and pointed to the centre of the activity. "Just look at the size of the foundations: that's going to be a massive building."

"I can't believe what's going on here," their leader marvelled, "when we left, it was the remains of the Royal Village, almost a barren patch of land, covered in grey soot and ash. Come on, lads! Let's report to HQ, if we can find it, and work out where we will live."

As they parted company Morris headed for the newly laid-out Abercorn Street where he and David had been allocated a stand near the centre of the settlement to conduct their trading business. He allowed his horse to walk through the settlement slowly as he took in all the activity that was going on around him. His eyes darted everywhere, taking note of what people were doing, what they were building, and, most importantly, who was doing what. He did not miss a thing, but what caught his attention (and caused not a little amusement) was the energy and fervour with which people were attending to their tasks. It was almost as if there was a race against time, or a race against their neighbours, to finish whatever they were doing. The rebuilding of the settlement was at fever pitch.

The building of structures was taking place all over the settlement, and the allotted stands were large and well-spaced. Together with the abnormally wide streets, the settlement looked sparse and under-populated, and from wherever he sat on his horse, Morris was able to see the furthest edges of the settlement. KoBulawayo looked very empty indeed, yet people were scurrying about endlessly between the structures like so many desperate ants seeking scraps of food.

Morris turned his attention towards Abercorn Street and looked for the three wooden structures they had built before he left for Mafeking. Two of the structures were the sample room and the warehouse; the third was a small, circular, wood-and-thatch hut: Nkosazana's living quarters, situated at the rear of the stand. At the time, the sample room and warehouse were the largest structures in the settlement, but now it seemed that those residents who were using bricks were building on a much grander scale. This worried Morris, because he liked to be the biggest and the best himself. He quickly located their stand and the three buildings, and noticed that a small wall of bricks on the eastern boundary had been started by David, who was even then laying more bricks at a feverish pace. Bronzed and sinewy without a shirt, David was quite conspicuous, because he was the only European settler Morris knew in the settlement who enjoyed hard labour and getting his hands dirty. Morris could not fault David's enthusiasm and had to smile. He could not have asked for a better partner.

"David," Morris called to his brother as he stopped in front of their plot.

David had his back to Morris and spun around at the sound of the familiar voice, almost toppling off the wooden crate he was standing on. "Morris! Welcome back, so glad to see you."

"Good to be back, brother, that I can assure you. It's a very long way down there and back again."

"Tell me about it!" he laughed. "Glad to see you are safe and well." David jumped off the crate and wiped his hands on a cloth that was partially tucked into his trousers. He quickly walked up to Morris and shook his hand, obviously excited to have him back. "So much has happened in the short time you have been away," David said, "we need to catch up."

Just then Nkosazana put her head around the corner of the Sample Room, broke into a wide smile when she saw Morris, and walked out gracefully to greet him. Her perfectly white teeth glinted in the sunlight, enhanced by the smooth, coffee-coloured skin of her face. Greeting her in siNdebele, Morris dismounted.

"I see you, Nkosazana,"

"I see you, Boss," she curtsied gently, looking at the ground and avoiding eye contact out of both shyness and respect.

"Has my brother treated you well?" Morris teased.

"Yes, Boss," letting slip a little laugh and making eye contact after all, pleased that the two brothers were reunited again. "I will make you some coffee, Boss."

"Nkosazana, I would love some of your coffee," Morris enhanced the word 'your,' "but I have been thinking about your shortbread since I crossed the Shashi River last week. That is something I would very much like with the coffee."

Both Nkosazana and David chuckled." I have made fresh shortbread this very morning and I will bring you some."

"Then that is good, and I am very pleased to be back in KoBulawayo. Thank you, Nkosazana."

Nkosazana curtsied again and seemed to glide back into the Sample Room. She was so graceful in her movements and character that the boys were convinced she came from royalty, but now it was David's turn to eagerly question his brother.

"How was the journey?"

"Tough, very tough." Morris shook his head in disgust. "Damn hyena wouldn't leave us alone for days. Even a pack of wild dogs had a go at us. I'm afraid I'm not cut out for trekking through the bush for days on end."

"Go freshen up," David encouraged him. "By then the coffee

will be ready and we can catch up on our news. I dare say we have lots to talk about."

"You're not joking," Morris looked around him at all the activity. "I'll be back shortly."

*

Morris took a sip of the strong black coffee and exhaled gently, savouring both the aromas and the gentle, but instant kick from the coffee. Having washed with the aid of a bucket of water, he had changed into a fresh set of clothes. His brown slacks had been pressed with a sharp crease that ran perfectly down the length of each trouser leg, and his cream shirt, which he wore open-necked without a tie, had been neatly ironed. He also sported a pair of brown leather brogues that were so highly polished they shone in the bright, morning sunlight. Having further shaved and combed his hair, he had been transformed from bushranger to businessman in an instant

"You didn't need to dress up for me, brother," David teased.

Morris was sitting awkwardly on an upturned galvanised bucket, cup of coffee in one hand and shortbread slice in the other. He looked at David sideways and smiled. "After nearly three weeks on a horse in the bush," he replied, "I need to feel a little civilised."

"Sorry I couldn't offer you a proper chair," David retorted, and took a sip of his coffee.

Morris nodded in the direction of the wall David had started building. "What's with the bricks?" he asked. "I see we are allowed to build permanent structures now."

"Yes. The day you left KoBulawayo, I was sitting with Phil Innes and Abe Kaufman, complaining that we didn't have establishments like The Grand Hotel in Port Elizabeth where people could meet, socialise, do business, and that sort of thing. Anyhow, the conversation turned to building and brick-making, and it seemed that Phil knew all about making bricks."

"That doesn't surprise me," Morris cut in, "Phil knows just about everything about everything."

"Well, it also transpired that Abe knows everything about rocks and sand and soil, and he had already found a patch of land on the outskirts of the settlement that had perfect clay deposits for making bricks."

Morris looked up at David with a grin. "Don't tell me Abe and Phil started a brick factory?"

"No, we started a brick factory: Phil, Abe, and Langbourne Brothers," David was smiling uncontrollably.

"Langbourne Bros? Our business has a share in a brick factory?"

"Yip!" David nodded once and looked at his brother for a reaction. Morris just stared at him in disbelief.

"These bricks," he gestured with his coffee mug, spilling some of its contents on the dirt, "do they come out of our brick factory?"

"Yip," David repeated. "I set up the business and the agreements. I got permission from Major Seward and Dr Jameson, and Captain Bailey registered the business: one third to Abe, one third to Phil, and one third to our company, Langbourne Brothers. It means you and I own our third jointly."

"Yes, I know what that means, and I'm impressed. Well done, David. I certainly didn't expect you to start a brick factory. But where did you get the money to set this up?" Morris was fascinated by his brother's unexpected entrepreneurial skills.

"Well, that's the thing: it didn't cost much to set up. We had some taxes and licence registration fees to pay, but Phil used what he had in his hardware yard to make up the moulds, and Abe built the kilns by himself, and all I did was go around to some of the settlers to let them know we were open for business. We can't keep up with demand, so I stopped telling people."

"What about profits?"

"I knew you wouldn't waste any time getting to that part," David chuckled. "Profits are rather small, but turnover is high, and expenses are minimal. It's a good business to be in. We had a meeting last week, and, don't worry, I'm keeping minutes of all our meetings, just like father taught us to do, so you will be able see what we have discussed and agreed. We decided to supply each other an equal amount of bricks at no cost so Phil could build a proper hardware store, Abe could build a dress shop for Sharon, and we could build a decent store for ourselves. Once we have each used up our equal quotas we will revert to cost price, which is not much, really."

Morris pointed to the wall David had just begun. "So what are you building?"

"Ahh…," David sat up proudly and pointed to the start of his little wall. "I thought I would start at the front corner of our plot and build a wall along the side up to there," indicating a lone brick that lay on the ground, "then across to there, there, and there. That is an area the same size as both our wooden warehouse and Sample Room combined."

"No, that certainly won't do," Morris said bluntly.

"Why?" David was obviously disappointed.

"Think about it, David." Morris stood up and walked over to the brick wall, followed by David. "It's all well and good for you to build a shop out of bricks, but you could put 10 or more of these structures on our plot. Why build something the same size that we already have? No, this wall needs to start here and follow the entire boundary we have been given."

As his eyes followed his brother's along the boundary line, David was confused. "Don't be silly, brother," he said, "that's way too big! How on earth do you think you will fill a shop this size with stock? We don't have the money to fill the sample room, let alone the warehouse."

Morris was not listening to David; his mind was racing at a pace that most people would struggle to keep up with. "True," Morris mumbled as his eyes swept the boundaries of their plot, "we can't afford to stock a warehouse this big… and yet…" As if being woken abruptly from a dream, Morris suddenly glared at David, a fire burning behind his eyes. "We need to have a meeting, just you and me. I need to discuss my plans with you."

"You want an indaba?" David scowled, a little irritated that his hard work in building the wall had just been hijacked by his older brother.

"Yes. Let's go and sit under the old tree at our original camp-site. I think better when there are no interruptions around me."

In the African tradition, an indaba was a very serious meeting, usually called by the chief of the village, to discuss matters of great importance. Often it was held under a large shady tree and only selected, important people would be invited to attend. Before the Langbourne boys were forced to move their business to the new settlement, they used to sit under a large tree just outside their sample room on two small rocks they had placed there. It had become the focal point of their camp and a place where they ate their meals, drank their coffee, and discussed all manner of business and personal issues. There was no doubt the tree had become the location of their most valuable indabas.

CHAPTER TWO
The Indaba

AFTER WALKING THROUGH the derelict and abandoned remains of what was once a thriving settlement, both Morris and David felt uneasy at the strange quietness that had settled on the area. In the few short months since the settlement had been hastily relocated to the site of the destroyed Royal Village, the vegetation had begun to reclaim what was rightfully its own domain. Grasses and small shrubs were already invading what were once paths and walkways, and the wildlife was beginning to move back into the area. Three small impala were grazing on the site of the old BSAC officers' mess, their flanks twitching sporadically to keep flies and other pests at bay, while four female kudu antelope stood alert on the old main road, cautiously watching the Langbournes' approach.

It was Morris who stated the obvious. "It didn't take long for nature to take over, did it?"

"Well we have had a lot of rain," David replied, "but I'm surprised at all the wildlife that's moved in already. I should have brought my rifle."

Morris looked around nervously for the first time. "Did you bring your revolver with you?"

"Yes, but I would be much happier with a rifle. A revolver won't be much use against a charging buffalo."

"Let's go back," Morris suggested.

"No, we'll be fine, and we are almost there." Since David sounded so confident, Morris started to relax. The old rocks that had been placed under the tree to be used as seats appeared to have waited an eternity for the boys' return. Nothing had moved at all, and the grass, having grown taller beyond the drip-line of the tree's outer branches, made the venue for their meeting even more secluded from the untamed bush beyond.

It was a perfect spot for an indaba.

After the two lads sat down on their respective rocks, Morris opened a tin of shortbread and offered a piece to his brother, before selecting a slice for himself. Wasting no further time, he bit into it, delighting in its salty-sweet taste, while David opened a kidney-shaped canister of coffee that had lost most of its heat, and poured the contents equally into two chipped enamel mugs.

Struggling to contain his curiosity, David asked, "So tell me, what happened in Mafeking?"

"I went to see Julian Weil and told him up front that, although we wanted to buy another six wagons of stock, we had lost just about everything in the Matabele rebellion and so we now had no money to pay for it. I think he was shocked – not just at how we had survived, especially you, David, but also at my boldness in asking for so much stock without so much as a down payment."

"What did he say?"

"He said I had some guts to ask for such a thing, using a Yiddish word I had never heard of before: 'chutzpah' - it means 'guts,' or 'gall,' apparently."

"Julian Weil is Jewish? I would never have guessed! Do you think he worked out we were Jews?"

"I don't know, but it seems being Jewish in Africa is not looked down upon as it was in Poland, so don't worry too much about it. Can you believe that he's related to Sharon Kaufman?"

"Abe and Sharon are related to Weil? Well, what do you know?"

"Anyway, Julian seems to have a soft spot for us and believes we will make a lot of money for him, so he agreed to let us have six wagons full of stock, but without a discount this time. We've had to agree to the normal wholesale price, with one year to pay him back, paying a portion each month."

"That's a good deal, Morris, well done."

Morris winked at his brother with a wry smile "Oh, it gets better. After we had spent about an hour negotiating this lot, I told him the deal was useless unless we had wagons, so I asked him to put pressure on Mr Gerran at Gerran's Coach Builders to give us the same terms."

David frowned. "He obviously did as you asked, because the wagons are on their way."

"Yes, he certainly wants the business. I was forced to agree to some interest charges from Gerran, but they were acceptable. It gets even better, though. When I walked past a builders' supply yard I noticed a pile of brand-new roof sheeting, and in the back of the yard, buried under a heap of scrap, I found a rusty old wagon that belonged to the owner, so I negotiated a really great price for the roof sheeting and for its delivery to KoBulawayo. I convinced the owner to fix up his rusty old wagon, load it, and send it up here with Daluxolo, and we only have to pay for it when Daluxolo returns the wagon to him. It will take at least six months for the wagon to get back there, so we have bought some much needed time."

David was amazed. "How did you manage to wrangle that?"

"Oh, he was easy to convince," said Morris airily. "I also ran into Mr Savage at The Standard Bank. I hadn't intended to see him but he spotted me in the banking hall and invited me into his office. Like everyone in Mafeking, he had heard about the rebellion and wanted to find out how we fared. I think he already knew what had happened to us and he tried to push me around a bit; he made it clear he would not loan us any money, and in his sarcastic way tried to make a fool of me."

"Typical. I would have expected that of him," David shook his head in disgust. "Bastard!"

"Mind your language, David," Morris scolded. "Anyhow, I just happened to notice he had made an error of addition on some deposits he had in a ledger on his desk, and they were deposits for Weil. The error was not much, but it was in favour of the bank, so I casually pointed out the error to him, and suggested that I would view that error as either stupidity on his behalf, or a deliberate attempt to defraud Mr Weil."

David slapped his thigh in delight. "Ha-Ha! Brilliant work, Brother. How did he respond to that?"

"Oh, he couldn't answer that one, so I simply walked out and let him stew over what I had pointed out. One thing I can assure you is, while he's in charge of the bank down there, we will never get a loan. As a result, our recovery is going to be slow. The good news is that, in seven to eight years from now, all going well, I have calculated that we will be in a much better position."

David allowed his brother's prediction to sink in before speaking again. "I don't mind waiting that long," he said. "I'm just worried that we may not be able to support the family back in Ireland until then. And the main reason for coming to Africa in the first place was to make money for them."

"That's true…" Morris stared at the ground and frowned, before suddenly looking up at David again. "I have a plan, though, and I can get us back to where we were much quicker than that, but we will have to take some very big risks. Not only that, but we'll have to work harder than ever before, while you, sad to tell, are going to have to carry the lion's share."

David's astonishment was obvious. "I don't know what you are going to say next, Morris, but I'll bet it will be outrageous. Go on, I'm listening," he shifted on his rock in anticipation.

"For starters, I don't trust this country. Father had a strange sense that Poland was on the brink of war, and he was right. Thank the good Lord he left for Ireland and took us with him. Then I had an inkling this country was on the brink of war, and – although I had nothing to go on except my gut feel – I was right. Perhaps I have inherited father's ability to foresee a war."

Morris looked up into the leaves of the shady tree, lowered his voice dramatically, and leaned closer to David, "I feel there will be another war in this country," he murmured, "I don't know why and I can't explain it, but I just feel it. You know that saying; 'Don't put all your eggs in one basket'? Well, never again do I want to put all we have into one basket. The BSAC is very powerful, masters at warcraft and well trained, and seem to be in total control, but there could be another rebellion for all we know, and then we won't be as lucky. Remember: King Lobengula is on the run and hasn't been captured yet."

"Oh," said David, with a dismissive gesture, "there's a rumour that he died of smallpox up near the Zambezi River."

"Rumour?" Morris cocked an eyebrow.

"Yes, just a rumour."

"As I was saying," Morris persisted, "if the Matabele nation rises up again, it will be a disaster, and I don't want to be caught short a second time: that will be financial suicide for us. It might be the death of us, too. What's more, the relationship between the Boers and the British is tense. Things could erupt in the south as well. They've already had a vicious war between themselves in the good old days."

"So, what are your thoughts?"

Morris smiled and shifted on his rock. He picked up his enamel cup, drank the last of the cold coffee, and threw the coarse grounds into the grass beside him. Then he began to set out his plans.

David was fascinated by the way Morris thought: all that his brother spoke about was amazing; not just what he planned, but the way he did it; the way he projected the direct result of a decision, and how that result would affect the outcome of an anticipated event. He had no control over acts of war, an act of God, or poor governance, but Morris considered all of these events and prepared for them in his planning. David deeply admired his older brother's business mind and ability to see an opportunity, to seize it, and capitalise on it.

Morris' plan was elaborate, and it required that David succeed in each stage he undertook. Although David's brick factory had changed some of his brother's plans, Morris commended his younger brother once again for his foresight and initiative. As from that very afternoon, Morris would convince Phil and Abe that time was not on their side and every brick that was produced would be allocated to Langbourne Brothers so they could build their store as soon as possible. Morris had the unusual ability of persuading people to his way of thinking, and even David felt he should have no problem with this task.

The new Langbourne Brothers' building would be constructed in earnest, making full use of every inch of their available land by erecting the exterior walls along their boundary lines, so they would end up with a massive structure. They would work around the existing wood pole and mud structures that would ultimately be surrounded by the new brick exterior walls, because the six wagons of stock would be arriving well before they could complete the building. They would continue to trade as usual from the existing wooden structures while construction went on around them, and when the wagons arrived with Daluxolo, they would stock the wooden storerooms as usual. Morris would then set up the empty wagons and accompanying oxen for wagon trading, just as he had done before. Once a sound roof had been completed on the new building the wooden buildings, including Nkosazana's round hut, would be demolished.

According to their calculations their two younger brothers, Louis and Harry, should be on their way already at this time from Ireland to Port Elizabeth. Once they had arrived, it would take about a month or so for a telegraph message to reach them in KoBulawayo. David would then head down to Mafeking and catch a train to Port Elizabeth to collect his siblings.

"Now this is where it gets interesting," Morris paused to ensure he had David's full attention. "By the time you get to Mafeking, I have worked out that we will need to restock our goods, so I will require you to drop in on Weil and place a new order. You will also have to buy more wagons. By then, however, we should have turned over enough in sales to keep Weil and Gerran happy and allow them to confidently extend the credit they have given us. It's important that you convince them to keep trading with us."

David nodded in agreement. "I think I can manage that."

"Once you have placed the order, just like you did the last time, head on down to Port Elizabeth and meet Louis and Harry. From there you must take them to East London."

"East London?" David's voice rose an octave in surprise. "Where's that?"

"It's a town not far from Port Elizabeth, just a bit to the north. You can get there by rail, and I think it's only a day or two's journey."

"Alright," David calmed down slightly, but he was never too sure what surprise Morris would have in store for him next.

"I need you to rent a warehouse there, as close to the harbour as possible, and open a branch of Langbourne Brothers, which must be based in that warehouse. Next register the branch with whatever authority handles business registrations, and open an account with The Standard Bank." Morris paused once again looking at David's facial expressions to make sure his brother understood. When David said nothing he continued, "Most importantly, set up a telegraph address, because we will need to communicate from Mafeking. This is vital. Port Elizabeth receives its ships from England after they have stopped in Cape Town. By then their cargo-holds are almost empty. But East London seems to be the first stop for ships from the Far East, the Spice Islands, and all those exotic countries before they get to Port Elizabeth or Cape Town. I want to have first pickings of whatever comes in on those trade ships."

"Okay, stop there for a minute," David put his palm in the air, "are you saying you want me to relocate to East London with the boys?"

"No," said Morris, "I just want Louis to run the East London business. You will have to show him how we do business."

"Morris, he's only thirteen or fourteen!" David objected.

"I know, but he's tall and can pass for much older. Also he would have had his Bar Mitzvah, so, in the Jewish tradition, he'd be a man by then. It's Harry I worry about."

This remark further troubled David, but he continued. "What do I do with Harry?"

"Bring him back here. I want to take him under my wing and teach him how to run the business in KoBulawayo. You will take Louis under your wing; he will be your responsibility. While you teach Louis in East London, I'd like you to show Harry at the same time. See if you can arrange all of this in one month."

"One month!" David exclaimed. "Are you crazy? I can't open a business, find premises, teach a thirteen-year-old how to run a business, and then get back here in one month."

"No, no," Morris calmed him down, "I meant for you to take a month in East London, excluding the travelling time."

"Oh, well I'm glad we cleared that up," David sighed sarcastically, looking up at the clouds for some invisible support.

"I told you it wouldn't be easy."

David looked his brother in the eye and realised he was being serious. "Alright, I'll do it," he responded, not knowing exactly how though.

"Good," Morris shifted on the hard rock, satisfied with David's response. "When you leave Louis in East London, make your way to Mafeking and load the wagons as you did before, getting Harry to help you. Engage Daluxolo and his men again, send them on their way with the wagons, and then get back to KoBulawayo with Harry as quickly as possible."

"Morris," David slowly stood up and stepped over to the tree trunk, turned his back to it and leant against the rough bark, frowning intently. "Let me get this straight: within this single year, you want to build a monstrous warehouse out of bricks, open a branch of Langbourne Brothers in East London, a town I had never heard of until a few minutes ago, and cut Weil out of the equation? We need Weil and his credit; we have no money to make our own cash purchases in East London. Are you aware of that?"

"Yes, I am fully aware of that, Brother. If business is the same as it was before the rebellion – and I believe it will be better now, mind you – then I have worked out the finances and the timing and it can be done. I have even factored in the purchase of another horse for Harry, since he will need one to get from Mafeking to KoBulawayo. And you are correct, we can't survive without Weil, so we will continue to use him, but he likes to add on his profit margin, which is quite healthy I might add, and he charges interest. Ultimately, we will have to become self-sufficient, which is more profitable for us, obviously, but remember, we mustn't put all our eggs in one basket, so we will become our own supplier and we will use Weil, only to a lesser degree."

David shook his head slowly and smiled, he had not considered the horse and saddle. "Trust you to think of that," he muttered. "And what about Louis? Are we going to give him a stipend for food and other expenses?"

"No, we can't afford that, but you will need to leave him some money to purchase his initial stock, of course. The warehouse in East London must not just be a warehouse to supply our business in KoBulawayo, Louis must actively trade from there as well. You will have to teach him how to use our black-rhino code and how to mark up the goods. The profit from his trading is what he can draw a stipend from. And you need to teach him how to keep a set of books, and tell him I will be checking them so he had better not make any mistakes!"

David laughed, because he knew how pedantic Morris was when it came to numbers and money. "That will keep him on his toes, if he doesn't become totally petrified! Alright, tell me then, how we are going to afford to build a brick warehouse? We are not professional builders; we don't really know how to lay bricks or how to make mortar; we will require building material and tools, and certainly we will need labour. It's one thing for you and me to build a wooden shack six yards by six yards with wire and string, but for a brick building a builder who knows what he is doing would be essential, and that will not be cheap."

"Good point, David," Morris agreed, "you are right, of course, and I want the building completed within a year. We will engage a builder, I'm sure there is one in the settlement. We will pay a deposit only and pretend we have enough money to pay him."

"Pretend?" David was horrified. "You can't do that!"

"Well, I don't mean 'pretend,' we simply won't tell him we can't afford him. Then, just before the building is complete, when we need to pay him out, we will sell the brick factory."

David looked shocked. "But it's a profitable business! And it was my idea," he pleaded.

"A fantastic idea, yes, I agree, and I am very impressed with what you did. But just like our cigarette business in Port Elizabeth, we only had it a year or so, it was profitable and we sold it," he countered, "bricks are not our main business, and we need the money. Your business will be worth a lot a year from now, make no error, so we need to sell our one third share and in return we get a beautiful building from which to operate our main business, which is trading – as both wholesalers and wagon traders. And the builder will get every last penny we agree on; I will make sure of that."

David sighed and weighed this all up. As usual, he could

not find fault with his brother's ideas and plans. "Alright, then, I agree," he said, reluctantly.

Morris smiled for the first time in a while. "Excellent. As I said at the start, it's going to be really hard work, and you will have to bear the brunt of it. I am sending you to Port Elizabeth and East London with the brothers because, honestly, I don't have the patience to teach them. We will end up yelling and shouting at each other and then they will be on the next ship back to Ireland."

"That's an understatement!" David laughed. "You don't tolerate much at the best of times."

"Well at least I recognise that," Morris defended himself, "but you are the diplomatic one in the family, and without you and your level head we would be lost."

David was touched to hear his brother admit to one of his failings in life. "I never expected to hear you say that, Morris."

"Well, it's true, and we work well together. If you can do what I have asked of you, David, we will soon be richer than our wildest dreams. You watch and see."

David stared at his brother in some disbelief at what had been discussed that morning. It was clear that their lives were about to round a bend in the slow, dark, winding river of life, and face a turbulent set of rapids. The question remained as to whether they could negotiate successfully the sharp rocks, whirlpools, and eddies that lay in their way.

David pushed himself off the trunk of the tree and sat down on his rock again. "Okay, Brother, let's do it," he said calmly.

Morris smiled. He knew he could depend on his brother to do the impossible. "In that case," he declared, "I pronounce the indaba finished."

CHAPTER THREE
Building

"SLOW DOWN, SENHOR Langbourne, slow down," the Portuguese man wailed at David. "You are too much in a hurry; the bricks are not straight."

David was pressing a brick into a rough mix of wet mortar, made from sand and clay, which was gently oozing off the wall and onto the dirt floor at his feet. He looked at the old man with a confused look on his face before stepping back and casting his eye over his handiwork. A number of the bricks jutted slightly out of alignment.

"Well, the bricks are not perfectly straight, I must agree, but the wall is straight, don't you think?"

"My father would break this down and rebuild it from the start, Senhor. One must work carefully, with pride in what is done."

"My father would probably have done the same," David confessed, "and would have given me a sound thrashing, too; but, Senhor Da Santos, we don't have enough time to work carefully and slowly."

Manuel Dos Santos was in his late 30s, with a rugged face that made him look older than he was. He had jet-black hair on his head, his arms, and his chest. He could have had a very full beard, but he shaved every day, and – although it was only eleven o'clock in the morning – he already sported a five-o'clock shadow on his chin and cheeks. He had come from a family of builders and had lived in the Portuguese East Africa territory for many years. Having become disillusioned with a lack of work, however, he had set off to the new country of Matabeleland, where he had heard there was a lot of opportunity for builders like himself. Contracted by Morris to oversee the building of the new Langbourne Brothers warehouse, he was not having an easy ride with David, who – like an over-fuelled steam engine – continued to push his team of six Ndebele employees to the limit, while throwing his entire being into the construction work, albeit a little haphazardly.

Morris spent his days selling off what little stock they had left in the temporary wooden sample room (which was slowly becoming swallowed up by the construction of the brick walls of the new building), and making sure bricks were constantly being delivered from their brick factory on the east side of the settlement. With Senhor Da Santos' guidance and instruction, David had begun to master the bricklaying art, but he was by no means neat and tidy.

Manuel threw his hands up in despair. "I no take responsibility if your building falls down, you unnerstand?"

"I understand, Senhor, and I accept that, but I am sure it will stand for a hundred years."

"A hundred years?" He turned to walk off and started muttering in his home language, then swung back to face his employer, "This building no last just one year, I tell you."

"What's the matter?" Morris asked as he rounded the side of the sample room.

"Your brother, he is a very bad builder. Your building will fall down in one year. I no take the responsibility."

Morris looked at David's workmanship and had to agree it was a bit tacky. Then he looked at David, who simply cocked an eyebrow in reply and shrugged. A slight smile caught the corners of Morris' mouth. "I tell you what, Senhor Dos Santos, if the building falls down, I will not blame you, but my brother will take the blame entirely. I will also sack him from the business. Please come with me, I have a very important job I would like you to do, and only you." Morris took the burly builder by the shoulder and led him away from David. "The front of the building, what do you call it?"

"The façade." His shoulders slumped as he walked away with his short, young client.

"Yes, that's right, the façade. It is the most important part of the building, the only part that the public will see."

David smiled as the voices trailed off around the corner of the sample room. He knew his workmanship was pathetic at best, so if Morris could convince Dos Santos to build the façade they would have something most respectable to front their building. The problem was simply that they were short of money and David's labour was free, so he and Morris had agreed to use their personal labour wherever they could to get the bulk of the bricklaying done in places that would not be visible to the general public.

Three days later, Dos Santos was working uninterrupted on the façade of their new building, and enjoying the free reign that Morris had given him to add a bit of his own imagination and character. The builder wasted no time in attending to his master-piece. Meanwhile, David had trained up two Ndebele men to lay bricks and gave them each a team to work with, while he carried on with his own team. Then he turned it into a competition to determine which team would lay the most bricks in a day, and before long the building was rapidly taking shape. After two months, all the bricklayers were standing on hastily made ladders along their allocated length of wall. As the walls increased in height, the standard of bricklaying was noticeably improving.

At around mid-morning on the first Thursday of April, when all the men were hard at work, a BSAC soldier sauntered up to the construction site and called out for Morris, who quickly went out into the street to greet him.

"Sorry to trouble you, Mr Langbourne, Sergeant Stanley is my name."

"Pleased to meet you, sir. How may I be of help?"

"I have just arrived from Mafeking on the postal run. When I passed through the old settlement, I came across a Xhosa man standing under a tree where your old shop used to be. I assumed he might belong to you."

"Oh, fantastic!" Morris couldn't contain his excitement, "that must be Daluxolo, right on schedule. Thank you Sergeant Stanley."

"Right-oh, glad I could be of some assistance. I have a feeling he has been standing under that tree since yesterday, so you might want to shake a leg and see what he wants before he disappears."

"Since yesterday? Oh dear, of course he has no idea where we have moved to. Many thanks. I'll get right to it."

Morris ran back into the construction site and told David that Daluxolo had arrived. In trepidation they both dropped what they were doing and hurried off in the direction of the Indaba tree, David throwing on his shirt as they ran.

"Do you think he has all the wagons with him?" David asked his brother nervously.

"I hope so, David, I really hope so."

As they approached the old tree, they saw Daluxolo standing under it, patiently waiting for them, draped in his traditional Xhosa robe with bright colours woven into the edges. He broke into a very broad smile when he saw the two young lads jogging towards him, which instantly calmed the nerves of the two brothers.

"I see you, Daluxolo," David greeted in Xhosa when he drew close. "Please tell me you are well and unharmed."

"I see you, Boss David," the muscled man's eyes shone in delight at this warm and genuine welcome. "I see you also, Boss Morris. My heart sings with happiness to see you."

"Our hearts are happy also, knowing you are well." Morris beamed and locked forearms in a traditional embrace. "The journey, are the men safe, too?"

"Yes, we are all together and happy."

With respect for the traditional ways of the African people, Morris and David did not dive straight into business and ask about their wagons and goods, but took time to discuss each other's health, their families and home life, even their cattle. David enjoyed this custom and relished in the news from his friend, but Morris, being more forthright, had to control his impatience in wanting to know about their wagons and valuable stock.

"Daluxolo," David continued, "when you left KoBulawayo, you told us that on your return you wished to take Nkosazana as your wife and wished to discuss this with your father. How were your discussions with him?"

"My father and I spoke well. My father now believes it is time for me to marry, and he has discussed the matter with the father of Nkosazana. I was blessed by the Great One and the two fathers agreed that Nkosazana should be my wife."

"This is good news for us, Daluxolo," David laughed, "then your bride awaits you in the new village. As you can see, the old village has moved."

"I can see," he looked curiously around at the abandoned settlement, "and I am told it has moved to the village of King Lobengula, but I cannot enter the royal village without an invitation from the king and so I thought it would be wise for me to wait for you here."

Morris shook his head slowly, holding his chin in sadness. "The king has run away, Daluxolo. There was a terrible battle near here and the king burnt his village down, so people say that he has died, and the white people live there now. A formal invitation is not necessary, because you are most welcome."

The fact that the men did not need to discuss the wagons, but every subject under the sun, indicated to the boys that everything was well. Finally, though, Morris could not contain himself any longer and turned the discussion to business.

"Daluxolo, is your news about the wagons good? Did you not have any problems along the way?"

"We had some problems, Boss Morris," the Xhosa man looked at the ground, avoiding eye contact.

"What problems?" There was some anxiety in Morris' voice.

"It is my hope that you and your men came to no harm with these troubles," David quickly stepped in before Morris erupted needlessly.

"We were not hurt, Boss David," Daluxolo smiled and looked him in the eye, "one wheel broke on one wagon. It was smashed and could not be fixed so we used a spare one."

"Were the goods damaged?" Morris asked sympathetically. He had realised what David was doing, so controlled himself.

"The goods are well and happy," Daluxolo looked pleased with himself. "Then the wood pole that joins the wagon to the oxen broke in half."

"The disselboom? Oh, my word!" David exclaimed in surprise. The disselboom was the heavy wooden shaft that connected the wagon to the team of oxen. It would have meant that the men needed to find a tree with a trunk roughly the same length and thickness, and most importantly, as straight as possible. Then, with what tools they had, they would have had to fell the tree and fashion each end to accommodate the team of oxen and the wagon. It would have been a massive job.

"We cut a new one from a tree nearby," said Daluxolo. "It delayed us for two days, but it is working fine now."

"Well done," Morris congratulated Daluxolo, "that would have been very difficult. I am very proud of you."

"Thank you, Boss Morris," Daluxolo said, beaming proudly.

"We need to bring the wagons to the place of business in the new village." Morris turned to his brother, "David, would you mind going to the wagons with Daluxolo and leading them into KoBulawayo?"

David smiled. "My pleasure, brother."

"Good show, thank you. I will go back and prepare for your arrival. I suggest we out-span the oxen at the front of the building and manhandle the goods directly into the two sheds. Meanwhile, make sure that Daluxolo walks ahead of the caravan so that he can give Nkosazana a surprise."

David winked with a mischievous grin. "Will do," he said.

*

The activity and energy emanating from the Langbourne Brothers premises over the previous two months had been relentless and seemingly unending. David was like an African Killer Bee, buzzing around the site, laying bricks, mixing mortar, checking on his teams, correcting mistakes, offering encouraging advice, and lavishly praising good work. He threw himself into the hard labour, carrying bricks with his team, shovelling sand, moving earth, and even joining his team in song when all was moving along in harmony. These were his favourite times. When the team broke into song, the mood leapt and productivity increased immeasurably. The harmonies and simple, circular beats filled David's soul with joy, and even Morris, from inside their wooden sample room, would walk outside to marvel at the camaraderie of these people, and to immerse himself in the beat of Africa.

Morris had his days cut out for him, too. He kept the shop running, selling goods whenever he could, running down to their brick fields, checking on the books, collecting whatever cash or cheques had been paid over the previous day, and getting Abe and Phil to put their signature of agreement against their takings. He was pedantic about ensuring there was never a doubt or a finger pointed at him when dealing with money. He kept the books of accounts of both Langbourne Brothers and Bulawayo Bricks between serving customers, as well as tending to the constant, and sometimes petty, demands of Senhor De Santos, who refused to deal with David. When his tasks were done and there was no one in the shop, Morris would scour the settlement for second-hand planks and wooden sheets that they could fashion into tables, counter tops, and shelves upon which to display their wares.

Now that Daluxolo had arrived, the activity had moved to a new level, a level that neither the boys could have imagined possible, and certainly a level that left Senhor De Santos ending his day in a state of nervous fear that he would be called upon to either keep up with them or be given additional tasks beyond designing and building a fancy façade, a project he hoped would be the envy of other shop owners who would then contract him to build their bigger and better shop fronts and give him a name that would be discussed for centuries to come.

It had been one week since Daluxolo and his men had arrived in the settlement of KoBulawayo and unloaded all the goods under canvas sheets within the walls of the growing building. Morris had used two of the team to help him unload some stock into the old wooden sample room, while David had asked Daluxolo and his remaining men to help him with the laying of bricks, which they readily had agreed to do. Although happy to help wherever possible, they set up camp just outside the settlement limits, as they did not wish to sleep within the walls of a building with corners, a superstition among the locals, who believed that evil spirits lived in the corners of a room. Even Nkosazana was beginning to get nervous as the rectangular building began to take shape around her traditional dwelling: a circular wood-pole structure with mud walls and a sloping, thatched roof. With the help of Daluxolo and some of his men, she had insisted on having a new dwelling built where the other amaXhosa women had their living quarters.

It had been a particularly tough day for the boys and their entire team. Fuming at some comment that Morris had made, Senhor Da Santos had just left the site. A plank had fallen on Morris' foot, which had caused him much agony, and David had received some mortar in his eye that gave him problems all day. Nkosazana had made the boys a meal of maize porridge with some boiled meat and a thin gravy and had put it in the sample room, as usual, before calling them to dinner and leaving for her hut. The announcement of dinner, which was always just before the sun went down, signalled to the boys that the day was over.

The brothers sauntered into the sample room and, picking up their enamel bowls of food, walked to the rear of the room, before flopping heavily onto their blankets. They slept on the floor at the back of the warehouse, which – for two young lads with little else to their names – was perfectly adequate, as far as they were concerned.

Morris sighed as he carefully put his bowl down on the floor beside him to light a candle on a makeshift shelf near the side of his pillow. "I can't say I had a particularly good day today, David,"

"It must be a full moon or something," David replied, stretching out along his bed, and also putting his bowl of food down by his side, "everybody seemed to be either clumsy or irritable. I'm glad to put this day behind me, brother."

"Well, the good news, if you can call it good news, is that Bulawayo Bricks is far more profitable than Langbourne Brothers and that includes all the production we are taking at no cost."

David grunted as Morris leant back against the wall and stretched out his legs on his bedding. He picked up a cashbook, opened it, and thumbed his way to the page with the last entry.

"Abe got a big order today," he continued, "Seems like the BSAC want to build some administrative block down on Selbourne Avenue. This will increase the value of Bulawayo Bricks when we come to sell it. I'm now in a position to recruit traders for the wagon-trading side of our business: the sample room is stocked, all the stock is coded, the storeroom is bursting at the seams, and all six of our wagons are empty. Three of our previous traders are anxious to get started, so I just have to recruit three more, which shouldn't be difficult. I'll start tomorrow."

He put the cashbook down in his lap and stared at the candle flame that was dancing joyously in the soft breeze that crept in through the gaps in the mud-and-pole walls. As his eyelids slowly drooped, he allowed himself to enjoy the evening peace. He was about to say how tired he felt when his mind started to think about something else, he wasn't sure what, and it seemed stupid anyhow.

Forcing his eyes open once more, he looked at the candle, but it was no longer there, having transformed itself into a molten mess of wax on the makeshift shelf. Although the flame had been extinguished, light was pouring into the room through every crack and crevice in the walls. His neck ached and his bladder was at bursting point. Without moving his head, which hurt his neck even more, he cast his eyes around the room, finally looking at his brother who appeared to be sleeping in the same position as when he had first lain down.

"David," he mumbled, "wake up."

David stirred and rolled his head to the side. "What?" he grumbled.

"We fell asleep, it's morning already."

"It can't be," his brother complained, "I haven't eaten my dinner yet."

"Open your eyes, David. There's daylight out there."

David opened one eye, then the other, and stared at the walls around him, then gradually heaved himself into a sitting position. He stared at his bowl of cold food for ages, trying to comprehend where the night had gone. He looked up at Morris, who was now sitting and moving his head up and down, and side to side, trying to loosen up the stiffness that had set in after a long sleep in a sitting position.

"Surely it's not the next day," David mumbled and carefully picked up his bowl of food. His hands felt weak and he nearly dropped the cold dinner on the floor. "You had better eat your food before Nkosazana comes in." David took a spoonful of the food, and discovered that it tasted exceptionally good.

"I'm bursting, I need a toilet first," Morris stood up very

slowly and stretched his aching muscles. "It's going to be a tough day, I can feel it already."

"Heaven forbid," David mumbled through a mouthful of food. "Hurry up, I need the toilet, too."

Despite ending each day utterly exhausted, both mentally and physically, they never had a night like that again. Morris' workload increased ten-fold as he set about getting the wagon-trading business up and running once more. He first located three Greek traders who they had used before the rebellion, and they were quick to sign on, using the same agreements that David had put in place with them before. All they had to do was choose a wagon, a team of oxen, and then decide what stock they wanted and how much. Morris kept a record of the goods they selected to sell from the wagons in remote settlements around Matabeleland and Mashonaland to the north.

Once they were organised (having had the first pick of the storeroom) and were on their way, Morris put word out that he had capacity for three more traders. Not surprisingly, he recruited this number within the hour, turning seven other hopeful men away in the hour after that, although he made sure that he kept their details for the next six wagons they would bring up from Mafeking.

Happy and confident with his choice of traders, and the fact that they had depleted his warehouse by well over half its stock, he was walking out into the sunlight to ask Nkosazana to make him some coffee when he saw David jogging towards him from the direction of the BSAC camp. He stopped to watch him draw nearer and noticed he was grinning from ear to ear.

"What gives?" Morris asked his brother, unable to contain a smile in return.

"Morris, I want to show you something; something incredible! You are not going to believe this. Come with me now, right now!" he urged excitedly.

"What? Tell me first," Morris objected, but automatically

joined his brother as they briskly walked down to the middle of the settlement.

"This, oh brother of mine, is going to make you the happiest man in town, and of that I am certain!" David laughed. "I can't wait to see your face when you see this."

"What? Don't be such a rascal!" Morris chuckled, enjoying the break from business and building that this little interlude with David was bringing.

David led him into the BSAC camp, where civilian men walked about with a distinct purpose in shirtsleeves and ties and often a shabby felt hat that did not fit the fashion of the day. Morris had not been in the perimeter of the camp for some months, and noticed that there were a few more canvas tents that had been erected since his last visit. David walked up to one tent and stopped. Conical in shape with a round base of no more than three yards, it ended in a single point at the top, which was only slightly higher than a tall man's head.

"This is it!" David exclaimed excitedly, pointing at the dull-grey, bell tent.

"What about it?" Morris was obviously disappointed.

"This, my brother, is either going to make you the happiest man in KoBulawayo, or the happiest man in the entire kingdom of Matabeleland."

"It's nothing but a tent." Morris sounded annoyed, but there was a look of expectant excitement on his face.

"Indeed, nothing but a tent. However…," David put his hands on his hips and drew himself up to his full height, "this is the back of the tent; the front is what will make you exceptionally happy."

Morris looked at his brother in confusion, but cocked his eyebrow as if to say he was game to play along with this charade. He turned and walked cautiously around to the front of the tent, his head pushed forward as he tried to look around the bend ahead of his body. As he rounded the side he noticed the entrance: a set of two flaps that had been drawn back, exposing a dull interior with nothing but a metal trunk placed on the earthen floor in the centre. Sitting outside on a simple wooden chair to one side of a flap was a gentleman, apparently sunning himself as if he had nothing better to do. He wore a white, long-sleeved shirt with the cuffs rolled up his forearms and beige, cotton slacks. The man, who slouched in the chair with his hands in his pockets, looked at Morris with curiosity. Morris looked back at him with confusion written all over his face, and then looked back at the metal trunk inside the tent.

Suddenly, he saw a sign that had been hung roughly above the apex of the entrance. There were only two words written on the wooden sign, in a stylish, black-painted calligraphy. Morris stared at it in silence for a moment, then looked back at the strange gentleman sitting on his chair, who had not taken his eyes off Morris the whole time. Morris began to smile. He looked over at his brother, who was still standing where he had left him, and started at first to chuckle, and then allowed the laughter to flow. David joined in, laughing more with his brother than out of his reaction to the sign above the door, which simply read "STANDARD BANK".

Starting to feel that Morris was laughing at him, the thin man stood up from his chair and folded his arms. "Would you care to explain yourself, young man?" he demanded indignantly.

"My apologies," Morris spluttered between bouts of laughter. Struggling to compose himself, he quickly tried to tuck the excess folds of his shirt into his trousers as he strode over to the thin man, before being joined by David. "Forgive me," Morris beamed, extending his hand, "I am just so delighted to see that the Standard Bank has opened in KoBulawayo. My name is Morris Langbourne; please allow me also to introduce you to my brother, David Langbourne."

Although somewhat cautious of Morris' sudden composure, the thin man extended his hand and introduced himself as Mr Wilfred Honey, manager of the KoBulawayo branch of The Standard Bank.

"Mr Honey," Morris confided, "You have no idea how pleased we are to see you and your bank here. We are traders and depend on the bank's facilities, yet we are beholden to the Mafeking branch. In point of fact, it is more than that: we are held hostage by our inability to deal with the branch."

The newly arrived manager remained cautiously formal. "I know of the acute shortage on cash out here," he replied, "I am well briefed on the situation. I am nevertheless sure that we, as a bank of good reputation, will be able to assist you in a number of ways now that we are established in KoBulawayo."

"Please accept my apologies for my unusual reaction at seeing your tent, sir, but it was one of pure delight. Forgive me, but do you know of the Mafeking manager, Mr Savage?" Morris ventured cautiously.

"Not personally, no, but he has a reputation of running a fine agency," he nodded.

This was not exactly the answer Morris wanted to hear and he stole a glance at David. "We... umm... did not get off on the right foot, unfortunately. It seems he has difficulty in dealing with, shall we say, a younger generation. His services to us are limited to simply accepting our deposits and honouring our cheques."

Mr Honey smiled, "Yes, I believe he can be a difficult man. I'm assuming you asked him for a loan and he refused?"

"No," David interjected, "we never even got the opportunity to ask for a loan. He made it quite clear that he would not entertain us, nor our business requirements. That's why Morris says the Mafeking branch holds us to ransom."

"Well, gentlemen," the new manager paused, looking them over, "the good news is that I am not answerable to Mr Savage, and that I will entertain all transactions, applications, and service requirements on their merit. The problem you have, however, is that I am answerable to a higher authority in Cape Town, and they will act on my recommendations. If you do indeed wish to approach me for a financial loan, then I suggest you provide me with some compelling figures to present your case to Head Office."

David locked eyes with Morris, who raised an eyebrow at him, a tiny smile appearing on one corner of his mouth. "We do need some assistance," Morris confided, "but please allow me some time to get my facts and figures together before I present them to you." A little embarrassed now, Morris patted the creases of his work clothes. "If I had known that my brother was going to introduce me to the new branch of Standard Bank, sir, I would have dressed accordingly,"

Wilfred Honey laughed. "Don't worry Mr Langbourne, but I must admit for a moment I thought you had come to ridicule me. After all, I'm not entirely comfortable having been given a tent as a bank! By all means, come back in a week or two when you have some financial statements for me and I will see what we can do."

Morris laughed, and shook hands vigorously with Mr Honey. "I'll be back as soon as I can clean up and put on some apparel more befitting a meeting with one's bank manager."

Still a little concerned, Mr Honey managed to force a laugh. "I suggest you take a bit more time to put your financial report together."

"Don't worry, Mr Honey," said David, also shaking his hand as they departed, "when it comes to finances, Morris is always ready."

As they walked back to their premises, Morris could not contain his excitement. "This changes everything, David. Do you realise that? Not only will we be able to grow the business that much faster, but others in the settlement will grow theirs faster, too, and – depending on the policies of the head office in Cape Town, some people who don't have a business yet will be able to start new ones, which will in turn grow our business even further."

David scratched his head before it dawned on him, too. "I didn't think of that!"

"Yes, this changes everything. I can't wait to get back to him with our future plans."

"Let's hope he lends us some money."

"Oh, he will; I have no doubt of that, but how much they give us will determine how quickly we get the business up to full speed."

Just then their attention was drawn by the clatter of a coach, drawn by a team of mules, rolling into town. Although they had seen such coaches in the big, southern towns of Port Elizabeth and Cape Town, they had never seen one this far north, and certainly never one that was drawn by mules in the settlement. The mules looked awkward as they trotted in front of the coach; mournful, uninterested and totally oblivious to what was going on around them. There was a sign above the door of the four-wheeled vehicle that said "Zeederberg Mail Coach". As the procession slowed to a halt by the BSAC camp, men folk stopped what they were doing and began to clap and cheer.

"What is that?" Morris wondered in surprise.

"I don't know," David replied, "but it looks like a mail service that has just arrived in town."

Starved of any entertainment and worthwhile news from the world beyond the dusty settlement, the boys quickly became side-tracked and wandered down to where a number of men were starting to gather around the strange arrival. The wagon looked very sturdy and solid, with two large open windows on each side and a door in the middle, also with a window built into it. There was a shallow rail around the roof upon which was tied all manner of baggage and sacks, and upon those sat six very bedraggled men covered in dirt and dust, one of whom was the driver, who commanded a lengthy whip.

As the vehicle came to a halt, creaking and groaning, a further six men emerged from the interior of the wagon. These passengers were as equally unpresentable as the men on the roof, but, unlike their fellow travelling companions, these men did not look at all happy; in fact, some looked decidedly ill. One gentleman, upon alighting from the coach, staggered off to the side of the road, bent over, put his hands on his knees, and dispatched his most recent meal to the ground. The crowd that had gathered too close to this man rapidly dispersed with some very undignified looks on their faces.

A gentleman on the roof of the coach drew their attention away from the sick passenger by extending his arms out to his sides as if making a major proclamation. "Lay-dees and gen'l'men!" he bellowed, "I announce to you the arrival of the Zeederberg Mail Coach Service. The Zeederberg Mail Coach Service will offer a regular mail service between Mafeking and KoBulawayo! Not only will we transport mail, we will transport a limited amount of fare-paying passengers! Luggage and parcels will also be carried at a separate rate, space permitting!"

The crowd mumbled and shuffled among themselves in return, by which time the two brothers had arrived at the gathering to examine carefully the signage and workmanship of the coach from a short distance. They couldn't help noticing the ten mules that stood silently in front of the wagon, completely aloof to what was happening around them, their ears swivelling backwards and forwards, accompanied by an occasional flick of their tails.

"How long does it take to get to Mafeking?" a lone voice called out from the crowd.

"One week, sir!" came the booming and authoritative voice of the Zeederberg Mail Coach Service. This caused a marked stir among the populace.

"Impossible! How can you do that?" the lone voice called out again, creating a murmur of agreement.

"I am glad you enquired, sir." The dusty man smiled, looking around at his audience and ignoring the questioner altogether. "We have established rest and watering points every ten to fifteen miles along our route here, and at each point we have a fresh team of mules. It is simply a matter of changing the old team of mules for a fresh and rested team, thereby keeping up the speedy momentum of our coaches and passengers. One week, ladies and gentlemen."

Then he paused for effect. "Our rates of carriage will be posted outside our office, the site of which is yet to be announced."

David walked over to the sick man who was now sitting on the ground, his head drooping between his legs. "Are you alright, sir? Can I find you a doctor?"

Looking terribly frail and lacking colour in his face, the man looked up at David. "Very kind of you, son, but I will be quite fine in a little while. I don't know why but sitting inside that damn coach makes me quite sickly," he grumbled. "Never again will I use their service, I will walk back to Mafeking if I have to."

David ambled back to Morris. "He'll be fine; he is just suffering that same movement illness we had during those first few days on the ship."

"I feel for him," Morris replied. "That was not pleasant at all; I thought I was going to die. Come on," he nodded towards their construction site and spun on his heel, "we have work to do, even faster than before. This settlement is going to explode with activity, now that we have both a bank and a mail service. Things are going to go crazy, and I need to see Mr Honey as soon as possible. Can you find a way to speed up the building of our shop?"

"Morris, we are going as fast as we possibly can. We cannot go any faster."

"You have to. See what you can do. I know you can do it."

As he tried to keep up with Morris' pace, David shook his head and muttered to himself. "Okay," he finally sighed, "I'll see what I can do."

"Good show!" Morris called over his shoulder, pleased with his brother's response, "I knew I could depend on you. Oh, and please run down to Bulawayo Bricks and bring me the cashbook and the ledger from Abe's office, I'll need those."

David stopped in his tracks and stared at his brother as the latter strode off in a hurry to get back to the Langbourne building site. He had just been told to increase his already chaotic workload without delay, and now Morris wanted him to run down to the brickfields and fetch paperwork for him. He shook his head and frowned, then immediately shrugged, turned right, and ran down to see Abe. There was no use arguing with Morris.

As he trotted into the brickfields he saw Abe and Phil standing among a fresh pile of bricks that had just come out of the kiln. They were discussing something unimportant, as they shared a laugh.

"Greetings, partner," Phil waved, "what brings you running all the way down here?"

"Morris – would you believe?" David stole a laugh before he began to catch his breath.

"What's the problem this time?" Abe scowled.

"Oh, nothing that concerns you chaps, or the production this time. He has an appointment with a new bank manager who has just arrived in town and he needs to show him the cashbook."

Phil looked concerned. "We don't need to borrow any money. Bulawayo Bricks is making lots of money; even Morris seems happy with that."

David wiped his brow and took a deep breath. "True," he agreed, "but Langbourne Brothers needs to borrow as much as possible, and our one third share in Bulawayo Bricks will help with this cause; it is important in their discussions."

"Fair enough," Phil nodded. "You okay, David? You look harassed."

"I'm okay, thanks Phil, it's just that Morris wants me to hurry up and finish building the shop even faster now, and I'm not sure how I can go any quicker."

"Any faster and you'll have an accident or something," Phil cautioned. "Even at the rate you are going I believe you won't be ready for at least another six months, if you're lucky."

Abe kicked a pebble nonchalantly. "That's why your brother is in such a hurry," he said, "that six months will take you to around November, which is when the rainy season starts."

David looked at Abe in surprise. "I never thought of that.

Actually, Morris believes that the settlement will boom with new business and activity and he wants to be ready to trade as soon as possible. As I mentioned, we now have a bank in town, The Standard Bank, and while we were down there only moments ago, a mail-coach service rolled in. They say they can get mail and passengers to Mafeking in one week."

Phil was intrigued. "One week? Well, that's interesting,"

"I don't know how you cope with your brother," Abe complained, looking David in the eye. "Please don't get me wrong, but with all respect, he is very demanding. I must confess that I get nervous when I see him walking towards the brickfields. He has an ability to ask me ten questions before I can even answer the first, and I honestly don't think he is aware of it. I'm working to full capacity and he always pushes for more. How you survive with him all day, and every day, beats the hell out of me!"

David took the remark as a compliment and simply laughed. He explained that he had grown up with Morris and knew how to handle him, including his moods and his outbursts. But, he said in all honesty, they would not be where they were without his brother's drive for business and for making money; his need to survive, both personally and financially; and his need to support his family in Ireland. He also understood and accepted that Morris had a very smart business brain on his shoulders and could see opportunities that most men missed. Yet most importantly, with all his quirks and nuances, Morris was his brother and the only family he had in Africa, so he would support him whenever, wherever, and however he could. Added to that, he was more than a family member: he was a friend and companion. David agreed that Morris could be a handful but admired his fast thinking; the mental, and sometimes physical challenges he threw at him; and his almost genius ability to understand and deal with business and finances.

Phil and Abe stood in silence, listening to their close friend speak from his heart. They had never heard him talk like that before and it touched them deeply. They were secretly in awe of

David's dedication to his brother and to their business and family, and of how hard he could push himself. They knew that – in his own right – David was also an excellent businessman, having a good command of the English language, which they noted when he had drawn up an impeccable agreement for their brick factory. They had quietly agreed that neither of them could have done that themselves. To top it off, they observed that David was a very fair and genuine person in all his dealings, and a great pleasure to have around in a social gathering, because he was humorous, quick-witted, listened to others intently, and laughed easily in conversations. He also took pity on the less fortunate and commended people for the smallest of deeds. In Abe's own words, he was a "born leader and a gentlemen extraordinaire", even at such a young age.

Phil cleared his throat. "As much as your brother is hard work, I feel very comforted that he is controlling the financial side of Bulawayo Bricks and I wouldn't have it any other way; he is a godsend. And apart from his quirks, he is a very likeable chap. I guess you are right, we just have to learn to accept him for who he is," he nodded at Abe.

Abe nodded in agreement and put his battered and sweat-stained hat back on his head. "I've been toying with an idea that might double the production of bricks, but I'm not sure if it would work. Give me a day or two to try something."

"Sounds like you're onto something, Abe," David enthused, which caused his partner to smile.

Abe slapped David on the shoulder and gave him a friendly nudge in the direction of the makeshift office. "Go and get your books for Morris, and let's catch up tomorrow morning. We might have a surprise for you."

"See you in the morning!" David laughed and trotted off towards the shed. He was pleased with their conversation, since he appeared to have circumvented any conflict that may have arisen between his two partners and his brother, and had somehow encouraged them to find a way to double production. In a very strange way, he had experienced nothing but an honest, heart-to-heart talk with them, and they had then somehow motivated themselves to perform better without him actually having asked them to do so.

*

By midday, while the sun was busy roasting the exposed backs of the building teams, David was a good five feet off the ground, standing on a rickety ladder and pressing one brick after another onto the growing wall. From that height he could see over the entire settlement and no structure appeared to be higher than his head, while he counted four other brick construction sites similar to theirs. Seeing that a number of large and empty plots of brown land had been marked out with pegs, he was sure that they would soon be filled with construction crews, as more and more settlers had arrived after the news of King Lobengula's defeat.

David paused for a moment to enjoy the view from his vantage point and wondered how much money the brick-making business might generate over the following years. It saddened him that they would have to sell the business to finance their trading operation, but he understood why Morris felt that they needed to do this. It pleased him immeasurably, though, that the brick idea was prosperous and profitable, especially so soon after its commencement, and that his brother was very impressed with David's business initiative. If he were honest with himself, he would concede that Morris' accolades meant more to him than the money.

David took a moment to listen to the sounds of the burgeoning settlement. He heard a horse neighing in the distance, and somewhere a man called out to a colleague, but that was all he heard. Sounds were quickly devoured by the wide, open spaces. The settlement area was huge, and as it was bare of any trees, shrubs or grasses, he heard neither a bird chirp nor an insect buzz or trill. There were no sounds of carriage wheels rumbling on the dirt roads below, no banter between men, or the tinkle of a womanly laugh, even the happy shriek from a child at play was absent. The air was still and clear, the silence all-encompassing. Suddenly he realised that even the scrape and grind of the trowels used to lay the mortar had fallen silent. He looked down behind him to find all his crews taking their midday break, lounging in whatever shade they could find, waiting for their womenfolk to bring them their daily sustenance of ground maize-meal porridge. Without his team of men throwing bricks up to him, there was not much he could do, so he put down his trowel and leant against the top of the new wall to enjoy the rare solitude that calmed his soul.

In the shade of a wagon that was parked near the new Standard Bank tepee, David spotted Morris and Wilfred Honey sitting on a couple of wooden crates, bent over some papers that lay on a third crate, talking in earnest. They leaned back a little and appeared to share a laugh before they stood up, shook hands, and Morris took his leave. From that distance David could not see if his brother was smiling, but he was certainly walking tall. He decided to climb down from the ladder, put his shirt on, and meet Morris along the street. He had decided that he needed a break from building the wall, anyhow.

Morris was definitely smiling when they met near Sharon Kaufman's shop.

"So?" David smiled back at Morris.

"Fantastic meeting, brother! Fantastic!" Morris beamed, "I wish you were there; so stimulating. Mr Honey is a very smart man."

"I wish I had been there too." David sounded disappointed. "Did he agree to give us a loan?"

"Absolutely!"

"Is he going to give us what we need?"

"Exactly what we need," Morris grinned, "I didn't tell him what we wanted, I just told him what we were capable of; what we wanted to do; and what we were doing right now; and I let him tell me what we needed. He just needs the authority from Cape Town and we are made."

"That was a clever tactic. Now he thinks it's his idea, and he will make it happen."

"Indeed, my thoughts exactly. It's a tactic father taught us, you may recall: let the other person think that it's their idea."

David laughed. "You're too smart, Morris."

"I know," Morris chuckled and winked at David, "but you know that it also means we will have to work harder, and faster. If the loan comes through, our plans will accelerate a lot quicker than we anticipated."

"I was afraid of that," David sighed, "I knew there had to be some sort of penalty for this. I'm not sure I can go any faster, Morris."

"I think you can, David. You're a smart chap; you can do amazing things if you put your mind to it."

The conversation seemed to naturally stop there, both boys lost in their own thoughts as they walked back together in silence, their minds in overdrive as they pondered the future of their business in KoBulawayo.

CHAPTER FOUR
New Arrivals

T HE OLD SAILOR, now wearing his formal white uniform, threw out a length of rope that was caught and fumbled by a man standing without a shirt on the dock. As the sailor fed the rope out, Harry noticed it was attached to a much heavier and thicker rope that snaked its way out to the slender dockworker.

"Look, Louis, they are going to tie the ship to the land!" he exclaimed, eyes wide with excitement, "and why are those men painted brown?"

Louis looked out at all the activity in the harbour. He had certainly not expected to see men only half-dressed and covered in a brown dye. "I have no idea," he admitted, not sure if he should be nervous. Since the other passengers were laughing with ease and smiling openly, they were apparently relieved that the journey had come to an end, so he assumed that what he was looking at was perfectly acceptable, and relaxed a little, too. Harry, on the other hand, was almost chatting to himself, so excited was he at the prospect at arriving in Africa at last.

"So this is what Morris and David saw when they arrived here!" he exclaimed.

Louis was not quite as pleased, since he was taking everything in rather, and becoming increasingly concerned as to what their next move would be. After all, he was responsible for his younger brother. "You stay close to me now, you hear?" he warned. "If you get lost out there, I will never be able to find you again, and you will be caught and eaten alive by some monster."

The ship touched the dock with a gentle thump and everyone on board involuntarily rocked in unison at the final halt in movement. They had finally arrived after almost 3 months at sea, and a small group of passengers briefly applauded and cheered. This comforted Louis for a moment, before he turned his attention back to the gathering group of African men waiting for the cargo doors to be opened. It was obvious that a practised routine was in place for when a ship arrived at port.

Keeping Harry close to his side, Louis located their two trunks, and the brothers made their way down the gangplank to set foot on Africa's shoreline. Louis was significantly taller and thinner than his younger brother, while his soft facial features, his porcelain skin, and his neatly combed and dark, wavy hair set him apart from most young men of his own age. His height gave him the appearance of being a young adult, yet his looks put him at being barely a boy. To the casual onlooker, it seemed obvious that he came from the upper class, because he was impeccably dressed in a tweed business suit, set off with polished, brogue shoes. Gentlemen couldn't help noticing that his necktie was perfectly knotted and tightened neatly to his shirt collar.

"We made it, Louis!" Harry beamed excitedly. He couldn't wait to disembark onto the foreign land with its population of brown people, and to explore the exotic sights and sounds it had to offer.

A wave of nervous anxiety crept into the depth of Louis' stomach. "I'm not sure where to go now," he muttered. "Stay close to me. I need to find that letter father wrote for us." Louis placed his trunk on the ground at his feet and noticed that the sea air had caused some of the metal edges to begin to rust during the voyage. He started patting all his pockets, searching for an envelope he knew was there, but could not hear the familiar crunching of stiff paper that he expected to emanate from within. A new fear began to take over. He quickly started plunging his hands into all the pockets of his jacket, and each time came up with mementoes of Ireland, but not the envelope he wanted.

"Don't tell me you've lost it," Harry frowned.

"I had it this morning, Harry. It must be here," he snapped, frantically searching here and there. Then, feeling something in his back trouser pocket, he literally ripped it out and sighed as he found the letter of introduction to the manager of The Standard Bank.

Harry also sighed. "That was close. What would you have done if you had lost it good and proper?"

"I don't want to think about that. Come on: let's get out of this harbour. There's a gate over there."

At that very moment, two things happened to unnerve the boys. First, a cargo door on the ship came crashing down onto the dockside, startling most people in the vicinity; next they saw a very large African man break away from the group and walk directly towards them with an unreadable expression over coal-black eyes that were trained unmistakably on Harry. He was by far the largest and strongest man in the group.

"Oh dear…" was all Louis could muster, as Harry took a small step closer to his older brother.

When the imposing man reached the boys he cocked his head and stared even harder at Harry, before looking at Louis with a very confused look. All the boys could do was to stare back at him. Suddenly, the scary look on his face melted, to be replaced with a wide smile, showing perfect white teeth.

"Boss Rangbon?" he said gently.

"Excuse me?" Louis had no idea what he had just heard, but was relieved that the giant of a man had a smile on his face.

"Boss Rangbon?" he repeated.

"I beg your pardon, sir," Louis looked flustered, "I only speak English."

"Boss Rangbon?" he said once again, "Boss Morris, and Boss David?"

"Yes!" Louis shouted at the top of his voice when he recognised his brother's names, before checking himself. "Yes, Langbourne, Langbourne; Morris and David Langbourne. My brothers, you know them?"

"My boss," Nguni smiled from ear to ear. "This one," he pointed to Harry, "this one like Boss Morris. Same father."

Louis wanted to hug the man. He had been standing on this – a new continent – thousands of miles and many months from home for barely two minutes, and someone recognised his brother.

"Gosh," Harry grinned, "everybody knows Morris and David. What a small town! I like this country."

Louis couldn't help smiling. He felt as if the entire weight of fear and trepidation had been lifted off his shoulders. "How do you do, sir?" he enquired, offering a formal greeting in his best English. "My name is Louis Langbourne," and extended his hand. Nguni promptly gripped the offered appendage in a traditional Xhosa handshake, which totally enveloped Louis' soft, thin hand and threw him off his train of thought.

"I am Nguni."

"Ingoony? Yes, well, alright. Well… this is my brother, Harry." Louis let go of the big, calloused hand and pointed to his younger brother.

"Boss Loo-ee, Boss Hurry," he shook hands with Harry in response, still smiling broadly.

"Well, Ingoony, Sir, we are in need of locating The Standard Bank of Port Elizabeth. I wonder if you would be so kind as to direct us to their location," Louis continued in his best English, not realising that Nguni hardly spoke much of the language at all.

Nguni looked at him, with his head cocked, confusion written all over his face.

"Standard Bank?" Harry repeated, emphasising only the words that mattered.

"Standard Bank... Yes. Come," Nguni smiled before turning to some of the other workers waiting to board the ship. He shouted at them in a strange language that was peppered with clicks and two men immediately sprinted to his side, picked up the boys' trunks, and hoisted them onto the tops of their heads.

"Good grief!" Harry exclaimed in surprise; but he was impressed. In the meantime, Louis had objected fruitlessly as Nguni and the two bearers walked towards the exit of the wharf. After a few yards, Louis gave up his objections and obediently and silently followed the procession.

The Standard Bank was not far, just a couple of blocks past The Grand Hotel. Nguni commanded his men to deposit the boy's trunks on the street outside the bank's main door and bid them farewell in Xhosa, believing they would surely understand that much. Leaving their trunks they entered the bank, they approached a teller, asked to see a Mr Jack Shiel, and then retired to the rear of the banking hall to avoid seeming conspicuous.

In less than a minute, a stocky man with very short-cropped, fair hair appeared from inside an office and studied the two boys who had asked for him by name. For a moment he looked at them blankly before smiling and walking over.

"Good morning, boys, I am Jack Shiel, and I would assume you belong to the Langbourne family."

"Yes," for the second time that day Louis was taken aback.

"I knew it," Jack laughed, "I can see the resemblance, particularly this young chap, who, I would venture to suggest, bears a perfect resemblance to Master Morris Langbourne." Jack proceeded to ruffle Harry's hair, at which the young man instantly withdrew in indignation, straightening out his now bedraggled hairstyle with his fingertips.

Introductions, however, were duly made and Jack invited the boys into his office where he poured them a cup of fresh coffee. Although they felt very insignificant in the presence of such an important bank manager's office, so far from home, in a strange land where they knew no one, and where the majority of the people dyed their skin brown, their feelings of insecurity were allayed by the comfort of being recognised by just about everyone they met.

As Jack handed out the coffee cups, Louis produced the important envelope his father had given to him before they had departed Ireland and handed it to Jack. When the boys were settled, Jack sat in his big leather chair and opened the envelope with a polished silver letter opener. Both boys stared in fascination, because they had never seen a man open a letter this way. The letter read as follows:

*

April 1894

Mr J, Shiel, Esq.,
The Standard Bank,
Port Elizabeth.

Dear Sir,

By means of this humble letter that you might currently hold in your hand, may I take the liberty of introducing to you my two sons, Louis and Harry Langbourne. I am led to believe that you are a friend of their older brothers, who are my two, first-born sons, Morris and David Langbourne.
It is at the request of their older brothers that you may be further encouraged to introduce them to a landlady, Mrs Sonja Du Plessis, who, if possible, will provide shelter for them. I then

*respectfully ask that you telegraph my eldest sons, at a place
called KoBulawayo, advising of their arrival.*

*I have given Louis a small amount of money to cover any
expense you may incur in arranging the telegraph and I would
be further eternally grateful for any assistance you might
provide for my sons.*

I remain, sir,

Your humble servant,

Jacob Langbourne.

*

Jack folded the letter and placed it back in its envelope. "Well,"
he smiled, before taking a sip of his coffee, "your father sounds
like a fine gentleman, but then, knowing your brothers, I wouldn't
have thought otherwise. What your father asks me to do is exactly
what David has already instructed me to arrange. I believe you
have some money that your father has given you to give to me?"

"Yes, sir," Louis pulled another envelope out of his breast
pocket and passed it to the manager, "five pounds exactly."

"David has already given me enough money to cover most of
your expenses, so keep this money and use it wisely. What you do
not use, I ask that you please give back to your brother when you
see him. Now, I need to take you down to see Sonja Du Plessis: she
will be your landlady until your brother collects you. Where are
your ports?"

"Ports, sir?" Louis questioned.

"Bags… luggage?"

"Oh, outside on the street."

"Good Lord!" Jack raised his eyebrows in horror, "don't leave
them there; bring them into the bank right away. I have a meeting

shortly and should be finished in an hour or so. Wait for me in the banking hall and, when I am finished, I will take you for a walk down to Mrs Du Plessis."

Quickly swallowing their coffee in two gulps, the boys rushed outside to rescue their trunks. It wasn't long, however, before Jack Shiel was walking the boys through the beautiful town of Port Elizabeth, enjoying a break from his office and the opportunity of showing them the beautiful settlement he lived in. The manager relished their facial expressions in response to the totally unfamiliar surroundings, while two African porters dutifully followed the trio, each with a trunk skilfully balanced on his head, an act that neither brother had ever seen and which they found immensely impressive.

Jack's first stop was at The Grand Hotel, where he walked them into the reception area and allowed them some time to marvel at the mounted trophies of various wild animals that hung on the walls. He took time to explain what each animal was and related some stories of how their various horns had fatally wounded many an experienced hunter. When he thought he had scared them enough, he led them to the dining room and explained that it was here that their brother's company, Langbourne Brothers, had begun. The next stop was the Post Office where he scribbled out a telegram:

*

TO: LANGBOURNE BROS, KOBULAWAYO, MATABELELAND

VIA: WEIL & CO., MAFEKING

ARRIVAL OF BROTHERS IN P E CONFIRMED

BOTH IN GOOD HEALTH STOP

SHIEL STOP

The manager handed the telegram slip to the postmaster, who worked out the cost. Jack paid the gentleman, pocketed the receipt, and continued on to the lodgings of Sonja Du Plessis. The path leading up to the house was lined with a few straggling plants that were in urgent need of a trim, while the veranda also looked as if it could do with some maintenance, but the house itself stood both soundly and proudly, amid the shrubs and small trees.

Jack knocked on the door and stood back, fastening a brass button on his business suit. A faint call was heard from inside followed by a series of footsteps approaching the door. When Sonja Du Plessis opened the door, she was all smiles at seeing the bank manager, and especially the two timid boys that stood politely behind him.

"Good morning, Mr Shiel, how wonderful to see you again!"

"Good morning to you, Mrs Du Plessis. It is indeed a pleasure to see you after so long. I must say you are looking quite delightful today." Jack always made a point of offering a polite compliment to any lady he met in town.

"Why, thank you," she beamed, attempting to pat down a stray hair that may have escaped her attention. Some time ago she had been blessed with flowing tresses of jet-black hair, but an advance-guard of grey streaks had begun to invade her temples in order to pepper the top of her head. "Let me guess," she said, "these two delightful boys must be the younger brothers of Morris and David."

"Indeed, that is correct, madam," he replied, stepping aside to introduce the boys. "Gentlemen, I'd like you to meet Mrs Sonja Du Plessis. She will be offering you board and lodging until one of your brothers returns to collect you. May I at first introduce you to young Louis Langbourne?"

Louis immediately stepped forward and gently took her hand, bowing slightly. "It is a pleasure to meet you, Mar'm."

Sonja raised her eyebrows, impressed by his formal response, and quickly stole a glance at Jack, who also raised his eyebrows at her in surprise. "The pleasure is mine, I am sure," she replied, and gave a little attempt at a curtsy.

"And may I introduce young Harry Langbourne?" Jack quickly continued, hoping that the brothers had not noticed his surprised look.

"It is a pleasure to meet you, too," said Harry, as he stepped up to meet her and copied Louis exactly as his father had taught them.

"Well, I never!" Sonja exclaimed, letting slip a giggle. "Yes, indeed, lovely to meet you, too, Harry." Then she invited Jack to stay for a cup of tea, but he politely declined, saying that he had to get back to the bank. He instructed the porters to deposit the boys' trunks on the veranda and gave them each a coin before dismissing them with his thanks in their own language.

Preparing to leave himself, he informed the young brothers that the telegram to KoBulawayo might take as much as a month to be delivered. It would get to Mafeking in a matter of days as the telegraph network followed the rail line, but the network terminated at that settlement, and the message would have to be carried further overland by a courier, which could take over three weeks. Then Morris or David would have to travel down to collect their brother, and that journey could take a month or so, depending on their circumstances. The net result was that it could take three months before they saw any of their siblings, so it was incumbent upon them to find employment as soon as possible to cover their living expenses. Nevertheless, until they were able to support themselves, David had given the manager enough money to support the boys' basic needs. Then he nodded at Sonja and reminded her to provide him with all board and lodging expenses due to her. Once she had agreed, he departed and Sonja told the boys to bring their trunks inside, after which she showed them to a small room with two narrow beds pushed up against adjacent walls.

"This will be your living quarters," she said. "It's where your brothers stayed when they boarded with me. You may use that cupboard, and the bathroom is down the hall. When you have settled in, meet me in the kitchen and I will have some tea and biscuits ready for you. I'll also show you where your brothers ran their cigarette factory."

"Thank you, Mar'm," said Louis, gratefully accepting her hospitality. "Unfortunately we know very little about what our brothers did when they got to Africa, so we would be delighted to learn more about them, and see their factory."

Sonja laughed heartily, "Well, I'm sure you will be surprised," was all she'd say.

Once the boys had freshened up and taken in their surrounds, they made their way to the kitchen where a cup of steaming hot tea was waiting for them. Before they sat down, Sonja took them outside to the back veranda. The railings were in need of a little repair, and the wooden deck had begun to fade to a pale grey, while the planks creaked as they stepped onto them. The veranda itself was bare, except for a small wooden crate, upturned and pushed up against one wall.

Sonja waved her hand at the empty veranda "This, my boys, where your brothers had their factory."

Louis and Harry's faces were equally empty of expression and Louis looked to see if Sonja was joking.

"Here?" he asked in amazement.

"Yes, it's incredible, isn't it? They had little cigarette machines tied all along the railings, and employed about twenty Xhosa women. It was such a bustling little business that they worked from sunrise to sunset every day." She smiled as the memories of those adventurous days came flooding back. "They would then sell their product at night, mostly down at The Grand Hotel."

Sonja remembered how Morris and David would sit on her veranda, working with their team of half-naked Xhosa women, sometimes singing and chanting along with them as they churned out cigarettes. She could vividly picture Morris collecting the manufactured cigarettes as they fell from their copper tubes into old and tacky cardboard boxes that were roughly tied to the railing, frowning intently as he counted them and entered the numbers into his journal, always looking very serious and concerned. She could almost see David as he sat at a makeshift desk, shirtsleeves rolled half way up his arms, wrapping boxes of cigarettes and addressing labels with an old fountain pen, taking time to laugh and joke with his female workforce when he resupplied them with cut tobacco, or paper glue, as the supplies ran low. The two brothers had such different characters, yet they both worked hand-in-glove with each other: the perfect team. Sonja missed those happy days. Since the boys had left for better opportunities, her days had become rather lonely and quiet. It had only lasted one year, but it had been a most memorable period in her life.

Louis looked at Sonja and noticed the sad look on her face as she stared silently at the empty veranda. "So why did they leave?"

"Oh, I'm not sure…" she smiled as she returned to the present reality. "Someone bought the business and your brothers decided there was more money to be made in Matabeleland. It seems they are very successful there too, but…." she broke off and became serious. "Come inside and have your tea. There are some things we need to discuss."

Once they were seated and began to drink their tea, Sonja became very concerned. "Boys, I'm not sure if you know but a war broke out in Matabeleland recently." When Louis shook his head, Sonja continued, "David came to see me a little while back as he needed to ask an African man to help him take goods and wagons up to Matabeleland. They had become friends from when they first arrived in Africa."

"We met a very large African man in the harbour who said he knew our brothers. Could it be him?"

"Yes, that would be him. Nguni is his name: a very big man. Well, he delivered the wagons all right, but no sooner had he returned from Matabeleland when a rather fierce war broke out between the Matabele warriors and the European settlers. Thousands of Matabele were killed, but not many settlers were harmed. We have not heard from your brothers since then, so we have no idea how they are, or even if their business survived the war, although we don't believe we have much to be concerned about."

"Is the war finished?" Harry asked, a look of worry on his face.

"Yes, it is, I believe. I'm just telling you what we know. Unfortunately, you won't have any news for about three months, just as Mr Shiel said. So I think it is best that you boys find a job as soon as possible and then let's wait out the next three months."

"We could start a cigarette factory on your porch like Morris and David did," said Harry, beaming at his great idea.

"Don't be silly," Louis scolded, "we have no idea how to make a cigarette. In any case, Morris and David want us to help them with their business."

Sonja smiled again. Although, she could see that the boys had a lot to learn, the older boy appeared to be quite sensible. Her first impression of Louis was that he was very similar to David in many respects: a good upbringing, charming and polite, well presented, good-looking, and well-spoken. Harry, on the other hand, was similar to Morris in looks, but she wasn't sure of his character. He seemed excitable when discussing business, except that, when Morris thought of an idea, he was instantly ten steps ahead, having considered the repercussions of his actions, the logistics of putting such a plan in place, the financial aspect of it, and – if other people needed to be involved – whether they were physically, mentally, and emotionally capable of doing what was needed to be done. Undoubtedly, even in his late teens, Morris seemed smarter than his entire family put together.

"Mrs Du Plessis," Harry had a curious look on his face, "why do a lot of men here dye their skin brown and black?"

She almost choked on a sip of tea. "Oh my goodness! You boys do have a lot to learn!" She started to giggle when she remembered how Morris and David reacted with sheer embarrassment when they met their all-female staff for the first time. The only garments the women wore were beaded cloths around their hips, and necklaces around their necks. Watching them deal with seeing partial nudity for the first time was, to her, the funniest thing ever. "Where, oh where, do we start?" she looked out the window trying – unsuccessfully – to suppress a laugh.

CHAPTER FIVE

Expansion – July 1894

MORRIS DIDN'T WANT to leave the warmth of his blankets: the winters in KoBulawayo were freezing cold, the previous day having greeted the residents with a thin layer of frost on the ground. A plant that Morris had attempted to grow in a small tin can had been burnt black from the frost and looked as though it would not survive through to another season. The only reason he forced himself out of his bedding was because he was in desperate need of a visit to the pit latrine at the back of their plot. The cold and discomfort reminded him of the winters in Ireland, the notable difference being that in Ireland he had always been very hungry and damp, as well as cold. Here, in Africa, there was no shortage of food, and his shortbread treats ensured he carried a little more weight than he had done in Ireland, where his frame had looked skeletal.

The boy's bedding was placed on the floor of their warehouse, and, sitting upright, Morris noticed that David was curled up tight in his blankets.

"You awake?" he grunted at David, who opened one eye and stared at his brother.

"No," David mumbled, and closed his one eye again.

"Man, it is cold! What is it with this place?" Morris stared at the floor for a moment, thinking hard about standing up. His bladder gave him some encouragement, so he reluctantly made the effort. "I need you to help me in the sample room today. Can you arrange to take a break from building?"

"Sure," David mumbled, motionless under the covers.

Morris left the warehouse to relieve himself and instantly caught the aroma of wood-smoke. Thembela, the young Xhosa lady who had replaced Nkosazana when she had returned to Mafeking to be married to Daluxolo, had already stoked the fire and placed a blackened kettle over the flames to boil the water for their morning coffee. Morris took a moment to praise the Lord for the abundant blessings he had received before striding off to the latrine.

Back in the warehouse, David fought an internal battle with himself. He knew he had to escape his blankets, but he was still so tired. His muscles ached from the previous day's labour, and the chilled air that drifted past his face and ears reminded him how comparatively warm his bedding was. In the end, common sense prevailed, and he crawled out of his cocoon, knowing full well that – once he had drunk a cup of very hot coffee and started moving about – he would be as good as new again. Leaving the sample room, he walked over to where Morris stood next to Thembela, as they watched the kettle coming to the boil together.

"I see you, Thembela," said David in the customary greeting to the beautiful young woman. "I hope the night was kind to you and that the cold kept some distance from you."

"I see you, Boss David," she giggled quietly. "The night was kind to me, yes, and the cold was not able to enter my home."

"Then that is good," David mumbled, "but I fear the cold has found my home very comfortable and will not leave." Thembela chuckled shyly again.

"David," Morris interrupted, "please would you run the shop for me today? I am behind on coding stock in the warehouse and

I need to get down to Bulawayo Bricks and catch up on the book-work there, plus I owe Major Seward a visit; I haven't spoken to him in a while."

"Sure, I could use a break from the brick wall." David had made a feeble attempt at sarcasm, but it was too early in the morning for Morris to notice. "How's Dos Santos progressing? I think it's looking quite good, actually."

"He's doing well. He seems happiest when he is not looking at your workmanship," Morris joked. "I estimate he will be done in about three months from now. The only problem we have is getting glass for the shop front windows. Most of it arrives in KoBulawayo completely smashed. And it is so expensive."

"Why don't we just board up the windows with wood until we can afford to buy glass, or the price comes down a little? It's not as if we are a high-street store that needs to display our wares to the passing public."

"Yes! Good thinking, David. We'll do that, then." Morris took a sip of his hot coffee and savoured the warmth that filled his stomach. "How long will it be before you and your teams finish the brickwork?"

"I guess we need about two more months," David replied, then maybe another month to fit the roof. I was going to suggest that I come off the walls now, anyway. My teams know what they are doing, and I would like to start looking into the roof trusses and assess the timber we will need for that."

As the discussion turned to the next phase of the building, they walked around their building site examining the progress. This time it was David who did the talking and Morris who did the listening. At this stage, timber was becoming a priority for door and window frames, and for roofing. To a lesser degree, painting was also about to start. By the time they had finished their assessment of progress on the building site, the bricklayers had arrived for work, Dos Santos was checking on his previous day's efforts, and their first customer was walking into the sample room. David excused himself to freshen up, put on smarter clothes, and have a shave: something he had not done in over a week.

Later that morning, David took over the trading arm of their business while his brother began his day down at Bulawayo Bricks, before Morris returned to the warehouse to deal with his administrative responsibilities. The original wooden warehouse and sample room were beginning to look insignificant as the brickwork around the two structures began to dwarf them. Morris made a note to talk to David about shelving and tables upon which to display their stock, especially the cumbersome bolts of fabric. He would have to ask David to apply his mind to designing a table specifically for the rolls of material: tables that would allow them to be easily handled and displayed to prospective customers.

At around noon, a short gentleman in his early twenties wearing a long-sleeved, pale-yellow shirt and dark-brown slacks arrived at the sample room and poked his head inside. "Mr Langbourne, sir?" he asked timidly.

David stopped what he was doing and approached the man. "Yes, indeed, come in, sir. How can I be of assistance?"

"Herbert Bachmayer at your service, sir. I come from the new Posts and Telecommunications Office. I have a telegraph message for you that was delivered last night by the BSAC postal run."

David's heart skipped a beat. "Oh, fantastic!" he almost shouted. He wanted to snatch the envelope out of Mr Bachmayer's hand and rip it open.

"Perhaps I could ask you to place your signature here?" Bachmayer produced a small book with lined pages in it, "To acknowledge receipt of the telegraph, of course."

"Certainly," David agreed and quickly scribbled his signature in a spot that had been neatly indicated with a tiny "x" alongside the name, "Langbourne Brothers".

"I believe this may be one of the last telegraphs the BSAC postal run will deliver," Bachmayer said with a little smile.

"Really, why would that be?"

"Well, as you know, there is a network of telegraph wires that connect most of the towns south of us, but the cable stops at Mafeking, along with the end of the rail line. However Mr Rhodes has funded a telegraph line to connect Mafeking with Fort Salisbury, up north. That line is now complete and working, and they have taken a branch from that line which they are leading towards KoBulawayo. The line is now only six miles away, and soon the KoBulawayo office will be connected. Very exciting news for the citizens of KoBulawayo, if I say so myself," he beamed. "Unfortunately we are still not connected to the rest of the world. I doubt that will ever happen, but certainly we will be connected to all the main towns in the Cape, Transvaal, Bechuanaland, Free State, et cetera, et cetera."

This was good news indeed! It would mean a very large sea-change for their business. The ramifications were immense, and David felt he needed to tell Morris as soon as possible. He thanked Mr Bachmayer and politely saw him out the door. The moment the postal clerk had left, David dashed into the warehouse to find his brother, where he burst out with excitement.

"Morris! Guess what?"

Morris was visibly annoyed, and quickly turned his attention back to his ledger where his pen had scratched through a number when David had startled him.

"Two bits of news," David continued, "firstly, a telegraph has arrived, and secondly, in a few days a wire will arrive in KoBulawayo that will connect us to all the big towns south of us."

This caught Morris' attention, and he immediately put his pen down. "You know what this means, David?"

"Yes, for starters we will be able to communicate with Louis in the East London office."

"And we can order goods from Weil without going down there every time we need to replenish our stocks."

"The possibilities are endless!" David was almost beside himself with excitement.

Morris nodded at the envelope that his brother was clutching tightly in his hand. "What's in the telegraph message?"

David tore it open and read the irregular typeface that punctuated the coarse surface of the dull postal paper. "It's from Jack Shiel in Port Elizabeth!" His face lit up with joy. "Our brothers have arrived, safe and sound."

"Well, that is also good news," Morris stood up from his desk and slapped his brother on the shoulder. "They say good news comes in threes. Two pieces of good news in two minutes is not bad, brother."

Just then there was a knock on the wooden doorframe, and the brothers turned to see who it was. It was Mr Bachmayer, who shyly poked his head through the doorway again.

"My apologies, Gentlemen," he said. "I forgot to advise you that Mr Honey of the local Standard Bank would be most grateful if Mr Morris would care to pop down and see him later this morning."

Morris looked at David, "I dare say that might be number three," he grinned, leaving Mr Bachmayer a little confused, but David quickly thanked Herbert and sent him on his way. Then, turning to Morris, he lowered his voice almost to a whisper even though there was nobody else in the room, "Do you think Mr Honey has approved our loan?"

"I'm sure he has," Morris replied, also in a hoarse whisper. "Mark my words, if that is so, we are going to make more money than you could ever imagine, because – believe me," Morris frowned in serious vein, "nobody is going to stop us now. David, we are going to build a business empire, and it begins right now."

*

When Morris returned from his meeting with Mr Honey, he found David standing outside the sample room with Abe Kaufman and Phil Innes, deeply engrossed in a conversation. "Greetings gentlemen," he almost sang, catching the trio off guard. "Have you ever considered making bricks of varying sizes? There may well be a market out there that has a need for bricks to suit different applications."

Abe tried to answer but Morris continued, "Perhaps you need to make your bricks slightly smaller. You would have to charge less for a smaller brick, but the customer will need more that way, and if you could cost them with a slightly better profit margin, that would increase your profits magically." Phil tried to say something but Morris kept going, "It might be worth doing the sums on cost and profit, have you tried that yet? And I was thinking, what about making some decorative bricks? You could charge higher prices for those, I would imagine. Profits would be a lot healthier. Abe, you're good with soil and matters of the earth, is there not some mineral around here that could be introduced into the clay to make them different colours without compromising the strength?

David winked at Phil and noticed Abe's look of concern. Before Abe could answer, Morris ploughed on, "and what about bricks that can be used for pathways and pavements? Have you thought about making bricks for different applications? Diversification is the name. There must be a magnificent market out there for that. Phil, bricks and moulds are your speciality. Do you think you could invent something to make pathway bricks? I think we could treble the production of the business in five weeks if we can get this going. David, I need to talk to you right away. Gentlemen, if you'll excuse me," he stepped through the group and entered the sample room alone.

"See what I mean," Abe grumbled, throwing his hands in the air in resignation.

Phil chuckled. "He's a handful, your brother,"

David ran his hand through his hair and sighed. "He's got a belly full of fire today, chaps, that's for sure, but I had better go and see what he wants. Stick to what we discussed and I'll handle Morris."

The group broke up and David followed Morris into the sample room. Thembela walked in, carrying a tray with three cups of coffee, originally intended for Abe, Phil and David. David thanked her in Xhosa and took a cup over to Morris who was packing some ledgers into a trunk, which he closed and then sat upon.

"I'm guessing Mr Honey approved the loan?" David smiled and passed the cup to Morris.

"Yes, we are in business, dear brother," Morris grinned, taking a sip of his coffee. "I have also set up a telegraphic address with the Postmaster. It could be a maximum of seven letters long, so I have used the address 'LANBROS'. Remember that address; if you send a telegraphic message and address it to LANBROS it will come here. It will save you typing long expensive addresses. A fantastic advancement in communications!"

"Very good, but did Mr Honey give you what you wanted?"

"Exactly what we wanted, yes. He thinks I needed a lot more, and apologised that he couldn't do better, but it is exactly what we wanted. Take a seat, I have a few adjustments to our business strategy and I want to go over it all with you," he cocked an eyebrow at his brother.

"Okay, I'm listening," David pulled up a wooden box and sat gingerly on it.

Morris explained that he wanted David to go to Mafeking in the next few days to visit Weil and Gerran, and pay them in full, including any interest owed. This would demonstrate that the Langbourne's were true to their word. Then he needed to arrange a further twelve wagons to come up before going to Port Elizabeth and East London. David was startled at the number of wagons – double what they had worked with in the past – and questioned whether Weil had the capacity to fill twelve wagons of stock, or for that matter, that Gerran had twelve wagons for sale in his factory. Morris had to smile at that because it had crossed his mind already. By the time David had returned to Mafeking from Port Elizabeth and East London, however, about three months would have passed, and they should have had time to fulfil their orders. It was Morris' hope that, if Weil and Gerran received full payment for their previous sale well before they expected payment, thanks entirely to the bank loan, they would be amenable to let twelve wagons and stock leave their premises on the same terms of credit.

Once David had arranged that, he was to travel by rail to Port Elizabeth and collect their two younger siblings. From there, he was required to make his way to East London and establish a procurement office; open a bank account with the Standard Bank; open another account with the railways; and set up a telegraphic address for the East London branch. Once that was done, he was to teach Louis how to manage the office, purchase goods, crate and ship his purchases, and then get them on the train to Mafeking.

It was vital that Louis understood how to use their black rhino code, and when to use it. Now that they had a loan from the bank, Morris calculated that Louis would not have time to sell to the public, as originally thought, so he would be sent a living allowance from KoBulawayo, leaving him free to concentrate solely on supplying the KoBulawayo business; by his reckoning, Louis's job was going to be all-consuming. Morris wanted David to introduce Louis to high society and to get him circulating among the business community.

"Start at The Grand Hotel in Port Elizabeth," he frowned. "Take him to a dinner with Jack Shiel; show him how to dress correctly in these establishments, and to use his best table etiquette. I know father and Bloomy have made sure he knows all this, but you must assess him. Then in East London, find some establishments where businessmen congregate, there must be many. Get him involved in the local synagogue, I'm sure there must be one there, anything, but get him mixing with high society."

"I thought we were going to keep our religion a secret," David frowned.

Morris thought about this for a moment, a look of concern very evident on his face. "You're right, ignore the synagogue, I'm not totally sure how Jews are regarded in Africa."

"What about Harry?"

"He is too young as yet. His voice will still sound like a child's and it will be embarrassing for you," he paused, concern washing over his face again, "I just hope Louis's voice has broken by now."

David chuckled. "It will be strange hearing Louis with a man's voice."

Morris returned the smile but continued with his plan. Once David was satisfied that Louis was established and the East London office working the way it should, he was to return to Mafeking with Harry, load the twelve wagons, or as many as he could arrange, and send them on their way with Daluxolo and his men. As soon as the wagons had departed Mafeking, David was to get back to KoBulawayo with Harry as fast as possible. By then, hopefully, the building would be complete and ready to receive the twelve wagons.

"How are you going to pay Dos Santos? Surely you would have used all our loans and credit facilities on the twelve wagons and whatever Louis purchases off the ships?"

"We have to sell Bulawayo Bricks, the sooner the better, I'm afraid."

"That is sad, as it will make good money once we stop siphoning bricks off it."

"We need all the cash we can get. I will offer it to Abe and Phil at a fair price, and make adjustments for what we have drawn off it, but – if they don't want our share – I'll sell it on the open market."

"You'll give them a fair price, will you?"

"Yes, of course: they have been very fair to us. I actually hope they do take it off us."

David smiled, because he was comfortable with what Morris had in mind, and he knew that their friends would get a good deal. "When do you want me to go?"

"One week from today. Take this week to finalise progress on the building site, and to sort out provisions for your journey, and maybe have a chat to Abe and Phil about what our plans are. They seem to like you better than me," he shrugged. "It's obvious,

David, I can see they are a little uncomfortable with me, but just plant a seed in their heads that I may approach them about us selling our share. It will give them some time to think about the value of the business and it will make negotiations a little easier when the time comes. I don't want them to think I will walk all over them."

"Thanks, Morris, they are good friends, as you say. I'll do that for you."

*

After just two days of preparation, David was ready and anxious to leave. There was a small BSAC mail run leaving the following day, so David took the opportunity to arrange that he accompany them. After calling on Major Seward at the BSAC headquarters and exchanging some pleasantries, David received permission to follow the run down to Mafeking.

Major Seward looked at David and smiled. "You'll be pleased to know," he said, "that the leader of the mail run tomorrow is your old friend, Captain Dent."

David could not contain his excitement. "Splendid!" he exclaimed, "I really enjoy his company. I could not have hoped for a better leader and companion."

"Yes," Major Seward agreed, "I must admit that I have found him to be a top-class officer."

Although David took a little more time to quiz the major on matters surrounding the settlement, and what Dr Jameson had in store for KoBulawayo, Major Seward was not that forthcoming. The doctor had been up in Fort Salisbury in the north for some three weeks now and communications were sadly lacking. Nevertheless, David could tell that Major Seward was secretly happier being free of Dr Jameson's presence. What David did discover was that the settlement of KoBulawayo was growing much faster than Fort Salisbury, and was in fact the fastest growing settlement north of the Limpopo River as far as anyone could tell. This was good news for David and filled him with encouragement. Even though the news of King Lobengula's death remained a rumour, as his body had not been accounted for, no threat of an uprising from the Matabele was foreseeable, so the situation across the land seemed stable. Major Seward bid David God's speed and safe travels as they parted company.

Reunited with Captain Dent the following morning, David joined the mail run down to Mafeking for the second time in his life. He did not look forward to the 18-day journey, but having Grant as leader of the company made it much more bearable. Kitted out with his trusted telescope, a tiny bottle of pain-relieving morphine, a blanket, and a small bag of formal attire, he bade farewell to his brother and pointed his horse southwards.

Exactly 18 days later, sporting untidy beards and looking very bedraggled, the men parted company as they entered the outskirts of Mafeking, all going their respective ways to have a well-deserved bath and shave. As David passed the cemetery on his left, he noticed that a few more fresh graves had been added since his last visit.

It seemed to him that people died easily in Africa. Apart from casualties of war, there were many ways a man could die, such as a simple accident, or a small cut that went septic. Broken bones would often take lives; the ravages of childbirth, and diseases of all types. Some snakes were sure killers though very few people were actually bitten by them, but by far the biggest killers were the animals. Men needed to respect the wildlife, even experienced hunters, because – if they didn't – their time on this earth certainly would be limited.

David checked into the same lodging he had used on his previous trip and was given the same room he had had before. After soaking in a tepid bath of dirty brown water, he shaved and made himself presentable before taking the familiar walk down to see his old friend and business partner, Julian Weil. He found him hard at work in his office, poring over a heavy leather-bound journal with pale-blue pages, filled with neatly written numbers and words. He was delighted to see David and instantly stopped what he was doing, giving him a hearty welcome and leading him down to the new hotel where he had met with Morris barely six months previously. He noticed that David had filled out across his shoulders and had developed a handsome physique. David realised that his business suit was decidedly tighter, especially around his shoulders and upper arms, and had grudgingly accepted that he was in need of another, which he would buy in Port Elizabeth when he got there. Tea was ordered, which came in a beautiful set of delicate bone china with exquisitely matched floral designs, as well as two portions of the chef's cake of the day: a sponge cake, with granadilla mixed into the creamy icing-sugar, giving it a tantalising tang, something he had never before experienced and but which he immediately decided to like.

Julian asked after Morris, and caught up on their news. David was as charming as always and a delight to talk to. Julian seemed very interested in the Matabele conflict with the British and how the BSAC supported the settlers of KoBulawayo. David explained what had happened, and how the general population of the settlement felt about the whole debacle, but he had to confess that he had been a little confused by the politics of it all. On one day they had appeared to be under the rule and influence of a Matabele King, and on the next day it seemed as if the Queen of England had dominion over the entire nation, but which was nevertheless administered by a public company run by one man: Cecil John Rhodes. Yet the result was a settlement that was booming; permanent structures were being built at an incredible pace; land was almost being given away; commercial stands had been allocated; and the infrastructure required to administer the settlement was busy forging ahead.

Julian lowered his voice and lent closer to David. "I have it on good authority," he murmured, "that they are thinking of renaming that country, from Matabeleland to Rhodesia, after Cecil John Rhodes."

Although there really wasn't anyone in earshot, David lowered his voice, too. "It wouldn't surprise me," he murmured back. "The settlers up there have already nicknamed the place 'Rhodesia'. I set up a brick-making company with two friends and dropped the 'Ko' in 'KoBulawayo', calling it Bulawayo Bricks, simply because it had a nice ring to it, and now a lot of people are doing the same thing. We now have Bulawayo Bakery, Bulawayo Barbers, Bulawayo this and that," he laughed. "Maybe they will change the settlement name to Bulawayo as well!"

Julian leaned back and briefly flashed one of his rare smiles. "That wouldn't surprise me either," he replied. "And to business: are you recovering? Morris apprised me of the horrid events leading up to the loss of your wagons and stock."

David sat up as straight as he could and then lent forward slightly, resting his forearm on the table. "Julian, we owe you a debt of gratitude for your trust and confidence in us. Without you, we would have been bankrupt." David paused to allow the sincerity of his statement to weigh in on Julian. "We have begun to recover quite well, thank you, and with Morris' careful planning, we are doing exceptionally well. So well, in fact," he reached into his pocket and pulled out a Langbourne Brothers cheque and passed it to Julian, "that I have come here to settle our debt with you in full, including all the interest that might have accrued over the period in question."

Julian took the cheque with his eyes wide, his eyebrows raised, and his mouth slightly open, as he stared at the words and numbers written upon it in Morris' untidy scrawl. He looked David in the eye and tried to say something, then looked back at the cheque. A moment later, he took a deep breath and studied David, who sat smiling proudly.

"If I bank this cheque, David, and it bounces because of lack of funds, you know that it is a criminal offence, legally speaking.

Are you certain you want me to bank it? I can hold onto this for a little while for you, you do know that?"

"Julian, I am aware of that, and I can assure you there are sufficient funds in the bank account to cover the cheque. Please feel free to deposit this cheque with Mr Savage this very afternoon."

Julian folded the cheque and placed it in the breast pocket of his jacket. "Very well, David. I must hasten to add, however, that I am rather impressed."

"Thank you, Julian. With Morris at the helm of the business, our prospects are very favourable. In fact," he reached into his pocket and withdrew another cheque, "after our meeting, I will be visiting Mr Gerran to repay our debts to him, in full."

Julian was stunned. David was hoping for this reaction, but didn't expect it to be so obvious. He decided to keep going while he had the upper hand.

"We do have another favour to ask of you, though, and that is if you would do us the honour of extending your credit terms with us once again. We have decided we want to accelerate our recovery, and need to push on at a cracking pace."

"Well, certainly, David," Julian shook himself out of his shocked trance. "Your credit with me is exceptional, and of course I have a personal liking for both you and your brother."

"Wonderful," David beamed, casually taking a sip of his tea, "we are honoured to do business with you and cherish our relationship. Our next order needs to be double what we took last time, twelve wagonloads. Your business can accommodate that, of course?" he threw the challenge at him.

"Of course," uncertainty was in Weil's voice as he glanced around the room nervously. "That's a very large quantity. When do you require all this?"

"Oh, no urgency this time, Mr Weil," David relaxed back in his chair, smiling. "I have to proceed to Port Elizabeth to collect my two brothers who have disembarked from Ireland. I have other business to do there, so I will return only in about two months. As usual, Morris insists that I personally load the wagons, so perhaps I could give my order to your manager, Mr Taylor? He can use the next two months to order from your other warehouses around the country what you don't have in Mafeking."

Julian quickly worked this out in his head and agreed that it was all a very simple matter for him and his business, although the uncertainty in his voice did not escape David's notice. "You might find that Gerran may not have enough wagons for you to purchase."

"I had thought of that, and I am sure that there may be other traders in town who would be willing to hire out some wagons to me, if necessary."

"Indeed," Julian mulled the response as he picked up his cup, staring at the tablecloth, but focussing on something far away as he tried to comprehend what this young boy had asked him to do. He seemed to freeze when his lips were just inches from his teacup.

"So," David said, hauling him back to reality, "please give Mr Savage my very best when you deposit the cheque."

Immediately, Julian looked concerned and put down his teacup. "Oh, he is no longer here, unfortunately. He left about six months ago, soon after Morris' visit, in fact: something or other to do with ill health. He said he was going back to England, but it happened rather suddenly; most peculiar."

*

Within the hour, David was walking into Gerran Coachworks, having decided that his two helpings of granadilla sponge cake had been far superior to any shortbread Gerran could have offered him. He didn't need to ask to see Mr Gerran, however, as the burly man spotted him from a small window in his office and hurried out to greet him. Although his actions were welcoming, there was a great deal of concern showing on his face.

"Welcome back to Mafeking, Mr Langbourne," he gushed, "I hope everything is well?

"Yes, everything is fine up north, thank you. I wondered if I could have a quick word with you?" David knew that he was playing on the poor man's nerves, believing that Gerran must have expected the worst from him, but Mr Gerran invited him into his office immediately and sat him down in a chair while seating himself behind his desk. He asked a few trivial questions about Morris and the BSAC in Matabeleland, but no coffee or shortbread was offered. David decided to get to the point as he could sense that Gerran was anxious about the wagons they had on credit with him. He reached into his jacket pocket and pulled out the cheque, passing it to him over the desk.

"I have come to settle our debt with you in full, Mr Gerran," he said, "and both Morris and I wish to extend our deepest gratitude to you for giving us a chance to get on our feet again."

Gerran's eyebrows arched across his brow in surprise. "In full?" he gasped, "and so soon?"

"Yes," David replied amiably. "We have been blessed with some good fortune, and as soon as we were able, Morris instructed me to personally hand you this cheque along with his gratitude."

"Well I never…" Gerran trailed off, studying the cheque. He even looked on the reverse in disbelief. "How on earth did you manage this so quickly? Actually, never mind, that's none of my business, is it?" he chuckled, placing the cheque in a drawer with a touch too much speed, concerned that David might snatch it back.

Coffee and shortbread were suddenly offered, but David declined this time, preferring to continue uninterrupted while the matter of business was at hand. "We have decided that the opportunity exists to grow our business rapidly, and we have a requirement for a further twelve wagons. We would like to ask if you would please extend your credit terms to us once more for the twelve wagons. As you can see, we are more than good for our word."

"Indeed, I can't fault your honour, Mr Langbourne, but twelve wagons is a sizeable amount of credit," he hesitated.

Quickly, David threw a challenge at his pride. "Indeed it is, a very large risk for you, I do understand, but I rather assumed that twelve wagons are not beyond the capacity of your factory?"

"Absolutely not," he faltered, then realised he had opened a weakness in his excuse not to take the risk.

"Well, it is a large sale for your company, and your terms are very lucrative for you, but do not forget that we have just now proven ourselves to be honourable in our business dealings."

"Indeed, indeed," Gerran muttered and looked out a window that overlooked his workshop and the assembly of his wagons. He wanted to open the drawer and look at the cheque once again, but knew that would be rude. David just sat, smiling gently at him.

"When would you need them?" Gerran asked at last.

"Two months hence, Mr Gerran. I am travelling to Port Elizabeth shortly and will require them only on my return. Mr Weil also needs at least two months to fill my order." Hoping that there might be a little rivalry between the two Mafeking business-men, David gently pushed a little competitiveness into the nego-tiations. "We have recently settled our debt with him, too, so he is more than delighted to meet our future requirements."

"You have settled with Weil as well?" Gerran's eyebrows arched again. "Alright, Mr Langbourne," he broke into a genuine smile, "you have a deal. I will have twelve wagons ready for you two months from today – you have my word on that – and the same credit terms will apply."

"Splendid! And thank you, sir," David beamed.

The men stood up and shook hands across the desk. That's all it took: a firm handshake and the deal was set in stone.

CHAPTER SIX
Port Elizabeth

A S THE TRAIN ground to a halt in the red-brick railway
station of Port Elizabeth, the giant clock that hung above
the platform showed that it was ten minutes past six o'clock
in the morning. The magnificent clock had been supplied On Her
Majesty's Service, and was renowned for its accuracy. David picked
up his meagre possessions in a small, soft-leather bag and bid farewell to his fellow passengers, before alighting and making his way
towards the exit without wasting any time. He had several hours to
wait in Kimberley on the journey down, and as he was decidedly
uncomfortable in his ill-fitting formal garments, he had found an
exclusive gentlemen's store on the main street and purchased a fine
business suit that would pass for evening wear as well. He took
an instant liking to a woollen felt, Derby hat that made him look
quite dapper, or so he thought, and purchased it without hesitation. Inadvertently, it would soon become recognised as his personal trademark.

Although the streets of Port Elizabeth, his favourite town,
were empty at that early hour, and all the shops securely locked, he
knew that The Grand Hotel would be open, and he had a purpose

for going there without delay. Making his way up the steep slope of Whites Road, he turned left into Belmont Terrace, and entered the opulent and welcoming warmth of that magnificent hotel. It seemed deserted and quiet, but there was some activity within. Upon entering the dining room, he found Shadreck, his favourite waiter and bar tender. Working his way through the very enjoyable Xhosa custom of greeting good friends, David revealed all the news in Matabeleland, and of his older brother. Shadreck shared his family news in turn, as well as the fact that he recently had become a father for the fifth time. Once the social formalities were over, David asked for a large breakfast, the way only The Grand Hotel could provide, and Shadreck set about placing the order in the kitchen while David made himself comfortable at his "usual" table, having collected a copy of the Eastern Province Herald that had been published on the previous Wednesday.

There was not much news in the Herald, most of it being taken up with businesses advertising their wares and services. David made a mental note to suggest to Morris that they should advertise in a newspaper in Matabeleland, whenever a newspaper became available. His attention was drawn from the paper when Shadreck produced a monstrous breakfast, consisting of three fried eggs, a piece of steak, lamb chops, a length of traditional boerewors sausage, some boiled potatoes, green beans, and two slices of thick toast, which was presented on a side platter as there was no room left on his plate.

David had been holding out for this meal for days, and he wasted no time in addressing the mountain of food in front of him. When Shadreck delivered a pot of steaming hot coffee, he treated himself to four spoonful's of sugar and savoured every mouthful of food, including every sip of the sweet beverage. Shadreck stood discreetly aside as he watched his favourite customer slowly devour the meal, using the most impeccable table etiquette – despite no one else being in the dining room – and smiling with each delicious mouthful.

Leaving enough money on the table to cover the cost of the meal, and a generous little extra for Shadreck, David left the comfort and security of the hotel for The Standard Bank, hoping to see his good friend and mentor, Jack Shiel. Jack would tell him where to find his brothers. Since the bank was not due to open for another fifteen minutes, however, David was obliged to stand in the doorway patiently, but filled with excitement and anticipation. Inside the bank, Jack saw this big man standing with his back to the door, but – although he thought it might be David – he had already decided that the man was far too muscular, and so ignored him. When the doors eventually opened, David walked in and Jack couldn't believe the transformation in his young friend. He had grown into a fully-fledged adult: his facial features were more defined, his shoulders had filled out, and he looked altogether extraordinarily handsome and distinguished in his fashionable business attire, Derby hat included.

"Good grief, David!" he exclaimed loudly, "I didn't recognise you for a moment. What are they feeding you up there?"

David pumped his hand and slapped him on the shoulder. "Good to see you again, Jack," he laughed, "hard work and fresh air, that's all."

"Come in," said Jack and led David into his office. "Margaret," he called over his shoulder to a pretty young teller, "I'll be in a meeting for a little while and can't be disturbed. And please bring us a pot of coffee."

While some further pleasantries were exchanged, the muffled outbursts of laughter coming from Mr Shiel's office told his staff that he was in the company of a really good friend, but David could hardly contain his excitement at the prospect of seeing Louis and Harry again.

"So how are my brothers, Jack?"

"They are well, David, I can certainly see the resemblance in your family - well, I could have before I saw you today. Louis is working as a clerk for Weil, down at his procurement office. As you well may know, Danie Coetzee left for Johannesburg and they have replaced him with a young man from Cape Town. Harry is working for Mr Smit, the same chemist that you and Morris started working for. I don't think either of them is enjoying it, but they know it's temporary. But I must be honest in saying that we were very worried about you two when the rebellion broke out."

David related what had happened when the Matabele had risen against the European settlers, and how they had borne witness to the rebellion. He told him how they had lost just about everything when the war erupted; how their wagons and stock had been destroyed in the countryside; and how he himself had narrowly escaped death when he and Abe had been chased by the marauding impi.

Jack was stunned with what David related. "I hadn't really wanted to think about it," Jack confessed," but yes, although I was worried, the reports claimed a decisive win by the BSAC and the European casualties were said to have been unusually low at the time, so that provided some small comfort to me.

"All is well, Jack: thanks for your concern." David then quickly changed the subject and smiled. "I'm very pleased Louis is working at Weil's. This is excellent news as he will get a good grounding on shipping and procurement. Can I assume you had a hand in this?"

"You know me well, David," he winked.

"I think you know us well, Jack," he laughed. "Morris has plans for our brothers, and you couldn't have put him in a better place to begin to learn about our business."

David went on to explain what Morris intended for the growth of Langbourne Brothers, and further sought Jack's advice on how he believed the plan would work, because Jack's wealth of knowledge and experience in the commercial field was always greatly valued. Jack listened intently and marvelled at what Morris had in mind, and how he intended to implement his business strategy. He was equally fascinated at how Morris had managed to secure such huge loans of credit from Weil and Gerran, especially without collateral to support him.

"It was done on trust and honour, Jack. That's all we had when everything was said and done. We even had our age against us."

"Well, I didn't want to bring that up, but yes, Weil must have put a lot of trust into you boys – I mean, 'you men'. Sorry, I must apologise," he said sheepishly.

"No offence taken, Jack. I know we are young."

"Well, I take my hat off to you chaps. If Louis can do what you ask of him in East London – and I must confess that it will be a huge challenge for him – then, yes, I feel that your plans are sound. But I must warn you that you are flying close to the wind with your cash flow. I estimate that you will struggle with cash for a good seven to eight years before you see the light of day, and only then will you have any hope of seeing any profit."

"Two years, according to Morris."

Jack shook his head, "Morris is a very clever young man, but I beg to differ on that one."

"Well, we took up six wagons in January, and now we are taking twelve wagons. By August next year we could well take eighteen wagons. That would surely put us on the commercial map."

"Impossible!" Jack spluttered. "Have you any idea what eighteen wagon-loads of stock will cost, let alone eighteen wagons? Then there are the logistics of getting them up there: extra oxen and men to drive them; food to feed both men and beast; the list is endless. In any case, you cannot grow a business that quickly without significant financial support."

"I know, but Morris has already factored this all in."

"Well, then he's a better man than me if he can get his plan to work."

"For Morris, numbers, business, and finance are like air, food and water to you and me: we can't live without them. It's his lifeblood; it's what he lives for. And to top it off, he is not scared of taking risks."

"Two years, David?" Jack laughed, but he was still shaking his head in disagreement, "I reserve my judgement on that I'm afraid."

"Sometimes I have my doubts too, Jack," he smiled. "Now, I have a small quantity of cash that I need to send home. We were unable to do it last year, and things might be a little desperate there now, but we have a loan and can spare a little for the family. Can you arrange this for me please?"

*

Half an hour later, David walked up to the old wooden office of Weil & Co., which looked over the bustling harbour. He quickly scanned the activity in the port, looking for the unmistakable hulk of Nguni, but could not see him, so he turned and entered the dilapidated office that he knew so well. Standing at a corner desk, pouring over a pile of paperwork was his younger brother, Louis, who took more than a second to realise it was his older brother.

"David!" he exclaimed in a hoarse whisper, excitement stealing his voice away momentarily.

David felt that, having escaped from the hungry clutches of Ireland, his brother had reached the same height as himself, possibly even taller. "Hello brother," he smiled.

"I knew you would come for us," Louis' voice came back, but this time uncharacteristically deep and manly. David was shocked at how masculine his voice was, and honestly felt it did not match his physique.

"Of course I would come for you, silly boy," he scolded in a joking way, "just listen to your voice! Where did you buy that voice from?" he laughed openly.

In two lengthy strides, Louis stepped over to his brother and shook his hand. He wanted to hug him, but it was not a gentlemanly thing to do, so he held back, awkwardly. David responded with a strong handshake while gripping him firmly on the shoulder with his free hand. "So good to see you, David. We all miss you and Morris," he confided.

"Yes, we miss the family too. But look at you," he stepped back sizing his skinny brother up and down, "you have grown so much."

"Well, you have changed too," Louis laughed as he admired David's bulging chest and shoulders. He was so happy to be with family again. The isolation and distance from any of his family was overpowering. Having left his father, stepmother and sisters in Ireland, he had endured almost a three-month journey by ship, while his two older brothers in KoBulawayo were equally two or three months distant by train and horseback, somewhere in the heart of Africa. Where he stood in Port Elizabeth, he could not be more distant from any of his family. Harry was his only family right now, but acting more as his guardian, so the younger lad was starved of relaxed conversation and company. Although his job had provided some distraction, loneliness remained a nagging problem for him.

They chatted at a fast pace for ten minutes, exchanging some news on the family. Louis admitted that there was some doubt as to whether both brothers in Matabeleland were even alive after the rebellion, but David assured him that he and Morris were in exceptionally good health. There was a lot they needed to talk about, but David felt he should not impose any further on Weil's company time, and arranged to meet Louis back at Sonja's house after working hours. Louis didn't think he could wait that long.

"Wait. Before you go…" Louis quickly stepped over to his desk and withdrew an envelope from a drawer. "Here is a letter from father for you and Morris. You'll be pleased to know we now have a new baby sister."

"No," David was shocked. "You mean, father and Aunt Helena?" he trailed off.

"Well, we call her mother now, because father married her, but yes, our sister's name is Rachel," he smiled innocently.

"No, surely not?" David murmured in disbelief. "A sister?"

"Well, she's a half-sister because we share the same father, but from a different mother. But she is a bit more than a half-sister, I suppose, because Aunt Helena is mother's niece. I'm not sure what that makes her, actually, a three-quarter sister, perhaps?"

David scratched his head in amusement. "Morris will love this!"

"Will you visit Harry now?" Louis asked as he walked David to the door.

"Yes," David pulled his thoughts back into line, "I'll pop down there and say 'hello'."

"Good. He will like that. He has not coped very well being away from the family. He desperately wants to go home."

"I can imagine that he was too young to come out to Africa, but Morris has plans for him and he can't go back. Anyhow, I have an idea how we can make him enjoy it here. Leave it to me," David winked. "Also, I need you to resign from Weil and Co. We have plans for you, too."

"I have to give a week's notice."

"Good, do it today. Make Friday your last working day here," David instructed Louis rather bluntly. Although he was usually diplomatic in his persuasiveness, now was not the time; he expected his plans to be actioned without question, especially by his younger brothers.

They shook hands again and David, with a distinct spring in his step, walked down to the chemist to pass his regards to Mr Smit and greet his youngest brother. He smiled as he thought of the last time he saw the pharmacist, he had just convinced Morris they needed to go to Patensie and buy tobacco. On that occasion they both resigned from Mr Smit. He was sure his reception would be a little cold, especially as he would tell Harry to resign also.

When he entered the chemist, Mr Smit was not to be seen, but Harry was standing on a short ladder, packing vials of some medication onto one of the many, rich-brown, wooden shelves. Believing that Harry might become a little emotional, David thought he would turn his arrival into a game. He knocked gently on the wooden counter to catch his attention, and the moment

Harry looked over his shoulder, David smiled and put his finger to his lips, indicating silence was needed. Harry nearly jumped off the ladder in excitement, but reacting to David's sudden gesture to stay put, looked around for Mr Smit. Keeping the situation under control, David put his finger to his lips again, looking carefully around the chemist for its owner, before quickly signalling Harry to come to him, silently. Wasting no time, Harry almost leapt to the ground and walked over to David as carefully, but as quickly as possible.

"Hello, Harry! Gosh, you have grown!" he whispered loudly, shaking his older brother's right hand vigorously.

"David! I've missed you!" Harry hissed back. "Some people thought you and Morris had been killed and eaten alive."

David shook his head and clucked his tongue gently, "Silly stories; we are all very well." He started speaking normally again. "Now listen to me carefully. I'm going to leave quite soon, before Mr Smit walks in."

"No…" Harry interrupted him, not wanting him to leave so soon.

"Yes, yes; listen to me," he put a firm hand on his brother's shoulder, "I'm going to see Sonja Du Plessis now. I will stay there tonight with you. We can have a long chat later with Louis. At precisely five o'clock, before Mr Smit locks up the shop and sends you home, I want you to tell him you are resigning and your last day will be on Friday. If he asks why, you just tell him your brothers have asked you to come and work for them."

"Oh, what wonderful news that is! I hate it here."

"And don't forget to thank him for letting you work in his establishment. Make sure you thank him," David reiterated sternly.

Harry having agreed excitedly, the details were quickly reconfirmed and, smiling like a Cheshire cat, Harry let his older brother slip out of the shop, unnoticed by the owner. David then put on his Derby hat, straightened his necktie, and made his way to see

Sonja, whistling a little ditty as he went. Their plans were falling into place nicely.

*

Sonja was just as excited to see David, and they chatted and laughed the morning away. She was appalled at the violence the boys had witnessed during the Matabele rebellion, and was shocked at David's story of how he had narrowly escaped a murderous party of Ndebele warriors who had been hunting him down. What impressed her most, however, was the change in his physique.

Bronzed by the sun and sporting broad shoulders, a proud chest, and arms that tested the seams of his long-sleeved, cotton shirt, he made it very difficult for the fairer sex to miss him. The only thing that looked out of place was his hands, which were calloused from the constant hard labour: his carrying loads of bricks, shovelling clay and sand, and tearing up and down ladders as he built the new Langbourne Brothers warehouse. Yet he was now outfitted in the finest garments which might befit the gentry in the highest classes of society.

Sonja could not help a quick glance at his hands before taking a more serious tone and looking him directly in the eyes. "David," she said, "Harry's not coping well without his family. I have often heard him weeping at night. This puts a lot of pressure on Louis, for he, too, is but he puts on a brave exterior for Harry."

"Louis did mention that; I'm sorry you've had to endure this, and I feel for Louis. Nevertheless, I do have some plans for the boys, and by the time I finish with them, they will never look at Africa the same way again."

"Now don't you go telling them that vultures hunt humans in packs. I will never speak to you again if you do!"

David burst out laughing. "And don't you go telling people that is what I believed before! No, I have one month to teach them how to ride a horse, shoot a gun, understand African customs, run a business, and mix with society a lot older than themselves. We also have to get to East London and set up an office there. This is exciting stuff for young boys: I know it was for me. That should take their minds off home."

David saw Sonja's look of disbelief but rather excused himself politely, since he wanted to get down to Solly Alhadeff's General Store to see what goods he might have in stock for their East London excursion. On his way to Solly's, he carefully opened the letter from his father and read his flowery script.

*

23 St. Kevin's Parade,
Wood Quay
Dublin,
Ireland.
3rd April 1894

My dear sons, Morris and David,

I pray that this letter finds you both in good health. Our family is well and we continue to live comfortably on the kind and most generous gift of money that you sent to us. We are forever indebted to you for all you have provided. I will never be able to thank you enough for enabling us to live at a little higher standard than most.
As you requested, I have found lodgings suitable for the family at the above address, and as a result we have blossomed and prospered with excellent fare on the table. Louis and Harry were enrolled at exceptionally good schools and your sister, Bloomy, looks resplendent in some fine garments, while Sally continues to flourish and provides us with much joy and happiness.
There has been a new addition to the family and you now have

a half-sister, Rachel Rae. She is a bundle of joy and keeps us eternally entertained. I am saddened that you are unable to meet her at this time.

Although we are not expectant of any more money from you two, I feel I need to let you know that if you have sent any more money over to Ireland, it has not arrived.

If you receive this letter, then you will know that I have carried out your request to send Louis and Harry to Port Elizabeth. I pray that they have arrived in good health and that they are put to good service in your business.

As letters take so long to traverse the oceans, I would be grateful for any news of you two whenever possible. We miss you dearly and ask that you keep your younger brothers out of harm's way.

Your stepmother, Helena, and myself, send our best wishes to you.

I remain,

Your loving father,

Jacob

*

David folded the letter and replaced it in his jacket pocket. He was still surprised that he now had a half sister, because he didn't know whether his father and stepmother could even have a baby. He decided that, before he left Port Elizabeth, he would write a letter back home, if only to let them know that everyone was safe and had not been harmed in the rebellion up north. He would nevertheless omit the fact that they were almost bankrupt as a result of it.

His visit to Solly's took longer than he expected as he ran into the kindly gentleman himself, who insisted that he stay for a cup of tea and tell him all about his travels. After exchanging news with Solly, he went down to the harbour to look for his old friend, Nguni. Failing again to locate him, he put the word out that he was looking for him and would return, and having achieved all he wanted to for the day, he went back to Sonja's home to wait for his brothers.

He did not have to wait long. Harry was the first to come home, squealing with delight as he bounded through the front door, excitedly stating that Mr Smit was not happy with his decision to leave, so had paid him out and told him not to come back. David had been confident that this would be the result and nodded approvingly at the news. Barely five minutes later, Louis entered the household with a little more restraint, but was still clearly bursting with excitement. The formalities of the morning in their workplaces were relaxed, and much laughter and giggling punctuated the incessant barrage of questions that the younger brothers threw at David.

Granting them some degree of privacy, Sonja retreated to that part of the room which formed the kitchen and listened quietly to the little family reunion, smiling and dabbing at a small tear as she stirred a lamb stew that had been simmering in a blackened three-legged pot. Eventually, she intervened by serving dinner at her small, wooden table and so joined in the conversation and excitement that carried on right through the meal.

David answered all his brothers' questions as best he could. He explained how they had set up their cigarette factory on the back veranda of Sonja's house, and how they had sold it for an unexpected small fortune. He told them of the gruelling, monotonous, yet dangerous three-month trek up to KoBulawayo, and how they had built two wattle-and-daub buildings to run the business. Skimping somewhat on the details of the Matabele rebellion, he explained that, because of the nature of their wagon-trading business, traders had taken their stock on consignment and only paid them for what they sold on their return from the outlying settlements. The brothers had therefore lost just about everything when the Matabele impi had attacked their traders, burning their stock, wagons, and all the takings to the ground.

"But why did you buy so much stock? Surely you must have understood the risk you were taking?" Louis was quick to understand their difficult business predicament.

David explained carefully so that both brothers would understand. "Yes, we did, but you have to understand that when we realised that it was going to take four to five months to walk with our wagons to Fort Salisbury, where we intended to trade, we needed to take as much as we could at one time or we would have spent our entire lives walking around the countryside driving wagons and replenishing stock. Just one month is an inordinate amount of time to walk alone in the bush and not even do any business, so when we got to KoBulawayo, which was three months later, we had had enough stock to last us a good year. The problem was that we did not realise how few people were living there, so we had too much stock for the amount of people in the settlement. We had no idea what problem we had created for ourselves; we had enough stock to last about three years."

"So what happened?" Harry asked impatiently.

"Morris had this idea to hire out our wagons to businessmen we call wagon traders, who would fill their wagons, our wagons, with our stock and go out into the countryside and sell to people in other settlements. We made a profit selling to them, and the profits they made would be their profits. We would also make a profit on renting out our wagons and our oxen, and by renting out the oxen, we didn't have to feed them or care for them, which costs money, the traders did that for us. It was a great business idea. The problem was that people in KoBulawayo didn't have a lot of money, so in order to get them to take our wagons, oxen and goods, we had to give them credit. When the rebellion broke out and our traders were attacked, they lost everything, and so did we, simply because they had not paid us for the stock yet. If the rebellion had not happened, we would have been in a very sound position right now, but we never saw it coming and I have no idea what got into the British and the Matabele. Politics is something I do not understand, and I warn you two," he looked at his brothers sternly, raising a finger, "and I mean this: stay well clear of politics, and never take anyone's side; you will get into a lot of trouble. Remember that you are Irish, not British, Dutch, Matabele or Xhosa. We are here to do business and to make money to support our family, just remember that."

There was a deathly hush as the enormity of their situation sank in.

"But you have a plan to fix all this, don't you?" Louis asked cautiously.

"Morris has a plan, yes. He always has a plan. Let me tell you something about your brother that you don't know: he is a very clever person."

"We know that, David," Louis interrupted, glancing at the ceiling in frustration.

"No you don't," David shot back. "Yes, he was clever in Ireland when we lived in the old cottage. He could answer all of father's complicated trick questions and he was good at his maths and all that, yes, I agree, but somehow he has just become more and more smarter while we have been in Africa. He is actually brilliant beyond words. You will find out," he smiled mischievously.

"How smart?" Louis looked concerned.

"Very! I've seen him confuse bank managers and he talks circles around the big company bosses, who are much older than him. He is quite something to watch when he gets started. If he has a plan, you can be very sure it will work." David leaned forward in his seat and stared hard at his two brothers. "Morris needs you to join our business now. Louis, we are going to a town called East London on

Saturday. We are going to start a branch of Langbourne Brothers there and we need you to manage it for us."

"Me?" Louis looked startled.

"Yes, and I have one month to teach you what to do. Harry, you will be coming with me to KoBulawayo, Morris wants to teach you himself."

"Are you going to leave me in East London on my own?" Louis objected.

"If I feel you are not able to run the business after one month, I'm going to take you to KoBulawayo with Harry, hand you to Morris, and come back to run the East London office myself." David winked at him. "Personally, I would far prefer to live in East London so I would suggest that you try your best." The insinuation was not lost on Harry, who suddenly looked concerned and opened his mouth to say something, but decided against it quickly.

"Right, then we start tomorrow. When you get back from work, Louis, I'm going to take you boys out a little way into the bush to learn how to shoot a rifle for protection and I need to teach you how to hunt for food."

"To hunt?" Harry exclaimed.

"You have a gun?" Louis seemed shocked.

"You won't live long in the bush without a rife, that's for sure," David winked at Sonja, who returned the gesture with a knowing smile.

"We're going hunting tomorrow, Louis. How exciting!" Harry bubbled with anticipation.

Louis looked David in the eye and smiled. He knew that his older brother had taken Harry's mind off his isolation and given him a renewed interest in their unfamiliar home. He had not seen that spark of excitement in Harry's eyes since they had landed in the Cape Colony, but he had a fresh concern of his own that now plagued his mind: how would he deal with even more isolation in East London, without even a brother? He understood fully that

David depended on him to succeed in East London; there was clearly no alternative.

"Oh, and I'll need some space on the floor of your bedroom tonight, my brothers," David joked. "I'm used to sleeping on the ground."

"You can have my bed, David," Harry almost insisted, "I'd like to sleep on the floor."

"Why, thank you Harry. That is so kind of you," David showered him with appreciation, although he already knew that Harry would make that offer, and as he enjoyed the comfort of a mattress, he gratefully accepted his brother's sacrifice.

Harry beamed with pride, honoured that his older brother would sleep in his bed.

*

Standing in the shade of a large gum-tree three miles from the town limits, David surveyed the land around him. He was dressed in his bush clothes – a long-sleeved, beige shirt and khaki trousers, with a wide-brimmed hat to match – while his Martini Henry rifle was perched over his right shoulder. Although freshly washed, his clothes carried with its many stains the odd nick and stray thread, a well-illustrated journal of the hard labour and close calls over the preceding months. From his leather belt hung a razor-sharp knife, made in England, and secured in a brown leather sheath, as well as his Webley revolver. By his side stood his trusted friend and companion, Nguni, dressed in his traditional robes and holding a long spear with ease. Like David, he scoured the distant landscape, looking for something as yet unknown. Although of widely contrasting cultures, the two men stood in a silent bond of friendship in a land that they both loved.

Louis and Harry stood a couple of yards behind, staring in utter fascination at their brother and the large African man. They could not believe what had become of their brother. When they had last seen him in Ireland, about three years ago, he had been a skinny boy of fifteen years' old, wearing threadbare hand-me-downs, and appearing a little unsure of himself. Now, here he stood: proud and content, as if an integral part of Mother Africa, carrying a host of lethal weapons, and looking as if he was quite comfortable in both the big towns and the wild bush alike. He had a physical strength they had not imagined possible in him, his boyish looks having been replaced by strong masculine lines, and a sense of confidence that was hard to ignore. He even spoke an African language, a strange language that had sharp clicks scattered among the words. Now he stood beside a very large and muscular African man, who seemed to be his best friend. Many times they had to remind themselves that he was the very same brother they had known in Ireland.

"The kudus look peaceful today, mfo wethu," David said softly in Xhosa.

"Perhaps the lions were well fed last night," he mused, scanning the veld for predators. They spoke without looking at one another.

"We will annoy the kudus when we teach these youngsters how to shoot this rifle."

A serious frown creased Nguni's brow. "Perhaps they will forgive you, if you do not point it at them,"

David allowed a smile to escape his lips. "If my brothers pointed the rifle at them they will be sure to miss. Do you recall the first time Morris and I tried to shoot a rifle?"

Nguni looked down at his European friend. "It is a day I try to forget, but I cannot," he chuckled. "Even the baboons were laughing at Boss Morris that day."

David started to laugh at the memory of the first time Morris pulled the trigger of the Martini-Henry. He had to admit that it was probably the most hilarious day he had ever experienced. He had never seen Nguni laugh so much either. Then he turned to his brothers who were silently listening to him conversing in that strange African language. They appeared eager to join in on the humour, but at the same time looked very out of place in their town clothes.

Making a mental note to get them down to Solly Alhadeff's General Store as soon as possible, David called them over and began to explain how to work the Martini-Henry rifle. He showed them how to load the weapon, how to aim, and how to clean it, a very important part of using a rifle. Safety was a big issue with David and his tone became very stern when he discussed this topic. He made his brothers hold the rifle, turn and turn about, aiming at a random target in the distance and "dry firing" the empty chamber. Each time one of the brothers passed the rifle to the other, he made them show everyone that there was no bullet in the chamber, such was his strict discipline when it came to gun safety.

He tried to explain how violent the kick of the rifle would be when they fired it, but knew they would be unprepared for what was to come on the first shot, so he made them stand correctly, aim the unloaded weapon, and pull the trigger. At the same time, he held on to the barrel and violently slammed the butt into their shoulder to simulate what would happen; of course their shoulders hurt, but they did not complain.

Finally the time came to load a real bullet into the chamber, and although it was second nature for David, his brothers were both anxious and nervous at the same time.

"Who's first?"

"Me please," Harry insisted.

"Go ahead."

Louis stepped back and put his fingers in his ears and David chuckled. "You can't shoot a gun with your fingers in your ears, Louis. Far better that you hear it for what it is. Don't worry: if you do as I say, it will be fine. Alright, Harry, show me what you have learnt."

As Harry placed a round in the chamber, David noticed Nguni surreptitiously take a few steps back and put some space between himself and the offending weapon. Following David's instructions and encouragement, Harry did what he was told and lined up the sites for a shot. When he pulled the trigger, the impact of the butt on his shoulder, the volume of sound in his head, and the blinding cloud of white smoke were overwhelming. Although a strong sense of pride overpowered his impulse to drop the killing machine and run for safety, he was not happy with what he had experienced and lowered the gun, while holding it at arm's length. When the smoke cleared David seemed to be congratulating him, but in very silent tones. He looked over at Louis, who was also speaking to him, but there was no sound coming from his lips, only a shrill ringing from somewhere above. He was deafened and dazed, and somehow, thankfully, David took the rifle from him.

Louis initially refused to fire the weapon, but with a little encouragement from David, and fear of humiliation from Harry, he took the rifle and went through the steps of loading, holding and aiming the rifle. Just before he pulled the trigger he closed his eyes tightly shut. The sound and the violence that erupted from the Martini-Henry was immense, but having seen what had happened when Harry pulled the trigger, he was more prepared and found the ordeal manageable.

It would take four days of practice before David was comfortable that they could use a rifle, although their aim was less than good. Meanwhile, he had his brothers fitted out with a set of bush clothes and walking boots, which he insisted they wear for a couple of hours each evening to break them in, and he had Louis fitted out with a new business suit as he would need this when they got to East London.

Friday came swiftly and on that evening David hosted Sonja, Jack, and his two brothers to a dinner at The Grand Hotel. It was partially a test to see how his younger brothers, especially Louis, could handle themselves in an upper-class establishment. At the end of the evening, he was comfortable that Louis could easily integrate himself in a situation like this, although he needed more confidence. Harry, meanwhile, was a little too sure of himself for his age, and David found him a little annoying, although he could not fault his table manners. While they were enjoying their dinner, many local businessmen and acquaintances who were also dining there took time to greet both Jack and David and to ask after Morris, which further impressed Louis and Harry with David's popularity.

On the following morning, the three Langbourne brothers boarded the train to East London, and that is when the hard work began.

CHAPTER SEVEN

East London

D AVID CHECKED THEM into a simple lodging a quick ten-minute walk from the port, close to the East London railway station, On the second day of their arrival, he located a small warehouse that was for rent one block away from the bustling harbour, and signed a lease agreement with the land-lord for one year. That being done, he found a one-bedroom flat on the first floor of a dull brick apartment with communal water closet and bath area, and negotiated a very good lease for one year, much to the disgust of Louis, who knew this would be his home for some considerable time.

"If you saw where Morris and I lived for the last year you would find this absolute luxury, trust me," he warned his brother. "In any case, we can't afford anything better."

"When we make lots of money, I'm going to build myself a mansion," Louis grumbled miserably.

"You do that," David laughed. "I'm sorry to do this to you, brother, and in time you will have the mansion you dream of, but right now this will have to be your home. Make the most of it."

"What's your house like in KoBulawayo? Will I have a room

like this?" Harry asked, pointing to the minute room that Louis would soon be occupying.

David burst out laughing. "Your room, little brother, is a roll of blankets on the floor at the back of a grass-thatched, mud and pole warehouse. And you will be sharing some floor space with Morris and me. But never fear, on our way up to KoBulawayo, you will get lots of practice at sleeping soundly on the ground!"

Harry was not amused, but Louis smiled. "Then I am delighted to call this room my home," he joked as he waved his arms at his sleeping quarters in mock pride.

The remainder of the month went by in a blur. David ensured that almost every evening they dined in good-quality eating establishments and hotel lounges, and showed Louis how to walk up to a group of gentlemen and enter their conversation with a warm smile and firm handshake. He also showed him how to ascertain if they were uncomfortable with the intrusion and how to politely excuse himself from the group, if necessary, which happened more often than not. Within that month, he had successfully forged a friendship with three groups of businessmen in three different establishments, who thoroughly enjoyed their company. He challenged Louis to align himself with two other groups in the next two months on his own.

The brothers spent a large amount of time at the wharf, visiting businesses in the harbour area, befriending the Harbourmaster and other key members of the shipping industry. Louis began to understand the movement of ships from various countries and what they supplied, and David spent hour upon hour drilling into his brother the type of goods they wanted and how to negotiate and bargain for a better price. He pretended to be a hardened trader and forced Louis to haggle with him in order to strike a deal. David made it downright difficult, sometimes leaving his younger brother perplexed at the weird change in character he could assume. It wasn't easy for David either because he did not like pretending to be someone he was not, but it was a charade, an act designed to ensure their future financial survival.

Following Morris' strict instructions, they bought a cashbook and journal in which David taught Louis how to enter all his transactions, threatening Morris' wrath if Louis were to neglect recording everything perfectly, or heaven forbid, to make a mistake. They further opened an account with The Standard Bank and, coupled with an introduction from Jack Shiel, together with David's welcoming personality, forged a strong business relationship with their manager.

Under David's guiding hand, Louis was given the lead in registering the company with the authorities and Harry watched in fascination as he began to learn all about company law and company structures. When David observed his brother's keen interest in the field, he proceeded to bombard him with as much information as he could, much of which he had learned from Jack Shiel in their early days in Port Elizabeth. The brothers opened a telegraphic address called 'LANGBEL', an anagram for Langbourne Brothers, East London, and sent a test telegram to Morris in KoBulawayo. It read:

*

TO LANGBRO

LANGBOURNE ESTABLISHED EL STOP REPLY LANGBEL STOP

*

David rented three horses for one month, with saddles and reins, and for the last two hours of sunlight at the end of each hard day, he would saddle up and take his brothers past the town limits and lead them through the bush, talking constantly about everything he had learned about the local wildlife: from the tiniest, creeping insects to the largest and most dangerous mammals. Secretly, he was preparing Harry for long hours in the saddle and to break in his boots. He remembered how, the first time he took off on a horse, expecting to ride for five or six hours at a time, he had lasted barely one hour after receiving raw patches on his backside and how the muscles and tendons in his thighs had taken several days to recover. Now the journey to KoBulawayo was looming and he did not want his young brother to hold him up.

In the third week, some unexpected news filled the boys with excitement: the Harbourmaster informed them that a ship from the Malay Islands was due to dock later that afternoon. Using a telescope, David could see her flag flying a few miles off the coast. They watched her dock and studied how she was unloaded and where the goods were being carted. Wasting no time, and with cheque-book in hand, David hustled his brothers to the respective warehouses, where they were shown what was available for purchase. David took the lead in haggling with the wholesalers, making sure that Louis followed his example. They didn't buy very much that day, but just enough to get a feel for what was required of them, what their competition was like, and a little something about the traders they would be dealing with.

Carrying what purchases they made to their own warehouse, Louis quickly entered their trades into his cashbook and reconciled the cheque-book. They implemented the same system of storing the goods that they used in Matabeleland so the goods might be located in a hurry when the warehouse was full to capacity. Most importantly, David made Louis record the cost price of each item into their black-rhino code both in the cashbook and on the goods themselves.

Each day David would speed-test his brothers on the black-rhino code until it became like a second language to them. Because the telegraph was their only means of communication at that time, the use of codes was a necessity in order to keep their sensitive information private. They thus invented a code for units of measure – including weights, lengths, distances – and other codes for colour, countries, towns, modes of transport, and people of importance, such as bank managers, station masters and even the prime minister. Even Cecil John Rhodes, unbeknown to him, received a secret Langbourne code word.

Finally, they gave each other code names one evening over dinner, and enjoyed a good laugh in the process. Louis accepted the code name "Giraffe", because of his tall, thin shape and lanky legs, and Harry went with "Badger", because of his black hair, small stature, and natural curiosity. David preferred a bird over an animal, and so he was given the name of the fearless "Eagle". Morris, however, had no choice in his code name, but – since he was the head of the Langbourne family in Africa – they named him after the King of the Jungle, "The Lion", and they were sure he would not argue with that.

Although comfortable with leaving Louis behind, David did not let up in the last remaining week together. Conversations about company law, company systems, business strategies, and administrative tests were carried out relentlessly. Although most of the discussions were aimed at Louis, Harry listened in and asked occasionally pertinent questions that David was able to answer at the drop of a hat. Bush walks and horse trails were constant and the socialising after hours continued every night. David had such endless energy that Louis and Harry struggled to keep up with him, both physically and mentally.

"Come on brothers, keep up!" David would laugh. "We have work to do; things to learn; places to go!"

One Thursday afternoon, as they made their way to the harbour, they called into the post office as usual, but this time there was a telegraphic message waiting for them. It was erratically type-written on off-white paper that was of a lesser quality than newspaper and there were only eight words printed on it:

*

RECEIVED STOP CONFIRM BL GRINDERS REQD URGENT STOP

These eight words were vitally important to the boys, each for their own reason. For Louis, it proved he had a connection and closeness to where his family would be in that distant country of Matabeleland, and so he felt less afraid of his future isolation and loneliness. For Harry, it was the fascination of communication and codes, while for David, it not only reconnected him with his brother, but also more importantly told him how things were going in KoBulawayo.

"Louis!" David thrust the telegraphic message into his brother's hand, "decode that. What does it say?" He couldn't contain his excitement.

Louis read the message carefully. "It says Morris confirms he wants twelve wagons urgently. Doesn't it?" he asked nervously.

"What do you think it says, Harry?"

"I agree with Louis, 'Grinder' is the code word for 'wagon', and 'BL' is 'twelve', so he wants twelve wagons rather urgently."

"Good, you've both got it right, but what else does it say?"

Louis and Harry both looked at the telegram and read it again. Louis shook his head and looked at David with a confused frown on his forehead. "I'm assuming the word 'received' means he received your telegram, but I can't see anything else."

"Me neither," Harry added.

"You are right, Louis, it does mean he received our telegram, but come on, chaps," David teased, "there's a story in there. Morris is telling us that business is good in KoBulawayo. It's better than good, it's booming! It's been just over four months since we received six wagons of stock and already he needs twelve more wagons, and urgently. It also tells me that in April next year we will need another twelve wagons, if not more."

"Now how on earth can you work that out from eight words?" Louis raised his eyebrows as he tried to work it out himself.

"Easy, if it takes four months for Morris to plough through

six wagons, then it will take eight months to plough through twelve, which takes us to about June next year, but knowing your brother as I do, he won't wait for the stock to run out and he will place a new order for twelve or more wagons around April, about two months before he gets desperate again. But of course, it all depends on how brisk business is at the time: it may be more, or it may be less, or it could be sooner or later, depending on our cash position, but what these eight words are telling me right now is that business is booming up north and we need to shake a leg or your brother will be like a cantankerous old elephant, and that's not pleasant to be around, believe me."

"David," Louis ruffled his hair in desperation, "it is obvious to us that you and Morris have your own language, and I fear I will never understand it. It's also plain to see that you understand each other even though you are a thousand miles apart, and I feel somewhat inadequate in stepping up to your level of understanding and teamwork."

"You will, don't you worry," he reassured his brother confidently. "Once you spend a bit of time in Morris' company things will start to make sense to you. It won't take long before you, Harry, Morris and I will be a perfect team. Now come on brothers,…"

"I know, I know," Harry interrupted David and sighed, "we have work to do."

*

The day came when David was ready to head back to KoBulawayo. One month had passed in East London and he was confident that Louis would cope on his own. He had given him clear instructions what the business was looking for, what they wanted, and what they expected. He had given him a budget to work with, and – although Louis was still lacking in confidence – he had succeeded in integrating him into some sectors of society. He had signed up with the repertory theatre, joined the local library, and applied for memberships with a host of clubs and organisations. He was able to shoot a rifle, albeit his aim was not exceptional, and could ride a horse with some degree of confidence. Wholesalers and traders at the wharf recognised him and were greeting him, even though he didn't conduct much business, and David had outfitted him with appropriate garments for daytime, evening, and bush wear. The business administration and systems were in place and Louis had a place to put his head down at night.

Although the farewell at the station was a little too emotional for Louis, he was excited about what lay ahead of him, being now in charge of the East London branch of the family business. Secretly, he was pleased to see his two brothers board the train and depart, but he needed a day off to rest and to gather his thoughts: David's intensity and uncontrolled energy, excitement, and enthusiasm had worn him out completely.

*

The train journey was exciting and invigorating for Harry. The fellow passengers were jolly and entertaining, especially when in conversation with his older brother, but he was not impressed with what he found in Mafeking, although he had little time to sulk about it. Almost as soon as they alighted from the train, David bundled him into a dim warehouse filled with boxes and cartons. He was briefly introduced to Ian Taylor, who commented on Harry's likeness to Morris, before he was thrust a wad of paperwork to start combing through and checking off crates of stock as they were loaded onto a wagon that had been wheeled into the warehouse.

As Harry's eye became accustomed to the paperwork – the layout of the numbers, the names, and the quantities of the items he was looking for, his efficiency began to speed up. It took a week to load the twelve wagons. It would have gone faster if David had helped, but he was too occupied in gathering his team of drivers and herders with Daluxolo, as well as organising the large number of oxen needed to transport the wagons north.

Unlike previous expeditions, David was a little wiser and purchased a small flock of goats. When he accompanied the wagons on their trek, he would provide fresh meat by hunting small antelope when food was required, but when Daluxolo led the wagons north, David would have to provide dried meat or bully-beef in tins for his men because they hunted by traditional means, and that was not as efficient as a rifle and bullet. Tins of meat took up space and increased the weight of the load on the wagons, and if the wagons ever got bogged down in mud or sand and required to be unloaded to lessen the weight, it caused a great deal of wasted time, effort and inconvenience. Goats, however, could feed themselves as they walked behind the wagons on the grass and vegetation of the bush. They would also provide good fresh milk, cheese, and meat when required. The chickens which were caged underneath the wagons would also supply fresh meat, but only when the travellers were desperate, because they also provided protein in the form of eggs.

By the time the wagons departed Mafeking, it looked like a mobile farmyard, much to Harry's amusement. Within hours of their leaving the town, however, David picked up the pace with Harry in tow and they moved ahead of all the shouting, moaning, creaking, bleating, and the cracking of whips. As they reached the crest of a hill, David stopped and looked back. There were twelve wagons of stock, three wagons of corrugated-iron roof sheeting, 43 goats, 32 chickens, 90 oxen and 31 men, mostly Xhosa-speaking, with some Ndebele and Tswana in the mix.

Harry marvelled at the caravan as it ground forward at a slow pace, leaving a cloud of dust in its trail. "I can't believe all that belongs to us," he murmured.

"Sometimes I can't, either," David replied, looking up at the clear sky. "The rains will be here in a couple of months. This might be a tough ride for the men if they get caught."

"Will we get caught in the rain?"

"No, I don't think so," he reassured his youngest brother. "The rains will be here around November or December, so we have two months up our sleeve. Then the rivers will flood about a month after that. Our own journey will take about 18 days, but they will take about three months: that's what worries me."

"Does Daluxolo know the way?"

"Oh yes, he's done this journey twice before. He knows where to go and where fresh water is. He is taking an easier route, but we are taking a faster, more difficult one. There are some things along the way I want to show you. Come on, your brother is waiting for us. Let's go now."

With that he turned his horse northwards and gave it a gentle dig in the ribs with his heels. Harry followed him obediently as they broke into a gentle canter.

Despite David's careful breaking in of Harry's equestrian skills, Harry still found the first four days tough on his bones and muscles, but pride kept him from complaining. Along the way, David's interest in birds, animals, plants, and insects did not escape Harry, with David making the most of the rest periods explaining to his brother what he had learned or discovered during his long spells traversing the plains and forests of Southern Africa. Around the campfire at night, he babbled excitedly about his experiences in the bush, his bruising encounter with an ostrich, the giant hairy spider that had crawled over his neck one night, or the ferocious sting of the scorpion that he had experienced on his baby finger. These stories left Harry nervously inspecting the ground by his feet every few seconds.

One afternoon, they arrived at a slight rise in the ground that was barren of vegetation, apart from one dry and gnarled tree. A dead log lay on the ground beside it among the light brown earth and broken white quartz rocks that littered the area.

"Let's stop here and take a break," David suggested, dismounting and securing his horse to the bare tree. Harry did likewise and looked around, seeing nothing different to what he had seen over the last nine monotonous days. Monotony was a terrible thing, especially for a twelve-year-old boy, and it tested his every resolve, but David had a patience that might have been classed as a gift.

"It's not a very shady spot," said Harry abruptly and David noticed a slight similarity between Morris and Harry's temperament.

"I know," David agreed and sat on a rock, indicating to his brother to sit on another rock beside him, which he reluctantly did. David nodded and smiled his appreciation.

David began to explain to Harry how the African people were very superstitious and believed in many spirits who could do them harm. As a result they constantly had festivals or rituals to appease the sprits, asking for good luck, good rains, or good health. Spirit mediums, who generally doubled as doctors, played a very important part in their societies and communities, and, David warned, they were not to be taken lightly. He related some fascinating stories about the exploits of these mediums, and some of the incidents that he had personally witnessed during his short time in Africa that were difficult to explain. The conversation certainly held Harry's attention until David finally paused, looked around, and sighed.

"The third time I passed here," he said, "I was on my own. Look around you, Harry: there is not a soul for hundreds of miles in any direction." Harry nervously looked into the bush and realised his brother was right, they were truly in the middle of nowhere.

"If you were to fall off your horse," David continued, "and break your leg, and couldn't mount her again, or maybe you didn't hurt yourself and your horse just ran away, which happened to me, incidentally; or maybe you got a sickness, or your horse got bitten by a snake – anything that might disrupt your journey – then the chances of your dying out here would be very good."

Harry was starting to squirm on his stone seat, but David continued with his lecture, "and I haven't even started to tell you what a lion can do to you or your horse, or an elephant, or a hyena, which is an animal that looks a bit like a dog and often hunts in packs. A buffalo is a terribly aggressive animal if it takes a disliking to you, and – unless you know exactly where to shoot it – it can still kill you even though it might have taken six bullets in its body."

"You're making me scared, David. I want to go back to Port Elizabeth."

"Yes, I'm deliberately making you scared. I want you to know what your brother and I had to go through, and we didn't have someone with any experience to show us. But you have me here to protect you, and I will do that, but I need you to protect me, too. I know this is terribly boring, everything looks the same, and every day is the same as another. I understand that, but if you took an interest in where you were and what you were doing, the days would go faster, and you could have some enjoyment out of it."

"How could I possibly create any enjoyment out of a land that is prepared to kill me?" he complained, his eyes welling up in despair.

David smiled calmly, pleased that his lecture had touched his brother's heart. "Start studying that which is around you. Look at the birds: see how they fly, their colours, where they perch, and learn their calls. When you see an animal, watch his behaviour; look at the marks they leave on the ground and on the trees; look carefully at the leaves of trees as you pass them, their shapes and colours, the type of thorns and their fruits. There is so much to see and learn. And then, watch my back, protect me, look out for predators, keep alert, and at night when we take turns keeping watch, don't fall sleep."

Harry smiled sheepishly, then sighed. He realised he had been a little inconsiderate during the journey thus far and resolved immediately to change his behaviour. After all, he was here for the family. "Alright, brother, I hear what you say. I promise to take a better interest in this place."

"Good," David smiled kindly. "I have named this spot 'Nomandudwane'; it means 'Place of the Scorpion'."

Harry immediately checked the ground around his boots. "You have been to this exact spot before?" he asked.

"Yes, I told you so. This is where I was stung by that scorpion. It was under that log," he pointed to the dead log lying beside them.

"I don't believe you. In this vast place of nothingness, you have found your way back to this very spot? How is that possible, David?"

"I just know the way, don't ask me how," he laughed. "Now, I want to share a very special secret with you that nobody knows but me. I have decided that every time I pass Nomandudwane, I will leave a coin as a token of respect for this wonderful continent of Africa."

To Harry's amazement, David stood up and took one pace to a small pile of stones that lay right in front of them. Very carefully he removed the three quartz rocks, checking for scorpions under each, and exposed three silver coins. There was also what looked like a small piece of brown leather lying among the coins. Harry's jaw dropped.

"These coins represent each time I have passed this place. The leather," David picked it up between his fingers and blew some dust off it, "is a piece from my belt. It represents me, as it belongs to me."

Harry looked at the tail-end of David's belt, and realised for the first time that he had a piece roughly cut off it. Jokingly, David matched the two pieces together to prove to his brother that it was from the same belt. Harry was speechless again. Putting the leather back in its place on the earth, David rummaged in his pocket and drew out another silver coin, which he placed next to the other three.

"This is my way of thanking Africa for allowing me to walk on her land, Harry. Now, would you like to join my secret?"

"Yes, please!" Harry almost leapt to his feet, "but I don't have any coins."

"Here," David extracted another coin from his pocket, "you can have this copper one, but first you have to leave with it a piece of something that belongs to you. Only once, never again."

Harry excitedly began to unbuckle his belt, but David stopped him, saying that he had to use something other than his belt.

"A piece of my boot?" he suggested. David laughed and nodded, passing him his sharp sheath knife. Harry removed his right boot and turned it over several times looking for a part of it to cut off, and eventually settled for a section of the tongue. Carefully slicing off a piece about one-inch square, he placed it on the ground with his copper coin, right next to David's three silver coins.

In absolute silence, the two brothers mounted their horses and turned their backs on Nomandudwane. Leaving five coins and two pieces of leather under a small pile of rocks, a secret bond between Africa and these young men had been irreversibly forged.

CHAPTER EIGHT
Plaque

THE YOUNG LADY'S shriek was so loud and blood-curdling that the entire street stopped in their tracks and looked at her in horror. Standing on the footpath of Abercorn Street, dressed in a long flowing turquoise skirt that reached down to her ankles and a delicate cream blouse with matching ribbons, the attractive young girl began flailing her arms uncontrollably, attacking her own face, throwing her long, ginger locks wildly about her head like a dog that has just emerged from a pond, shaking drops of water from his coat. Her second scream was louder and more desperate and she began stamping her feet in panic as men and women in the street ran to her assistance, wondering what disaster had befallen this poor woman.

A gentleman wearing beige trousers and a white, long-sleeved shirt with a thin, black necktie reached her first and began to grab for something in her hair. Having dislodged and thrown the item on the street, he quickly grabbed the distraught woman in his arms as her legs began to buckle in a faint. Two other women reached her and took over from the man, talking gently to her as they eased her into a sitting position.

"It's okay, Miss," Harry heard the man say as he ran out onto the street, "it's just a locust. It's harmless. Don't worry, Miss, it's gone now," he soothed.

David and Morris came tearing out of the warehouse and into the street behind Harry. Morris, like Harry, was wearing smart work clothing, whereas David was shirtless, having tumbled down a ladder and run outside the moment he heard the screams of distress.

"What happened?" Morris exclaimed.

"A locust flew into her face, I think. Looks like it got tangled in her hair," Harry ventured.

"Poor girl, she must have been frightened out of her wits," Morris sympathised.

"What's a locust?" Harry couldn't take his eyes off the fuss being made over the young lady who was sobbing openly as she was helped to her feet. "Are they poisonous? Will she die?"

"Oh Harry," David scolded, "no, of course not. A locust is like a giant grasshopper. She would have got a terrible fright, though, especially if it got tangled in her hair. Poor girl," he repeated.

"It's lying there, on the road. I'm going to have a look at it," Harry said as he walked off.

Just then, another locust crash-landed heavily at David's feet. "Hold on, here's another one," he bent down and picked it up cautiously by the thorax, careful to keep his fingers away from its spiky hind legs.

Harry came to look at the offensive insect and was intrigued by its size and evil looks. Although it displayed some fascinating variations of colour, he turned his nose up at it. "I can well imagine how frightened she must have been, this creature is awful. This must be the other locust's mate; they probably fly around in pairs." Harry looked back at the shadow of the first locust that still sat in the dust, poised to jump.

Suddenly, a cloud moved overhead and the light was darkened

in an instant. A faint buzzing could be heard, but it was direction-less, and people began looking all about them.

"Oh my word…" Morris said slowly, looking up at the sky.

A massive swarm of locusts was flying above KoBulawayo, so thick and dense, that it had dimmed the bright sunlight. At that moment, another locust crashed into the wall of the Langbourne Brothers' building, landing clumsily at their feet, then another on the foot-path, until – just like large raindrops before a tropical storm – locusts began tumbling down all about them.

The population of KoBulawayo stared silently at the sky in both horror and fascination.

"Run!" bellowed a man's urgent voice, followed for just a very brief moment by silence. Then some women began screaming wildly, men were yelling desperately, dogs were barking, and chil-dren were wailing in horror. People began bolting in every direc-tion, some careering into each other, others falling over their own feet, almost everyone doing their best to cover their heads with their hands.

It was pandemonium.

"In here!!" David grabbed a man and a woman as they ran past the entrance of Langbourne Brothers. He led them into the sample room along with his two brothers and instantly closed the door behind them. All five people stood panting, wide-eyed in surprise at what had just happened.

Morris was in a mild state of shock. "Have you ever seen any-thing like this before, David?" he gasped.

"Never! Did you see the size of that swarm?"

Harry needed confirmation. "They are harmless, aren't they?"

"Yes, as far as I know they only eat vegetation."

It was not a swarm, it was a plague. Dark clouds of locusts settled mercilessly over the land, and any plant that was green and edible was relentlessly mown down in their wake. Women stayed indoors, or were cocooned in their tents and wagons. Only the brave and curious children came out to play when the locusts were not swarming. The herds of grazing animals – impala, kudu, zebra and other antelope – started moving away to find food, while the happily insectivorous birds feasted well on the gift from the skies.

Despite the infestation of millions upon millions of locusts, David continued to work on the Langbourne building, although his teams of builders were less than interested in a day's wages, and often did not arrive for the day's tasks. The building was now almost complete; all that was needed was a roof, the galvanised sheeting of which was on its way with Daluxolo. Housed inside the roofless building stood three wood-and-mud, thatched struc-tures where the Langbournes conducted what business they could. The plague had not only reduced food supplies and demoralised the settlers, but businesses throughout the settlement almost came to a standstill. The Matabele nation grumbled as their crops van-ished, and they cursed the Europeans, believing that it was they who had upset the ancestors and so brought this plague upon them. Tensions in all spheres of society began building.

The plague lasted almost two weeks, and the landscape in its path was transformed from lush, green bushes, grass, and trees, to a barren earth devoid of greenery. All the Matabele crops and harvests had been decimated, their cattle herds began to face star-vation, and hunger became a real threat. Development of the set-tlement, however, continued unabated. A second brickfield had been established by a Portuguese family on the south side of the settlement, and Morris negotiated the sale of their own Bulawayo Bricks to a small consortium of Englishmen. He initially offered the Langbourne Brothers' share of the business back to Phil and Abe at a very acceptable price, but surprisingly they preferred to go with Morris' advice of selling outright at the best possible price. As much as they were cautious of Morris and his abrupt mannerisms, they trusted his honesty and business sense. Even David was sur-prised with their decision, but welcomed it. The deal turned out to be very favourable and Morris was satisfied that even he could not have hoped for a better outcome. Likewise, Abe and Phil were very happy with the capital gains and channelled their profits into their own businesses.

Brick and mortar buildings were springing up at an incredible rate and the population was growing steadily, with wagonloads of new families arriving every day. A newspaper, The Chronicle, had been established, which covered a little news of the southern colonies and some sporting results. It also had a large section devoted to advertisements for businesses in Johannesburg or Cape Town, which were of little use to the local population. Infrastructure was developing rapidly, schools were being built and business was increasing apace. Settlers were calling themselves residents, and once the settlement of KoBulawayo had become known as a town, it was officially renamed Bulawayo.

As a result of this boom in settlement, Morris once more began to fret that they were going to run out of goods to sell before their resupply from Mafeking arrived. So concerned was he, in fact, that he attempted to send David out to find Daluxolo and the wagons and to report back on their progress and position.

"Be patient, Brother," David reasoned with Morris, "the road to Mafeking has many forks and side-roads. I have no idea which route Daluxolo would have taken; it changes from month to month with the weather, as you well know. If I miss him, I could be out there for weeks, even months, and he may arrive on time, and then you won't have me to help you unload, code the stock, stack the shelves, or sign up traders. It will be just you and Harry. It's best to wait."

Morris sighed in resignation. "You're right, and I do need you here. It just takes so long for the goods to get up here and we needed the stuff weeks ago. If Daluxolo is not here in two weeks, will you consider going out and looking for him?"

"Sure, that sounds fair. I'll do that for you."

Five days later, the lone figure of Daluxolo appeared at the entrance to the new Langbourne Brothers building. All three brothers rushed out to meet him and they clasped arms in a warm greeting.

"I see you, Daluxolo," David greeted this trusted friend with the broadest of smiles, which Daluxolo reciprocated.

"I see you, my bosses," he beamed, standing proudly in his traditional garb as he greeted each of them in return.

"You were very slow in getting here this time, Daluxolo. Did you have problems?" Morris politely asked the Xhosa-speaking man.

As Daluxolo frowned and shook his head, Morris's heart skipped a beat. "Hawu, nkosi! The journey was not so good this time. One wagon is broken and, because we were not able to fix it or move it, we have hidden it in the bush under sticks and grass."

"But you know where it is?" Morris asked quickly.

"Yes, nkosi, I have found a new road, a much better one that few people know. It is a bit longer, but it is kinder to the beasts. You need to bring some pieces to replace the broken ones. I can show you what pieces we need. It is Wagon Number Four that is broken."

"I will help you, Daluxolo," David soothed, "you have done well to hide the wagon and to find a better road. Any other problems?"

"We had many this time, and we fixed them all but for the one wagon. Also, the Great One sent many, many insects to slow our journey. They ate all the grass and leaves. The oxen are very weak. Seven have died and we have eaten more goats than before."

"That saddens me, but I am more concerned about you and your men." David showed genuine concern and spoke slowly and softly. Harry watched how David carefully and gently edged his shoulder ever so slightly in front of Morris and took the lead. Morris was looking very agitated, but David was in command, controlling not just the flow of the discussion, but also his brother. He smiled quietly as he admired David's many qualities. He certainly understood Morris exceptionally well.

"We are well, Boss David, but we are tired and weak."

"Then you shall rest. Outspan the oxen and make camp

outside the town in the same place as before. No more work today. We will bring food and umqombothi for you and the men tonight. We need to celebrate your safe arrival."

Daluxolo smiled appreciatively and took his leave before the brothers walked back inside their roofless building.

Morris frowned. "You handled that nicely,"

David grinned back, "I know you well, brother, and I could tell you were about to explode. No, we got off lightly. Tonight I'll find out how far out Number Four is and make plans to retrieve it. Hopefully it's not too far away. Harry, you packed Number Four back in Mafeking. Would you please get the paperwork out and tell me what's on that wagon?"

"Sure," Harry agreed quickly.

"I know what's on that wagon," Morris frowned again, "and there's some stuff on there that Phil Innes needs."

"How do you know?" Harry asked in surprise.

David laughed loudly. "That's your brother for you, Harry. He's read your packing slips and invoices, and he knows. Not so, Morris?"

"Yes, of course," Morris retorted indignantly.

"And I'll bet you know the value of stock on each wagon?"

"Down to the last penny. Why? Don't you?" He looked at Harry and winked at David. "Come on, Harry, you need to know these things," he mocked.

Harry went to a small cardboard box and shuffled through some papers he kept in it. Pulling out the manifest of Wagon Number Four, he looked at the total value that he had written upon it before they left Mafeking.

"Okay, my smart brother, how much stock is on the wagon?" Harry teased his eldest brother, feeling somewhat more relaxed and confident in his company.

"Four hundred and thirty-seven pounds, and six shillings," he declared, and as Harry stared wide-eyed at the same figure on the paperwork, Morris stole another wink at David, who simply smiled, holding back a laugh.

"I don't believe it," Harry was dumbfounded.

"By the way, you made a mistake in your addition, the correct figure should be four hundred and forty-two pounds, eight shillings and tuppence. You need to be more careful in future, my young brother."

At that point David could not hold back his laughter, slapping his thighs he doubled over and roared uninhibitedly.

*

That evening, the boys took a wheelbarrow from the building site and filled it with meat, crushed maize meal and a bunch of spinach-like vegetables, called merogo. In another wheelbarrow, they loaded some gourds of fresh, traditional sour beer that they had bought from a nearby Matabele village known as Kumalo, and then walked down to the outspan site on the edge of town. The welcoming party was greatly appreciated by the men and many stories were told of their journey. As Harry didn't understand the Xhosa language, he struggled through the conversations, with David and Morris translating the more important facts from time to time. The boys had a quick look over the wagons, and their excitement soared when they realised the completion of their building was imminent, now that the roofing sheets had arrived.

When the locust plague had struck, the main part of the building had been virtually completed. All that had been needed was the roof sheeting, and David estimated it would take less than a week to install it. Mr Da Santos had proudly completed the facade of the building, in which temporary planks of wood had been tastefully secured where glass windows would one day be installed. Had it not been for the guidance and assistance from Phil Innes, the tolerance and willingness to help from Abe Kaufman through Bulawayo Bricks, and the exceptional grants from Major Seward of the BSAC, they would never have been in the position they were in now. Morris and David were the happiest they had ever been in their lives. The debts they owed weighed heavily on their minds, but they were filled with such excitement and expectation that they allowed these negative thoughts little leeway.

*

Early the next day, the Langbournes initiated a plan which they had devised during the previous month. Morris would keep the shop running and trading while David and Harry, together with a small team of Daluxolo's men, would complete the shop's roof. The first of the wagons containing the roof sheeting having rolled down Abercorn Street just as the sun rose above the horizon, Harry and David were hard at work on the roof long before breakfast. After just three days, the roof was finished, which effectively marked the completion of the building. With much excitement, the three temporary wooden structures, now dwarfed inside the main building, were first emptied of stock and then demolished and removed. The patches of bare earth upon which they had stood was covered with the last of the paving bricks. While David finished the paving, Morris and Harry began restocking the shop, working from the back to the front and calling for more wagons as they progressed.

David, as was his way, worked very hard and fast with the paving and kept ahead of the growing inventory within the shop. As soon as he had completed his task, he attempted to join his brothers in unloading the wagons and restocking, but news of their resupply had spread like wildfire in the community and potential wagon traders began to apply for the remaining wagons. From a temporary office in the front corner of the new building, David's attention turned to forming agreements and contracts with the prospective wagon traders. No sooner had the stock moved in, the traders worked at taking the stock out. Business could not have been better.

Daluxolo's stay in Bulawayo lasted only three weeks before

the Langbourne boys hosted a farewell party for the men with fresh meat and traditional beer, and then sent them on their way to Mafeking with letters and some cheques for Weil and Gerran. This time, however, David went part of the way with them. The broken wagon was only three days out, so, with some spares and a small team of Matabele herders, David set off to repair and retrieve the stricken wagon. It took him eight hours to repair it, barely concealed under what sparse foliage the locusts had not denuded. Once repaired, a team of oxen was hitched up, farewells were said, and the teams parted company. Daluxolo and his men began the long trek back to Mafeking while David journeyed with the once-stricken wagon back to Bulawayo.

*

"Shut the door, Harry," Morris called out from the back of the warehouse. "It's after five o'clock and it's time to close the shop."

Harry quickly obliged, closing the wooden door and throwing a bolt in place. "We had a good day today, didn't we, Morris?" he shouted to the back of the building. With timber for windows, it was dark and gloomy indoors, but he could easily make out Morris, moving about the benches, while laden with various stock items.

"Yes," Morris agreed, but seemed to be talking to no one in particular. He straightened a bolt of material that lay on a cutting table. "Yes," he said again, but his mind was far from the present as he moved to another bench and straightened some enamel teapots that were out of alignment.

David was standing at the back of the shop and pushed the large delivery doors into place, threw two bolts into it, and gave it a firm shove to make sure it was locked tight. The warehouse was plunged into almost total darkness. "I think it was our best day yet, Harry," he agreed, calling out to his younger brother at the other end of the shop.

With the shop shut for the day, David and Harry walked over

to where Morris was fussing about and heaved themselves onto an empty wooden display bench, swinging their legs freely in the air.

David broke the silence, suddenly remembering they had sent a telegram to their younger brother in East London almost a week prior. "Have you had a reply from Louis?" he asked.

"Yes," Morris stopped what he was doing and noticed his two brothers were watching him intently. "We got a reply today. I forgot to mention it, sorry."

"And…?" David urged.

"He has made some interesting contacts with shipping agents. I'm not sure what he was on about. I have a feeling he has not had too much opportunity to buy anything since you left him because his value of stock has hardly increased at all."

"Well, I instructed him to buy quality, not quantity, so maybe he is being fussy."

Morris suddenly changed the subject, as he was wont to do. "I need to have a serious discussion with you two."

"I was waiting for this," David looked at Harry with a slight smile. Harry straightened up. He never knew what his two older brothers were going to come out with.

"I have a plan…" Morris began.

"I thought so," David interrupted.

"No, seriously: this is important. The business is well established, and now it is time to make money."

"I thought we were making money already," Harry looked confused.

"Not enough. Not nearly as much as we could be making."

"So, what's the plan?" David fidgeted in excitement, knowing that what was to come would be interesting. He did not think there could be anything more dramatic nor physically and mentally demanding as the last six months had been, but with Morris one just never knew.

"We have a good business here. The locals are supporting us well, and the population is expanding rapidly. We have traders selling our stock all over the country. Money is coming in now and we are repaying our debts. Our suppliers and the bank are happy with us. The country is stable, the BSAC is in control, but…?" he paused and looked at his brothers.

"We have a procurement office in East London that is under-utilised?" David ventured.

"Yes. Exactly! What else?" he looked at Harry, who looked at David for help.

"The shop is half-empty?" David continued, beginning to see where his brother was heading.

"Exactly. But it is more than half empty. It only looks well supplied because we have our stock spread out all over the place. We need more stock," Morris exclaimed excitedly.

"You are thinking eighteen wagons this time, aren't you?" David smiled knowingly.

"No, thirty."

"Thirty!" David shouted in shock. He jumped off the table and ran his fingers through his hair quickly, trying to come to terms with what he just heard. "Thirty?" he repeated. "That's impossible, Morris. Have you any idea…?" He broke off and looked at Harry, who sat motionless, eyes wide in confusion. "Have you any idea," he looked for the words again, "how much money we need for thirty wagons?"

"Yes," said Morris simply.

"Morris, for heaven's sake, thirty wagons will need about two hundred and fifty oxen, for starters, and…"

"Two hundred and forty," Morris corrected David. "Yes, I've worked it all out. We have settled most of our debts, thanks to Bulawayo Bricks. This building has great value now, so the banks will lend us good money, using it as collateral. I've already had a discussion with Mr Honey and money is starting to flow in from our off-the-street trade, not forgetting the fact that our wagon traders are starting to come in for resupplies and they are paying us in cash. We are already ahead of where we were before the rebellion started, and, I might add, there is a queue at the door with wagon traders wanting to join our team. The town is booming, and we are at the forefront of it. We cannot stop now."

"Morris, you don't have to be a genius to know we certainly cannot afford to bring up thirty wagons in one fell swoop. That's ridiculous!"

"I've checked the finances, and we can manage thirty wagons if the bank will loan us money on the collateral of this building, and if Weil and Gerran will extend our credit, but it is going to be very risky. There will be no room to fail, and we will be putting everything we have on the line, but we can do it if we plan the finances and negotiations properly. I'm going to need your help, David."

"When do you want to arrange all this?" David sighed in resignation. "You know Gerran certainly won't have thirty wagons for us. I'd be surprised if he has the capacity to manufacture thirty wagons all year. In any case, regardless of how big Weil and Co. are, they can't fill thirty wagons at once."

"I know, but we have Louis in East London now, and we must utilize that. We need to get the wagons here before the rains; Daluxolo left about a month too late last time, so time is against us now. Here's my plan," Morris smiled. "Sit down, both of you. I need you to listen carefully."

David stared at Morris for a moment, then reluctantly walked off with Harry to find some empty crates before returning and sitting down between benches laden with material. By this time the shop was in almost total darkness so, before taking his seat again, Morris lit a single candle that cast some very ominous shadows.

"Alright," Morris began. "Firstly, when we buy from Weil he adds on his mark-up, but if we buy directly, that mark-up belongs to us, therefore our profits would be better."

"So you want to cut Weil out?" David wasn't sure how to interpret this.

"Heavens, no, we need him. He will always be an alternative, and, besides, he offers us good credit that is vital at the moment.

Of the thirty wagons, I want Weil to supply another twelve. He's done it before and he will be expecting us to order them again. So will Gerran. Now, I'd like you, David, to go down to East London and help Louis procure the remaining eighteen wagons' worth of stock, which I would like sent to Johannesburg by train. I don't want Weil to know what we are doing."

David looked shocked. "Johannesburg? This is getting complicated and we haven't even begun! Why Johannesburg?"

"Listen to me: before you go to East London, I want you to go to Johannesburg and find Danie Coetzee. I need to open an office, a warehouse, like the one in East London, and I would like you to ask him to set up the company for us. I believe that's what he does now with his uncle. Then I need you to find a company that manufactures wagons and place an order for eighteen of them before you go to East London. Businesses and factories are bigger and better in Johannesburg, I'm told, and so you should have no problem there. After procuring the goods in East London, send them to our new warehouse in Johannesburg and load up there. Remember, the warehouse needs to be big enough to fit at least eighteen wagons in it."

"That is a massive warehouse!"

"Only half the size of this building," Morris glanced around the shop.

"You want me to bring them up to Bulawayo from Johannesburg?"

"Yes, avoid Mafeking altogether. I don't want Weil and everyone in Mafeking to see what we are doing. Not yet, anyhow. If they see how fast we are expanding they will also jump into the action and start setting up their own stores, and then we will have serious competition on our hands. Just look what happens when people find gold, or diamonds: word gets out and then it's a total disaster and nobody makes any money. I don't want people in Mafeking to see the scale at which we are moving stock up here. We have to do this secretly and with as little fuss as possible. The last thing I want is for Weil and all his trading customers to get wind of our expansion. On the other hand, it might go the other way and if Weil discovers what we are doing he might freeze his credit, fearing we won't be able to pay him."

"Morris," David was still looking a little shocked, "I don't know the way to Bulawayo from Johannesburg; nobody does. I doubt you can even cross the Limpopo River that far downstream."

"True, but you can cross at our usual place, David, upstream," Morris waved his arms in frustration. "You know how to navigate the bush. Didn't your friend, Bob Baden, or whatever his name was, show you how to use a compass? I will go down to Mafeking and load up the twelve wagons there as if it is business as usual, and send Daluxolo on his way, but I will instruct him to stop at the Limpopo River and wait for you. Meanwhile you and Nguni must take the Johannesburg wagons and join him there. After that, Nguni and Daluxolo know the way, so you don't have to be with them. Between Nguni, Daluxolo and their teams, they can manage thirty wagons, and you can return to Bulawayo."

David clasped his head with both hands, took a deep breath and stared blankly through the brick wall behind his brother. He was shattered at the thought that Morris could expect him to simply take eighteen wagons out of Johannesburg and walk through the bush in unknown territory and meet Daluxolo at a single point hundreds of miles away. To add insult to injury, he was also expected to secure a warehouse in Johannesburg, buy eighteen wagons, and then stock them with goods from East London. It was simply an impossible task. He pictured a map in his head of where Johannesburg was in relation to Mafeking and the Limpopo River, and figured that if he took a bearing generally North West, he would hit the Limpopo River well downstream from their crossing point. All he needed to do was turn left when he reached the river and eventually he would find Daluxolo. He decided that that part of the plan was achievable, but eighteen wagons of stock? Louis could help him in East London, so that could be done. He could enlist the help of Nguni before they shipped the goods by rail to Johannesburg. He realised that if he broke each part of the plan into smaller, achievable chunks, he might be able to pull it off.

"Alright," David was throwing himself into the plan now, his excitement growing by the second as he thought this all through. "I can do that. I just need to make sure I don't get lost between Johannesburg and the Limpopo crossing. And yes, between Daluxolo and Nguni, they can manage thirty wagons between the Limpopo and Bulawayo. It can be done."

"What about me?" Harry interjected.

"You stay here and run the shop for us. When David heads for Johannesburg with the East London stock, I will be going down to Mafeking to load up there. I need you here."

"On my own?" Harry looked horrified.

"You can do it, Harry," David said calmly, then returned to Morris as though Harry was suddenly not there, "but where will I find Danie Coetzee?"

"How do I know, David?" Morris sighed, looking at the roof, almost disgusted at the question; that wasn't his problem. "Oh, when you pass through Port Elizabeth, please pass my compliments on to Jack Shiel and ask him to send £200 back to father. Now let's get something to eat, I'm starving. We can discuss the finer details tomorrow."

David looked at Harry with a frown, cocked an eyebrow, and shrugged as if to say silently, "That's Morris for you!" before obediently following him out of the warehouse.

*

Louis donned his business suit and a chic hat to complement the fine garments David had chosen for him, then strode out the door of his humble bedroom and headed down to the bank to check on the finances. He had been hoping to see a small deposit from Morris in Matabeleland, as his spending money was getting quite tight. With not much to do to occupy him during the day, he frequented the numerous clubs and establishments David had signed him up to, in order to create a presence and glean information in conversation that could hold him in good stead in the commercial world. Visiting these establishments, however, always cost a penny here, or a shilling there, a tickey for a raffle or tuppence for a charitable organisation. Although not much individually, they did add up in time and he was beginning to find it annoying, especially as it cut into his eating allowance. Explaining to Morris that he needed a little more personal cash was not easy, especially via telegram that in itself was about the cost of a meal!

Walking past the post office as he always did, he entered the large wooden doors and joined a small queue. When he got to the window the teller greeted him with a smile, passing him a small brown envelope.

"Good news today, Mr Langbourne," he smiled cheerily, "you have a telegram."

"Oh wonderful! Thank you kindly, sir." Louis's spirits soared.

"I think there must have been a crossed line in the wires, if you'll forgive the intrusion, but I could not decipher the transmission correctly," the man in the peak cap and thick glasses admitted.

"Oh?" Louis looked confused, and opened the envelope.

*

LANGBEL

EAST LONDON

REQUIRE BI GRINDERS URGENT STOP EAGLE RETURNING EGGS STOP

*

Louis stared at the text with a worried look. He read it over three times, and each time it said the same thing: "Require eighteen wagons urgently. David returning East London."

"It can't be," Louis mumbled to himself, but the teller heard him.

"Confusing, isn't it, Mr Langbourne? Almost comical, actually."

"Indeed," Louis shook himself out of his stupor. "Perhaps you might be so kind as to respond to this for me, sir?"

"Certainly," the myopic teller pulled out a blank telegraph form and pencil. "Go ahead, sir."

"To Langbro, KoBulawayo. Confirm BI stop." Louis used the silly telegraphic word for full stop.

The teller passed the form to Louis. "Is this correct?"

Louis looked at the form. He had written 'LANGBRO KOBULAWAYO CONFIRM BI STOP'

"Yes, thank you." He paid the teller and left the building, both annoyed and confused. It didn't make sense, yet the message was very clear.

Arriving at the bank Louis greeted the attractive young lady behind the glass pane and asked if any money had been deposited into his account. She obligingly walked over to some shelves on the wall behind her and Louis watched her page through a large leather ledger she had retrieved, with some difficulty, from a shelf above her head. She ran her finger down a column of numbers and then closed the book, returning to her window.

"Yes sir, there has been a substantial deposit."

"How substantial?" he asked nervously.

"Four thousand, two hundred pounds, sir."

Louis felt vaguely faint. "Oh," he paused, trying to comprehend what she had implied. "Well," he suddenly felt stupid, "may I trouble you to withdraw three pounds today, please?"

The teller smiled condescendingly, and, politely avoiding eye contact, gently plucked a withdrawal slip from a wooden holder on her counter. "Certainly Mr Langbourne, no trouble at all."

Louis broke into a cold sweat; he was not sure if it was caused by the surprise of the overwhelming increase in the value of his bank balance or the stunning beauty of the bank teller in front of him. Whatever the reason, he couldn't wait to get out of the building.

When he stepped out of the banking hall, taking a deep breath of fresh, chilled air, Louis looked over towards the railway station. It seemed quiet, almost deserted. He knew beyond any doubt that David would soon be arriving on that platform, and then life would become extremely chaotic. A wave of almost tangible excitement, such as he had never before experienced, seared through his body. As he walked back past the post office he decided he did not need to check in for the reply to his telegram, he knew it would contain just one word:

"YES."

CHAPTER NINE
Wagons for Africa

ONLY FIVE MONTHS had passed since David had last trodden the dusty roads of the isolated and dull outpost of Mafeking. After meeting with Julian Weil and Mr Gerran, he returned to his lodgings and removed his jacket, his tie and his Derby hat. Loosening his collar and rolling his shirt-sleeves up his forearms, he walked off to the African village on the west of the town to locate Daluxolo, There he spent two hours in his company, drinking tea and talking about the old days. In the meantime, his lovely wife Nkosazana had given birth to a beautiful daughter. She was delighted to see David and, in her meek and gentle way, enjoyed the attention David gave their little girl.

David was particularly pleased to have the opportunity to see Nkosazana after all this time; she had been a godsend to Morris and him when she had lived in Bulawayo, cooking for them and attending to their laundry. She would buy their food and tidy around the sample room when she was not otherwise busy. Graceful in her movements, humble and somewhat shy, she seldom spoke, yet smiled constantly. Her name meant *Princess*, and both Morris and David believed she was the epitome of one, both lads respecting her as such. As the wife of Daluxolo, David felt that they were well suited to each other. It made him happy to see the two of them starting a family, and it was a real joy for him to see their little daughter - the cutest child, David thought, he had ever seen.

Once family affairs had been discussed and news of the village, crops and livestock had been considered, David turned the conversation to business, to the next journey up to Bulawayo. David explained the departure from the norm in the plans for this trip in that Daluxolo and his team would halt at the Limpopo and wait for Nguni and David to join them with more wagons. It was going to be a huge exercise, and he needed to know if Daluxolo was up for it. He deliberately avoided telling him how many wagons Nguni's team would be in charge of because he didn't want word to slip out into the community, thus somehow reaching Julian Weil. As he expected, Daluxolo was keen to do the job and looked forward to the challenge. Logistics were discussed, as well as wages. When all was agreed, David took his leave and returned to his lodgings to turn in for the night on a very comfortable mattress.

The following day was spent with Ian Taylor, placing orders, working out quantities, and negotiating prices. His meeting with Gerran went well and David found him agreeable to the requests for wagons and payment terms. The hard work that Morris had done in establishing solid business foundations during his visit at the beginning of that year had paid dividends, and this was not lost on David, who made a mental note to congratulate his brother when he next saw him. When he was happy that all his arrangements were in place and everyone crucial to his plans knew what was needed, he bought himself a train ticket to the sprawling and rapidly expanding town of Johannesburg, where his hunt for his old friend Danie Coetzee began.

*

Johannesburg was a hive of activity. Big, solid buildings made of stone or brick were springing up all over the place and David hardly recognised many of the streets he had visited when he was selling cigarettes for their factory in Port Elizabeth. He spent a good few hours asking people if they had heard of Danie Coetzee, but with no luck. Feeling despondent and rather irritated, he stopped at a café-type restaurant on a side street, planning to have a light meal before resuming the search. Most of the gentlemen inside wore smart business suits, presenting a very professional aura for the various vocations they pursued. While standing in line waiting to order, David struck up a casual conversation with the man in front of him, and, as he had with everyone he had met that day, David asked after Danie.

"Never heard of the gent, I'm afraid. What line of business is he in?"

"Accounting, I believe. Last I heard he was going to work in Johannesburg for his uncle," David sighed.

"Well," the gentleman grinned, "have you tried looking for him at Coetzee and Coetzee Accounting?"

David laughed and shook his head. "Actually, no, I haven't. Any idea where I might find this esteemed establishment?"

"It's on the corner of Commissioner Street and Simmonds Street, just past the Johannesburg Stock Exchange. Big, grey, stone building: you can't miss it. They're on the second floor. There is a small sign in their window, so you have to look up a little," he winked. "Good luck, I hope you find him." David immediately thanked the man and left without ordering any food.

Simmonds Street was abuzz with life, as men in suits walked briskly between makeshift tents filled with desks covered with papers and files, seemingly doing nothing but hurrying about from tent to tent. David found this somewhat amusing, but at the same time rather fascinating, watching everyone's urgent attention to their invisible task at hand, together with their almost universal frowns. No one looked happy or relaxed. A section of the street had been closed off with chains, preventing wagons and horses from entering, and paperwork littered the ground between the canvas offices.

Nothing made sense.

Strange chalkboards with numbers written upon them were interspersed between the various tents. This unusual activity was contained within just that block on the street, as more chains at the next intersection confined the hustle and bustle. Just as the gentleman in the food store had said, David saw a blue and white sign indicating the offices of Coetzee and Coetzee Accounting in the window on the second floor of a building just beyond the temporary barrier. Finding his way into the building and up the stairs, David entered the office and spoke to a young lady behind the large, wooden reception desk.

"I'm looking for a gentleman called Danie Coetzee, previously from Port Elizabeth."

"Do you have an appointment with him, sir?" she asked with a beautiful smile. David's heart skipped a beat, uncertain if it was caused by the magical smile of the receptionist or because he may have located his old friend.

*

Later that evening the two friends met at a prestigious hotel close to the Johannesburg Stock Exchange and together enjoyed a very extravagant meal at Danie's expense, exchanging stories and catching up on each other's news. David found that Danie had changed a little, having put on a bit more weight to lose his former, gangly appearance, while also seeming slightly taller. His pinstriped evening suit, moreover, was well tailored and looked very expensive, making him stand out among the crowd. He sounded more learned as he spoke a little more slowly than before and chose his words carefully.

"So," David brushed a bread crumb off the pristine tablecloth after a sensational meal, "Morris wanted to expand the business with an office in East London, with the intention of buying directly off the ships and agents over there, thereby easing our reliance on Julian Weil and Company."

Danie was listening intently. "And that is where you have established your younger brother?"

"Yes, Louis seems to have been making the right contacts, but has not been actively buying stock, probably for a number of very good reasons. But, now that Morris wants to increase our trading more rapidly than any of us expected, I am on my way down there to accelerate that side of the business."

"So why have you been looking for me?"

"Morris wants to open another office here in Johannesburg, and we would like you to set up the administrative and legal aspects of this for us, through your accounting firm, of course. Our intention is to have three offices: Bulawayo will be our trading arm, East London our purchasing arm, and Johannesburg will be the distribution warehouse and administrative centre of the entire business, should we open more purchasing offices in the Cape."

"Interesting," Danie observed, "I can certainly set up your Johannesburg Company, with all the legal and administrative commitments that might be required, and it won't cost you a great deal. My uncle and I do this type of thing all the time."

"There is another reason we have been looking for you specifically," David lent forward in his seat and dropped his voice slightly. "We hear rumblings that the mood between the Boers and the British is beginning to sour once again. Is this true?"

Danie looked about him to see who was in earshot, and equally leaned forward and dropped his voice slightly. "The Boers and the British don't like one another – that is plain to see – and both hold grudges dating back to the previous war between them of 1880, which was very brutal. Why do you ask?"

"As you know," David also glanced around quickly, "we almost lost our entire business and all our savings, including our ability to recover, in the recent conflict between the British South African Company and the Matabele. We lost wagons, oxen, stock, profits, and even two of our wagon traders were killed in the rebellion. We don't want to put ourselves in that uncertain position again, hence our plan to open more offices in different towns. If war breaks out in the country, we will have more than one office that we can depend on." David paused and took a sip of his coffee. "War is a terrible thing, and affects more than just soldiers' lives. We have seen that first hand."

Danie thought about this for a moment, then reached for his coffee. "I can't fault your strategy, David. It seems as though you and Morris have put a lot of thought into this."

"We have a further consideration to take into account. If relations between the Boers and the British degenerate into war yet again, we have concerns that, if the Boers win, they may make business difficult for British-owned businesses, or that – if the British win – they would make business difficult for Afrikaner, or Boer-owned businesses."

Danie scowled. "There'll never be another Anglo-Boer war, David, heaven forbid! I think you are overreacting, to be honest."

"Nevertheless, as they say: once bitten, twice shy, and we never want to be in that position again. Let's just say Morris is over-cautious."

"But you're Irish, not British, so why are you worrying?"

"Irish, yes, but with an Anglicised name that sounds very British. We want to ask if you will be prepared to act as a silent partner with us, to attach your surname, which has a Dutch ring to it, to our surname. We would also like to invite you to have a seat on our board and be a director of the company. We would like to call our company in Johannesburg "Langbourne Coetzee". This would confuse any nation that wins a future war here."

"I really think you are being overly cautious, David."

"Perhaps, but we would be very comforted by this. We trust you implicitly and value both your principles and your knowledge of business. We also value your advice and, above all, you are neutral, you have no family connection, and that may be vital to future decisions we may make, now that we have other members of our family joining our ranks."

Danie considered carefully what David had asked of him. He was slightly shocked that the Langbourne brothers were thinking so deeply about their financial survival and future. These thoughts were well beyond what the average businessman on the street would contemplate. To sit on their board was an honour in itself, and carried with it big responsibilities, yet little financial risk. On the other hand, they would have access to his business knowledge, and he would have an insight into how they operated. Probably the most important consideration was that the Langbourne brothers were very dear friends of his, and he placed a high value on their friendship.

"'Langbourne Coetzee, Johannesburg'? Is that what you want to call your business here?"

"Just 'Langbourne Coetzee'," David smiled and leaned back in his chair.

Danie also leaned back in his chair, reaching for a cigarette. "And will you pay me for my services?"

David laughed. "Oh no! We would never be able to afford you!"

A smiled hovered at Danie's lips. "Yes, they say I am a little expensive. So you will be running this Johannesburg office?"

"Not really," David looked serious for a moment, "I am needed by Morris up north. Harry will run the Johannesburg office for us. He doesn't know this yet, but Morris is training him all the same. They are very similar in character and I fear they may clash one day - so does Morris. They will be fine when there are a thousand miles between them. In fact, they work very well as a team when they are apart. Harry is young, I must admit, but he is no fool, and both Morris and I agree he will make a fine businessman.

"You fear another Anglo-Boer war, David?" Danie laughed, "I think you should fear a Langbourne-Langbourne war!"

David let out a hearty laugh. "You don't miss a thing, do you Danie?" he chuckled. "No, our family is very close, despite some short tempers and sharp words that may escape from time to time… from some of us," he winked.

The two good friends parted company, having enjoyed a warm and long overdue reunion. Danie knew what he had to do in establishing the new Langbourne Coetzee business, obtaining the necessary registrations, paperwork, and even opening a new bank account; time-consuming tasks that David would have had to do under normal circumstances. Now David was free to tend to other pressing matters, such as looking for a warehouse near the rail yard; finding coach builders and negotiating prices; and planning and purchasing supplies that would be needed on the long trek north with the wagons.

*

The warehouse David found was slightly bigger than the one in East London, and came with a mezzanine floor and a slightly higher rental. Nevertheless, since it was all that was available, he promptly signed the lease agreement, paying his deposit and two months' rental in advance. The warehouse was a rather dingy affair, with a cement floor and unfinished brick walls. There were no windows set into the side walls, as they formed part of the adjoining warehouses on either side but there were some small windows on the front and rear walls. The glass in the windows were intact, except for a pane in the window at the mezzanine floor level, which had been smashed by a half-brick that someone had thrown at it, since he could see the offending brick still lying on the floor among the shards of glass.

At each end of the warehouse was a solid wooden door that slid to one side and was big enough for wagons laden with goods to be wheeled in and out. These doors were painted dark green in colour and were locked by metal bolts and padlocks from the inside. Personal entry to the warehouse was via a normal-sized heavy wooden door, also painted dark green, just to the side of one of the sliding doors. It needed a chunky, heavy key to turn the tumblers of the internal lock, which impressed David enough to make him happy with the security of the warehouse. Outside the rear of the building was a small courtyard that was walled off from the alleyway that serviced all the other warehouses. Here he found a tap which fed running water into a crude cement hand-wash basin, as well as a very dirty, porcelain toilet bowl with a cast-iron cistern above, which could be flushed by yanking on a length of rusty chain. David turned up his nose at the toilet in its present state, but realised that, with a little cleaning, it would be quite acceptable. After all, he had been accustomed to less in Bulawayo.

On his last night in Johannesburg, David met with Danie for another quality meal, this time at a hotel that had just recently opened, and discussed what had been accomplished since their last meeting. Danie told David what he had achieved so far on the administrative side of the business, after which David entrusted him with their Black Rhino code and all the other code names they had invented. This fascinated Danie all the more because he was intrigued by the unorthodox planning and strategies of the Langbourne boys. As they walked out of the hotel to head for their respective accommodation, David allocated the code name of "Zebra" to his friend (because of his pinstriped suits), which Danie accepted with mock horror but secret pride. Before David left Johannesburg, he sent a telegram to Morris with the address of the new warehouse, and hoped Morris would realise that Danie's code name was Zebra.

*

NEW WAREHOUSE AT 9 RAILWAY ROAD GOLD STOP

ZEBRA LOCATED STOP LANGCOE ESTABLISHED STOP

TO EGGS NOW STOP

*

Pulling into the East London railway station, David saw Louis from his compartment window, standing patiently on the platform, while scanning the passengers who alighted from the train. Louis was dressed in his business suit with the trouser legs looking a little too short and showing a hint of his white socks. David felt sorry for him, since his younger brother must have waited for the train every morning for the last two weeks. He did have to smile, though, as the code name "Giraffe" suited him, and it seemed equally obvious that he had not stopped growing.

Jumping from the carriage door, David watched Louis's face light up when he spotted his brother. Shaking hands and exchanging pleasantries, the two mismatched brothers walked away from the platform, talking in earnest. Over breakfast, David filled Louis in on all their plans and what was expected of them over the next two months. Louis confided that he had not bought much stock, mainly because he was concerned about the budget he had been given, and that he might have bad judgement on stock items that would sell in Bulawayo. When they arrived at the warehouse, David looked over what he had bought and was pleased, boosting his younger brother with praise and encouragement. Louis made up for the slow buying with the influential contacts he had made, and this impressed David immensely.

Over the next three weeks, five merchant ships docked in East London and David and Louis got busy making a name for themselves among the traders and merchants. They enjoyed the challenge of negotiating and bargaining, and most of what they bought was high-quality merchandise. One ship carrying exotic Chinese and Persian carpets caught David's attention. The prices were already very agreeable, and, with some persuasive bargaining, he managed to secure a very acceptable quantity of goods along with a cash discount from the agent. The weight of the carpets, however, caught the boys by surprise and caused some concern as to how they would transport them back to their warehouse. After hiring a horse and cart, they moved their purchases to their premises, leaving Louis physically worn out and complaining of blisters on his hands and the fact that he would never be able to stand up straight again for the remainder of his lifetime.

Although David managed the physical exertions more easily, he did rip a shirtsleeve when he hoisted a rolled carpet over his shoulder, and certainly the rough pile on the underside of these carpets was a problem as they caused painful blisters on hands and knuckles. When ships were not in port and trading was quiet, the boys worked late into the night packing their purchases ready for shipment by rail to their Johannesburg warehouse. David stayed in East London for three months until he was satisfied they had purchased enough to fill 18 wagons. After having the stock delivered to the railway station and loaded onto a freight carriage that was due to leave the following day, David bought two first-class train tickets to Johannesburg, one each for him and Louis.

"I want you to come to Johannesburg with me and help load all this stock into our new warehouse."

"Really?" Louis was beside himself with excitement.

"Absolutely, you have worked hard and I'm pleased with what you have done. Besides, I want you to meet Danie Coetzee."

"That would be wonderful." Louis began to feel he was truly becoming a part of his brothers' business.

"It's also time for you to see Morris again. It's been a few years for you, and we will need his help too. Let's go down to the Post Office and send him a telegram, but I want you to code it," David said, since he never missed an opportunity to provide Louis with a business lesson.

When they arrived at the Post Office, Louis scratched out a telegram and showed it to David. "How does that look?"

David took the paper and read what Louis had written:

*

RETURNING GOLD WITH EAGLE STOP MEET AT LANCOE
SOONEST STOP

"Not bad," David smiled. "Ten words and all codes correct, well done. If I were Morris I would read it as 'Returning to Johannesburg with David. Meet at our Johannesburg warehouse as soon as possible'."

"He would understand that, wouldn't he?"

"Yes, he will, make no error. I have one other telegram I need to send. Please pass me that pencil."

David scratched out another telegram, but this time it was not coded:

*

TO JACK SHIEL STANDARD BANK PORT ELIZABETH STOP PSE ADVISE NGUNI ARRIVING PE WEDNESDAY MORNING STOP David

*

Morris stepped onto the Johannesburg railway station platform and looked at the blackened brickwork and steel pillars that were in desperate need of another coat of paint. People and piles of luggage littered the concrete platform as copious clouds of steam from the coal-fired engines drifted aimlessly among the activity, but there were no familiar faces. Although he had not expected anyone to meet him, because none of his brothers knew when he would be arriving, he was still a little disappointed by the lack of a familiar face in the crowds.

Buttoning up his black, woollen overcoat against the winter chill, Morris sought directions to Number 9, Railway Road and, slinging his old leather duffle bag over his shoulder, he strode off in search of his two brothers and their new Johannesburg warehouse.

Johannesburg in May was cold, and, being quite elevated on a high plateau, the wind was particularly icy at this time of year. Morris could not believe the size of the town: multi-storied build-ings towered over him, which brought back memories of his brief visit to London before he and David had departed for Africa. Horse-drawn carriages navigated the streets, the hollow sound of the horses' hooves giving him a strange feeling of belonging. The place looked drab and unexciting, yet there was a sense of excitement in the air, and somehow he loved being there. Perhaps, he thought, he had been isolated in Bulawayo for too long.

Railway Road was not far from the station and he easily found Number 9. It was like most buildings - a very plain and very dirty, single-storey, industrial-brick warehouse, roofed with rusty corrugated-iron sheets. He took in the grubby walls and the many spider webs that stretched over the windows, signalling the length of time since anyone had even considered cleaning them.

Morris walked up to the door and tried the handle, but it was firmly locked. Knocking hard, he stepped back and hoped that his brothers were inside, otherwise he could be in for a long wait, and, in this cold he was not looking forward to that. To his delight, he heard a noise behind the door as a key was turned and a chain rattled. When the door opened he was greeted by beaming smiles from his brothers.

"Good Lord!" Morris exclaimed when he saw Louis, "look at the size of you. You're a good head taller than David."

"Hello, brother," Louis grinned and shook Morris' hand as he entered the building.

"No wonder they call you 'Giraffe'. You're so thin! Are you eating properly? David, we need to feed the boy. And that voice? Heavens, where on earth did that come from?"

"Yes, I know," Louis looked sheepish, trying to cut in before the next barrage of questions hit him, "David has already complained about it."

"Nothing to complain about, David. Nice deep voice. I like it. So, this is the new warehouse, is it? Is it big enough, David? Show me around." Morris did not greet David, and David did not expect him to. They were so close that greetings and farewells were somehow just not necessary, since it was always as if they had never parted company. To meet after a fortnight, or even a month, was as if they had only seen each other earlier that day.

"Yes, this place is perfect, Morris. It looks abandoned from the outside, which has its advantages, but inside it is filled with treasure," David laughed. "The rent is very acceptable, and it is as solid as a fortress. This warehouse is near the railway siding, and most importantly, it can house at least twenty-five wagons."

"Very good," Morris marvelled as he walked around the interior, seemingly ignoring his brothers as the prospect of business overshadowed all else. In the gloom were eighteen wagons standing silently, calmly, waiting for their call to action. All but two wagons were loaded to the hilt and covered with a thick black tarpaulin that had been coated with a linseed-wax substance for protection against the rain. The smell was pungent, but not offensive.

Three weeks had passed since the goods had arrived by rail from East London, and in that time David and Louis had set about coding and tagging the cost prices on each and every item. As they coded the prices, so they created the dockets that indicated upon which wagon the goods were allocated. With Nguni and six of his tribe who accompanied them from Port Elizabeth, they had loaded the wagons, secured the goods, and tied everything down with ropes and tarpaulins.

Morris was impressed with their progress. What they had done in preparation for their departure would also save them considerable time when they arrived in Bulawayo. This way, the goods could be moved immediately into the warehouse and no time would be lost before trading.

"You men have done well," Morris beamed. "Thank you very much. Tell me, though, why are there two empty wagons?"

David immediately apologised. "We underestimated, that's all. When we are done, however, we will have only one empty wagon and we have enough carpets to load into that wagon and fill it," he pointed to the last wagon.

"Carpets?" Morris raised an eyebrow, "that's a good idea. I never considered carpets."

"From China, mostly," Louis added. "They vary in price but average around £3 each, and we have two hundred and fifty of them. They are difficult to load and pack. One needs gloves as they cause terrible blisters, and their weight is frightening, but we can pack many into a wagon, making it a very efficient commodity to transport."

"Show me," Morris was suddenly curious.

Louis took Morris over to a pile of carpets on the floor that had been covered by a tarpaulin and pulled it back. In the gloom of the warehouse Morris looked at the designs and vibrant colours, and ran his hand over the pile, feeling the density of the weave and its weight. His eyes lit up.

"These are marvellous! What a splendid purchase," he exclaimed. "These are from China?"

"Well, I believe China is renowned for their carpets, as are the Persians it seems," David said, also running his hand over the carpets, feeling their texture. "We also bought some Persian ones, but they look and feel very different, thinner and lighter; easier to handle," he frowned.

"Average price?" Morris didn't mince his words.

"£1 and six shillings each," Louis looked serious. "We have about two hundred of them."

"About?" Morris asked abruptly.

"Well, two hundred and four to be exact," Louis replied nervously; he had heard that Morris could be forthright. "The supplier was so fed up with my persistent bargaining he threw four of them in for free."

Morris smiled and looked at David. "I like this lad," he quipped, before slapping Louis on the shoulder. Louis took that as a compliment, especially when David smiled at him and winked. "I must say that I think you boys have hit the jackpot with these carpets. I am sure they will sell fast, and we can name our price.

I'm not too sure about the Persian ones, but these Chinese carpets, well I think we could mark them up by a multiple of ten."

"Ten times?" Louis exclaimed in shock, "do you really think so?"

"I know so!" Morris said confidently.

"Wow, we are going to be rich!" Louis exclaimed excitedly.

Morris looked at his younger brother condescendingly. "Well, that *was* the purpose of coming to Africa, wasn't it?"

To save money, and much to the disappointment of Louis, David had decided to live on the premises, making a fire in the courtyard outside the rear of the building and using the flames to heat a bucket of water with which to wash themselves. David would often remind Louis that conditions were worse in the bush, and – having a roof over their heads and a door to lock out lions and other predators at night – at least they could sleep soundly. Their beds consisted of blankets under one of the wagons. It was not comfortable, but then it was all they could afford, having committed more than their entire financial net worth to their business expansion. Morris did not complain either that night, although he remarked that once they had sold through their stock they could stay at a hotel of their choice, and price would not be an issue.

In the morning, Morris insisted they have breakfast down at the Johannesburg Stock Exchange. He was very keen to understand more about trading in stocks and shares. After breakfast, he wanted to see Danie and make arrangements for the company, and then he wished to go to the outskirts of the town where Nguni was looking after the oxen, goats, and chickens they had bought. He wanted to see his old friend and to make sure that the men and oxen were fit and ready for the journey to Bulawayo.

The following three days were spent loading the last of the wagons. Morris decided that the final wagon should be filled with food items. Although they did not, as a rule, supply edible goods for resale, they were easy to buy in bulk from the multitude of vendors in Johannesburg, and tinned goods could always be sold in Bulawayo at a later date.

As the sun went down on the fourth night of Morris' visit, Nguni and his men began arriving at the warehouse in pairs, each with a team of oxen. Wagons were hitched up and moved back to the outskirts of the town. They had expected to move all the wagons to the campsite that night, but events did not go according to plan. The third wagon that had been hitched up was passing the railway station when a steam engine blasted its whistle. The oxen got such a fright they bolted, tipping the wagon over and causing some damage that needed repair where it lay. The stock, having been strewn all over the street and pavement, had to be collected, the wagon up-righted, repaired, and reloaded. It took until almost daylight to sort out. What they thought would be a one-night exercise became a three-night exercise. They didn't dare move wagons during the day because of the human and mechanical traffic, and the numerous intermittent blasts from the various trains.

"I hope this is not a sign of what's to come," David muttered, as he crawled into his blankets in the early hours of the morning.

"Don't think like that, David," Morris objected. "In any case, the worst is over now."

"Sadly, I think that was the easy part," David sighed, and closed his eyes.

*

Sunrise found the brothers back on Commissioner Street, watching the hustle and bustle of the Stock Exchange before it opened. Pulling themselves away from this new and exciting form of business, they called on Danie Coetzee to finalise all administrative issues with the new Langbourne-Coetzee Company, and then visited the Johannesburg branch of The Standard Bank to ensure there would be no problems with the account they had just opened while they were away in Bulawayo. Later that morning, they walked out of town to where Nguni was camped, for the final check on their wagons, drivers, and oxen.

Seeing the brothers approaching from some distance, Nguni instructed some of his men to stoke the campfire and make some fresh tea for his bosses. He also arranged for a simple meal, consisting of maize meal and soured milk, to be prepared. Upon entering the campsite, the brothers greeted the men heartily and, sitting on the ground around the fire, they gratefully shared in the sustaining meal Nguni had provided. After the meal was over, they inspected their wagons and the enormous herd of oxen needed to pull the load up to Bulawayo. Louis was fascinated by the enormity of the operation, being still quite new to Africa and in some disbelief at what his older brothers had achieved in the short time since they had left Ireland. David spent most of his time in the campsite, checking the oxen, the wagons, and the harnesses, as well as the horse that he would need for the journey from the Limpopo River to Bulawayo. Morris checked the ropes holding down the tarpaulins and their valuable goods. Finally satisfied that all was ready, they made their farewells to Nguni and the team.

"I will see you when the sun greets us tomorrow, Nguni," David shook the big man's hand. "We will leave as soon as we have daylight."

"We will be ready, Boss David," Nguni smiled approvingly. "My heart will sing when we turn our backs on this town; it is too cold here and our blood needs to move. The oxen will be harnessed and ready to go."

"I will see you in Rhodesia," Morris shook his hand in farewell. "May your journey be safe and pleasant for you."

"I wish you a safe journey too, Boss Morris." Nguni's handshake was firm and solid.

Louis bade Nguni farewell, but neither of them knew when it would be before they saw each other again. Louis would be returning to East London, and was somewhat disappointed that he could not be part of this adventure to the end.

Nguni was quick to notice Louis' disappointment. "Perhaps we will journey together next time," he murmured.

"Perhaps," Louis smiled, but remained unconvinced.

The brothers strode back to Johannesburg as quickly as they could. The walk was well over an hour long and daylight was fading rapidly. On the Highveld of Johannesburg, dusk was short-lived: day turned to night with uncomfortable speed. On entering their warehouse, each brother immediately set to work in closing down the premises. They packed their personal belongings, making sure nothing was left behind, and swept the floor with an old broom that they had found abandoned in an alleyway. When they awoke at four o'clock the next morning all they would have to do would be to roll up their bedding and close their baggage. Morris and Louis would wear smart business attire as they would be travelling by train, but David would be dressed in his khaki bush clothing, as he would accompany Nguni and the caravan on the trek northwest to meet Daluxolo at the Limpopo River. Climbing under their blankets, they were fast asleep within minutes.

*

The three brothers took one last look at their empty and dingy warehouse, illuminated only by the faint glow of the streetlight seeping in through the broken windowpane near the roof, before walking out into the gloomy back road. The gentle radiance of the rising sun was only just beginning to show on the eastern horizon. A lone, horse-drawn carriage rattled noisily by under the dim streetlight as David turned the key in the heavy wooden door, locking down the Johannesburg branch of Langbourne Coetzee until their return.

David addressed Louis and shook his hand. "Safe travels, young brother,"

"Same to you, David. It was good to see you again." Louis shook hands with him and turned to Morris, shaking his hand firmly. "Good to see you, too, brother. I look forward to meeting up with you again soon."

"Don't forget to send us a telegram when you get back to East London," Morris jokingly warned, "and thanks for your help. You did well." This compliment meant a great deal to Louis, who smiled openly.

David handed the key of the warehouse to Louis and then turned to Morris, shaking his hand in farewell. "Are you sure you have thought of everything? We have never done anything like this before – nobody has ever done something of this magnitude, nor with such secrecy, and the risk of sending up so many wagons at one time is immense."

"I am also uncomfortable with putting all our eggs in one basket, but I have thought of every contingency I can, David," Morris replied. "We have spare parts for the wagons, and extra oxen, and enough men with ample food. Our team is competent, well trained, and they have travelled for us before, albeit on a different route - several times, in fact. And we have not one, but two excellent and trusted leaders. The rebellion is over; there are no hostilities; the country is stable and the rainy season is on our side. The men know how to deal with predators and protect the wagons and oxen. There are plenty of medical supplies in case of an emergency and I have shown each leader how to use them, if necessary. I don't know what else to consider."

"We've had to borrow heavily from Weil; we owe Gerran a fortune, and we are up to our neck in debt with the bank. The risk is enormous."

"I know," Morris shrugged his shoulders in resignation, "but – if we get this right – we will never look back."

David looked silently at his older brother for a moment. He knew he could trust Morris' judgment implicitly, but for the first time he had a nagging reservation about this entire exercise and he just couldn't put his finger on it.

"Okay," he sighed, "I will meet Daluxolo at the Limpopo

River in about six weeks as planned, and then, all going well, I'll see you in Bulawayo shortly after."

"Six weeks as planned," Morris repeated and nodded seriously.

The three brothers, two dressed in business suits, and one dressed in safari gear, turned on their heels, and without looking back, walked off in different directions, slowly blending into Johannesburg's dark and lonely streets.

CHAPTER TEN

The Plan

WHILE THEY WERE busy loading 12 wagons in
Mafeking together, Morris was driving his brother
Louis and Ian Taylor demented with all his demands
and incessant questions. At the same time, however, David was
working even harder, driving his team of 18 fully loaded wagons
towards an unknown point in the northwest of the country, where
he hoped to find the banks of the Limpopo River.

David's task was far from easy: the 18 wagons stretched out
for almost a mile at times and the lead wagon was cutting through
virgin grassland and bush because there was no sign of any road,
track, or path ahead. The scouts who ran ahead to check the route
would often come running hurriedly back to inform Nguni that
the way was blocked, only to be sent running in another direction looking for an alternative route in order to avoid the lead
wagon having to halt unnecessarily. On numerous occasions, the
lead wagon would have to stop, causing the others to bunch up
behind it. David would then call the procession to a halt, form
a laager, and allow the beasts to graze and rest, while a new route
was searched for.

To add to the frustratingly slow pace, the wagons would constantly break down, requiring David to canter back on his horse and help with the repairs. On other occasions, he would need to dash further ahead to help remove a wagon that had been caught in a rut. Most of David's day was spent on horseback, sprinting up and down the line of wagons, solving problems. Many times, a wagon would have to be painstakingly unloaded, repaired, or freed, and then re-loaded. Nothing was quickly solved: every problem seemed to demand an inordinate amount of time to sort out. Day after day, the only sounds David heard were the protesting bleats of the oxen, the crack of whips, and the cries of the herders and drivers, always mixed in with the monotonous drone and rumble of the iron-rimmed wagon wheels.

Whenever David's patience began to test his resolve, he would find Nguni, who was always with the lead wagon, and talk to him about their progress, their problems, and even their victories. Nguni knew when David needed consoling and, with his soothing baritone voice, would gently ease the frustrations and worries of his friend. Sometimes not a word needed to be said; with his face smeared with dust and grime, his hands and fingernails impregnated with the vile black grease from the wagon axles, David would ride up to Nguni, dismount, and walk with him for a while. Then, nodding his appreciation for his company, David would mount again and ride towards the last wagon, hoping he would find all well, but knowing in his heart there would be a problem somewhere along the line.

One morning, they came across a small river and Nguni's scouts reported that it was not flowing swiftly, nor was it deep. Referring to parts of the body as individuals, the statement that *'the knee, he did not get wet'* was an accepted way of saying the river was shallow and navigable. What they did not know until they began to cross the river, however, was that the bottom of the river was covered in treacherous boulders, two of which immediately snagged the lead wagon. Even the oxen began to slip and fall into the water when their hooves could not find purchase on the smooth rock surfaces. It was only Nguni's swift action in freeing the oxen from the wagon and leading them out of the river that saved a near tragedy of broken legs and wounded beasts.

It took four days to find a new route that enabled them to cross the river safely, and by now David was becoming very concerned not only at how far behind they were in reaching Daluxolo, but also that they may have become entirely lost. He was not sure how far west they had travelled and was worried day and night that they may have missed the Limpopo entirely, or that a river they had recently crossed was in fact the upper reaches of the Limpopo and they had already crossed it.

"Well," David mused as he stared at the flames in the campfire one night, "at least if we hit the Atlantic Ocean we'll know we have gone too far west."

"Boss?" Nguni looked at David very confused.

"Oh, nothing, Nguni," David apologised. "I was just wondering if we are still going the right way. I was worried that the last river we crossed was the Limpopo after all, in which case we need to turn right, not left as I had planned."

"It was too small for the Limpopo, Boss. The Limpopo is still far, far away."

David smiled as he took in what Nguni said. If, in their custom, *near-near* could be several days away, then only heaven knew how distant *far-far* was. "You're right," David sighed and ruffled his hair, "we have many days, if not weeks to go."

After another week of relentlessly driving forward, one of their scouts came back and urgently spoke to Nguni, who in turn halted the lead wagon and sent word down the line to ask David to come to the front with the same urgency. David was busy untangling a stray rope that had caught in the rear axle of one of the wagons and solidly locked up the wheel. The tangled knot was so tight that, although he did not want to waste such a valuable commodity, he was about to cut his way through the rope with a knife as a last resort. Upon receiving the message from Nguni, however, David handed his sheath knife to the driver, instructing him to cut the rope and finish the job, before nervously making his way back up the line of wagons to hear about Nguni's problem.

"I see you Nguni. What is the problem this time?" David asked, trying to hide his anxiety.

"I see you, Boss David. Yes, I am sorry to tell you there is a problem over that hill," he pointed over his shoulder. "There is a village there and their chief will not allow us to pass on his land. He sends message that we must turn around and go back."

"How far back must we go?"

"Four days back."

"No, surely we can't do that?" David was horrified at the thought. "Do you think if we gave him a gift of some chickens or some goats he might let us pass?"

"I think he will," Nguni nodded slowly.

"Maybe we should send the scout back with a chicken and a goat and see what he says."

"No," Nguni rumbled as he shook his head, "that is no good. We must send the scout back to say *you*, Boss David, would like to give him a present, and ask his permission for you to see him. It is better that the two leaders meet. It is a good custom. Then you can ask for his permission to pass. If he refuses, then you need not give him the present."

"He might chop my head off then," David joked.

"Yes, it is possible." Nguni saw the humour in David's quip.

"Then what you say is good and we must do as you say, Nguni."

Nguni sent his scout off once again, and three hours later he returned to say the chief was agreeable to meeting David and receive a gift, but only in seven days' time.

"Seven days?" David exclaimed when he received the response. "Is he mad? Why on earth does he want two hundred oxen to spend seven days on his land, eating his grass?"

"I feel he is showing you who is the more powerful chief," Nguni said solemnly, "he is making you wait under his terms."

"Or he wants me to better my 'present' to him."

"It is possible."

"Or he is mobilising his *impi* to attack us and steal all our wagons." Suspicion seeped into David's voice.

"It is possible." Nguni repeated without any emotion.

David thought about his predicament for a while. "Nguni, bring all the wagons together and assemble them so that they all point backwards as if we will go back. Then when this is done, please send your scout to the village again with seven chicken eggs. He must give these eggs to the chief as a token of my respect for his authority over his land and my apologies for trespassing on his territory, but the scout must say we cannot wait seven days and I will find another way. We will leave immediately."

Nguni nodded his agreement. "I will arrange this, Boss David. Do you think he will attack us?"

"No, I think he is just playing games with us. If he wanted me to wait seven days, and I give him seven eggs, it will stir his curiosity to see what kind of person I am. Also, once his spies see we are turning the wagons around and making ready to go back, I believe he will send a message to invite me to see him tomorrow."

"Do you think he will send spies to watch us?"

"His spies are already watching us, Nguni," David winked and nodded to his left. "There are three of them over there, whom I have been watching with my telescope."

"Ghaw!" Nguni hawked in anger.

"Don't look now," David warned with a smile, "they don't know we have seen them. It is good that way. When they see we are turning around, they will know we are serious."

"I do not like these people," Nguni scowled, before barking some orders to turn the caravan of wagons to face the southeast.

*

The following morning found David sitting on the bare earth, cross-legged, as he drank some traditional beer with the chief of the village. Nguni stood proudly next to his boss, looking decidedly dissatisfied. Surrounded by half-a-dozen, semi-naked young women of his village, the chief sat pompously on a chair, which had been fashioned out of a piece of dry timber. Four intimidating young men with spears knelt at his feet. Communication was very difficult, but Nguni somehow managed to understand most of what was said, or intended. David exchanged some presents in the form of a goat, six chickens, and four, pale green enamel mugs. The chief accepted these gifts and shared his sour traditional beer with David, who feigned enjoyment while he struggled to force it down his throat.

"Nguni, please ask the chief in which direction the Limpopo River lies."

Nguni obliged and after much consultation with his spearmen, they swept their arms west and north, and agreed it was basically in the direction they were travelling, beyond the village.

"Please ask him which direction is Mafeking," David asked again with a pleasant smile, not taking his eyes off the chief. He was hoping they would point somewhere in a southwest direction.

There was a great deal of head shaking and frowning, then Nguni reported that they had never heard of Mafeking.

"They have never heard of Mafeking?" David was both surprised and amused. "Johannesburg?" David pressed, taking a gulp of the brew and forcing it down his throat, smiling back at the chief and looking ever so pleased with the meeting. He wanted to gag, but forced his smile. He knew if he could just get some direction on a key place, a town, river, or mountain, he would know roughly where he was.

After more head shaking, Nguni cleared his throat. "They have not heard of Johannesburg," he mumbled.

Cape Town, Kimberley and Port Elizabeth were also never heard of, but the moment David mentioned Matabeleland, they all started pointing north in earnest, smiling excitedly at having heard a name they understood.

"That way?" David pointed north to reaffirm the direction.

They all pointed northwards again, babbling with excitement.

"Well, that will have to do, Nguni. I think we are still on track."

"They say we should not go there as it is ruled by King Lobengula and we will be food for his spears."

David didn't want to complicate anything; it was obvious they were a very isolated tribe with very little outside news. "Tell them we are not going there, Nguni. Also, please tell them we must start our journey before our oxen eat all their good grass, and thank them for their hospitality." With that David stood and bowed, trying his best to look humbled and pleased with the chief, but feeling decidedly queasy in his stomach. He wanted to get some distance between himself and the chief before he threw up.

*

On a slight mound on the edge of Mafeking, just beyond the cemetery, Morris and Louis stood silently with their hands in their pockets and watched the procession of twelve wagons grumble their way towards Matabeleland, with Daluxolo, as always, in command. He had done this several times now and he knew exactly what to do and what his boss expected of him. His team regarded him with utmost respect and Morris had absolute faith in his abilities. Morris' instructions to him had been clear: go to the Limpopo crossing, then out-span and wait for David and Nguni, who would be arriving with more wagons. Just as David had done before him, he did not say how many wagons.

"You know," Louis spoke to Morris without taking his eyes off the convoy, "once David joins that lot, it's going to be quite a spectacle."

"That's for sure," Morris agreed lazily. "That's one of the reasons I didn't want them all to depart from here; the community will think we have gone crazy. Also it spreads the risk a little. Furthermore, any more than that might take the fancy of some looters looking for an opportunity."

"Huh," Louis suppressed a laugh and looked over at his older brother, "even I think you're crazy. I still can't imagine how you got the loans to fund this exercise. I agree it is good to spread the risk, but you do realise the risk is unevenly spread between Johannesburg and here. Not only that, the biggest risk is the Johannesburg shipment. What if David doesn't make it? That will ruin us forever."

Morris looked at Louis with slit eyes. "Of course he will make it! You underestimate your brother."

Louis shrugged and sighed, "well, even so, splitting the risk is all well and good but once they cross the Limpopo the risk is no longer split. All the wagons will be together."

"That's true, brother Louis, that is true. I am well aware of that, but I feel more comfortable with both Nguni and Daluxolo working together when there are more than twelve wagons involved. To keep them separate will mean David has to stay with them for three or four months, and I need him in Bulawayo."

"Are you ever going to take me to Bulawayo?" Louis asked, anxious to join his brothers. He was not keen to go back to East London; the only thing that held any interest for him there was the pretty young girl who worked at the bank, and even she was slightly older than him and probably married.

"Yes, of course. You are a big part of my plan."

Feeling a little more comforted, Louis took a final look at the receding procession. "Whatever possessed you and David to walk three months in that direction will always be a mystery to me."

"Sometimes I wonder that myself," Morris chuckled, staring at the dust cloud that was now enveloping the wagons. "You know, this is the exact spot David and I stood on when we decided to go to Rhodesia. It was called Matabeleland then. It was a big decision," he reflected as his mood turned pensive. "It was the right decision, but we were a year too early." Morris fell silent as he drifted off in thought. Had they gone up a year later they would have missed the brutal Matabele Rebellion, and they would not have lost almost their entire wealth and business. They would have been well ahead of the game by now, but he nevertheless had exciting plans, and they were all coming to fruition.

"This is going to make our family a lot of money, isn't it, Morris?" Louis queried, with just a hunt of consternation in his voice

Morris looked over at Louis and cocked an eyebrow. "Absolutely, Louis, absolutely. Just you wait and see," he smiled. "Now, let's get back into town and finalise the paperwork with Weil and prepare to leave. You have a long train journey back to East London in the morning and I have to catch that dreaded BSAC run back to Bulawayo."

"I can handle the paperwork if you like? I know what to do," Louis offered.

"I believe you do," Morris smiled. "Alright, young brother, you do that for me, I would really appreciate that. I believe you and I will make a good team," he laughed and slapped Louis on the shoulder as he turned to walk back into town.

Louis smiled as he watched his diminutive brother walk away. For the first time in over a year, he felt as if he was a part of the family again. Wrenching his hands out of his pockets he quickly trotted off to walk beside his mentor.

*

"What is it now?" David called over to Nguni as he dismounted, frustration evident in his voice.

Nguni looked troubled. "My scout says there is much water ahead,"

"Is it the Limpopo?" David's spirits began to lift.

"No," Nguni looked very troubled, "it is not the river. The scout cannot see the other side."

"What?" David exclaimed in shock. He could not believe they had missed the Limpopo altogether and reached the far side of the continent, the Atlantic Ocean. According to his rough calculations, they would only have traversed one quarter of the continent's width, not the entire continent. "Please ask your scout to take me there now. Bring the wagons to a halt and set up camp; we have done enough for one day."

Nguni obliged and began to form the overnight laager while David and the scout, dressed only in a flowing white robe and totally barefoot, led David to where he had seen the body of water. About a half-hour later, the two men appeared through some tall grass on the banks of a vast expanse of shimmering liquid. The guide stopped and David walked a further ten paces to get a better view. Its beauty caught David by surprise, and he unconsciously allowed himself some time to admire another of God's wonderful creations, before reality caught up with him and he realised he was in a most awkward situation.

It was not the ocean, as there were barely any waves. It was not a lake, as the edges were not well defined, with dry grasses stretching for many hundreds of yards into the water before being swallowed up by the flood. The ground was soft and almost muddy; totally unsuitable for wagons. *No*, David thought, *this was not the ocean, but a marsh,* and there was no way whatsoever they could pass through it. To his right, in a northerly direction, the expanse of water reached the horizon, and to the south, the prospect of crossing did not look any better. To make matters worse, there were millions of small insects flying frantically around the edges, mosquitoes, midges, and other unknown species of insect David had never seen before. Something bit him on his neck and he slapped it hard. He studied a small winged insect that was still sticking to the palm of his blood-spattered hand, not sure if it was his blood or that of the insect. A strange feeling overtook him and he began to feel decidedly uncomfortable.

He turned to leave but his feet refused to move. Looking down he saw that his boots had sunk into the mud up to his ankles. A wave of horror overtook him as he realised he was rapidly sinking further into the muck. As he wrenched at one foot, the other buried deeper into the mud. He instantly knew he was in trouble and the ground was relentlessly sucking him into its bowels. He was about to turn to call out to his scout for help when something caught his attention – a small movement just off to his left. Standing motionless, he looked in the direction of the movement, and horror suddenly gripped him in his gut. A very large black snake was slithering past him only a couple of yards away. It stopped, as it seemed to sense David's terror, and locked its eyes in his direction. Both snake and human froze in fear, believing each other to be a deadly threat.

A new sensation alerted David to his dire predicament, and that was of cold water dribbling into his boots. His feet had now sunk to the height of the top of his boots and water from the saturated mud began to flow freely down his ankles and around his toes. Very slowly he looked down as a wave of panic overtook his sense of reason. He was sinking into a black, muddy mush, and a venomous and potentially lethal snake appeared to have him in his sights. He was frozen with fear and found he couldn't even call out to his scout.

Realising the real possibility of death within minutes if he didn't think clearly, David took a deep breath and forcefully calmed himself down. Remembering that someone had once told him that snakes don't appear to see slow movements, but are attracted to fast and intermittent actions, he very slowly reached for the revolver at his right hip. Withdrawing it ever so carefully, he aimed at the ground just in front of the cold calculating eyes of the snake, whose forked tongue flicked back and forth as it tasted the air, and gently pulled the trigger. The sound of the gun exploding into the silence of the swamp, and the resultant blast of white smoke, served its purpose and scared the snake off. When the smoke cleared, the reptile was nowhere to be seen.

Without wasting a second, David holstered the revolver and reached for his bootlaces. He was up to his calves now, and he had to literally dig for his boots. Loosening his laces one boot at a time, he found he was still well and truly lodged in the thick mud; he didn't have the strength to lift a leg vertically out of the mud without some form of support. Taking a chance, he leaned forward, further towards the depth of the swamp, hoping to get come leverage as he dragged his heels out of the boots. It began to work, and soon he was on all fours, hands and knees in the mud. As soon as he had freed his feet painfully from his boots and dragged them out of the mud with very pronounced sucking sounds, he desperately crawled back the way he had come, and as he turned, noticed that his scout was nowhere to be seen.

Reaching firm ground, David took stock of himself. He was covered in foul- smelling, black mud, and had no boots. He also realised, with some fascination, that not only had the swamp claimed his boots, it also had taken possession of his socks as well! Then, as he looked back to where he had escaped, yet another reminder of the dangers of the wild African bush hit him in the stomach with such force he wanted to be sick all over again. Not twenty yards from where he was, he beheld the eyes and snout of a monstrous crocodile staring back at him. Not wanting to be anywhere near this terrible place, David turned and followed his tracks back to where he had left the wagons.

Having realised the lethal predicament that David had been in, the scout had rushed back to find help, only to have met Nguni and six other men halfway, crashing through the bush in a desperate hurry to save their boss after hearing the single gunshot. In the end, David was very relieved to see the rescue party, while assuring them he was well and unharmed. That night, around the campfire, David thanked the scout whose quick thinking would have certainly saved his life had he not managed to free himself. "Nguni," he added, "I am not happy with that swamp. We cannot cross it. It is filled with snakes and crocodiles."

"The animals are the smallest problem, Boss," Nguni lamented as the dancing flames from the fire reflected in his face.

"Why do you say that?"

"Water from a place like that is said to be very poisonous. They say people die if they just smell that water. The insects also drink that water and when they bite people, it is said you get the water sickness from them. You chase away the animals, but you cannot chase the smell or the insects."

David reached up and scratched at an itchy spot on his neck where he had killed the bug that had bitten him earlier.

"We need to find another way. The water stretches as far as I could see both this way," David pointed north, "and that way," he indicated south.

"I can send scouts both ways to find a way around."

"That will be good, Nguni. I will not go this time, I will work on the wagons," David said uncomfortably. He was physically tired and needed a rest, and his encounter with quicksand, a snake, and a crocodile all at the same time, had unnerved him, but what worried him the most was that he had been bitten by an unknown insect, and was not sure if he had contracted that waterborne disease Nguni spoke of.

"I will send four men in each direction for four days."

"That will mean a delay of eight days, with no promise of a way forward," David shook his head in despair. "There must be a better way."

All the men around the campfire were silent as they could sense the despondent mood emanating from the tones of their leader and their boss, there was no joking or teasing this time, nor earnest discussions, laughter or lazy reminiscing; the sound of the crackle in the fire was the only comfort.

"We are told that water can only walk down the hill, but not up the hill," Nguni looked up at David with a frown.

"Yes, I believe this is true, Nguni."

"When the sun comes up, then maybe we should find a very

tall tree and climb it. Then we must look to see where the land rises, or where there may be mountains. Then that must be the way and we can continue our journey without waiting eight days?"

David stared at his leader in awe. "You are right, Nguni." He allowed a broad smile to brighten his face, "I think that is a very good idea. Thus it shall be done."

The first light of the following day found David in the canopy of a tall Acacia tree. The view was spectacular, and the size of the swamp was truly amazing, but it only took a few seconds for David to work out that they needed to take a northerly direction. There were mountains in almost every direction he looked, but certainly the closest peaks were to the north. Nguni's idea had saved them many days of delay and much wasted energy in trial and error.

They began their detour early the next day, but not long after commencing the journey, David began to feel a little off-colour. He had developed a throbbing headache, and the joints in his knees and fingers were beginning to hurt. By mid afternoon he was feeling nauseous and found the intensity of the afternoon sunlight hard on his eyes. Mounting his horse was becoming such a chore that, sitting atop his mount, he had to wipe the sweat from his forehead. Although he was sweating profusely, he felt strangely chilled. It was then that he realised that he was ill and needed to let Nguni know.

Riding to the front of the procession of wagons, he located Nguni and headed straight for him. It only took one glance from that trusted friend for him to realise that Nguni was concerned by what he saw. Dismounting with difficulty and handing his horse to one of the herders, David asked Nguni to help him onto the lead wagon where he needed to rest. There was also a medicine chest in the wagon and David foraged about looking for a bottle of medication for fevers. Frustrated by his blinding headache, he eventually found the elusive bottle, uncorked it and took a large swig from its contents. It tasted foul, but he didn't care.

"Nguni," he turned to the large Xhosa man. "I must rest as I am unwell. I fear I have got the water sickness."

"It is good that you rest, Boss David. I will look after the wagons."

"Thank you Nguni," David forced a smile. "Four times a day I must have this *muti*," David handed him the bottle of medication, "it is the English *muti* for this sickness. If I am sleeping you must wake me when the sun is there," he pointed to the horizon, "there, there and there," he moved his arm in an arch to indicate where the sun would be every three hours or so.

"I will wake you, Boss."

"Good, thank you. I will rest here in the wagon. Keep moving, there is no reason to stop."

David drifted into a fitful sleep almost the moment he put his head down on a sack of corn. The rocking of the wagon and the intermediate thumps and knocks from the wheels on the rocks and stumps did nothing to coax him out of his unconscious state. Soon the hideous dreams began in colours of red and black: black trees with black leaves that were bent and gnarled against a blood-red sky. The silhouette of a scorpion appeared on a branch of the black tree and flicked its tail at him. His fear of the scorpion was so intense that he could feel something like lightning crackle down his face – he could even hear the lightning. The black, bent leaves grew grotesque scorpion-like stings and flailed at him relent-lessly. They started to crack and spit at him; the scorpion began to scream; and suddenly there was a black snake hissing at him with cold, evil eyes, the sounds becoming louder and so intense that David began to scream back at them. It went on and on – he was trapped in a nightmare that never ended and he began to sob through the terrible sounds and pain that seared through his body. He wanted Nguni to wake him from his nightmare, but he couldn't find him. Everything was black, even the red sky became black, and with it came more pain.

Then suddenly, it went quiet – deathly quiet. The pain had

gone too, just as suddenly. The wagon was not moving either, and the world was still and at peace. David lay calmly, trying to understand what was going on. He thought he might have died and was safely in heaven with his Lord. With much trepidation he carefully opened his eyes, fearful of what he might find. He saw the canopy of a beautiful, leafy tree with a rich, blue sky behind it, while a brilliant-white, fluffy cloud drifted lazily past.

"Boss?" he heard Nguni's deep comforting voice.

David gingerly looked to his left. His neck was stiff, but there was no pain. Nguni sat on the ground by his side.

"I see you, Nguni," David croaked, and managed to smile.

"I see you, Boss David," Nguni grinned, obviously happy to see his friend smile.

"Why am I not in the wagon?" David's brain began to try and piece all the events together, but he was confused.

"You have been very sick with the water sickness. You have been sleeping."

"How long have I been sleeping, Nguni?"

"It is four days now."

"I have been asleep for four days? How can that be?" David tried to sit up, but he was so weak he could barely lift his head.

"We will wait here another two days, Boss. You need some rest. Also seven of our men are also sick. They will be better soon."

"Did you give them some of that *muti*, Nguni?"

"Your *muti* is no good for the water sickness, so I have given you and the men some of my traditional *muti*. My *muti* is good."

David lay back smiling and closed his eyes. He knew he should not question African traditional medicine over European medicine. The fact was that it worked and he was on the mend. "Thank you for looking after me and the men, Nguni," David muttered as he drifted into another deep sleep.

After a month of trekking through unexplored bush land, coupled with his illness, David had neglected to keep his journal up to date, and as a result, had no idea how long they had been on the move. He assumed they had been walking for two months, but couldn't be sure. They had negotiated their way through five villages, trading gifts for safe passage, encountered countless wild-animal threats, and had lost five beasts due to injury or illness. Their chicken and goat population had increased slightly, and the teams of drivers and herders were in good spirits. For two weeks, David had been expecting to hit the Limpopo River, but each day brought the same disappointment. His weakened state merely allowed him to sit on a wagon and watch its progress as he went along for the ride, since he could not mount a horse. All he could do was trust his men to make running repairs, and, to his relief, they managed very well.

Finally a scout came running back as camp was being set up for the night to say there was a very wide river up ahead. With much excitement the men turned in that night believing they were close to their destination. At first light David, a little unsteady on his legs, together with Nguni, stood on the banks of a riverbed that was, indeed, very wide.

"Do you think this might be the Limpopo, Nguni?"

"It is hard to tell, boss, but for sure it will a big river when the rains come."

Just then the scout who was standing beside them mumbled something, and Nguni simply nodded his agreement without looking at him.

"What does he say?" David asked Nguni, likewise not looking at him but continuing to stare at the far bank.

"He says he has been here before with his uncle. He says the other side of this river belongs to Lobengula."

David and Nguni remained silent, but, like two naughty children, smiled at Rhodesia's southern border.

*

Morris tethered his horse to a lamppost outside Langbourne Brothers and strode into the large double doors that welcomed their customers. The windows were still boarded up, but Morris was very proud of their building and their achievements. The structure was among the finest in town, and he marvelled at the fact that it belonged to them, even though they owed a lot of money on it. There were no customers in the store, and, standing in the doorway waiting for his eyes to adjust to the gloom within, he scanned the interior for his youngest brother.

"Harry, I'm back!" he called out, "where are you?"

"Morris!" came the immediate response from deep within the building, and, like a puppy eager to greet his master, Harry came bounding from behind a stack of cartons. "Welcome back, Brother! How wonderful to see you again! How was the journey?"

"Long and boring, as usual. So, what's been happening? Fill me in. Have you been making sales?" Morris never wasted time on pleasantries but always got straight to business.

"Business has been good, Morris," Harry beamed proudly.

"Good, good," he smiled in response. "Now show me the books, let's see what you have done. Are you banking money? What about our wagon traders? Have any come back for resupplies?"

"Yes, yes, and yes," Harry quickly interrupted the barrage of questions. "Three wagon traders have come back and restocked, and have also paid the rent on the wagons." He quickly walked over to a table and opened a large leather-bound ledger, running his finger down a line of numbers. "Here, this is what they paid, and this is what I banked; you can see the figures balance like you showed me. Oh, and here is the value of what they took. Then on this page," he flicked some pages over, "I have recorded all the sales I have made from the store. Look, not bad business, don't you think?"

Morris looked at Harry sideways, rather surprised by his enthusiasm, before studying the ledger pages carefully, frowning all the time. He thumbed through some of the pages, then went back a few before, breaking into a smile. "Not bad, Harry; not bad at all."

"Oh, and I've started a filing system for all our contracts and agreements, as well as for our banking, income and expenses, that sort of thing. I must say you and David are not very good at keeping your records in order – there are documents all over the place. Nevertheless, all the contracts and agreements have been filed in that box in alphabetical order, and all the cheques, receipts, invoices and matters that involve numbers are numerically filed in that box," he grinned, proud of his work on the administrative organisation.

"Well I'll be…!" Morris trailed off, looking at the neatly placed boxes, ledgers and files. "You did all that while I was away?"

"Oh yes, and more," Harry began to walk towards the back of the building. "Follow me, I've created a space for your office. You need an office, you know! It's not big, but it's private. It is where you can keep all these records and not worry about a member of the public paging through some files that we might have left on the counter. I have also created a similar office at the back where we can have meetings with our traders, or with important customers or businessmen, without being interrupted by the general public."

"I'm amazed, Harry," Morris was genuinely surprised. "Where did you learn to do these things? Who taught you? Father?"

"Mostly, yes, but I have been watching you, and David. When I was in Mafeking I saw how organised Mr Gerran was, but have you ever looked at Mr Weil's office?"

Morris burst out laughing, "Yes, there's hardly a space on his desk to place a teacup!"

"I have no idea how he knows what he is doing. I doubt he could tell you how much stock he has in any one warehouse, let alone the four he has in Mafeking. And if he doesn't know what he has in stock, how would he know what he has in the bank."

Morris instantly frowned, "Oh, believe me, he has no idea what's in his bank account, or should I say, what is *not* in his bank account."

"What do you mean?"

"I inadvertently saw an error that the bank had made in his ledger. I doubt he will ever know what cash of his has gone missing."

"So why don't you tell him?"

"It's none of my business, that's why. In any case I should never have looked at his ledger, it was just open in front of me, and that, my dear brother, is why I like your idea of keeping all our records and paperwork in a private office. After all, we have a code for numbers and names, so well done to you: I like what you have done."

Harry was very pleased with his older brother's remarks. This was panning out to be the happiest day he had had in many years. "So when are our wagons going to be here? I have customers waiting."

Morris was impressed with Harry. He had shown initiative and drive. "Not long, Harry, not long," he slapped him on the shoulder, "your brother should be crossing the Limpopo very soon now."

"Some other things you should know, Morris, is that the administration has run a copper water pipe down the back alleyway. I had to pay a small fee, but we now have a connection of water into the building. I also paid a Portuguese plumber to connect a tap to our connection, and dig a small drain out the back. I hope you don't mind? I found an old iron trough used to provide water for sheep and goats, which I have placed under the tap. It leaks a bit, but it means we can bath and keep presentable. The water is a little cold, but refreshing. I've stacked some boxes around the trough for a little privacy."

"Outstanding!" Morris exclaimed in amazement. "This administration is doing some wonderful stuff. All we need now is a classy eating establishment and we might even have a settlement we can be happy to live in."

"There are some, actually," Harry puffed his chest out for no apparent reason, apart from the fact that he was enjoying giving his brother some well needed good news, and feeling important in the process. "They are hotels: one is called The Charter Hotel, which I believe is very prestigious, and the other is the Maxim Hotel, frequented mostly by the BSAC chaps. I have not been there, but I hear they are very respectable."

"And how do you know all this?"

"It's in the newspaper," Harry smiled smugly.

"What newspaper?" Morris demanded, very curious now.

"We have a registered newspaper in town now. They are quite expensive at sixpence a copy, so I borrowed one from Phil Innes, which I have to return tonight. Here, have a look." Harry stepped over to a small box within which he kept some of his personal effects and pulled out a small bundle of papers that he placed on the counter top and gently flattened with the palm of his hand. All the pages were of slightly differing sizes and shades of beige or pale blue.

"There you go," he announced, "*The Matabele Times and Mining Journal,* registered in Bulawayo as a Newspaper."

"My word," Morris marvelled as he gently picked up the small collection of papers and scrutinised the front page. "It's all written by hand!"

As there was no printing press in town, an ingenious entre-preneurial gentleman had decided to register a newspaper and to handwrite one edition each week. It had the format of a basic newspaper, with a bold heading listing the name of the paper, the volume and edition number, date, and price at the top of the page, the remainder of the editorial mostly consisting of advertisements and notices. The bold and capitalised headings were filled in using freehand and a simple pen. The front page had the bold letters filled in as well, but as the pages progressed, it was obvious that the Editor became rushed, or tired, and the bold characters were not quite so neatly done. The effect was exceptional, though. The remainder of the content of the newspaper was handwritten in a very neat and flowery script.

"Look on Page 6," Harry urged, "there is an advertisement for the Maxim Hotel, and they boast a splendid dining room with first-class cuisine, liquors, and cigarettes. The Central Hotel has a spacious Bar and Billiard Room."

"This is magnificent!" Morris gushed as he looked at the print on Page 6. "There must be a shortage of paper because, look, you see these faint red lines running down the right side of the page here," he traced his finger gently down the sheet of paper, "this is a page out of an accounting ledger, and this page," he flicked back to page 3, "has been ripped from a publication of sorts; note the torn edge."

"I must give the Editor his due to handwrite a newspaper every week on paper he has had to pilfer from books and other publications."

"Indeed," Morris continued to study the pages of the newspaper as if he had been given a mathematical problem with no solution. "Well then," Morris suddenly put the newspaper down, "I think I will test out that makeshift bath of yours, and then perhaps you and I should sample one of these new establishments. I might suggest the Maxim Hotel with its fine cuisine?"

"Splendid!" Harry beamed.

*

Daluxolo was tending to one of the oxen when he saw his young cousin return from a scouting venture east along the river. He was jogging a little faster than usual so Daluxolo assumed he was carrying some good news.

"I see you, cousin," Daluxolo greeted the slender man. "Your face shows you have some news for me."

"Yes, cousin. I see much dust rising on the horizon. It is moving slowly. Such dust can only be caused by many animals, and animals that are not moving fast."

"So you think these might be the oxen your uncle is bringing to us?"

"Yes, cousin. I think they will be here tomorrow, but one," which was his way of saying *the day after tomorrow*.

"You have done well. I thank you. Let us prepare food for their arrival, then."

"I will prepare the food, as I feel you, yourself, should go there tomorrow to greet them. It will be good for their hearts to see you."

"Your suggestion is sound, my cousin, but my job is to protect the oxen and wagons at every hour. It must be you that goes to greet them. You must leave at first light."

"It shall be done," his cousin agreed without complaint, and politely took his leave.

At around noon the following day, Daluxolo's cousin and Nguni's scout met along the banks of the Limpopo River. Greeting each other as brothers and quickly exchanging vital family news, the two cousins jogged back to the approaching caravan of wagons. Both Nguni and David saw the two slender young men approaching and immediately knew that not only were they on the right track, but that they did not have far to go. Nguni looked up and smiled knowingly at David, who was sitting with the driver of the lead wagon. David, still recovering from his illness, spent many hours just sitting with one of the drivers as his joints continued to ache, and he tired very easily. Each day saw a very slight improvement, but it had been a slow recuperation. He had lost much of his weight, and found he needed to notch his belt up a few holes just to keep his trousers from slipping down to his knees. He nodded back at Nguni and smiled; they didn't need to talk much, so well did they understand each other.

Just as Daluxolo's cousin predicted, the two caravans finally joined the following day. The reunion was particularly enjoyable for everyone concerned. Nguni's team was delighted to end a journey through a section of bushveld that had never been traversed by ox-wagon before, and most importantly, to find that they had arrived at a destination where the camp had already been created and food prepared. For almost all the men, the reunion was between family and friends, which added to the hubbub of excited chatter when the wagons finally formed into one unit.

Daluxolo, who was particularly close to David as a result of the many weeks they had spent in the bush together, sharing experiences and learning from each other, was appalled at the sight of his friend when he watched him gingerly climb down from one of the wagons. He was thin and gaunt, and his clothes hung loosely from his shoulders and hips. When they gripped hands in a traditional embrace, Daluxolo put a hand on David's shoulder and realised his sickness had taken away most of his bulk; his bones were like those of a young adolescent boy – protruding through his skin.

"I see you, my friend," Daluxolo could not hide his sadness, "but I see only half of you. I am saddened beyond words."

"I am very pleased to see you, my old friend. Even my bones are pleased to see you," David smiled trying to make light of his companion's genuine distress.

"Boss David was struck by the water sickness," Nguni shook his head in dismay. "There are also seven men in the last wagon who cannot walk for long and need to rest often."

"Ghaw!" Daluxolo spat in horror, "it is not a good place you have travelled. You need to sit and rest, Boss David. I have prepared some tea for you. It is waiting for you by the chair that you left here a long time ago."

David laughed. His favourite place at this river crossing had been one where, overlooking the banks of the Limpopo, he had sat on an old wooden crate that he had salvaged, so he was thrilled that it was still there. "Then let us sit and drink tea together. I would like to drink tea with you and Nguni. The sickness tried to kill me, but to drink tea with both of you is the sign that I live."

Without a word, the three men walked over to the banks of the tranquil Limpopo River and sat in the shade of a luxuriant tree. David did not sit on his wooden crate, but chose to sit in the soft river sand with his two good friends, both of whom, on many occasions, had unknowingly saved his life. They sipped tea from old enamel mugs and discussed many things together until it grew dark.

*

It was a pristine morning that greeted all the men who were camped on the sandy banks of the spectacular river. With not a cloud to be seen, even the leaves on the trees seemed greener and appeared to sparkle, the sand seemed whiter, and the green of the remaining pools of water reflected the surroundings upside-down, as if in a perfect mirror. Whether it was because David was among his friends, or in a place he knew intimately, or simply because he had completed the mission given to him by Morris, he felt that his health seemed to have improved overnight. Physically, he was still very weak, but his mental approach had strengthened immensely. He was determined to get all the wagons across the river before nightfall, and then plan his journey to Bulawayo to be reunited with his family again.

When he joined his leaders and drivers around a fire, and sat among them as if an equal, the men could sense there had been a change in his condition; the very slight, and ever-present, smile that was so much a part of his character had returned.

"We cross the Limpopo today, Daluxolo?" David asked after a careful sip of blazing-hot coffee.

"Yes Boss," he grinned.

"Nguni?"

"My men are ready." Nguni straightened up and nodded gravely.

"Then so it shall be," David declared with authority, nodded, and returned to his coffee.

The trek across the river was a monumental affair. Thirty wagons, dozens of men, over 200 oxen, goats, and chickens traversed the 200 yards of white, sandy riverbed. Whips were constantly cracking, men shouting and whistling, pushing and shoving, goading the oxen forward over the soft sand. The beasts put their backs into their heavy loads with little complaint, and when the wagon wheels sank too low in the sand and became hopelessly lodged in the soft silt, more oxen were added to the teams and soon the cumbersome procession was on the move again. Although everyone knew that the wagons were grossly overloaded, nobody dared to say anything about it. Rather, when the wagons became so bogged in the sand that no quantity of beasts could dislodge it, the wagon was unceremoniously unloaded onto the dry riverbed, shifted, and then reloaded.

It took the entire day to move just a mere 200 yards, and by the end of it, every man and beast was exhausted, particularly David, who had been annoyed at himself for being so hopeless during the exercise. All the same, he was very proud of his leaders, his drivers and his herders. The chatter around the fire later that evening reflected the many incidents that occurred during that day. A little grumbling was heard about the stupidity of some of the oxen, and some laughter at the clumsiness of some of the men, but all in all David believed that he and his team had been richly blessed by his Lord. He was very happy.

"Nguni, Daluxolo," David caught their attention, "tomorrow I will leave you and make my way to Bulawayo. Are you ready to make your journey?"

"Boss," Nguni became serious, "we are ready, for sure, but you are not. We have concern for you. We all believe that you are too weak to travel in the bush alone. You shall certainly die."

"Nguni is right, Boss David," Daluxolo continued, "if you must go tomorrow then one of us must come with you."

David shook his head in objection, "No, Boss Morris insists the two of you must stay with the wagons and the men all the time and drive them to Bulawayo. It is most important to get there safely. Thirty wagons need two leaders. One alone cannot manage; Nguni and myself have proven that."

"Then you shall die," Nguni said bluntly. "You have no strength to hold a rifle straight if a hyena comes for your throat, and as a man alone, he will surely come for you."

David knew Nguni was correct. At night he was so tired he would not even hear a charging buffalo ten yards from him.

"You are right," David sadly admitted. He knew he had to get back to Bulawayo as quickly as possible. For one thing, Morris would be beside himself if he didn't show in the next few weeks, but in his weakened state he simply couldn't make the journey on his own. Suddenly he had an idea. "Daluxolo, how often does the BSAC postal run pass here nowadays?"

"Every three or four days they have passed me, Boss."

"When was the last time they passed?"

"I expect them to pass again tomorrow."

"How many riders?"

"Two, sometimes three. They can protect you, but you cannot keep up with them. They ride fast." He understood what David was thinking.

"Yes," David smiled, "they will give me protection." He knew this would be the answer to his dilemma, but he would struggle to keep up. Then he had another thought, "Do you remember that very tall man with the BSAC?"

"Yes, I know him." Daluxolo's teeth flashed through a smile in the firelight as he recalled Captain Grant Dent crossed the river some weeks ago. "It was more than two weeks; he went that way," he pointed in the direction of Mafeking.

"Then he should return very soon, I think," David mulled in his thoughts. "I will cross the Limpopo again in the morning and wait for him. He is a good friend to me. When he sees I am sick, he will protect me and go slowly for me."

"It is good," Nguni rumbled his approval at David's plan after giving it some thought.

"Tomorrow I need you to in-span all the oxen and begin moving north. This will make me happy."

"It will be done," Nguni nodded solemnly, "but we are not happy that you stay on the other side on your own. I will tell two of my men to stay with you until the horses arrive."

It was a sound idea, and David could not argue that. He agreed, and plans were made for him to wait on the southern bank of the river while Nguni and Daluxolo began the six-week trek to Bulawayo with all the wagons. It was also agreed that the two men who remained behind to care for David would be from Daluxolo's team from Mafeking. When Grant Dent arrived, or whomever the BSAC sent, then Daluxolo's men would leave David and catch up with the procession of wagons. At the wagons' rate of travel, this would not take more than a day or two. With all leaders satisfied with the planning contingencies, they turned in for the night.

Daylight saw the plans fall seamlessly into place. The oxen were hitched up to their respective yokes and the procession began in earnest. David bid each of the men farewell in person and finally shook hands with Nguni and Daluxolo.

"I wish you a safe journey, my friends. May the road be straight and smooth for you."

Nguni clasped David's forearm firmly. "May you return to Bulawayo in good health." He was sad to part from this small, but brave man.

"On my last journey," Daluxolo added as he shook hands with David, "I found a way that was easier, but longer. I will take that way again. No European knows that way. They will not see us until we are but one day from Bulawayo. When we reach that place we will stop and send a man to show you where we are."

"That is good, Daluxolo," David smiled, "I am happy with that. Go well, my friend. Do not rush, because what is on those wagons is very important to Boss Morris."

"Do not worry, Boss. Nguni and me, we will protect the wagons very well."

With that, David crossed the Limpopo for the second time in two days with two of Daluxolo's trusted men.

*

"David!" Captain Dent exclaimed as he dismounted, "I hardly recognised you. What on earth happened?"

"I took ill along the way, but I'm much better now, thanks,"

David smiled heartily. He had heard the horses coming and stood in the sunlight awaiting their arrival without a shirt on, enjoying the healing embrace that the sun seemed to impart. "How are you my friend? I was hoping it would be you that came with the postal run."

Shocked at seeing the emaciated form of his young friend and hearing a voice that held little volume, Grant shook hands with David and introduced him to the two colleagues riding with him. They sat around a fire that David's carers had made and shared a pot of coffee, discussing many subjects but often returning to David's health. The soldiers rummaged through their meagre possessions looking for medical supplies they had brought along, and plied David with various concoctions that they thought might help.

"I need to get to Bulawayo, Grant. I'm too weak to go on my own, so was hoping I could ride with you. I calculated, from my men, that it would be you coming through this crossing around this time."

"Of course you can ride with us, David, of course, but – looking at you – I fear you won't find it easy."

"Well, I was hoping you might not push the ride too hard. I know it's a big thing to ask, but if you went easy I would keep up."

Grant looked at his two companions who immediately nodded their acceptance of this request. "Alright," Grant sighed, "We'll give it a go. I also think you need to see Dr Jameson as soon as you get back. I must say you are very lucky to find us here; the company is going to use that Zeederberg coach service to run the mail from now on and we are probably the last of the riders."

"It was meant to be, then." David smiled his appreciation at the group. "Thank you, gentlemen; I am most grateful. Although I am improving every day, I do need to see a doctor. My joints ache like hell and I have very little strength."

"I wonder what it was that made you so ill?" one of the soldiers commented, concern written all over his face.

"Poisonous water, my men tell me. I never drank any of it - fell in it, but never drank it, and it sure made me sick. If it wasn't for their traditional medicine I can guarantee I would have died out there."

"That traditional medicine of theirs is pretty potent stuff, make no mistake," Grant shook his head in awe. "Maybe you got bitten by a venomous spider while you slept."

"I got bitten by a mosquito, and a few other insects that I couldn't identify; I remember that." David subconsciously scratched at his forearm and neck, "but I don't have much memory of the whole ordeal. They tell me I was delirious for four days."

"A mosquito would never make you that sick, but a spider could give you a nasty headache," the other soldier mumbled. "I think we should all be very careful of touching stagnant water from a swamp, if you ask my opinion."

It was Grant who changed the subject. "The day is still young, David; are you ready to start moving?"

"Absolutely, I can't wait to get back. Allow me to break camp and send my men off, then let's go. Thanks again, gentlemen." David showed his gratitude once again, as he stood up and shook their hands once more. He was in good spirits as the first part of Morris' plan was now complete: they had united the two caravans without loss, he and some of his men had survived the mysterious sickness and he would soon be under the care of a qualified doctor. Above all, the wagons were now on their way to Bulawayo under the protection of two very competent men along a route they had travelled before. It would be plain sailing for the wagons from now on; the worst was over.

For the third time in as many days, David crossed the Limpopo once more, and – as he emerged from the dry riverbed onto high ground – he turned in his saddle to look back at the magnificent river and his makeshift camp on the far bank. It crossed his mind that this day may have been the last time he ever visited the faithful camp. He had never seen the river in flood, and probably never would, but he felt it would be a most spectacular sight when it was flowing.

A few years later, a poet stood at the site of the camp and marvelled at the river in flood. Indeed it was magnificent: flowing strong and steady, the torrents of water gently pushing up to the calm surface, belying its formidable strength below; the eddies forming quickly, then slipping silently into oblivion. Standing with his hands on his hips and one foot on an old crate that lay abandoned on the ground, the poet deeply contemplated the magnificence of something he later described in a story for children: "the great grey-green, greasy Limpopo River,…"

CHAPTER ELEVEN
Catastrophe

C ARRYING A SMALL parcel, Morris walked into the tented hospital area and greeted the nurse. She was tending to a soldier who was lying prostrate on a very thin mattress with bandages wrapped around his head, both arms, and one leg. A brownish stain on the tourniquet near his knee suggested that this injury was particularly nasty.

"Good morning, Sister," he almost sang out, "how's my brother today?"

The nurse smiled back at him. "Slightly improved, Mr Morris," she said quietly. "The doctor is happy with his progress."

"Splendid! May I see him?" Morris asked. It was merely a courteous request, since he was already striding past the nurse on his way to David's bed with no intention of stopping.

"Of course, Mr Morris, of course," she chanted, already distracted by the needs of the wounded soldier before her.

By this time, David had spent a week in the BSAC infirmary. The doctor in charge had been unable to pronounce on the nature of his patient's ailment, although he had several far-fetched theories, but rather chose to experiment on David with all sorts of medication. Something in the panoply of drugs seemed to help, because David was making slow, but steady progress towards full health.

"Good morning, brother," Morris greeted casually. "Feeling better today?"

"Yes, a little… thankfully," David grinned, pleased to see Morris again.

Morris sat on the end of David's bed and handed him the parcel of shortbread that had been made earlier that morning. Still warm, it did not escape David's attention that Morris had already helped himself to a few pieces of the buttery treat.

"I have made arrangements for you to go by coach tomorrow to Fort Victoria to be seen by a new doctor, Dr Hamish Hamilton, who has recently arrived there. I hear he is excellent and has been studying tropical diseases in Harley Street in London."

"We can't afford that, Morris," David objected, "and I am getting better."

"You can't put a price on health, David," Morris scolded. "In any case, I don't believe the doctor who is treating you really knows what he is doing, and I am very much concerned about your health. If Dr Jameson could look at you, I am sure he would have had you on your feet by now. Furthermore, the wagons will be arriving in a few weeks and we will need all hands on deck."

Knowing that the business depended on his being in good health, David was willing to concede a trip to Fort Victoria, if it would speed up his recovery. "Alright, brother, I'll go if I must. How long does it take to get there?"

"Good, that's settled then. I understand that it's a two-day trip by coach and an easy ride at that. Dr Hamilton wants you under his care for a full week, so I have made arrangements for your lodgings accordingly."

Morris quickly turned the subject to business and affairs of the new town. Activity in Bulawayo was at fever pitch, with new shops opening up every day, including a few attractive eating and drinking establishments. The population now stood at around 4,000 people, with many more expected to arrive in the coming weeks, and the Company was performing miracles in town planning and management: new roads, piped water, storm drainage, even a new suburb was being laid out for residential housing, which, for a lack of imagination, Major Seward had proposed to name "Suburbs".

"You think we might be able to build a house in Suburbs?" David asked.

"No, we certainly can't afford it, not for a long while yet. The warehouse is comfortable enough for now, though."

"Harry did well, it seems. You have spoken very highly of him."

"Oh yes, I am very impressed with him. Our young brother has drive and ambition, and, above all, he is very loyal to the family business. He'll do anything for us."

"That is good to know, because – I must be honest – I thought the two of you would clash."

"Make no error: we will, David… make no error. But deep down, he means well, and I like that." Morris winked through a smile.

"Morris," David lowered his voice, "sit closer." He patted the bed to coax him to within whispering distance.

Morris suddenly looked concerned as he shifted closer, he could see his brother was worried. "What is it?" he asked.

David lowered his voice even further, "I've been listening to some of the soldiers and staff who have been passing through the ward. They don't talk openly, but I have overheard some things. What have you heard about the Boers and the British, south of the border?"

"Not much, although it is obvious they don't like each other, why do you ask?"

"There seems to be some almighty antagonism going on between them at government level. I even heard that the British want to annex the Transvaal – kick the Boers out, they say. Then, last night," David looked over at the wounded soldier and nodded in his direction, "you see that fellow over there?"

"Yes, he was here before you got here. What happened to him?"

"He was attacked by a buffalo: it ran over him and broke a lot of bones. The horns missed him, but he's in a bad way. Last night he was totally delirious; I think an infection is setting in. Anyway, he was moaning and performing and blaming Dr Jameson for letting this happen to him."

"Why Dr Jameson, for heaven's sake?"

"Well, that's what I find so curious," David shuffled in his bed. "He was saying that Jameson sent him to cut the telegraph wires, and while he was kneeling on the ground, snipping through the two wires, the sound attracted a buffalo that attacked him."

"Well, one thing for certain is that he is delirious," Morris stated condescendingly. "The telegraph lines have only just arrived in Bulawayo, and at great expense and effort. Why would Jameson order them to be cut? And, in any case, if he were cutting through telegraph wires, he would be high off the ground on a ladder and well clear of any buffalo. The wires are at the top of tall wooden posts. Furthermore, the wires are working – I received a telegram from Louis this morning."

"Yes, I know. It's all a little confusing. Where is the good doctor, anyhow?" David asked as he took a bite of the inviting shortbread.

"Nobody knows. He arrived in Bulawayo last week with a contingent of reservists or regular soldiers from Fort Salisbury, gathered up a whole bunch more from here, and took off again. Not even Major Seward knows where he went."

David cocked an eyebrow. "So how many BSAC soldiers are left in town?"

"Hardly any. I would say you would be lucky to see thirty men in the camp. There's hardly a uniform to be seen in the streets. For a population of four thousand, it seems weird that there are only thirty-odd administration and law-enforcement staff."

"I wonder what Jameson is up to?" David scratched his head,

before glancing over at the unconscious soldier. "If he is up to something and ordered that man to cut the telegraph lines so that whatever he is doing would be a secret, or a surprise, and that man cut a fence line, thinking it was the telegraph wires, that could really upset Jameson's plans."

The two brothers sat silently for a moment thinking this scenario through, then Morris began to chuckle.

"What's so funny?" David grinned.

"So who's more stupid: that soldier who can't tell the difference between a fence wire and a telegraph wire, or the doctor who sent an incompetent man to do such a critical job?"

*

During the last few days of the year 1895, the Langbourne brothers suddenly found themselves embroiled in a series of most peculiar events. It all began during a normal working day when Harry, who had been sent down to the bank to run an errand for his older brother, came bolting into the storeroom with a look of panic, mingled with excitement, etched across his face. Harry had taken to wearing braces instead of a belt, which was fast becoming his trademark within the community. His black leather shoes were a couple of sizes too big, being the only size available in Bulawayo at the time, so watching Harry run was almost comical.

"Morris!" Harry shouted. Morris was serving a customer and became totally distracted by his brother's ungainly and raucous interruption. Ordinarily, Morris would have scolded him for his unseemly behaviour, but the look in Harry's eyes told him that something was wrong.

"What?" Morris exclaimed.

"Your friend, Dr Jameson – he's been captured by the Boers!"

"Captured?" Morris couldn't believe what he was hearing.

"It's all over town. He took an army of men to Johannesburg and tried to overthrow the Transvaal Republic! Somehow they were expecting him and ambushed the soldiers long before they got there."

"What are you saying, Harry?" Morris was as uncomprehending as the customer.

"They say about thirty men were killed; horses, too! Those that survived the ambush surrendered, were captured, and taken into custody."

"Excuse me, Mr Langbourne," the customer turned to Morris, "I think I need to get down to the BSAC offices and find out what's going on. This sounds totally inexplicable."

"I'll come with you. Harry, lock up the shop. Let's go and find out what's going on."

The townsfolk were huddled in groups along the streets, discussing whatever piece of news they had heard. Morris found it almost unbelievable that such a gentlemanly person as Dr Jameson could even consider the idea of leading an army to overthrow another country's government. Breaking away from his customer after the latter had joined one of the many groups, he and Harry made their way to the BSAC camp to find Major Seward. When they reached his office, the orderly announced their arrival and showed them in.

"Major Seward, thanks so much for seeing us at such short notice. You know my brother, Harry?" Morris quickly introduced his younger sibling.

"Come in, Morris, come in. I know of Harry: how do you do?" The flustered major shook Harry's hand quickly. "We've never actually met, though."

Morris got straight to business, as was his wont. "Major," he said, "what's this I hear about Dr Jameson?"

"All true, I'm afraid, all true," the major replied, flushed and concerned.

"Well, I never thought he had it in him. Now what?"

"Indeed, now what?" Major Seward shrugged his shoulders. "A rather complicated issue, I'm afraid."

Morris pulled up a chair and sat down without being invited to do so. "I just can't believe he would do this," he said. "Why, for heaven's sake?"

Major Seward also pulled up a chair and sat upon it heavily. "It is not for us to question why," he replied.

"Hah!" Morris exclaimed, adding a line from Tennyson as an afterthought: "'Theirs but to do and die...' hey?"

Seward raised an eyebrow, somewhat amused that someone as young as Morris knew the line at all. "My duty is to ensure this town functions properly until I get orders from Mr Rhodes. My *problem* is that the good doctor took most of my men, about six hundred of them, and now they are all locked up in Johannesburg, or Pretoria, or who knows where?"

Try as Morris might to find out why Jameson had taken it upon himself to test the mettle of the Boers of the Transvaal, the major sidestepped the subject very diplomatically, and eventually managed to change the subject to David and his recuperation.

Morris told the major that he had sent him up to Fort Victoria for a week to receive what he believed would be better treatment from the new doctor, but that he would have no more news until he returned in three or four days' time. They continued to discuss trivial matters, although Morris repeatedly tried unsuccessfully to turn the subject back to Dr Jameson and his failed attempt at a *coup d'etat*. In the end, Morris decided he would get no further and politely took his leave along with his brother. As the two walked back to Langbourne Brothers, they occasionally stopped by a gathering of citizens to see if there was any more news, but all they heard were varying theories about the motive behind the good doctor's foolhardy excursion.

As they turned into Abercorn Street, Harry saw an African man dressed in typical Xhosa robes jogging steadily towards them. He was still some distance off, but he was definitely a Xhosa man.

"Morris, isn't that Daluxolo over there?"

Morris strained his eyes and picked out the man. "No, it can't be, the wagons aren't due here for at least another three weeks."

They continued to walk together, not speaking, but nervously watching the figure of the Xhosa man drawing closer to them, and the closer he got, the more like Daluxolo he seemed to be.

"Oh no," Morris almost sighed, "it *is* Daluxolo."

"Do you think something is wrong?"

"I hope not," he muttered to himself, and felt his stomach turn so badly he almost heaved involuntarily as the real possibility of a serious problem hit him square in his gut. Without thinking, he broke into a run to meet his faithful employee with Harry following clumsily behind.

"Daluxolo! What's the matter? What is the problem?" Morris exclaimed as he reached the exhausted man.

"Boss Morris, I see you," he gasped and gently, with respect and almost with relief, knelt down on one knee to catch his breath.

"What happened, are you alright? Tell me, what's the matter?" Morris was getting desperate for news.

"The oxen, Boss," he took more gasps of oxygen, "the oxen, they have all been killed by the spirits of Lobengula."

"What?" Morris exclaimed, not knowing what Daluxolo was implying, and looked at Harry in case he had misunderstood what he had heard.

"The oxen, Boss, they are all dead; every single one of them. All at once," he spoke to the ground, not wanting to look Morris in the face.

"Daluxolo," Morris bent down and lifted his friend, "come, let us sit in the shade. Come with me. Harry, please run into the shop and get some water for Daluxolo. Come, Daluxolo, come with me." He led the hapless man to a step in the doorway of a clothing shop that was shaded by the sun and carefully sat him down.

Morris sat beside his wagon leader and allowed him to catch his breath as Harry, still shaken by the events of the morning, ran over to Langbourne Brothers to fetch a mug of cooled water. When he received the water, Daluxolo swallowed the contents of the mug down so fast he almost choked, thin rivulets of the liquid escaping the corners of his lips.

"Alright, Daluxolo, now tell me, what happened?" Morris requested, desperately trying to control his temper.

"Lobengula's spirits are angry with us. Last time we came he sent locusts to eat all the food so that the oxen nearly died from starvation. Now he has sent more spirits and this time they killed all the oxen. Every single one is dead."

"I don't understand. How does he kill them? Does he send Matabele spears from the sky?" Morris knew he was being facetious, but was thinking that perhaps the Matabele had attacked the convoy with the intention of looting it.

"No, Boss, he sent a sickness that made the oxen die before the sun was down. When the sun was up, the beasts were weak. We did not in-span, and we were keeping the laager; we could not move. When the sun was high, all of them were sick and lying on the ground and dying. Before the sun was down that same day, they were all dead."

"Oh my word!" Morris sighed into his hands, before looking Daluxolo straight in the eye. "Maybe they drank bad water from the same waterhole?" Morris suggested.

"But we, all of us, we were also drinking the same water, and we, all of us, we are all good, even to this day," Daluxolo replied earnestly.

"It's not spirits, Daluxolo," Morris tried to calm the frightened man, then stood up and paced about the pavement, trying desperately to calm himself and find a solution to this dilemma. He ran his fingers through his hair. "There is a very simple reason why this happened. It is not spirits, Daluxolo, I promise you."

"It is, Boss. The men are frightened. They have run away."

Morris stood motionless in stunned silence, staring at Daluxolo who was now starting to tremble. He stole a glance at Harry, who looked almost as frightened as Daluxolo. "What did you say? The men have run away?" he demanded, although it was really a question.

"Yes, Boss," he cowered.

"Where did they go?"

"They have gone, all of them. We are frightened of the spirits."

Morris stared at him, in disbelief more than anything else. Their family business was teetering on the brink of annihilation because over 200 of their oxen simply died, all at once, for some mysterious reason. Firstly, he thought it was such a tall story it was laughable, but Daluxolo looked genuinely petrified. Strange things happened in Africa, but this was totally inexplicable. Morris knew that Daluxolo would never do anything dishonest; he was very loyal to the family, especially to David. How he wished David were with him right now. *He would know what to do,*" Morris thought.

A thought suddenly came to Morris. "Where is Nguni?" They had not discussed him.

"He is frightened of the spirits too, Boss, but he did not run. He remains, but near-near, not with the wagons. The spirits are still with the wagons."

"So there is no-one looking after the wagons?" Morris could no longer contain his anger and raised his voice sharply. Both Harry and Daluxolo were caught off guard by his outburst. "This is madness! An entire herd of oxen cannot die all at once. What kind of cock-and-bull story is that?! You can't leave my wagons unattended in the bush! This is my business, my life! I owe the world for those wagons and now you say they are abandoned in the bush?!" He threw his arms in the air, searching for something to say. "It is your job to protect the wagons!" he burst out.

"Calm down, brother," Harry timidly interjected, "calm down. There must be an explanation for this, an answer."

"Don't tell me to calm down!" Morris shouted at Harry in English, pointing a finger at him menacingly. "Our entire future is dependent on these wagons. My reputation hinges on this. The entire family's future is dependent on it, and now I'm being told all the oxen just up and died and our entire workforce have run off into the bush, thinking evil spirits are after them! Don't tell me to calm down!"

While Harry was shocked at the tirade, some people on the street began to stop and stare at the trio. Glancing at the onlookers with some embarrassment, Harry was at a loss for words. "Morris," he murmured, "people are watching."

When Morris took a quick look around, Harry was encouraged to continue. "David would know what to do – he understands Daluxolo well and might make some sense of all of this. Could you not send a telegram to Fort Victoria and ask him to return? It will only take him two days."

Morris glared at Harry, his eyes burning into his brain. He looked at Daluxolo, who was still cowering on the step, then back at Harry. His fists were tightly clenched. Suddenly, without another word, Morris turned on his heels and strode off to the Post Office, fuming with rage and with determination in his stride.

Herbert Bachmayer, who was quietly filling out a form behind the teller's counter, looked up suddenly when he heard the wooden door to the Post Office burst open with such force he thought the brass bell attached to the door would be knocked off its mounting. He was shocked to see Morris storm inside looking as angry as Hades, his face almost scarlet.

"Good morning, Mr Morris. Are you alright?" he asked timidly.

"No!" Morris responded bluntly, "I need to send an urgent telegram."

"We are a little backlogged right now, what with the news of Dr Jameson. I could possibly get it off by..."

"This is more urgent than Dr Jameson and his folly, Mr Bachmayer. I need to get this off immediately."

Herbert could tell by the resolve in his tone that Morris was serious, and he certainly didn't look very happy. "Very well, Mr Morris, I'll do it for you immediately."

"Thank you, sir. It will be brief," Morris was blunt, and tore a form out of its holder, scattering others on the floor, which he ignored in his haste. Scribbling hastily on the unfortunate form in his hands, he wrote:

*

DAVID LANGBOURNE
FORT VICTORIA HOSPITAL
URGENT PROBLEM WITH GRINDERS STOP
RETURN LANGBRO IMMEDIATELY STOP
LION

*

He handed the form to Herbert, who scanned through it quickly and told Morris how much it would cost. Morris dug into his pockets and duly paid. Feeling a little more relieved now that he was doing something about the situation, Morris thanked Herbert for his kindness and apologised for his curt entrance. Herbert accepted his apology without reservation, and went to the telegram room, watching Morris thunder out the door just as he had entered it.

As Morris walked back to Langbourne Brothers he was so consumed by his thoughts that he didn't notice citizens staring at him, and even those who greeted him were unintentionally ignored. Stepping into the warehouse, he was confronted by Harry, who looked very worried, and almost fearful of Morris.

"Where is Daluxolo?" Morris demanded.

"He's gone."

"Where?" Morris almost shouted.

"Back to guard the wagons. He hurriedly took off the moment you went to the Post Office. I don't know who he is more scared of: you or the evil spirits."

Their conversation was interrupted once again by the arrival of Phil Innes. "Good morning, Morris... Harry," he nodded, "I'm sorry but I couldn't help notice a little commotion on the street. Is there anything I can do for you?"

"Morning Phil," Morris sighed through his greeting, "indeed, a spot of bother, sadly. More like a catastrophe, really."

"Oh dear, I am so sorry to hear that. May I ask what the problem is?"

"Come into my office, Phil, take a seat. I really don't know where to begin or what to make of all this. I am in a conundrum." Morris walked off to his office with Phil and they sat down at the desk, while Harry stood at the door, keeping an eye out for potential customers. Morris told Phil the story of the events that had unfolded on Abercorn Street just half an hour previously.

"I really don't know what is going on, Phil. I can't possibly believe this yarn Daluxolo has spun me, yet I must believe there is a massive problem out there with our wagons and stock."

"It's a perfectly logical story he has told you, Morris," Phil said calmly.

"I beg your pardon?" Morris straightened up in surprise.

"Sadly it looks like your team of oxen has been hit by the *rinderpest*."

"*Rinderpest?* What in heaven's name is that?"

"It's a disease that affects all species of bovine animals, such as cattle, bulls, oxen, even buffalo. It's a terrible disease that spreads among them like wildfire. Once affected, the animal can die within a single day."

Harry expressed his shock from the doorway. "I've never heard of that," he said.

"It's a very bad and contagious sickness. The poor animal starts producing mucus from every orifice" – its nose, its mouth, its eyes – and then its lungs fill up with mucus and they literally drown in their own fluids."

There was a deathly hush from the room before Harry broke the silence. "That sounds disgusting!" he said.

"Once it breaks out," Phil continued, "it's almost impossible to stop. It will wipe out just about all the cattle in an entire country very quickly. I think it can be contained, but cattle herds need to be isolated and quarantined until the plague has passed. But, as I said, it is highly infectious. I really think you need to report this to the Administration as quickly as possible."

"So how would our team have become infected?" Morris pressed.

"Who knows? Maybe an infected buffalo crossed the path of your wagons and one of your oxen touched an infected piece of grass, or ate an infected piece of grass. Once one is infected, within the hour they will all be affected. It really is a very nasty disease. Fortunately, humans are not affected by it; at least, not that I am aware of."

"Phil," Morris slumped in his chair, "I have committed our business entirely to this load of wagons. I have borrowed so much money from so many people I cannot afford for anything to go wrong."

"How many wagons, if I may ask?" Phil asked politely.

Morris looked at Harry in desperation, then rocked back in his seat and took a deep breath. "Thirty."

"Thirty!" Phil exclaimed. "How are you going to manage to fit thirty wagon-loads of stock into your warehouse?"

"You see my dilemma, Phil?" Morris looked truly despondent, "now you understand what financial risk I have on my hands."

Phil tried to console him. "At least your wagons are intact and not going anywhere. Unfortunately, however, you will have to wait for the plague to pass, because, if it is the *rinderpest,* you won't find any oxen to hitch up to your wagons, and if you do, the Administration will not allow movement of oxen, you can be sure of that."

"But the wagons are vulnerable to looting and theft. How do we know if it is this *rinderpest* plague?" Morris was grasping at straws.

"There is one sure way to find out,"

"How?"

"Report this to the Administration urgently – you need to do this regardless – then simply ask them if there have been any other cases reported in Rhodesia. If there is just one reported case out there, you can be very sure your team has been hit by the *rinderpest.*"

"I will do that right now, but Phil, I need to ask you a very big favour," Morris looked at his friend desperately, "please do not discuss this with anyone. If word gets out that we have thirty wagons of stock stuck in the bush with just two Xhosa men guarding them, we will have every treasure hunter in the land looking for these wagons."

"Don't worry, Morris," Phil reassured his young friend, "what we discuss is always confidential." To indicate his word was good, he stood up to leave and gave Morris a very firm handshake.

Morris left Harry in charge of the business and made his way back to the BSAC camp, to Major Seward's office. Although busy, Major Seward was happy to see him for the second time in as many hours.

"Good lord, Morris, you look dreadful. What happened?"

"Dave," he addressed him by his first name as they were alone, "we have a couple of wagons coming up to Bulawayo, and my driver has just run into town to tell me that all the oxen perished in one day. Have you ever heard of a disease called the *rinderpest?*"

Dave raised his eyebrows in shock, "Not you as well? Where?"

Morris heart sank. Phil was right: the *rinderpest* was in the country. "North of the Limpopo, between here and Mafeking."

"Oh Lordy, you are the third case, and the first south of here. This is serious news, Morris, serious news," he repeated. "Come with me, we have an agricultural and veterinary department and you need to report this as soon as possible. Oh Lordy, first Dr Jameson and now the *rinderpest*. This is terrible!" he muttered as he stood and reached for his hat.

*

As David alighted from the Zeederberg, he waited for the driver, who now stood on the roof of the coach, to find his duffle bag and throw it down to him. He did not have many possessions in it so he caught it with ease and turned to walk to the family's shop. He was feeling a lot better than that time when he had last left Bulawayo, but knew that he still needed some recuperation. It had been two days since he received the disturbing telegram from Morris, and – although he was very keen to get to the warehouse as soon as possible – he also realised that the extra two or three minutes it would take to walk over there slowly would not affect whatever Morris was going to tell him.

Both Morris and Harry fussed over their brother when he entered the warehouse, and David was happy to tell them that, although the new doctor was still at a loss as to what exactly made him so ill, a combination of quinine and other drugs had helped immensely. All he was in need of now was good food, plenty of water, and some outdoor exercise to get him back to a good, healthy condition.

The pleasantries having been completed, Morris rapidly filled David in on the events that had taken place almost three days previously. David was stunned by the news, horrified to find that – in one single day – they stood once more on the brink of irreversible bankruptcy. What troubled him the most was that they could not tell a soul the degree of trouble they were in for fear others would seek to strip their wagons by force.

"I've told Phil Innes, he knows, but he won't tell anyone," Morris confided.

"This is terrible news, Morris. Soon the bank, Weil, and Gerran will start wanting a payment. Then what?"

"We can make payments for another two to three months from sales we have made so far, but – if we don't get the wagons up by then – we will run into trouble."

"So," David scratched his head, "if they have quarantined the movement of oxen, which could probably go on for a couple of years, how do you think we will get our wagons up here in two to three months? A team of a hundred men can't push one of those wagons up here."

"Mules," Morris said, "they are not affected by either the plague or the quarantine."

"You'll need a lot more than six mules per wagon to move that weight," David objected, "the strength of one ox is equivalent to three mules, and you'll need new harnesses. It could be an expensive exercise."

"We did some calculations," Harry interjected. "If we buy enough mules to move just two wagons, then we can bring them up here two at a time and keep the warehouse stocked. We don't need all of them at once."

David nodded slowly as he worked his mind around this suggestion. "Alright," he paused, "that would work, I suppose. So, how far are the wagons from Bulawayo?"

Morris and Harry looked at each other, and David noticed a blank stare on each of their faces.

"Oh," Morris looked at David, the blank expression still present on his face, "I don't know."

David cocked his head at Morris, before looking over at Harry. Both of them looked back at him, blankly.

"Hold up, hold up!" David put up his right hand before standing up, leaning against a wall for support, and addressing his brothers again. "Did either of you think to ask Daluxolo how many days he took to get to you after the animals died?"

A deathly hush enveloped the room. Morris and Harry simply stared at each other, then back at David. David's eyes shifted rapidly between the two brothers, and realised that neither of them were about to say anything. He looked up at the roof and took a deep breath. He realised their problem was dire. With two steps he took his seat again on the chair and lent forward in desperation.

"Brothers, please tell me you asked Daluxolo where the wagons are. The name of a river, or a mountain, a fort, a village, anything…."

"Harry sent him back to guard the wagons while I was sending you a telegram. I didn't ask him." Morris admitted.

"Don't blame me!" Harry exclaimed, "You're the one who told him to get back to the wagons to protect the goods, and he left immediately."

"I told him it was his job, his responsibility. I didn't tell him to go, you did! Don't you put the blame on me!"

The next moment all hell broke loose, with Morris and Harry exploding and verbally raising the roof of the warehouse as their anger and frustration and their extreme stress finally reached boiling point. They were soon on their feet hurling abuse at each other, with David pushing himself between the two shouting as loudly as he could to make them stop and settle down. When David finally got the upper hand, he placed the palm of his hand on Morris' chest and firmly pushed him back into his seat, and immediately did the same to Harry.

Without sitting, David pointed to Harry and Morris in turn, "Blaming and shouting at each other is not going to solve the problem. We are family, we have a problem, and we have to fix it," he paused, "together."

There was a long, embarrassed silence. Satisfied that his brothers had vented their frustrations, David very slowly took his seat, keeping his eyes fixed firmly on his siblings. Both Morris and Harry looked chagrined at what had happened and sat forlornly, not making eye contact with anyone.

"Let me explain how serious our problem is," David began, "I can tell you right now our wagons are lost…."

"But….." Morris began to object.

"Uh-uh!" David cut him off sharply, raising his hand, holding his palm at his brother's face to cement the fact that he was in charge of this conversation. When Morris shrugged his acceptance, David lowered his palm and continued. "Now listen to me…" he paused again, and, when he was sure he had their attention, he resumed.

"Obviously, you were both overwhelmed by the situation, especially by what Daluxolo said. To be honest, I would have been equally confused and dumbfounded. No person in their right mind would ever have expected an entire herd of oxen to die within hours of falling ill, especially as we had never heard of this *rinderpest* sickness. I understand how you both feared the financial impact this would cause on our business and our lives. I also understand that you didn't fully realise what Daluxolo was saying, or why he and the men reacted like they did. So I understand that you both got caught up in the situation and forgot to ask Daluxolo certain questions. I understand, but really can't believe you did that.

"Now, you have both walked and ridden the route north from the Limpopo River with me. You both know how dense the bush can get in certain places, and how treacherous the track can get. Need I remind you," he looked Morris squarely in the eye, "that with all the forks and dead ends, the track can be as wide as seven miles across in places?"

Morris nodded, he clearly recalled what Captain Marcus Bailey had told them on the banks of the Limpopo River the first time they had crossed it.

"When I left Nguni and Daluxolo at the Limpopo, and waited for Grant Dent to rescue me, Daluxolo told me he had found a new route, one that was a little longer, but easier to navigate. He said very few people appeared to travel that route, so our wagons would more than likely not be seen by any European until he was about a day or two outside Bulawayo." David paused and looked at his two despondent brothers sitting slumped in their seats. "You can take that two ways: firstly, that the wagons will be hard to locate by potential thieves or looters, which is good news; and secondly that they will be almost impossible to find by *anyone*, including us, which is the bad news."

"I'm assuming you don't know this route either," Harry asked quietly.

"Of course not, Harry. So that is why I am saying, and I say this again very clearly, our wagons are well and truly *lost*, somewhere in the Rhodesian bush."

The three brothers sat in silence for what seemed an eternity. The reality of the situation finally confronted them head on. Never before had Morris felt so dejected, or felt such a failure. Harry was angry with himself for not thinking this through and asking Daluxolo more questions.

"Is there a way we can locate our wagons, David?" Morris asked, his voice quavering slightly.

"Not unless we get on a horse and go look for them, but it could take years, if we are lucky. If I knew how long Daluxolo had taken to get here, I would have a starting point, which alone might be seven miles wide. If he did happen to mention how long it took him to get here, it would have helped if we knew if he walked or ran all the way, or partly walked, partly ran. Do you see what I mean?"

"The search area could be hundreds of miles wide," Morris slumped even further in his seat.

"No Morris, *thousands* of miles wide. Remember, the wagons are probably laagered."

"Yes," Harry interrupted, "he did say the sickness began in the morning, so they were still in laager."

"Great, well, that's something at least, but as I was saying, if they are in laager, which they are, then they are in one small place, not stretched over a mile or so, so hunting them down will prove even more difficult. We would have to search behind every forest, every rocky outcrop – no matter how small – in every valley and below every gulley. There will be neither sound nor spoor to follow as all the beasts are dead. We cannot ask people, African or European, if they have seen anything, because as soon as word gets out, every failed prospector from as far as Kimberley will be on the hunt. Our wagons are fair game, but at least they are practically invisible."

A heavy silence descended on the three brothers, and remained that way for several long minutes. Finally, a customer entered the warehouse and the meeting reluctantly broke up, as Harry walked over to assist him. Later that evening, the brothers sat silently eating the meal Thembela had provided from their old wood stove. The only sound was that of an occasional metal spoon scraping the enamel bowls from which they ate. After washing their plates and brushing their teeth, the boys rolled out their blankets and settled in for the night. Just as David was about to drift off to sleep, he thought of something.

"I have an idea," he spoke softly into the darkness. He heard Morris and Harry sit up in their blankets.

"What?" was the eager response.

David gently rolled over onto his back, before speaking. "There are two signs we could follow. Two hundred dead oxen in one place would cause a dreadful stink of decaying flesh. Also, it would attract hundreds of vultures as well as hundreds of scavengers, like hyena. If I were to look for a lot of vultures circling in the sky, it might lead me in the right direction. These are very long odds, because all these signs could well be gone by now, depending on how long ago the oxen died."

"It's all we've got," Morris mumbled. "Are you fit enough to go back out there?"

David heaved himself into a sitting position, "I have no choice. The longer I leave it, the less chance there is of finding anything, but I will take Harry with me. I need someone to watch my back," David knew he was not well enough to go out alone, but he would be all right if he had some backup.

"One other thing," he said, "if we never find these wagons, we will be out of business forever. I suggest you send a telegram to Louis and tell him to ship whatever he has bought up to Mafeking immediately, then close the East London office down, settle the debts, and come to Bulawayo post haste."

"That is a sound idea," Morris agreed, but it was obvious he was very disappointed by having to close down a business idea he had conceived.

"You have a very good business brain, Morris," David said wearily as he lay his head down on his pillow. "You look after the business and keep it alive while Harry and I find those wagons. We are not losing Langbourne Brothers. Not in my lifetime."

Morris frowned in the dark. He was touched by what David had said. "I'll do that, David, don't worry," his voice was very gentle.

"Night, Morris. Night Harry," David muttered, and within a few seconds he was fast asleep.

CHAPTER TWELVE
M'Limo

I T HAD BEEN just over five weeks since David and Harry
left on horseback in search of the missing wagons. They dismounted outside the rear entrance of Langbourne Brothers,
harnessed the horses to a pole, and walked into the warehouse.

David had fully recovered his health and he had also regained
his strength, although he never would get back the striking physique he had developed when he was building their premises.
Harry lost all his boyish fat on the five-week excursion in the bush,
and actually started looking more adolescent, his facial features
sharpening slightly and his voice deepening. Both brothers had a
shock of unruly hair and were in desperate need of a haircut, and –
as always when he returned from a lengthy expedition – David had
a full growth of hair on his face.

When Morris saw them walk in, he dropped what he was
doing and rushed to greet his brothers, shaking their hands heartily, being very pleased to see them again. He asked how they were
and commented on how well they looked, but did not ask if they
had found the wagons. He did not need to: their faces told the
solemn story that they had failed dismally.

It was David who finally broke the brief joy of their reunion. "Nothing, Morris, not even a clue. We did find a lot of cattle, though: all dead."

"This *rinderpest* is frightening," Harry chimed in, "almost every day, we came across carcasses of cattle. It's totally out of control. Soon there will be no beef to eat in the entire country, possibly the entire southern continent."

Morris shook his head in disbelief, "I have heard it is a national tragedy. The BSAC are actually slaughtering all cattle that have not been penned and isolated from other animals that are roaming the countryside, to try and contain the spread. They have orders to kill every stray cow they find. It's open season on cattle out there."

"We never even saw a live ox, for what it's worth," David lamented, before Morris cut the conversation off suddenly.

"Go and clean up," he said, "I'll take you two down to a new hotel that has opened up and we can have a proper meal. We have much to discuss. Have a shave and a haircut while you are at it, we must look presentable in town."

*

In the five weeks that David and Harry had been searching through the bush country, the town of Bulawayo had changed. New buildings were springing up with great frequency and velocity. Almost every building was made of brick under a corrugated-iron roof, with a very wide veranda, and very little architectural flair. The streets were exceptionally wide, which gave the new town an air of grace, and a feeling of calm and peace. Leafy trees had been planted at regular intervals, and, although only about waist height, their green hues provided a striking and welcome contrast to the dusty streets and reddish-brown brickwork of the buildings. Many of the signs on the various buildings that advertised the different wares on sale and encouraged the citizens to visit were proudly painted onto gables and bare walls with cheap paint. Almost every building was a single storey, but there were a few that boasted a second floor.

When the boys sat down at a table in the new single-storey Charter Hotel, with extra-wide verandas wrapping around two sides of the building, not much was left to discuss, since everything that David might have told Morris had been related during the short walk over to the restaurant. Morris therefore took the opportunity to go over his plans to protect the company from insolvency. Almost everything he needed to do relied on deception, making customers believe that all was well in their business world. As much as David didn't like the ideas put forward, he had no option but to agree with Morris because there was no alternative. The simple fact was that within the next two months they would be called upon to start repaying their debts.

Morris played with the food in his plate, avoiding eye contact. "I will have to visit Julian Weil personally in Mafeking," he muttered, "and tell him the truth."

"Surely he would understand that the *rinderpest* scourge was not our fault?" Harry suggested.

"I'm hoping he will see it that way. Our debt to him is just six wagons of stock, so hopefully he will be a little lenient on us."

"*Just* six wagons?" David exclaimed, but kept his voice down, "last year two wagons were a massive quantity in anyone's books. When we loaded up six wagons for the first time they all thought we were crazy and started taking bets on us. We have *thirty* wagons out there!"

"I know," Morris looked sheepishly at David, "unfortunately it gets worse."

"Oh, Lord," David leaned back in his chair and looked around the room, hoping none of the patrons could hear them, "how can it get worse?"

"Four of our wagon traders have been hit by the *rinderpest*. Their oxen," Morris sighed and corrected himself – "*our* oxen all perished in one night and they became stranded. I had to purchase, at great expense I might add, a team of mules to rescue them and bring them back into Bulawayo. Those who escaped the *rinderpest* are too scared it will happen to them and have refused to go back out again until the plague is over or we can supply donkeys, which we can't afford."

"So what you are saying is that we have no income from our wagon traders now," Harry added, very concerned. Even David nervously ran his fingers through his hair.

"Correct," Morris placed his knife and fork together and rocked back in his chair. His chicken was so tough it was almost inedible.

"How many wagons are still out in the land?" Harry asked.

"Only two. Everyone else is back. Since the time of the rebellion, I have kept a record of where every trader goes. Only the chap in Fort Victoria and an old fellow in Fort Salisbury are away. There is some good news, though."

"Well, that's a nice change," David said sarcastically.

"Three bits of good news, actually. Firstly, because the traders are returning their wagons, I have been replenishing the warehouse with their unsold stock."

"I noticed our stock levels looked good, actually," Harry frowned.

Morris nodded his approval of his younger brother's powers of observation with a curt smile, "and sales from Langbourne Brothers are steady. Also, because of the *rinderpest*, everything is in short supply, so prices throughout town are increasing. As a result, I have put our prices up quite considerably, so our profits have increased, because our purchase prices are still the same."

"What's the third bit of good news?" David looked at Morris intently.

"We are one of the few people in town who have any oxen that have not been affected by the *rinderpest*. Their value has increased dramatically. I have been ordered by the administration to have them quarantined on land acquired by them just outside town."

"Sell them, Morris," David implored, "before they die."

"They'll be safe there, David, don't worry."

"You haven't seen how this disease can spread," Harry

intervened, "David is right, take your money and run – now. I reckon that within a fortnight every beast in that quarantine area will be dead."

The look of horror in Morris' eyes was unmistakable. After thinking through what his brothers had just said, Morris nodded slowly, "Alright," he agreed, "I have a buyer, I'll sell them this afternoon. I was hoping to use them to bring our wagons back once we find them."

"Morris, please don't pin your hopes on finding those wagons," David scowled, "they may never be found. Yet I've been thinking about going to see Phil Innes after this meal. He sees things from a very different perspective, and he may have an idea as to how I can find our stock. He is very smart in all matters under the sun, and I somehow feel I am missing something. I have had five weeks in the bush to think about it and I believe my mind is stuck in a loop."

"Good idea," Morris enthused. "When do you think you might go back out there?"

David sighed. "You know, Morris, as much as I enjoy the bush, there are limits. Give me a couple of days to enjoy some civilised company and then I'll go out for another five weeks."

"I'm quite fed up with the bush myself," Harry grumbled.

"Sure, David," Morris agreed sympathetically, ignoring Harry. "Of course, I quite understand." He knew that without David there would be absolutely no chance of the wagons ever being found. He was in a very awkward situation, and was not comfortable with it.

*

"Morning Phil," David called cheerfully, as he poked his head into Phil Innes' office across the street from Langbourne Brothers.

"David!" Phil jumped to his feet and shook hands vigorously with his old friend and ex-business partner, "you're back? It's been a long time. Any luck?"

"Sadly, no… none whatsoever."

The two friends wandered out the back of the office into Phil's hardware yard, which seemed to contain a considerable amount of building material, much more since David's last visit. Phil seemed to be running a very successful enterprise. They discussed a number of topics, but each time a customer walked in, Phil would break away quickly to serve his client, leaving David to ramble aimlessly in the roofless area around the iron sheeting, plumbing pipes, and other bulky goods used in the construction industry. Because Phil believed it was cheaper and that it certainly did not warrant paving the area, the floor of the yard consisted of raw dirt. Some of his stock was therefore decidedly dusty and even splattered with mud from the occasional downpour, and it made David smile at how different businesses had differing priorities. Langbourne Brothers needed a warehouse with a good roof and a solid floor from which to sell their stock.

Once the two were alone again, David asked Phil if he had any ideas that might help him find his lost wagons. Phil began by asking him to recall every last detail before he parted company with Daluxolo and Nguni, and then they discussed the difference between the dates the wagons were last seen, when they left the Limpopo River, and when Daluxolo arrived in Bulawayo.

"You have a very unique problem, David," Phil commiserated, "your search can be done in two ways, either in a north-south fashion – if you knew the route he took, which you don't – or an east-west fashion, if you knew how long the wagons had been moving northwards, which also you don't."

"There is a third option, which is what I tried - unsuccessfully I might add." David picked up a short piece of copper pipe and then scraped the dirt with his foot, as if wiping a slate clean. "May I?" he asked, holding the pipe as if he were a school teacher with a pointer."

"Go ahead," Phil nodded.

David pulled his compass out of his pocket and laid it on the ground, then, walking around it for a moment, etched a rough map in the dirt with the end of the pipe, finally drawing a straight line at his feet.

"This," he pointed to the line, "is the Limpopo River. This," he prodded a spot near the top of his diagram, "is Bulawayo. Somewhere between here and here are our wagons. However, between these points," he scratched the earth in two small places, "the route is approximately seven miles wide among thick bush, hills, and valleys."

"So what you are saying is that the wagons could be anywhere in this area," Phil took the copper pipe off David and drew an oval in the dust."

David sighed in response. "Assuming, that is, that the wagons travelled an average distance per day, and that Daluxolo half ran, half walked when he came to Bulawayo, which is what I think he did. So what I did was search this area," he took the pipe off Phil again and drew a zigzag line across the imaginary routes.

"So you went north and south, east to west? Good thinking, but unless you have the correct area, you will miss the wagons entirely."

"Which is what happened – after I had wasted five weeks traversing all that terrain, dodging buffalos, elephants and lions, and sleeping with spiders, snakes, and scorpions," David muttered sarcastically.

Phil let a chuckle escape, "Rather you than me. It is entirely possible that you may have been in the exact area, but if you skirted a small forest the wrong way, or went around a hill on the wrong side, you would have missed them completely."

"I know," David sighed again, "and that thought depresses me immensely. One of the reasons I took off so quickly, five weeks ago, was in the hopes that I might pick up a sighting of vultures that would lead me to the dead oxen, but there were circling vultures in every direction; it was hopeless. I thought the stench of the decaying carcasses might lead me there, too, but that was a joke: the bush is littered with dead animals."

"The vulture idea was good, I'll give you that, David," Phil patted his friend on the shoulder showing genuine concern for him, "so that gives me an idea. Firstly, send a telegram to Weil in Mafeking and ask if Daluxolo has returned."

"No, Morris won't allow that," David quickly objected, "Weil will instantly know there is a problem, and he will immediately go into a panic, and we can't let word out that our wagons are missing. Half of the Transvaal will migrate here looking for them; for them it will be like striking gold. In any case, I had considered that and, while Harry and I were scouring the bush, we took a couple of weeks off the search to dash down to Mafeking and get more supplies, but he wasn't there. We did look."

"Ok, fair enough, but it may be that you missed him and that he is there now. I'd hate to think your simplest solution is sitting waiting for you in Mafeking, and we mustn't ignore that," Phil paused. "Would you mind if Abe Kaufman knows about this? I ask because he is going to Mafeking tomorrow and he could make some discreet enquiries for you."

"Not at all. Indeed, I trust Abe completely."

"Good. So, if Abe can confirm that Daluxolo has returned home, you can get him to lead you to the wagons. If he is not there, then there is a good chance he has remained with the wagons with Nguni, not so?"

"More than likely, yes. What are you getting at?"

"You gave me an idea about the vultures," Phil smiled broadly, "what else in the sky can guide you to your wagons?"

David cocked his head and stared at Phil, who was grinning from ear to ear, "I give up. What?"

"Smoke!"

"Smoke?"

"If Nguni and Daluxolo stayed with the wagons, they will have to eat, every day, twice a day, morning and evening. Every morning and evening you must climb up a tree with your telescope and compass and scan the horizon. Then you just follow the smoke!"

David suddenly burst into laughter and doubled over, slapping his knee before straightening up. "You genius!" he said through his laugher, "you absolute genius."

Phil just smiled, "You'll have a lot of false leads as there are bound to be many villages in the area. You'll have to work out a plan as to how to isolate those smoke trails you have visited previously."

"You'll show me how to do that, I'm sure. Come on. Let's find Abe before he departs."

Finding Abe was not difficult. Their first stop was at his wife's clothing store, where Abe's characteristically thin, lanky shape could be seen at the rear of the shop, moving some boxes about. He still wore his grubby, sweat-stained felt hat, even indoors. After greeting both Sharon and Abe, and exchanging some pleasantries, Abe, Phil and David excused themselves to the back of the shop and David confided in Abe what had happened to their wagons. Abe was shocked to hear the news and scolded David for not telling him sooner.

"If I had known," Abe shook his finger at David, "I would have accompanied you on your search. Your brother Harry is too young to go out there with you for five weeks at a time."

"I know," David confessed, "but he did well, and he grew up very quickly. It was very good for him, actually."

"So, what must I do if I find your man in Mafeking?" Abe questioned.

"Please send me a telegram the moment you know, but it must be in code. No one must know what has happened, absolutely no one."

"Don't make this complicated, David. What code?"

"Alright," David grinned, "if you find Daluxolo, then that is really good news, I will be happy, just as Phil would be," he slapped Phil on the shoulder. "Send me a telegram and say *'Advise Phil stock available'*. That is all happy news."

Abe frowned, but nodded.

"If you don't find him, then imagine Morris will be grumpy,

so send a telegram saying '*Advise Morris no stock available*'. That is all bad news. Got it?"

"Yes, of course," Abe still frowned, "I thought you wanted me to learn some weird new language or something. I can do that for you, certainly. Now," he placed a fatherly hand on David's shoulder, "if you have to go out in the bush again, or you need any help, you make sure you call on me. Do you understand, David?"

"Of course, I'll ask you, but Sharon may not like it."

"David," Abe sighed and looked around nervously, "I'm a man of the earth, a prospector first and foremost. I like the bush and I like hard work. Moving boxes from this side of the shop to the other side of the shop, and listening to women talk about dresses and frocks all day is driving me crazy. In any case, I am indebted to you for my life, and I want to help you.

David and Phil chuckled. "I understand, Abe. I won't go anywhere until I hear from you. I wish you a safe journey, my friend."

For the first time since David had faced death in the quicksand he felt whole again. These two men were his best and truest friends. His spirits had soared and he felt young and new once more. This day was a turning point in his life, and he needed to tell his brothers. After all, they needed a lift just as much as he had.

"Smoke?" David said, looking at Phil and shaking his head in disbelief. "Smoke!" he repeated, and then, giggling mischievously to himself, he took his leave.

*

Three hundred Matabele warriors sat in nervous silence among the massive, grey granite boulders, the bald-headed hills of the Matopos. They all stared at the entrance to the sacred cave of their appointed leader, the M'Limo, who had been concealed inside the dark cavern for three days. The cave was slightly higher than where the men were gathered, and occasionally a blood-curdling scream was heard echoing from the entrance. Not one of the 300, all dressed in full battle gear, knew if it was a male or female scream, nor if it was human or animal. The men had been waiting since sunrise, and now, in the heat of the afternoon sun, a sense of anticipation began to cloak the assembled commanders.

Suddenly, a very slight movement inside the shadowed entrance of the cave could be seen, and almost immediately the low rumble of anxious men's voices reverberated off the granite walls surrounding the secret meeting place. The movement edged closer to the entrance of the cave, and the rumble grew louder. Finally, the M'Limo emerged, and all the warriors knelt on the ground in unison, instantly showing their respect for the leader of their nation.

The M'Limo was a small man, and he looked fierce and angry. His eyes were so wide open that the whites of his eyes flashed fear and terror into the hearts of the brave commanders. A leopard skin, reserved only for leaders, was draped over the man's shoulders and down his back, the front legs of the creature tied together to keep the shimmering mammalian shawl in place. On his chest was a splattering of brown mud and white paste, and around his hips he wore the tails of twenty leopards. To the men gathered there the most frightening sight was the fresh red blood that stained and dribbled down his chin and onto his chest. The head of a baboon was somehow attached to his crown, appearing to be asleep, but it had obviously died a painful death. The pungent scent of decaying flesh drifted across to the nostrils of the men in the front ranks.

The M'Limo screamed that ghastly death cry again, and immediately all the gathered soldiers fell with their faces to the dust, wailing and chanting, hitting the ground with their mottled cowhide shields. The muffled din was spectacular. A second cry from the M'Limo and the noise stopped abruptly, the soldiers obediently standing to attention. Silence descended upon the sacred meeting place. The feared M'Limo walked threateningly from side to side in front of the cave entrance like an angry and frustrated wild leopard, never taking his unblinking eyes off the mass of humanity below.

"The spirits are disappointed in you, the warriors of our nation," he exploded, "you have become cowards!"

The soldiers shuffled in nervous discomfort. They did not know what was to come, but their fear of being put to death was real and very probable. In the days of King Lobengula, if the king had thought a warrior to be a coward, he would be brutally and painfully killed. The men had all witnessed the king's brutality and murderous moods. On some days he would have hundreds of soldiers put to death within a single hour simply because he thought they were weak or had been possessed by an evil spirit. Indeed, the gathered soldiers were petrified at being summoned by the M'Limo.

"Have you not seen what the European settlers have done to our land?" he paused and walked about menacingly again. "Do you not see that they have chased our king from the Royal Village and taken it for themselves? Have you not seen the houses they build on the Royal Village? They have forced us off our land and made our men work in mines, or till the land for their own, and our men get very little reward for this!"

The soldiers silently mumbled their agreement and shuffled uncomfortably, unable to take their eyes off the hideous apparition in front of them. This was the first time any of them had laid eyes on the M'Limo.

"Is this wrong?" he demanded of the warriors.

"Jhee...." the low cry of agreement went up in unison.

"Is it wrong?" he shouted so loudly his voice gurgled.

"Jhee!" The call went up loud and strong this time.

"They bring a plague of locusts to eat our crops. Our cattle starve and stop giving us milk. There is no seed for our chickens so they stop laying eggs. These locusts ate our crops of maize. Our children starve; we all starve. Is that not so?"

"Jhee!" reverberated off the boulders, and this time there was emotion in their voices. The M'Limo was pleased with this response. He knew that he could quickly whip them into a frenzied state.

"Now they bring sickness to our cattle and they die in the thousands," he thrust his fist into the air. The warriors cried out, driving their spears into the air; they understood their leader well. Cattle were a measure of wealth among the African people. They provided food and milk, and their hides furnished cloth, and when treated differently, their hardened hides gave protection from the enemy's spears in the form of shields. In marriage, a man would offer a dowry to the prospective father-in-law in the form of livestock, depending on the wealth of his family, and a good cow was of high value, fetching the most beautiful bride. Among the African people, the possession of cattle provided the cornerstones of their existence.

"But this is not enough for the European!" the tirade continued. "The cattle that live, they kill with bullets!" He went silent, and a strange, expectant quietness followed. Not a soul twitched as the religious leader stared hard at his subjects with his abnormally wide, unblinking eyes. "They kill every one of our cattle that they see. And when they kill them, they leave their bodies in the dust to rot. They do not even take the meat to eat. Is this not evil?" he demanded as a question.

"Jhee!" the shout of agreement went up, louder and more powerful.

"The spirits *command* you to take our land back. We must drive the European settler out of this land forever, and the time has come. Are your spears thirsty for blood?"

"Jhee…." they responded, beating their shields with their spears. The deep vibration could be felt within the men's chests and it stirred in each and every one the need to prove their manhood: to kill, to see blood, and take what was theirs, to right the gross injustices inflicted on their proud nation. Despite their fear of the European and his lethal weapons that cut and shredded their bodies with many bullets in an instant, they would go back to war for their nation, and to appease the spirits of their ancestors.

"The spirits have sent the European leader, the man they call the Doctor, from Matabeleland, and the spirits have made him take his army with him. There is no army to protect those that remain. Now is the time!" he punched the air with his fist, and the crowd roared, stamping their feet in the dirt and raising a cloud of dust, blood-lust rising quickly in their hearts and minds. They had heard that the European leader had run away with his army, but they had not known that their ancestral spirits had arranged the departure. Now they were jubilant.

"I will cast a spell on the European's bullets. Their bullets will turn to water, and their cannon's bullets will turn to chicken eggs, and your spears will drink the blood of the settlers. You need have no fear of their weapons."

"Jhee!" was the cry from the men. They were in awe of the power of their M'Limo. No other leader before him could do that, and they were filled with courage, and the need to kill. It would be like the days of King Lobengula again, and their hearts were consumed by joy.

By now the gathered commanders of the Matabele army were in a frenzied state. They pounded the ground with their bare feet, rattled their spears on their cowhide shields, and shouted their war cry in earnest. They were desperate to leave, to run to their legions and spread the good news, to finally give the young warriors the command they had so long waited for.

"Go to your men!" the M'Limo commanded when silence eventually prevailed. "Go prepare your troops and sharpen your stabbing spears. The day before the full moon you must surround KoBulawayo in secret," he used the old name of the Royal Village, "and after the big dance on the night of the full moon," he paused to make sure everyone was listening carefully, "the sunrise will be your command for the attack on the settlers."

Again a roar of approval erupted in the natural amphitheatre, and the dust rose in sync with the adrenalin of the war-hardened and bloodthirsty army leaders. They were young again; their hearts were singing joyously.

"The spirits have spoken to me," the M'Limo raised both arms, commanding silence, which he received almost immediately, "fifty thousand must surround KoBulawayo, but no attack must take place until sunrise after the big dance. I command you to leave only one way out for these settlers, the way to the south, from where they came – we must show them that we want them to leave. When the European settler sees the road open for them to leave, they will understand. Those that do not leave, we will attack, and you must kill every man, woman and child. Spare no one."

Another blood curdling roar went up, and again the M'Limo raised his arms for silence.

"All other warriors must go into the countryside and kill every European they find. Burn their houses, destroy their farms and their mines. Let no settler remain in Matabeleland. When we have driven out the European we will claim the Royal Village for ourselves once more, and then we will help the Shona people rid the settlers from their land in the north."

The roar was deafening; the M'Limo was deeply satisfied.

CHAPTER THIRTEEN
Siege

MORRIS AND DAVID found that, when they walked side by side along a path, or down a pavement, it seemed natural to discuss their business in great depth. Whether they spoke more freely without eye contact or were out of earshot of those around them, they neither knew nor questioned, but – whenever they needed to discuss anything of importance – they would simply go for a walk. It was a habit that stayed with them their entire lives.

On this particular day, they were expecting a telegram from Abe Kaufman and had just reached the edge of town, close to where two Greek brothers had opened a wholesale business, called "Divaris and Co." Standing in their shirtsleeves and business trousers, while David had rolled his sleeves half way up his arms as was his custom on hot days, they had paused to stare out into the African bush beyond. They had been discussing the role Louis would play in the business, especially as they expected him to arrive on the Zeederberg Mail Coach at any moment.

Morris pushed his hands deep into his pockets and jingled a couple of coins. "Phil's idea of finding Daluxolo in Mafeking is a clever idea," he remarked.

"I did go looking for him in Mafeking, as you know, but once I had realised that he wasn't there, I gave that idea up," David replied. "I never thought about looking for smoke, though. One way or the other, I feel we have a fighting chance of finding those wagons now."

"Any idea how long it would take?"

"Hah," David tried to force a laugh, "it could take years, Morris. The land is vast out there - you know that."

"Yes, I know, it was a stupid question. I'm just very worried that we are running out of time to meet our debts."

"I must admit, brother of mine," David stole a brief glance at Morris, "your idea and the risks you took were good. Who would ever have anticipated the *rinderpest?*" he whispered the word as if it were unmentionable.

"The idea was good, but the consequences of failure were greater," he paused, "perhaps even more dire than I had imagined. I had never even heard of the *rinderpest* until now."

"I would say that goes for just about everyone on the continent. How could you have known?" David shrugged. He, too, stood with his hands in his pockets, but he had no coins to play with.

"We'll get through this, don't you worry." Morris was as resolute as always.

Just then David saw a movement beyond the trees, a slight movement, on the crest of a hill in the distance. His prolonged time in the bush, and the lessons he had learned from his old friend Piet van Tonder, the tobacco farmer in Patensie, as well as from Daluxolo, had made him acutely aware of any sudden movement, especially in the bush. He observed the place intently, trying to work out if it was a kudu or an eland antelope.

"If we find those grinders," Morris continued, "business – and profits – will be exceptional. If that happens, I'm thinking of sending Badger to take over the Gold warehouse on a full-time basis."

Speaking in their own code was almost second nature to the boys now. "I'd like Giraffe to remain here at Langbro with us. I think – "

"Morris," David cut him off mid-sentence, holding up his hand slightly to silence him, "there is something moving out there, and it's not characteristic of any animal I know. In fact, it looks decidedly human. Let's go back to the shop; I'd like to get my telescope."

"Sure thing," Morris needed no further encouragement: when his brother sounded concerned about something, he usually had reason to be.

Whether it was out of curiosity or adrenalin or because they remembered vividly the Matabele rebellion of a couple of years before, the brothers immediately picked up their pace. When they arrived at the warehouse, David wasted no time in extracting the treasured brass-and-leather telescope from his worn duffle bag. Within moments, both he and Morris were back on Abercorn Street and making their way to the east side of town. As they rounded a corner, they almost ran into Captain Charles Rudge of the BSAC.

"Good morning, gentlemen," he greeted them cordially, slightly out of breath.

"Greetings, Captain. Very pleased to see you again," Morris extended his arm. "How's your hand? Fully recovered?"

Captain Rudge shook Morris' hand very gently, "Indeed, but sadly a couple of fingers don't work as well as they used to. It seems I'm allergic to Matabele metals," he joked. "Very sorry, however, but I can't stay to chat. I have just received a report that some Matabele warriors may have pitched up on the west side of town, so I need to get back to headquarters at the double in order to have a look."

"Funny that," David frowned, "I saw something on the east side, so we're off there right now to take a closer look with my telescope."

The captain looked troubled, "Would you fellows mind coming with me to the Market Square? Let's go to the top of the bell tower so we can have a good look around. Bring that telescope, David, if you don't mind."

As they walked briskly to the tower, Captain Rudge told the

boys that, two days beforehand, a family had come bundling into town on their wagon. They reported that they had been attacked by a group of Matabele warriors, which he had found perplexing because he knew of no reason for them to have been attacked. Now that a report had been received of some activity around the perimeter of the settlement, however, he was very troubled.

In no time at all, the captain and the two Langbourne brothers were standing in the bell tower, all three panting from the exertion of climbing the steps at pace. The space was very confined, but the view was spectacular. Though not particularly high, the tower was the tallest structure in town. From that height, the extraordinarily wide streets carved a series of perfect rectangles out of the corrugated-iron blanket of roof sheeting. At that time, Bulawayo was a very flat settlement with only a handful of buildings exceeding one floor, but Morris knew it was only a matter of time before that would change.

Meanwhile, Captain Rudge had his telescope out and was scanning the western perimeter of town, while David scanned the eastern side with his.

"I don't see anything," Rudge muttered. "Anything your side, David?"

"Nothing," David grunted, "I've found the place where I thought I saw something, but no, sorry, false alarm."

"Let's swop sides," Charles suggested. Morris sidled around the bronze bell to allow the other two to change places and the captain broke the silence after about five minutes.

"Any luck?" he called out.

"No, nothing," David replied. "It must be simply that the citizens' nerves are on edge."

"What about north and south?" Morris suggested.

"Good idea," Rudge complimented Morris and the trio shuffled around.

Apart from Morris knocking the bell gently with his knuckle to test its resonance, the men crouched in total silence as they scanned their allotted horizons.

David broke the serenity after about two minutes, "I've got something," he mumbled softly.

"What?" Morris asked anxiously, tension rising rapidly and a touch of nervous heartburn catching him in his chest.

"Where?" Rudge demanded as he shuffled over to David and trained his telescope on the horizon.

"There," David continued without moving, "you see that rock on the ridge with the two sharp points, just behind that large green tree, at about one o'clock?"

"Yes, got it," Rudge was abrupt.

"At the base of the two points, it looks like feathers. Keep watching them, they'll move."

"I see them, but they're not moving."

"Keep watching, I thought I saw a movement. I think they are feathers from a warrior's headdress. There! You see it?" he exclaimed.

"I see it. It could be a bird," Rudge mumbled, and then gently said "Oh, hell!" making Morris' skin tingle.

"What?" Morris asked urgently.

"A warrior armed with a spear has just stood up and moved behind another rock," his brother said calmly. "Do you think they plan to attack us, Captain?" David put his telescope down.

"I certainly don't expect them to, not after the last defeat they had. What worries me, though, is that we have no men to defend ourselves. That idiot, Jameson, took everyone capable of defending us with him to Johannesburg."

"How many soldiers have you got?" Morris sounded agitated.

"Here? In Bulawayo? About twelve, and about thirty men countrywide, that's all. I think we only have about ten rifles in the armoury. Damn Jameson! Now look what he's done!" Rudge grumbled to himself; he was very angry. "I need to get this town into a laager and protect the citizens, but I don't want to overreact; all we have seen is one detachment."

"One sighting to the north and two reports from the east and west sides of the town," Morris bluntly interrupted, "in my view, we are surrounded."

"Well…" Rudge tried to find an argument in reply, but couldn't. "I'll send out a couple of scouts to look around. If they come across anything, I'll take rapid action, don't you worry. Let's go; we don't have any time to lose."

As the boys parted company with the captain and hurried back to their shop, they heard the Zeederberg Coach arriving behind them, the driver shouting wildly at his team of stubborn mules to slow down and stop.

Morris suddenly stopped and grabbed David's arm. "If the Matabele are going to attack us," he murmured, "Louis could be caught out there in the thick of it."

"I'd completely forgotten about Louis," David sounded shocked, "when are you expecting him?"

"I've been waiting days, already; he should have been here by now."

"Let's go over to the coach and see if he's on that one."

"Let's pray to our Lord God Almighty he is," Morris looked horrified.

As eight men pried themselves out of the overloaded carriage the unmistakably lanky shape of Louis emerged, much to the delight of his older brothers. Although covered in dust and looking as if he had walked most of the way, he wore his business suit and a thin black tie, his white socks – now coated in a fine layer of orange dust – appearing starkly under the trouser legs that he had outgrown.

The brothers greeted one another with hearty handshakes, slaps on the back, and copious jokes about Louis' appearance, but they could not have been happier that he had arrived safely and that his timing had been perfect. As they walked back to their warehouse to see Harry, they totally forgot about the anxiety they had been subjected to only minutes earlier. This was the first time in over five years that all four brothers were together. It was a most joyous occasion for them all.

Although Louis already knew much of the news about the lost wagons through receiving their cryptic telegrams, the brothers quickly filled him in on what had happened, particularly the expedition that David may soon venture on, to hunt for smoke, if Daluxolo was not found in Mafeking.

"You didn't see him there, did you?" Morris asked Louis.

Louis shrugged his shoulders in a typical gesture of guilt. "I didn't think to look, to be honest."

"Don't worry. Abe Kaufman, a good friend of ours, is on his way there. He's going to have a look for us."

As he looked at the roof and all the stock on the tables and shelves, Louis' bright smile returned. "You have a fantastic warehouse, here!" he said.

Morris proudly slapped David on the shoulder. "Your brother just about built it himself," he said, but then their conversation was suddenly cut short as the bell in the Market Square tower began to ring.

David jumped to his feet "I thought so," he said, "I had a feeling there was trouble out there."

Both Harry and Louis were taken aback. "What's wrong?" they asked.

"We have to get to the Market Square post haste! I'll tell you on the way," David said as he whisked the door key off the desk, "Sorry, Louis, this is going to be one hell of a welcome that Bulawayo will be giving you."

Every citizen knew that the bell sounded some sort of urgent alarm and they wasted no time in flocking into the town square, arriving to find Captains Rudge, Bailey, and Dent frantically organising a defensive laager in the centre of the town and blocking off the streets. The citizens joined in without question and helped wherever possible, since the danger was perfectly clear. While Captain Rudge was in command of constructing all the defences, Captain Bailey took control of all available armaments, which included sending those men who owned hunting rifles scurrying back to their homes or places of work to collect them.

The remainder of the afternoon was spent in setting up further fortifications and in protecting the centre of the settlement. Wagons were set in place and loaded with sandbags, their undercarriages jammed tight with logs, thorn bushes, or whatever else was available. Knowing that the *impi* always fought barefoot, bottles and other glassware were rapidly collected from homes and businesses to be smashed across the streets in front of the wagon barricade; nails were swiftly hammered through planks and pieces of timber; as well as any other means of injuring a barefoot warrior and slowing his attack.

Explosive charges that were normally used for prospecting and mining were placed in buildings on the outer edges of town to prevent the enemy from occupying them and setting up vantage points for attack, and all available barbed wire from every hardware and farming supplier had been strung across roads, paths, alleyways and any area that could be used to access the laager. Booby-traps were made from wire and rope, including some ingenious trip-wire alarm systems to sound an alert or ring a brass bell if they were disturbed.

Phil Innes and some of his hardware competitors joined forces and rapidly made up some Maxim gun look-alikes using lengths of iron tubing and broken, discarded wagon wheels, which they positioned around the perimeter of the laager, hoping that – from a distance – they might be mistaken for lethal weapons.

*

That evening, all 4,000 citizens were confined within the fortifications. It was a very long night, but no attack came. The four brothers had fallen asleep late into the night and awoke to the sound of human movement - some grumbling and the cry of a distressed child. With bare earth as a mattress, and no blankets to keep the cold night air off their bodies, their joints ached and they all felt pretty miserable.

Morris sat up and rubbed his eyes. "Seems like we've done this before…" he mumbled.

David yawned in reply. "Only last time we weren't surrounded,"

"But we thought we were at the time," Morris retorted, "I hope our shop is alright."

Harry joined the conversation after sitting upright and taking in the scene that was unfolding in front of him. "Are they going to kill us?" he asked a little apprehensively.

"I hope not," Morris muttered. "What is it with Africa? Everybody wants to kill everybody all the time."

"We'll be alright," David consoled his brothers. He saw Louis sitting quietly behind Harry, "Nice welcome, huh?"

"I didn't like East London, but this place is worse than a sewer. Please send me back there."

David chuckled, and then nodded in the direction of the entrance to the BSAC building that bordered on the Market Square, "Come on, brothers, looks like someone is going to tell us something at last."

Captain Rudge stood tall on the steps with three large men sporting bushy beards behind him. As the civilians gathered close, his unmistakably commanding voice rang out, "Ladies and Gentlemen, I need your attention," he paused until the hubbub died down and not a sound could be heard from the assembled mass of humanity.

"We have evidence that the Matabele nation has once again risen up against the Europeans. We have been surrounded and our town is under siege. There is no way in, and no way out." This statement caused a brief rumble among the townsfolk, who quickly went silent again so as not to miss a word their commander and protector was saying.

"We have managed to get a message out to Mafeking and Fort Salisbury before they cut the telegraph wires, and they will be sending reinforcements. Unfortunately, it will not be easy for support to arrive, as they will be encountering hostile Matabele along the way. We could be here for several days.

"We have been consulting with Messrs Burnham, Selous, and Gifford," Rudge turned slightly and pointed out the three burly men behind him, "and we have decided that we will not wait for reinforcements as an attack by the *impi* appears imminent, possibly immediately after the full moon tomorrow, so *we* will go on the offensive and attack first. The Matabele warriors will not be expecting us to do that."

A deep rumble undulated through the civilian crowd. David nudged Morris with his elbow, looked at him briefly then cocked his head at the men standing on the stairs.

"We will form an attack force, to be called the Bulawayo Field Force, and we will go out and engage the Matabele. At the same time, we will attempt to rescue our own men, women and children who are undoubtedly under attack in their stores, their homes, on their farms, and on their claims. Time is not on their side, nor is it on ours.

"We will need volunteers for the Field Force to go with Selous, Burnham and Gifford," Captain Rudge announced, "forty men, each with a rifle or handgun and a horse, are needed to go with each of these men, so we are looking for one hundred and twenty volunteers. It will be extremely dangerous and I cannot guarantee your safety."

"How many Matabele are out there?" a lone voice rang out.

Captain Rudge cleared his throat and half turned to look at the three men behind him. They did not budge, but Selous gave a barely noticeable nod. "We don't know. Fifty to seventy thousand; we can't be sure."

Another low rumble engulfed the crowd as these numbers took them by surprise.

"How many have surrounded us?" the same voice echoed off the building walls.

"As I said, we don't know. We estimate fifty thousand."

That statement caused an immediate uproar among the population, which the captain battled to subdue. When he finally got back everyone's attention he continued, "We need volunteers, one hundred and twenty able-bodied men with weapons and horses. Volunteers may form up at the base of these steps immediately."

Morris and David locked eyes and stared at each other. To any bystander, they would have simply noticed the stare, but very gently, almost invisibly, David shook his head from side to side. Morris responded with a virtually indiscernible frown, his eyes burning deep into David's head. Harry, however, noticed the secret conversation his older brothers were having in their own silent language, and a grim fear overtook him. He grappled with the need to cry out that he wanted to go back to Ireland, but his terror was so strong it prevented him from saying anything.

It was Louis who unknowingly broke the telepathic conversation. "What's going to happen?" he blurted out.

David broke off his stare with Morris and turned to his younger brothers. "The situation is not good. The Matabele seem to have thought this through, and these blokes," he pointed his thumb over his shoulder at the BSAC officers, "have been caught with their pants down. We will not be volunteering for –"

Morris abruptly interrupted and pointed a finger at Louis and Harry. "None of you will be volunteering!"

"I must remind you," David continued, "this is not our war and we are not trained soldiers. If we go out there, we will die."

"We will sit it out and pray to our Lord God Almighty for His protection," Morris wound up the lecture to his siblings.

*

In the early afternoon, three contingents of the newly-formed Bulawayo Field Force rode out in different directions to face the Matabele and take them by surprise. The townsfolk watched silently as these brave men took off in clouds of dust, and within minutes the horror and seriousness of their predicament confronted the citizens of Bulawayo as gunfire erupted just beyond the tree-line that indicated the town limits. Just before the sun was about to set, what was left of the three patrols, returned. They had each lost several men, over-run by a force of significant numbers and stabbed to death by the *impi's* lethal spears.

As fortifications were hurriedly opened to allow the volunteers back into the relative safety of the laager, townsfolk were dumbstruck as they saw the horrendous injuries sustained by the lucky survivors, their clothing shimmering with fresh blood and their faces smeared with dirt and sweat. The look in the eyes of some of these men showed that they had looked death in the face more than once; it was obvious that many would have recurrent nightmares about this day for the remainder of their natural lives. One man in his thirties, who stood aside to let the patrol pass, went pale and fainted, crashing to the ground in a small cloud of dust.

As the group of exhausted men rode past the Langbourne brothers, their equally spent horses covered in foam, Morris stole a look at David, but this time it was Morris who shook his head from side to side ever so slightly. David responded with a miniscule nod; nothing more needed to be said.

A newly constructed building within the laager was hastily converted into a hospital, and womenfolk, without being asked, began treating and nursing the injured. They quickly created a roster for shift work and gathered all the medical and nursing equipment they could muster. During that night three men and one horse would succumb to their injuries. Wads of cloth were gathered and stuffed into old, dented metal buckets, which were each filled with a quart of oil. As night began to set in, a number of men left the laager, running down the streets and weaving in military fashion, to drop the buckets with the oil-soaked textiles in strategic positions, lighting them, then making a zig-zag dash back to safety. These would give the night watchmen some light, allowing for some sort of warning if an attack began, and would also assist with their aim in the dark. Many doubted, though, that the flames would last until daybreak. As the severity of the situation became clear, more strategic plans were suggested, then either rejected or implemented.

After the first week of the siege, many members of the Field Force had been killed, and many more wounded, some critically. Some encouragement was provided, however, when a number of civilians, trapped in their homes when the war began, were rescued, and a great cheer went up in the laager when the Field Force cantered in with the freed victims. Sadly, these were few and far between, since the majority of outposts visited by the Force had revealed entire families who had been brutally murdered at their homesteads, their mutilated bodies decaying in the hot African sun.

As the days of the siege dragged on, conditions within the laager became difficult, almost unbearable. Because food was scarce, it was tightly rationed. Fresh water, however, was plentiful, owing to a prolific well that had been dug in the Market Square gardens. Nevertheless, proper sanitation remained a problem and sickness soon began to spread. This prompted Major Seward to appear on the steps of the BSAC building one morning, and, with the help of Captain Rudge's booming voice, he called the civilians together.

"Ladies and gentlemen," Seward's voice rang out, "it is obvious that the Bulawayo Field Force is having an impact on the Matabele as there has been no attack on the town as yet," he paused to make sure everyone could hear him. When there was no comment, he continued, "and as conditions within the laager are becoming difficult we have decided that, despite the fact that Bulawayo remains surrounded by hostile Matabele and under siege, you may all go back to your homes and places of work during the day, but you must all return to the laager at night for safety.

"If our scouts feel an attack is imminent, we will ring the Market Square bell. If you hear the bell ringing, you must return to the laager immediately and with some urgency. If you decide to delay your appearance, you may be locked out and thus make it impossible to let you enter should an attack be in progress. It is absolutely imperative, therefore," he paused to make his point, as he looked at the people standing silently before him, "— *imperative*, I say, that you get back to the laager at once! If you are uncomfortable leaving the laager, you are welcome to remain inside," he concluded. Then, after a final, brief look at the blank faces, he silently mouthed the words "thank you" and walked back inside the building.

*

During the daytime, life almost returned to normal. Business trading continued, although at a much reduced pace, and socialising at hotels and clubs resumed. At nightfall, though, the population regrouped inside the laager and defences were strengthened. Food and other necessities were becoming increasingly scarce, and what was available was almost unaffordable. For the Langbourne Brothers, business was very slow. Since their stock consisted mainly of luxury goods and not basic necessities, many a day went by without a soul walking into the store.

A few days after the civilians were allowed back to their homes and places of work, the Matabele began launching raids into the town. Civilians would come tearing into the laager at breakneck speed when the warning bell rang out, some bringing their pets with them. The BSAC soldiers and civilian volunteers would beat off the attacks, and then, when all was clear, the daily routine would resume. Occasionally, there would be two or three attacks in one day. On the odd occasion, the bell would ring out in false alarm and the entire population of Bulawayo would come bolting back into the laager and anxiously wait for the attack. Tempers were pushed to breaking point: men argued with men, women snapped at each other, and tolerance towards misbehaving children was at a low point. Not only were conditions difficult and uncomfortable, but the awareness of the thousands of warring Matabele on the outskirts of town also made sleeping very difficult for everyone.

As the town entered its third week of the siege and the population grumbled at having their day constantly threatened with violence, the Langbournes sat in the dirt in the shade of the east wall of the makeshift hospital. David spotted Captain Dent standing on top of a wagon wheel peering through his telescope down Main Street. He touched Morris lightly on his shoulder and nodded at Grant.

"I'm just popping over to Grant to have a chat. Back in a minute," he grunted as he stood up. Morris nodded his approval.

Grant was a very tall man, and standing on top of the wagon wheel in his BSAC tunic and slouch hat with a rifle slung over his shoulder he presented an impressive sight, catching the eye of almost every woman in the settlement. Even gentlemen gravitated towards him believing he was their best hope for repelling a close hand-to-hand skirmish.

"Seen any elephants today?" David joked.

"David," Grant looked down towards his ankles, "good to see you."

"Would you like some company?"

"Absolutely, grab a wheel," Dent returned the humour.

David stepped over to the rear wagon wheel and hauled himself up with ease, briefly enjoying the view of Main Street that the extra height afforded him.

"Any idea when the reinforcements are coming?" David asked without looking at his long-time friend.

"I do know they are on their way, but they are being forced to fight to get here. There's a full-scale war going on out there."

"How long can we hold out? How are our supplies of ammunition?"

Grant lowered his telescope and looked directly at David. There was a look of serious concern on his face. Before he replied, he glanced behind him to check that no one was in earshot, which made David realise his answer was not going to be encouraging.

"Not good, I'm afraid. In fact, more than serious," he admitted in hushed tones.

"How long have we got?"

"A couple of weeks, at best," Grant sighed. He did not mind talking openly to David; their friendship was strong. "The Field Force is out there every day, as you know." He was referring to the constant and lengthy battles from which rifle, cannon and machine-gun fire could be heard in the distance. "The good news is that Rudge and the boys are constantly making plans and working on the situation. I take my hat off to Rudge, he's very astute. Further good news is that Cecil Rhodes himself is on his way here with a contingent from Fort Salisbury."

David was impressed. "How do you know that?" he asked.

"Telegram, yesterday. He's coming with your friend, Bob," Grant grinned and then resumed his vigilance of the street.

"Bob? Major Baden-Powell?"

"The very one," Grant was smiling as his telescope scanned the far side of Bulawayo.

David went silent for a while as he thought this through. "Are you telling me that the Matabele have not cut the telegraph wires yet?"

"Well, that took you long enough to work out," Grant chuckled and lowered his telescope. "Indeed, we still have communication with the outside world, and that, my dear friend, is our saving grace. Think about it, it seems as though the Matabele actually don't know what the wires are used for."

"Well, I'll be...." David marvelled.

"There's something else we can't figure out. Bulawayo is totally surrounded, except for the way out through the Mangwe Pass to the south, back to Mafeking."

"I know the Mangwe Pass. Why would the Matabele leave us a way out? Surely they would have cut off our escape. That's the first thing I would have done, if I were in their position."

"Indeed. We have absolutely no idea why. We think it's a trap.

Selous, he's that chap with the big white beard, is an incredible scout and has found that the Mangwe Pass is not guarded at all, and this has got us all worried. We are not even going to attempt it – something is just not right. It's too easy for us to escape. We are beginning to think these people have given this siege a lot of thought."

"Seems to me as if the Mangwe Pass is a trap I must admit," David scratched his head. "It's perfect for an ambush. This seems most odd."

"Sadly, the big boys don't think there are any more European survivors out there. It looks as if we are the last ones left in Matabeleland, and we'll soon be out of food, medicine and bullets. The situation, I must be honest, is pretty desperate. We've lost a lot of men, and, as you know, the hospital is overflowing. We are losing horses, too."

David stayed with his friend for another twenty minutes, giving him some silent moral support as they both stared into the distance, seeking the elusive enemy. After leaving Grant, he re-joined his family, filling them in on what he had learned.

"I really hope the reinforcements get here soon," Morris complained. "The Matabele are playing this war very well. Not only are they physically wearing us down and picking us off bit by bit, they must know we are running out of ammunition."

"And they are starving us," Louis added. "I am so hungry I could fold in half."

"I didn't know a man could get so hungry," Harry moaned.

"We felt hunger in Ireland, didn't we, Morris?" David frowned sadly. "Here, drink some more water," David handed Harry a metal container with a fat cork stopper in the neck, "it will help with the hunger pangs."

Morris looked at his three brothers. They were painfully thin, dirty and scared. He knew that they were in Africa because of him, and therefore found themselves in the midst of a war. It was because of his decisions that they were all sitting in the dirt, starved, miserable, and waiting for the inevitable invasion of tens of thousands of men with broad-bladed spears, hell-bent on brutally killing each and every one of them without an iota of compassion. He blamed himself for this, and vowed that, if they survived the conflict, he would never allow any his family to witness a war again.

Ever.

*

It had been six weeks since the siege began, and morale was extremely low. Louis had developed a fever and was finding it hard to run between the shop and the laager whenever the alarm sounded. The warning was going off three times a day, on average, so some days Louis just remained within the laager resting in the shade of the hospital building so that he did not need to exert himself. David used all his charm to try to get medication for his younger brother from the nurses, but there was none. All three brothers would give a portion of their food ration to Louis, and this did seem to help his general wellbeing.

One morning, as the population came running into the protection of the laager to the sound of the bell clanging overhead, David was holding a thin branch from a tree. It had been roughly broken off at one end, and at the other there was a fork that also has its ends roughly broken off. The straight thin branch had a young leaf or two that had begun to sprout.

"What's that for?" Harry asked inquisitively as the four brothers sat on the ground in a patch of shade.

"I'm going to whittle a staff for myself," David grinned and pulled out the razor-sharp pocket knife that Major Bob had given him on that same evening that he had given Bob a brass compass.

"Let's see that knife," Louis demanded, thrusting his hand out, "Where did you get it?"

"My friend, Major Bob, gave it to me in return for a telescope

I gave him," David opened the shiny and impressive knife and passed it to his brother. "Be careful, the blade is as sharp as a razor."

"How are you going to make a staff out of that branch?" Harry chuckled. "A staff has a large hook on the end that shepherds use for catching sheep around their necks. You can't bend that stick!"

"In England and Ireland you might use it to catch sheep and pull them closer, I understand that, but here in Africa," David cocked an eyebrow and grinned, "you want to keep animals away from you. It is the opposite here. You see this fork," he flipped the branch over and picked a leaf off the stem, "I'm going to trim this down and it will be the top of the staff. I can pin snakes down with the fork, and if an ostrich attacks me, all I have to do is put the fork on its neck and hold it away from me until it breaks off its attack."

"Ostriches are birds, David. How can they be dangerous?" Louis looked surprised.

"Let me tell *you* a story," Morris laughed.

"Not now, Morris," David said seriously, then began to chuckle. "Please hand me that knife, Giraffe."

As David whittled his custom-designed staff, Morris related the story of the ostrich attack that left David battered and bruised. He enjoyed embellishing the incident, making light fun of his brother, much to the amusement of Louis and Harry. David just smiled as his brothers had some fun at his expense.

"And, where were you, Morris?" David laughed when Morris had finished telling the tale, and looked at his younger brothers. "No wait, I'll tell you. He was kicked into a thorn bush by the bird, so hard I had to cut him out of the bush with a knife!"

It was rare for the boys to enjoy a good laugh together, so they just let it flow and continued the banter for the duration of the morning's siege. After two days, David had completed whittling his staff, and, to finish it off, he found a long piece of dirty twine that was being utilised to prop up a flimsy shrub, and wove an intricate knot about three quarters of the way up the shaft, to be used as a handgrip. He passed the finished item around and his brothers genuinely admired his craftsmanship.

"If I were you," Harry turned the shaft over in his hands and felt its balance, "I would carve my initials on the bottom of the stick so that, wherever you go, people tracking you will know it's you."

David glared at Harry with some confusion, trying to find a response, then looked at Morris and cocked an eyebrow.

"Good idea," Morris shrugged.

"Give me that staff," David smiled as he pulled his knife out of his pocket.

*

Soon after the laager had calmed down after yet another concerted attack, Captain Dent happened to walk past the four brothers as they were sitting propped up against the rear wall of a brick building. He noticed David, who appeared to be dozing with his brothers. All four had their eyes closed, and Captain Dent wandered over, crouching down on one knee as he greeted them.

"Rough night?" he grinned as he gently tapped David on the sole of his shoe.

"Greetings, Grant," he smiled as he opened one eye, then the other, "yes, a bit tired of sleeping in the Market Square Garden Hotel," he joked tiredly.

"Morning Grant," Morris sat up and stretched his arm out to shake his hand, "You've met my younger brothers, have you?"

"Not formally, no," he shook their hands, stretching across David. "I thought I might update you on a bit of news."

"Oh, lovely," David shuffled into a sitting position, "I hope it's good."

"It's a bit of good and bad I'm afraid; the bad news is that the Bulawayo Field Force is down to two days of ammunition. After that, they start taking my ammunition from the laager defences, which will buy them another day, that's all."

David was genuinely concerned. "You had better get to the good news fast, Grant, because that doesn't sound encouraging at all."

"Indeed, it is troubling, but, last night when the Field Force came back, they said they heard artillery to the north. They think that Rhodes' relief force are fighting their way through and are almost here."

"Good show," Louis said drearily, causing everyone to stare at him in surprise.

"Yes, good show, and just in time, because really, we are at the end now," Grant stood up and they could see that his knees were troubling him.

David and Morris also stood up, but – because they were so weak from lack of sufficient food they needed to roll onto all fours before they could stand, Morris using the wall for extra support and grunting in the process.

"How soon before they get here?" Morris asked.

"If it is them," Grant cautioned, "it depends on what resistance they encounter on the way and how far away they actually are. We estimate two to three days."

"That is taking it a bit close, don't you think?"

Grant shrugged, "it is, I must admit, but those fellows in there," he nodded at the building, "are doing the best they can. I would say their military strategy, their plan of attack, is about to change to help Rhodes get here as soon as possible."

"Thanks, Grant," David smiled weakly, "I know you didn't need to tell us that, but we really appreciate it."

"No problem my friend," Grant grinned as he turned to leave, "if I hear any more I'll let you know."

Morris and David slowly lowered themselves to the ground again, wrapping their arms around their knees. They sat in silence for a moment.

"We'll be okay," David reassured his younger brothers who were looking at him expectantly. "Not long now."

"Look," Morris nodded towards the gate of the Market Square enclosure, "there's Herbert Bachmayer from the Post Office with a piece of paper in his hand. Do you think he's looking for us?"

"Could be," Harry mumbled. "Do you want me to go over and say 'hello'?"

Just then Herbert seemed to spot the brothers sitting in the shade and began walking over to them. David raised a hand in greeting and Herbert responded similarly.

"Relax, Harry," Morris mumbled, "he's seen us."

"Greetings Mr Bachmayer," David called out without shifting from his sitting position. "Please, take a seat," he said, indicating a spot in the dust in front of him, and chuckling gently at his own humour.

"Thanks Mr David," Herbert smiled, but only dropped to his haunches, preferring to keep his trousers free of dust. "Morning, Messrs Langbourne," he nodded genially at the brothers.

"So, what brings you to our office this morning, Mr Bachmayer?" Morris smiled, continuing with the dry humour. Being confined to a laager that was under constant threat, humour of any sort was given and accepted readily by the citizens. For Morris to show some light-heartedness, however, was particularly surprising to his brothers since he rarely joked in front of others. Yet Herbert was particularly pleased, because the last time he had seen him, Morris had been abrupt, to the point of being rude.

"I have a telegram, Mr Morris," he announced, flashing a smile and handing a mustard-coloured envelope over to him, "from Mr Abe Kaufman, in Mafeking."

"Thank you," Morris said politely and in one fluid motion extracted the coarse postal paper from the envelope. He unfolded the paper, flipped it right-way-up, and read the contents quickly, 'ADVISE MORRIS NO STOCK AVAILABLE'. He then folded the telegram and put it in his shirt pocket.

"Smoke," Morris said to Herbert with a mischievous grin,

deliberately confusing the hapless telegraph master and sending a one-worded message to his brothers.

David looked at Morris sideways; he and his brothers knew exactly what Morris was saying, and it was that David would have to search for smoke, if they wanted any chance of finding their wagons.

"I'm afraid I don't smoke, but thank you," Herbert smiled his appreciation at Morris. "Well, I must be off, gentlemen. The telegraph wires are burning red-hot right now, as you can well imagine."

The Langbournes thanked Herbert for delivering the telegram and wished him a pleasant day. As he disappeared into the milling crowd, the boys sat in silence, contemplating how the telegram from Abe would affect their future, or if indeed the wagons would ever be found now that Daluxolo and Nguni were more than likely staying with the wagons, or, for that matter, if the Matabele hadn't already found and looted them, killing the two men in the process.

Harry broke the silence with a soft chuckle, which escalated into a gentle laugh. Louis began to join him, and very shortly all four boys were laughing together.

"What's so funny, Harry?" Morris quipped, knowing quite well what the joke was about.

"I'm sorry, I don't smoke," and Harry exploded with laughter, causing the close-knit family to follow suit, much to the amusement of many men and women nearby. It later intrigued David that, despite the fact that the family had been half-starved and very close to a brutal death, or that – if they had survived, they would have been on the brink of a massive bankruptcy – they had managed still to find some laughter in their lives. Indeed, since that incident, he noticed that many citizens would find time to laugh about their dire situation. Mankind, he thought, was an unusual lot.

*

Captain Dent had been right. The relief force from Mashonaland in the north had been only two days away, and the sound of gunfire and artillery had become more evident as they had fought their way into Bulawayo. The spirits of the citizens of Bulawayo had begun to lift, and the Field Force had turned their attention to cutting a route open to assist the advance.

When the relieving force had broken through, finally, there was much cheering and jubilation as they rode into the safety of the laager. Seven hundred rescuers had arrived with food, medicine, and ammunition, led by the famous Cecil John Rhodes himself, the man the new country was named after. Riding next to him was his commander and chief scout, Major Robert Baden-Powell. As they rode past the smiling faces of the welcoming citizens, Bob, as David knew him, recognised and pointed directly at him, acknowledging David's presence. David grinned back.

The protection of the laager was immediately strengthened, and the commanders of the relief column inspected the defences that had been put in place. They were in awe at how effective the improvised fortifications had been, and how much had been achieved by so few against so many.

The following day, distant artillery fire had been heard just to the southeast of the Matopos Hills, and a cheer went up in the laager when the population realised that the relief force from Kimberley and Mafeking were on their doorstep. Because the Matabele commanded such a powerful stronghold in that area, however, it would take another four full days before the southern force broke through, even with the help of the northern force. The relief force strengthened the embattled town with a further 600 soldiers, more food, vital medicine and armaments.

With some confidence restored, the two military contingents having briefly rested before being fed and fresh battle plans having been devised, they wasted no time in going on the offensive yet again with daylight attacks beginning in earnest in order to break the Matabele's resolve. Each day, the men would thunder out on their horses, and each night they would return, all weary and many soldiers bloodied and wounded. As was expected, each day meant more lives lost on both sides. Horses were not immune from the violence either, many being killed in action or returning badly wounded, unable to fight another day.

Like the AmaZulu of the southeast from whose ranks they had broken away, the Matabele had a particular style of fighting: a style that the Europeans found very difficult to challenge. They would form up in the shape of the horns of a bull, the *boss* in the middle where the horns met, charging at the enemy head on, with the left and right horns flanking the main battle area and curling in on the fighting, almost surrounding the hapless attackers. Those who became caught in the horns of the bull learnt very quickly that they were about to die. Undaunted, and with heavy losses, the BSAC continued their assaults on the Matabele, but because of their sheer numbers, it seemed an end to the fighting was a long way off. The M'Limo sent word to the Mashona in the north to come to Matabeleland and help them defeat the settlers, offering in return that, when they had won the war, they would go north to help rid Mashonaland of their settlers. The Mashona answered the call and the Matabele numbers swelled. The Matabele began a tactic of sniping with their numerous Martini-Henrys, and the BSAC responded with seven-pound Hotchkiss cannons and Maxim machine guns. The war was ferocious and deadly.

Intelligence reached the BSAC command that the M'Limo himself was inciting the aggression, preaching prophecies of their victory and promising ancestral and spiritual intervention, and it was thought that his capture might be the key to the end of the war. As it happened, the BSAC commanding officers soon received a tip-off as to where the M'Limo's sacred cave was located in the Matopos Hills, and two scouts were sent out at night to find him, skittering undetected through the dense bush, before hiding in the cave to await the spiritual leader's arrival. The intended capture, however, soon turned into an assassination when the M'Limo was shot dead in the cave after which the two scouts found themselves desperately fleeing for the safety of the Bulawayo laager. With the loss of their leader, the Matabele quickly became disillusioned and disorganised. They realised that not only were the European bullets not turning into water, but cannon shells also were not turning into eggs, and they knew they were in trouble.

Overnight, the Matabele offensive became defensive, and around 50,000 men, women, and children hurriedly retreated behind the gigantic granite boulders of the vast Matopos, while others went north towards Mashonaland. As in the days before the M'Limo, the chiefs took back command of their people and although the siege of Bulawayo might have been suddenly over, the bloody and violent war continued.

CHAPTER FOURTEEN
Negotiations

WITH THE SIEGE of Bulawayo now broken, and the fighting contained in the Matopos Hills just twenty miles away, the population of the town was finally able to move around freely and to go about their daily routines, although a keen ear was always trained on the Market Square alarm. It became a war of attrition; the Matabele had the numbers, vast numbers, but the BSAC had the weaponry and training. The ratio of men killed or maimed on both sides was staggering, especially when ratios of casualties in wars before this one were compared.

Life in Rhodesia was not easy. Persistent drought put the population on the edge of hunger; the beef industry had been decimated by the *rinderpest* plague, and the knock-on effect of the *rinderpest* meant that the transport of goods from the Boer republics and British colonies further south was at a virtual standstill. Mules could be used in wagon transport, but – since they were nowhere near as powerful as the mighty oxen – more animals were needed to pull less weight, and a good two-thirds of a wagon had to be filled with food just for the mules. Because the goods carted up from Mafeking became so very expensive, the cost had to be passed on to the consumers, making even the most basic commodities extremely costly and therefore practically unaffordable.

Five days had passed since the siege had been lifted, and for the Langbourne brothers only one small sale had been conducted from their store over the entire period. As the evening drew its cloak over the settlement, Louis closed the doors to the warehouse as a patrol of BSAC troopers came thundering into town on their horses after yet another bloody and terrifying day in the Matopos Hills.

"When you have locked the doors, come down to the back," Morris called to Louis from the makeshift office.

As the youngest brother entered the office, he found Morris sitting behind his desk, and David opposite, perched on the only other chair they owned. Harry was sitting on a wooden crate. The small wooden box that Louis used as a seat was a little low for him, which had the effect of pulling his already short trousers even higher up his ankles and exposing his white socks to the point where his skin was now clearly visible.

Morris addressed the miserable faces of his brothers. "We have a really big problem on our hands. Unless we do something, we may have to close the business and then we will be literally on the street."

"What can we do?" Louis moaned as two seven-pounders rumbled in the distance. He pointed his thumb over his shoulder in the direction of the Hotchkiss cannons, "Who wants to spend money when all that is going on?"

"I agree," said Morris, "if we had a store that sold food then we would be doing great business."

"Well, we don't," Harry interjected.

"Yes, I know. There's very little food to buy." Morris picked up a pencil and opened his ledger. "Unfortunately, the bank is going to take action against us very shortly, but I have spoken to the manager and he feels that, under these circumstances, which he agrees are most unusual and very much not of our doing, he might be able to give us some grace."

"How much grace?" David asked curiously.

"Two months, depending on what Cape Town says. He has written off to them seeking authority."

"Have you told him about the wagons?" David cocked an eyebrow, wondering what the response would be.

Morris sighed, "Yes, and no."

"Huh?" David exclaimed with a curious smile. "Explain that one, please."

Morris wanted to smile back, but the seriousness of the situation prevented him from doing so. "It doesn't take a professor to work out that our oxen must have been stricken by the *rinderpest,* so I was honest and told him that all our oxen died and our wagons are stranded."

"And?" David prompted.

"I didn't mention that we had no idea where they were."

"Morris!" David stood up and walked to the wall, leaning against it as he shook his head from side to side. "You are sailing very close to the wind, brother. That's misleading," David scolded.

"So he thinks we know where they are?" Harry asked.

"He didn't ask, so I didn't tell him," Morris defended himself.

"I have to go and find them," David mumbled, then pushed himself off the wall to resume his seat. "I'll leave tomorrow."

"No," Morris was quick to object, "it's still too dangerous out there. I know the fighting is confined to the hills, and north of us, but we don't know what's to the south. Even the Zeederberg coach has an armed escort when it travels between here and Mafeking. Our problem is Weil. I need to go down there and speak to him personally. If we default with Weil, our entire reputation will be in tatters with every trader on the continent."

Louis frowned. "I thought the bank would have been more of a worry," he murmured.

Morris leaned back in his chair and took a deep breath. "The way I look at it," he replied, "we owe the bank a ton of money. If we have to tell them we have lost the wagons, they would be crazy to let the word out because they, as well as we, will run the risk of losing our stock to looters. If that happens, they will never see their money again. They have as much to lose as we do, and, besides, they have a professional responsibility to keep this confidential. Weil, on the other hand, will panic if he finds out and will start talking to his friends, trying to find a way to recover his money, but – if I personally go and talk to him – I am sure he will understand our predicament and give us time to try to sort this out. I have a close connection with Weil. He's a Jew, so I feel if he knows we are also Jews, he will be a little more sympathetic."

"Doesn't he know we are Jews?" Louis asked.

"No, I have never told him. I'm too nervous to tell anyone."

"He knows, Morris," David sighed, "he knows."

"You never knew *he* was a Jew," Morris looked at David in surprise.

"True," David shrugged, "so, what's your plan?"

"I will leave tomorrow on the Zeederberg Coach for Mafeking. I'll have a man-to-man discussion with Weil. If it goes well, then we will have some time to work this mess out. If not, we may soon be on our way back to Ireland."

"We won't have a penny between us to buy a ticket back home," David scowled. "Our home will be the streets of this god-forsaken town."

Morris glared at his brother. "All the more reason to get it right," he snorted.

Having ended the meeting with that statement, Morris left for Mafeking on the following day.

*

Morris greeted his friend nervously as he poked his head around the office door.

"Good morning, Julian!" he said, pretending a little cheer.

"Good grief!" Julian Weil exclaimed as he looked up from the copious ledgers and cashbooks that lay scattered about his desk.

"Morris!" he exclaimed again and stood up, skirting his desk in one fluid motion, despite his portly stature.

"Good to see you again, Julian, believe me," there was genuine feeling in Morris' statement.

"What happened up there, in Rhodesia? The news here is awful. Are you alright? And your brothers, are they safe?"

"Yes, yes, we are all well. Hungry, but well. Let's get some tea down at the hotel, Julian, I have much to tell you."

"Indeed, let's go now," he whisked his jacket off a peg on the wall and took Morris by the shoulder, leading him out of the building, "but we will have a good meal, not just tea. Come, come...."

*

Morris pushed his empty plate back slightly and dabbed his lips with a crisp, white serviette. "So, Julian," he continued, "I told Daluxolo to go back to the wagons immediately. Sadly, we simply cannot tell when conditions up north will allow us to retrieve them."

Julian shook his head gently, staring at a painting on the wall that was slightly crooked. "Well,' he sighed, "it's a very unfortunate situation, Morris. I completely understand your predicament."

"Who would have thought there was a disease in this world that killed oxen in hours? I certainly didn't. At first I thought Daluxolo was possessed by one of their traditional evil spirits; it made no sense to me whatsoever. We had valuable wagons abandoned in the bush and the only man who could protect them was cowering at my feet, thinking Lobengula's ghost was going to curse him. Then Dr Jameson...."

"Oh, what a fiasco that is!" Julian cut in. "An idiot extraordinaire. Whatever possessed him to try and take on the Boers in the Transvaal? Now he languishes in a prison somewhere with all his surviving men. And worse, he has triggered diplomatic hatred between the Boers and the British again. Can you imagine if there is another Anglo-Boer War! Heaven forbid."

"Indeed," Morris shook his head, "and if that wasn't enough,

Jameson also triggered the Matabele war. Terrible, terrible stuff that. It's still going on."

The conversation went on for over two hours. Julian Weil insisted Morris stay with him until his wife could at least fatten him up a little, an invitation that Morris accepted with polite hesitation and heartfelt gratitude. If Morris had been honest, he would have said that he was unable to afford a room at the lodging down the road, but Julian understood that Morris' situation had not arisen through any fault of his own, so he gave him the break he needed.

"Morris, I have done business with you for a long time now and you and your family have conducted your affairs very honourably with me. If you can pay me the interest on the outstanding balance, I will extend your credit for a full year."

Since Morris had never expected Julian to be so generous, he had not anticipated an outcome this good, and it made him determined that Julian's would be the very first debt he would pay back, well ahead of the bank's.

Over the three weeks that Morris resided at the Weil's home, he helped Julian to better understand his books and to implement some new procedures that were aimed at keeping a tighter control over his cash flows and inventories. He also convinced him to employ a bookkeeper in order to keep his records both current and accurate.

"You have twelve companies throughout the colonies, Julian. You can't keep your books in order and run your businesses alone at the same time," Morris scolded politely. "You need someone who understands numbers to report to you every day. Bookkeeping is the rudder of your ship. Without your rudder, you have no way of knowing which direction your business is going. You also become limited in your business decisions, too."

"I can manage, Morris," Julian objected with his hands in the air. "In any event, I don't trust anyone but myself.

"Remember your bank manager, Mr Savage?"

"Of course, a good friend of mine. Unfortunately he took ill and returned to England."

"Oh, he was a good friend of yours, of that I can assure you," Morris smirked sarcastically. "Let me show you something. You see this deposit?" Morris flipped back several pages of Julian's ledger for the Mafeking branch of his business, and ran a finger down one column, "This date here?" he pointed to some numbers written in blue ink.

"Yes, my takings for that day. What about it?"

"I would guess," Morris said, scratching his head and staring wistfully out the window, "if you went down to the bank and asked to see their record for *this* deposit on *this* date, it might be about, let's see, eight shillings and tuppence short of what you think."

Julian immediately pushed himself back in the chair that squeaked angrily under his weight. "How can you tell by looking at that?" he demanded, a look of total confusion on his face.

"I'm good with numbers, Julian. You know that," Morris smiled.

"What about the next day?" he looked horrified.

"Ah, Julian, it is not right for me to look at your business records. You really need a confidential bookkeeper you can trust."

When Morris left Mafeking the following day on the Zeederberg Coach Line, Weil had extended his credit indefinitely. As for the interest charges, well, they were dropped too.

*

David slapped his brother on the shoulder. "Congratulations, Morris! You surely have gotten us out of a very tight corner."

"We owe a lot to Julian, and not just financially," was the honest reply.

The discussion that afternoon in the office of Langbourne Brothers was much more flippant and jovial, but it quickly, and inevitably, turned back to the war that was raging in the vicinity. Throughout the day, the burst of intermittent machine-gun fire could be heard between the low rumble of the Hotchkiss cannons, and on the occasional morning, the faint but foul stench of sulphur from the black-powder rifles would waft through the town.

David had met his good friend Bob, or Major B-P, as he was known around the settlement, and they ended up enjoying a cup of unsweetened black coffee down at the Officers' Mess, since sugar was completely unavailable in Bulawayo. David had later reported on the discussion to his brothers.

Although Major B-P believed that all the fighting had been contained in the Matopos Hills, a threat had emerged up north in Mashonaland, where a contingent of escaping Matabele warriors had incited the Mashona to rise up and join their cause. Because most of the BSAC were busy fighting the Matabele, moreover, few BSAC troops were to been seen in the north, so the Mashona had seized the opportunity to join the fighting, and this had made conditions very difficult for the BSAC. Settlers, including police-men in remote outposts, were in grave danger, and further lives were being lost on all sides every day.

In the south of the country, it seemed as though Mr Rhodes was looking at the Matabele situation not so much from a military, but rather from a political point of view. He had sent some scouts into the hills to determine if the Matabele chiefs would be willing to talk about peace, because this war was not doing either side any good.

"How are they going to do that?" Morris asked with some sarcasm.

"Quite clever, it seems. The scout they sent out took two flags with him, one red, and the other white. They gave both flags to one of the Matabele warriors they had captured with instructions to give to their commander-in-chief. If the Matabele wished to continue fighting, they were to place the red flag on top of one of the rocky hills, and, if not, they were to display the white flag instead."

"And?" Morris asked.

"That happened yesterday, so I have no idea what the outcome will be. We will find out soon enough, I'm sure."

"I wish they would hurry up," Harry moaned, "food is scarce, and people are not spending money."

"Once peace has been restored, everything will return to normal," David said calmly, "and on that note, I'm going to prepare for another trip south to find those wagons."

"It's not safe," Morris instantly objected, "I won't allow it."

"I agree, but if the Matabele show that white flag I think the war will stop almost immediately, and I want to be ready to go. I have spoken to Abe to see if he would come with me. He insists, actually, which will allow you three to run the business while I am away."

A heated discussion ensued among the four brothers, all opposing David's decision. In the end, David agreed that he would go out only if Major Bob were comfortable that the hostilities had actually ceased. Firmly believing they would, David began his preparations immediately.

His first plan was to find Major Bob and ask him to draw up a map of Matabeleland between the Limpopo and Bulawayo, and pencil in the rivers and mountains as best he could. It turned out to be a most remarkable experience as Bob was a proficient artist and spent many hours sketching in a book that he often carried with him, which he now proudly showed to David. He had sketches of Ndebele warriors in full wardress and of their homesteads, and further intricate drawings of some of the Matopos Hills. He also had a rough drawing of Mafeking, with its more important features, such as the cemetery and where the railway station was, and of course many of the nameless streets. He had sketches of trees, wildlife, and a few birds, and David could not help but marvel at Bob's talent.

They visited Captain Bailey, who appeared swamped with paperwork, and secured from him, albeit with a little resistance, an obsolete plan of a building, the construction of which had been abandoned. The back of the plan was clean, and on this was going to be drafted the map that David so desperately wanted. Armed with a sharpened pencil, Bob spread the old plan face down on a large desk, and began to trace out the Limpopo River at the bottom of the back page, while scribbling a number of black dots and circles at the top.

"These," he exclaimed, as he wrote two words at the top on the dots, "are the Matopos Hills. We are here." He inserted an X just below the hills.

From there he deftly sketched in rivers and hills, adding a number of Matabele villages in the form of crude symbols for a hut. Some of the villages he named after their chiefs whom he had personally visited on his various forays into the bush. He drew in the occasional waterhole that he could remember stopping at, and sometimes he recalled a story of some exciting event that had happened at a certain place.

As the map evolved, it seemed to come to life in the eyes of the two unlikely friends. David took the pencil off Bob at one point and added in a few depictions based on his own personal recollections, inserting them in the approximate vicinity he thought they had occurred. The map was by no means accurate, being based solely on the two men's memories, but to Bob and David, it took on a life of its own and captured a thousand memories in a series of simple squiggles, lines, dots, and circles.

The two spent several hours building their map, and only stopped when it became so dark that they could no longer see their work without lighting a candle. In the bottom left-hand corner of the sheet of paper was a sketch resembling a leopard's footprint. To any onlooker, it would look just like that, a leopard's footprint, but it held a secret code for Bob and David, a code that neither of them would ever share with anyone else.

*

The white flag duly appeared at the peak of a granite outcrop and flapped lazily in the gentle breeze. Hearing the news, Mr Rhodes himself rode out to the base of the goliath rock and, in the midst of vehement objections from the officers who accompanied him, he disarmed himself and walked out, alone, onto the open plain, vulnerable, and in full view of the enemy, simply wearing a day suit, a grey tie, and black leather shoes. Finding an anthill almost as tall as himself protruding from the hard earth, he sat upon it and waited, staring at the formidable, but most spectacular, Matopos Hills for the next hour.

Nervously, and very suspiciously, several tribal elders walked out from between the rocks in single file and approached him. Formal introductions were made, and one of the leaders among the elders spoke for almost two hours, relating the history, trials, and tribulations of the Matabele people, going back over nearly two hundred years to the rise of the amaZulu King Shaka, through to the breakaway General Mzilikazi and his successor, Lobengula. Listening patiently, Mr Rhodes was touched by their plight and, as a result, a preliminary peace accord was struck with further negotiations planned to take place at the anthill on a later date in order to formally end the war.

*

On the following day Abe Kaufman and David Langbourne left the town of Bulawayo on a secret mission to find the lost wagons.

CHAPTER FIFTEEN
The Search

A LAST HOUR OF sunlight lay ahead of them when David and Abe pulled their horses to a halt under a sturdy Mopane tree. They sat quietly in their saddles, scanning the African bush for predators, a routine they had followed since the trip had begun, since a customary caution had become second nature to them both.

"I'll climb this tree," Abe offered.

"Good show," David agreed and dismounted.

Having followed suit, Abe tethered his solid horse to a smaller tree, and began to search for suitable footholds in the dark, furrowed bark of the first one. After securing his horse to a green shrub, David pulled out his map from its improvised leather scabbard and unrolled it on the ground. He then pulled the brass compass from his pocket and placed it on the map, pausing for the needle to stop swinging from side to side and to find its magnetic north. When he was happy that the map was perfectly orientated, he weighed the corners of the map down with stones that were scattered around him, before looking up into the canopy of the tree.

"I'm set, Abe," he called out. "What have you got?"

"Almost there," Abe grunted as he hauled himself up another branch.

"Stop!" David said suddenly, a ghastly sense of urgency in that single word, and Abe froze instantly, barely breathing. "There's a thin grey snake just above your head. Come down slowly."

By the time David had finished the word 'slowly', Abe was already on the ground. He looked terrified, staring into the tree-top, looking for the reptile and unconsciously wiping imaginary snakes off his shoulders and arms. David couldn't contain himself and rocked back, rolling on the ground in fits of laughter.

"I hate snakes," Abe almost spat. "Next time I climb a tree I'm going to set it alight first!"

When David had finally composed himself he apologised for his lack of compassion and assured Abe that no harm would have come to him. What he didn't tell Abe was that the snake appeared to be cornered in the canopy and had begun to recoil, which didn't bode well.

"Just as we check the bush before we dismount, I think we should check the trees before we climb them," David chuckled.

"Absolutely," Abe concurred, "now let's move to another tree, but this time you can climb it."

Each evening, an hour before sunset, one of the pair would climb a tree while the other would lay the map on the ground underneath and orientate it to face north. The man in the tree would then search for signs of smoke and point to them, calling out its approximate distance. By working out where they stood at the time, based on where they had been in the morning, they found that they were beginning to accurately map out where several villages were.

The mapping of various rivers, mountains, and other landmarks that David and Major Bob had originally sketched on the map, however, had not been quite as accurate as David had hoped. Another tactic that David and Abe used was to mark out one or more of the smoke plumes of a village they had passed earlier that day. This gave them some comfort that where they thought they were, was indeed correct, thus making David and Abe feel more confident that they were on the right track. They would then pencil in the location of a column of smoke on the map, and record those plumes they had already visited, thereby eliminating the chance of searching the same place twice. All these search tactics had been carefully explained to them by Phil Innes, and seemed to be working well.

Although, after six weeks of searching, David was beginning to give up hope, each evening brought the addition of new smoke plumes to their map, bringing with it a fresh breeze of enthusiasm and a quiet conviction that the next day would reveal the jackpot. Averaging two or three villages per day, some would invite them to share a meal or a pot of traditional beer, while others would be very suspicious – some to the point of open hostility – in which case the two would beat a hasty retreat. David's biggest worry was that he was keeping Abe from his wife, and felt they should return, but Abe would have none of it, insisting that he was enjoying the adventure, and learning a great deal about the African bush and its inhabitants. Abe also owed his life to David, and felt that by helping his friend he would be able in some small way to express his gratitude, because he believed he would always be in David's debt.

"We'll find your wagons, David," Abe assured his friend as he lay on his blanket, head propped against a tree. The fire was dying down and it was a very dark night.

"I like the prospect of that new smoke column to the southeast. We didn't see it at first light," David smiled, his eyes starting to droop.

"Yes, promising I would say. We will check it again in the morning. If it's there, I think that should be our first port of call."

"Good idea," David mumbled, and gratefully fell asleep.

The following morning the smoke trail in question was still visible in the distance, and, with renewed excitement, the two set off. It took seven hours to get there, and when they arrived all they found were cold ashes from a cooking fire, with a set of wagon wheel tracks leading from it.

"New migrants, I would say," Abe sighed dismally.

"Yes, on their way to Bulawayo, it seems," David agreed. "A young family of four."

"Show me how you see that," Abe was inquisitive and never questioned David's ability to read bush signs.

""See here," he got down on his haunches and picked up a stick, pointing to a mark on the ground, "this is a print from the shoe of a small child, probably about five or six years old. Here's another, slightly bigger. The toe is slightly more pointed, so I would say a girl," he looked up at Abe with a knowing smile.

"What about this?" Abe waved his hand at a patch of grass that had been flattened.

"Oh, that's obvious," David looked concerned, "that's where a heavy-set man wrestled with two lions."

"What?!" Abe exclaimed, shocked at the revelation, hunting the ground for signs that might explain the event.

"I'm joking, Abe," David laughed, "it's just where someone slept in his blanket last night. Sorry, I couldn't resist that," he continued to laugh.

Abe grunted his displeasure, but took the humour in good spirits. "Well, that was a waste of time. It would have been nice if they had spent another night here. It would be good to catch up on some news from Mafeking, and send word to Sharon and your brothers that we are still alive and well."

"Yes," David agreed. He was beginning to feel very isolated from the real world, and he missed his brothers and the hustle-bustle of civilised life. "What say you that we start heading back to Bulawayo and give this lark a break?"

"Hmm…." Abe pondered, "It's up to you David, although I must admit I'm ready to go back."

"Then it is agreed. I suggest we head west about twenty

miles, then turn north and head home, that way we won't pass the same villages."

"My thoughts exactly," Abe smiled.

Although some disappointment hung over the men, they also felt a sense of excitement that they would soon be home and in the company of those they loved. David estimated they would take about ten days to get back if they traversed a general line north. They knew they would constantly see smoke plumes along the way,, but agreed that once they were at their furthest point west, they would only investigate smoke to the north and east of them. In David's mind, his wagons could never be any further west than they were already: it was simply too far off the beaten track.

*

It was an exceptionally warm afternoon at the beginning of October, three days after the decision had been taken to return home. The men had been searching for over six weeks without the slightest sign of the wagons having materialised. As they walked their horses down a gentle slope, they noticed that the base of the meandering valley was lined with green vegetation and trees. It was a sight that was common, indicating that there was a river in the valley, and usually meant that water could be found for their horses and to refill their partially empty water canisters. As always, the men scanned the distant horizons for something that might lead them to the wagons, but, as always, there was nothing obvious.

"I think there's flowing water in that river," Abe commented. "Look how deep the line of vegetation is. You see that range of hills to the west?" he pointed off to his left, "I would guess the river flows all year round from that catchment area."

"I would never have noticed," David covered his eyes and looked over at the distant mountainous region.

Abe was right: a thin stream of crystal clear water ran through the bottom of the shallow valley. The vegetation was luscious and green, providing ample shade and a cool breeze that felt soothing and comforting on the men's skin. They dismounted and let their horses suck noisily on the refreshing water while they crouched on their haunches, scooping up water with their bare hands and drinking just as noisily. When they had satisfied their thirst, Abe rested against a leafy tree while David filled his water bottle and splashed water on his face and over his neck, running his wet fingers through his hair and enjoying the rare comfort.

"How far to the next village?" Abe asked lazily, not actually caring what the answer would be, because it really didn't matter; time in the African bush didn't have a lot of meaning.

David shook the excess droplets of water from his hair and walked over to his horse. "We won't get there before dark," he replied. "I'm going to mark this river on the map," David pulled the now tattered scroll from his saddle.

"Maybe we should spend the night here. It's hot out there today."

"Yes, let's do that," David readily agreed. In fact, he was about to suggest it. "We are a bit low on meat. Would you mind looking after the horses while I take a walk upriver and see if I can shoot something for the pot?"

"Great idea," Abe smiled, "see if you can shoot a chicken for roasting," he joked.

David let a belly laugh escape, "I'll be no more than three or four hundred yards up and I'll stay on the north side of the river. I saw a big clump of trees and bushes spanning the river there when we were on top of the hill. I'll see if I can flush out a guinea fowl for dinner."

It was a strict rule that they let the other know exactly where they would be at all times, and an even stricter rule that they never deviate from what they had agreed. It was simply a matter of safety and survival. Before he left, David flattened the map on the ground, laid his compass on it, orientated it to magnetic north and pencilled in where he believed they were and where the stream ran, inserting a small arrow depicting the direction of flow. He then put the map back in his saddle and retrieved his rifle before crossing the river, turning left and following the stream.

As he progressed forward, the vegetation became thicker, as he had expected from when he had been elevated on the opposite hill, but he hadn't realised how intense the foliage would be. It became darker under the thick canopy and he had to pick his way through carefully, sometimes crawling under twigs and branches, and at other times stepping over them. The ground was gently rising, and – while he kept the sound of the trickle of the river to his left – every ten paces or so he would pause and listen for the sound of a bird or an animal, looking as hard as he could through the foliage, but there seemed to be no living creature in the entangled undergrowth.

Exhausted from all the leopard crawling on his belly, elbows, and knees, David took a moment to rest, listening to the soothing sound of the stream not far from him, the dappled sunlight barely making it to the damp ground upon which he sat. He suddenly realised that the sound of the trickle had evolved, and he was actually listening to the sound of water dropping from a slight height into the stream, a small waterfall perhaps. Carefully picking his way through the vines and branches, he aimed for the sound, and in less than a minute he found himself on the edge of a precipice about the height of two men. He stared into a pond of crystal clear water, stark sunlight pouring through the open canopy above. To his right the stream gently cascaded into the natural pool.

He felt as if he had discovered the Garden of Eden, shimmering in beauty, with thousands of hues of green and blue pressed right up to the edge of a pool surrounded by grey, granite rocks which were covered in magnificent shades of orange, red, green, and blue lichen. On the far side of the pond, a large granite rock had an overhang, with the smooth floor of the rock cavity sloping gently into the water. David could not see the back wall of the cave, so had no idea how deep it was. What he could see was that there was no way to enter the cave unless by swimming up to its mouth.

Certainly, one could not reach it from the slippery rounded top of the boulder and, in any event, they would not be able to see the cave from that angle. He looked down into the water through the reflecting ripples and saw clearly the smooth rocks and the occasional log from an old tree that littered the depths.

Excitement overtook him, and he was eager to get back to Abe and share this discovery immediately. At first he unceremoniously ploughed his way back through the overgrown bush, then, taking control of himself, calmed down and picked and crawled his way out the way he had come. As soon as he was clear of the thicket, he took off at a sprint, arriving at Abe and the horses out of breath and babbling with excitement. When Abe first saw David sprinting towards him, he stood up and considered grabbing his rifle, but was confused by the look on David's face, since it did not display shock or horror, but something else.

"Whoa, slow down, slow down!" Abe exclaimed, trying to calm David down by gripping his friend's shoulders. "What's the matter? What's wrong?"

"Abe! Come quick, I have something amazing to show you."

"You've found the wagons?" Abe asked curiously, a frown forming quickly.

"No, no, I have found something else! Come, come, and bring the horses. We can't leave them here, they'll be vulnerable to predators."

Abe tried to question David as they mounted up and retraced David's steps, but he would not be drawn out. When they got to the thicket, David dismounted and, with his machete, partially cut a way through for the horses. When he had gone about ten yards deep he cut a clearing, then instructed Abe, who was now beside himself with curiosity, to lead the horses into the clearing. Using the cut branches and foliage, David blocked the entrance he had just created. Once the horses were safe and the two had secured them on lengths of rope, David faced his friend and smiled.

"Now we have to crawl, but prepare yourself for something quite incredible."

"I've never seen you like this, David," Abe shook his head in confusion. "But let's go."

David carefully scrambled through the overgrown bushes, following the route he had taken earlier, constantly checking to see that Abe was right behind him. When he arrived at the precipice, he shuffled sideways and allowed Abe to move up beside him.

"Well I never…!" Abe stared at the scene that unfolded in front of him, falling silent as he absorbed the radiant beauty, the full sunlight from directly overhead bathing God's secret garden in a magnificent splendour.

"Isn't that too wonderful?" David beamed, staring at the spectacle below as he lay propped up on his elbows. For a full ten minutes the men continued to lie there, enjoying the incredible contrast that Mother Africa had provided for them.

It was Abe who finally broke the silence.

"I'd love to spend the night here," he murmured, "in that cave, by the edge of the water, listening to the sound of that waterfall."

"So would I," David dreamily agreed.

"I wonder: how could we get to that cave?"

"There's no way over to it, I've thought about it already."

"We could just jump into the water and swim over there."

"You can, perhaps," David looked at him over his shoulder, "but I can't swim."

"You can't swim?" Abe sounded surprised."

"I grew up in Poland and Ireland, don't forget. Nobody swims there. It's just too cold most of the year."

"You don't know what you're missing," Abe grunted as he sat up and pulled off his boots and socks. Then, stripping off the remainder of his clothes, he sat on the edge butt-naked, his thin, pale body reflecting in the stark sunlight.

"You're going to jump into that water? You're mad."

"I can't wait," Abe said simply. Then, in one fluid movement, he pushed his posterior off the precipice and plunged into the water, legs and arms flailing wildly, hitting the surface with a massive splash and disappearing in a torrent of white and aquamarine bubbles, before the silence descended once more.

David stared into the water, desperately looking for his friend, but all he could see were the remaining bubbles rising to the surface and bursting with a gentle hissing sound. As the bubbles gradually thinned, he saw the dark, lifeless shadow of Abe lying face down and naked on the bottom of the pool.

"Oh no! Oh no!" David panicked and quickly jumped to his haunches, *what have you done? I can't swim,* he thought.

David looked around for something he could use to fish Abe out; a branch, a vine, anything. He stared at the unmoving form of his old friend lying on the bottom and decided he would just have to jump in and risk his life, too.

Suddenly Abe jerked alive, tucked his feet under his body, and lurched himself upwards and out of the water. "Whooee!" he yelled as he broke the surface and burst into laughter. "It is beautiful!"

"Abe!" David bellowed furiously, "You scared the living daylights out of me."

"I got you back, my friend," he laughed some more. "Now, get your clothes off and jump in, it's not deep. Look," he stood straight and touched his chest at the height of the water. You're taller than this."

David began to chuckle; he thought he deserved that from Abe. He was about to take his shirt off when Abe called up to him.

"Actually, wait!" Abe shouted, throwing his hands in the air, "from here I have just noticed I can't climb out. If you jump in we will spend more time here then we anticipate. Get a rope and tie it to a tree before you jump."

"Sure, Abe, that was close," David agreed in secret relief; it could have been disastrous if they had been both trapped in the natural quarry.

By the time David returned with the rope and secured it to

a tree, Abe had waded over to the cave and – with some difficulty – had crawled out of the water, to end up sunning himself
on the warm rock. David tied some simple knots in the rope to
use as hand-holds, then threw the loose end into the water. He
stripped off and crouched on the edge of the cliff. His torso was
well defined and bronzed from working so often in the sun without a shirt, but his buttocks and legs were baby-white.

"Come on, don't be scared," Abe's voice echoed off the smooth,
granite rocks, "it's not deep. Jump in, and when you feel the bottom, just stand up."

David looked down into the water, his heart racing and panic
almost overwhelming him. Yet he didn't want to look like a coward
in front of his friend, so he took a deep breath, composed himself,
and lurched himself off the edge. No sooner had he committed
himself than he regretted it, clawing at the air for something to
hold onto, and plummeting down uncontrollably. He desperately
tried to take a deeper breath of air, but the fear took control and
hindered his breathing.

Crashing into the water, the world became silent, weird and
eerie, and a shocking cold surrounded him. He opened his eyes,
surrounded by turbulent bubbles. Thrusting his foot down quickly
to find the bottom, he stubbed his toe on a smooth rock, then,
forcing himself up, he breached the surface and daylight flooded
his world again. Coughing and spluttering, David wiped the water
from his eyes, only to hear Abe laughing a short way off.

"That wasn't too difficult, my friend, was it?"

"It was decidedly horrid!"

"No it wasn't. Now come here, I want to show you something," Abe insisted, taking David's mind off his personal trauma.

David waded over to Abe, who helped him climb up the slippery granite slope to the cave. It was warm in the sun, yet there
was a cool, pleasant draft that engulfed them. David looked back
in awe at the beauty of the oasis they had found in the middle of
the African bush.

"I wonder how many of these wonderful, isolated and undiscovered places there are out here?" David marvelled.

"I have no idea," Abe shrugged his shoulders, "could be hundreds, who really knows?"

"I wonder how this pool formed like this?" David continued to question, his voice echoing gently off the opposite rock wall.

"I've been giving it some thought, actually. I think what happened is that many years ago that big rock over there," he pointed to a large boulder that protruded from the pond where the stream exited, "was probably on top of this boulder that we are standing on, and for some reason it rolled off and blocked the stream. Then, in times of floods, debris and stones and stuff gathered at the base of the rock and formed a blockage, causing the water to rise, eventually forming this pool. It is constantly topped up and kept at this level by the stream. Look at this," Abe distracted David, "we aren't the first people to visit this place."

On the roof of the cave were drawn many simple figures. Rhino, kudu and elephants were easily identifiable. They were mostly painted on the rock surface in red and orange tones, and some appeared to have been drawn using grey ash.

"It's very easy to tell what they have painted. The drawings of the animals are very clear," David noted.

"This is interesting," Abe announced as he peered closely at a figure on the roof.

"What is it?" David was now very curious and stepped over to Abe's side.

"These are human, not animals: hunters. This one has a spear, and this one here," he pointed to another figure beside it, "is carrying a bow and arrow."

"I must be honest I haven't seen Matabele with bows and arrows," David commented as he studied the red-brown images on the roof.

"Maybe it was a tribe that lived in these parts before Lobengula's time. Perhaps they were driven out, or moved out themselves, or simply perished." Abe looked closely at another one of the drawings. "Look at the shape of their bodies, very distinct in each painting: that's not a Zulu or Matabele trait. I wonder what they used for paint?"

"Blood?" David offered.

"It looks like these people are hunting these animals. Perhaps it is a recording of the way they lived."

"I think these are paintings of animals that have already been killed," David ventured, "not animals they are chasing."

"And what makes you so certain of that?" Abe looked over at David, intrigue written all over his face.

"Well, just look at their hooves, Abe," he pointed to the feet of several paintings. "If the animals were running in flight, their hooves would be at an angle to their legs, as if they were standing on the ground, yet here the hooves are mostly pointing down, as if they were lying on their sides, sleeping, or dead. When I shoot an animal for food, that's what they look like when they are lying dead on the ground."

"Trust you to notice that," Abe grunted and returned his stare to the images. "I believe these paintings were here before that rock blocked the stream, or else how would they get here unless they swam? Whatever the case, this country is full of mysteries."

On closer inspection, they found that the cave was not that deep after all: barely four yards of rock protected the overhang and the paintings that were contained within. No bones were visible, nor ash from any fires, and so it was obvious that the cave had not harboured any visitor, whether animal or human, for a very long time.

After they had decided that they would spend the night in the protection of the cave, David – being the more agile of the two – volunteered to climb out of the natural quarry to collect their clothes and sleeping blankets. He then carefully threw these down to Abe in small bundles, who waded back in turn to the cave, holding the bundles above his head to keep them dry. David, still butt-naked, was going to climb back down the precipice with the rope but changed his mind and took the plunge again. It was worse the second time around, as he knew what was coming.

As the night set in, the men were dressed in their bush clothes and wrapped up in the warmth of their blankets. They sat in silence, surrounded by the mystique of their unusual dwelling-place, and the soothing song of the small waterfall. They had decided to spend a few more days in their own new world, simply to enjoy the total secrecy it had to offer from the world beyond, secret from all civilisation, secret from all animals.

By the time the sun rose in the morning, a number of small errors of judgement had become evident. Firstly, the cold of the rock on which they slept had sapped them of their warmth, and they woke up icy cold, stiff, and aching. Another problem they had not considered was that, unlike the natural dirt, often sandy or covered in dry grass, granite rock had no give whatsoever; it was solid to the absolute, and that made their night very uncomfortable and somewhat painful as their bony protrusions and joints caused them to shift often in the night, keeping them awake in trying to find a comfortable position.

After waking, thankful for the sunrise, and grumbling about the uncomfortable night, their biggest *faux pas* of all was that – if they wanted a cup of life-sustaining, hot coffee – they would have to swim across some very chilly water. Being already chilled to the bone, they suffered a great deal of resistance to making the effort, so the two of them continued to grumble and argue, as each time one of them emerged from his blanket, he rapidly retreated into the minimal warmth it provided. It was a tug of war between waiting for the sun to warm the rock, which would be around mid morning, and making the break through the water to get to a fire, their horses, some nourishment, and a cup of coffee.

In the end the coffee won out, and a strategy to strip down, wade over to the rope and clamber out, was put in place. Abe wrapped all the clothing in a blanket and held it over his head as David very reluctantly entered the water. After an agonisingly cold struggle to get to the other side, he battled to climb up the rope, his energy having been sucked mercilessly away firstly by his rock mattress, and then by the freezing water. Once out, however, Abe tied the bundle of blankets and clothing to the rope and David pulled it up. Then, throwing the knotted rope down to Abe, he began laughing as his friend struggled to hoist himself out of the water. It was the first time he had climbed out since he had jumped in the day before.

"Come on, old man," David jibed.

"I'm not as strong as you," Abe complained, but laughed at the same time causing him to loose his grip and slide down the rope into the water again. He stayed dry from his chest up, "and I'm freezing cold. I have no strength: you will have to carry me out!"

"You're half-dry. Who are you to complain? I'm short and so I'm wet to my chin. Come on," David chuckled.

"Oh, you be quiet," Abe replied as the banter continued, each laughing at the other.

With much grunting and groaning, and with a little help from David, Abe finally made it to the top and over the edge. As he took a moment to catch his breath, the two looked back at the cave and the mesmerising stillness and perfect reflections the pond shared with them. David picked up a white quartz rock the size of an orange and gently lobbed it into the water to watch the ripples form.

"Wait!" Abe exclaimed the moment the stone left his hand, but it was too late.

"Sorry," David apologised as the projectile hit the surface with a pronounced hollow splash, "I just wanted to see the ripples."

"That rock, I saw something in it. Where did you find it?"

"Right here," David looked around for another, "I'm sure there are more around here."

As they stared into the clear water, the white quartz stone was clearly visible among the dark rocks and rotting vegetation at the bottom.

"Never mind," Abe stood up, "let's get dressed and warm. I'm freezing cold and could really use a hot coffee."

"Me, too," David needed no encouragement.

"Leave the rope, if you don't mind, I'd like to come back here at mid-day and retrieve that rock."

David was immediately curious. "What did you see?"

"Not too sure if it was my imagination or not, but I thought I saw a flash of gold just as you threw it in. Regardless, I'd like to have another look to satisfy my curiosity."

"No problem at all, Abe," David smiled, "but I think we give that cave a wide berth tonight, I'm in no hurry to sleep there again."

"For sure, never again," Abe grumbled his agreement.

After leading their horses into the sun, with both man and beast enjoying the warmth on their bodies, the men put their clothes on, lit a fire, and put some water on to boil. While they were waiting for the coffee, they resumed the monotonous routine they had practised for the last seven weeks of climbing a suitable tree to search for columns of smoke.

On this day, only the one smoke column could be seen, and this was the same plume they had been aiming for the previous day, before the cave distracted them. David estimated that it was a good twenty miles away, and that they would probably get there on the following day, considering that they would stay another night to allow Abe to satisfy his curiosity regarding the rock in the pond. By then it would be too late to break camp, but, to avoid a waste of a day, David suggested that they explore the area a little more and follow the river downstream for a couple of hours.

Following the stream at a leisurely pace on horseback was a most enjoyable experience. They had no time constraints that day, no destination to reach before nightfall, just a relaxed morning in which to look at the scenery unfolding on either side of them and to watch out for new birds and different animal species, occasionally crossing the gurgling flow of water to allow their horses to stop and drink at their leisure. The stream took a gentle bend to the right at the base of a low hill and a vast plain opened up before them, covered with low scrub and bush, the stream gathering pace as it meandered into the distance. David stopped to pull out his telescope, scanning the far reaches of the valley. The view was impressive, the brown grasses speckled with green.

"Anything out there?" Abe asked as he enjoyed the scenery. It was very similar to what he had been looking at for well over a month, but he never tired of it.

"No, not much," David mumbled softly, "no wildlife, a couple of eagles. I can see a woman fetching water down at the stream."

"Where?" Abe was curious.

"See where the river kinks to the left a touch? Just there."

"I see her now," Abe confirmed, shielding his eyes from the sun with his hand.

"She's got a child strapped to her back, and there's a little one next to her too. Looks more like a Xhosa speaker, not Ndebele, by the way she is dressed, wearing a skirt and some beads around her neck. Here," David passed the telescope to his friend.

Abe took the brass instrument and searched for the kink in the river. "Alright, I see her," he mulled, "She's leaving now. Walks very gracefully, and is a little taller than the average Matabele, so I would say you are probably right."

"Come on," David looked at the sky, "let's get back. The sun will be high by the time we get there and you can go for another swim," he joked.

The men turned around and leisurely wandered back. By the time they arrived at their camp, the sun was directly overhead. Just as they were about to dismount, a small flock of guinea fowl appeared, foraging for food on the edge of a thicket, their speck-led plumage perfectly groomed, apart from their unattractive mis-matched blue and red heads. In one fluid motion, David drew his Martini-Henry from its scabbard, took aim, and fired a shot. His aim was true, as it often was, and the two men smiled gleefully.

After a hasty meal, David and Abe made their way back to the pond at the cave. The water was still and inviting, and the white quartz rock lay where they had left it, tantalising Abe at the bottom of the pool of clear water.

"Off you go," David chirped.

Abe stripped off his clothes, and then, without hesitation, launched himself into the air, splashing heavily into the calm, cool water. Wading over to where the stone lay, he took a breath, dipped under the water and surfaced with the rock in his hand. He ran his fingers through his hair, shaking the excess droplets off his face, and then began to examine the stone, turning it over in his hands as if it were of great interest to him. David saw him look at one part of the rock intently; then, submersing it underwater, he shook it, and rubbed it with his thumb before bringing it back up to study it carefully again. Abe was a man of the earth, and David had seen him do this on many occasions.

"Anything interesting?" David called down, unable to tell what Abe was thinking.

Abe looked up at David, "Possibly," he replied, wading back to the rope. "Here," he cocked his arm, "catch this, I'm coming up."

David caught the rock easily and studied it while Abe clambered up the rope. He needed no help this time, and was up in a jiffy. Taking the rock back from David, he held it in a shaft of sunlight and brought it close to his nose. David leaned forward to get a closer look.

"You see this," Abe pointed to a hairline mark that was only slightly below one of the surfaces of the quartz, "that's a fine line of gold."

"Is that gold?" David exclaimed, "It looks black to me."

"You have to hold it in the light just right," he passed the rock to his friend, "and you will see a hint of gold."

David turned the stone over in his hand, and at precisely the right angle to the sun, when a very slight sheen, a golden sheen, reflected back at him.

"There's not much gold in there," David observed, "it's no thicker than a hair."

"They thought they would find a lot of gold in this country, but that's what they have been coming up with: such small quantities, it's not worth the effort; that's why I have given up prospecting. In all the time I have been digging around this godforsaken country, this is the first time I have even laid eyes on any gold, and look how much I found," Abe waved the back of his hand at the rock in disgust.

As they ate what was left of the unfortunate guinea fowl that evening, Abe told David about his prospecting days, and – since David seemed so interested in the many ways that gold was mined, Abe explained as best he could how small-time prospectors like him used pans to look for deposits in rivers and how the bigger companies used stamp mills to crush the quartz, after which they would dump the debris on sorting tables to catch the heavier particles of gold that broke free. Gold, being a very heavy metal, always found the lowest point, which was one reason why it was often found in riverbeds where the granules had become trapped.

"So, my understanding, then," David pondered, "is that – if there is gold in this area, and over thousands of years very small granules broke out of the quartz and made it into this stream – then a logical place to pan for gold would be in this river bed."

"Yes, my thinking exactly," Abe nodded his agreement.

"Well, that boulder blocked the water, so it must have blocked any gold that came down stream too."

"Hmm…." Abe pondered, and nodded gently.

"Go on," David encouraged his old friend; he could see his thoughts were troubling him. "Let's stay here another night, and tomorrow, when the sun is high, take your enamel plate into the pond and scoop up some mud and see what you find."

"You think so?"

"Of course. You're a prospector, Abe. You need to do what you do, and this is the first time you have seen gold in this country. If you don't do it, you will regret it all your life."

"Alright," Abe was hesitant, "if you really don't mind waiting another day."

"I'd far rather wait here another day where we have shade and fresh water. What's one day after seven weeks? In any case, I'd like to go back to where we saw that Xhosa woman with the baby on her back; something is bothering me about her."

"What?" Abe sounded curious.

"I have no idea, I just know that something is bothering me about it."

"Alright then," Abe rolled out his blanket, "you do your thing tomorrow and I'll do mine. I didn't sleep at all well last night, so I'm off to bed." Abe wrapped himself in his blankets, put his hat over his face, and drifted off to sleep almost instantly. David rolled out his blanket and lay for a while, thinking about that woman and her children by the stream earlier that day, but sleep overtook him equally quickly.

*

David covered his eyes and looked up at the sky. He was about two hours ahead of the time when he had seen the woman the previous day. Cautiously, he walked his horse in the water to cover his tracks, scanning the banks constantly. When he reached the place where he thought he had seen her, he dismounted and, still standing in the water, studied the ground. Indeed, the footprints indicated that either a woman or a young male had been there, and there were traces of a child's footprints, together with imprints made from a traditional bowl for carrying water. Everything else looked quite normal. Peering into the bush, he could see a well-worn path leading into the foliage. No sign of humanity, neither footprint nor path, was visible on the opposite bank. Satisfied with what he had seen, he walked back up the river, leading his horse by the reins.

He kept asking himself what it was that had bothered him. It had all seemed very normal, and something he might have seen on any given day, but somehow he felt he was missing something. Perhaps it had something to do with the terrain. Maybe he had been this way before, and he recognised something about it, in which case they would be well off track. *No*, he thought, *it's something to do with the woman.*

He stopped and looked over his shoulder at the place where she had gathered water, but, no matter how hard he thought about it, nothing came to mind. Not wanting to go back to camp and then realise in the morning what it might be, David put about 300 yards between him and the footpath downstream and tethered his horse out of sight. He backtracked to where he had a good vantage point behind a small boulder and settled in to wait with his telescope. A quick glance at the sun told him he still had a while to go, if the woman was a creature of habit and routine, which, in his experience, she would be.

He heard her before he saw her, or rather, he heard the excited squeal of a child just before the small family appeared out of the bush. The woman was carrying deftly a clay pot on her head which she then carefully lowered, bending with straight legs so that the infant on her back was almost upside down.

Suddenly it dawned on David what it was that was troubling him so much; the smoke plume! For almost three days they had plotted the smoke trails in the area, morning and evening, and never had they seen one east of the direction they were travelling. With a toddler walking to the river, the village had to be close by, and yet there was no smoke column to indicate the village. They had checked and double-checked at least six times in the last three days.

Very carefully, David extended his telescope and trained it on the woman. Dressed only in a skirt, she was bathing the infant in the stream, sitting on a rock with her back to him. The telescope brought the vision of her so close to him he could even see a fly land on her bare shoulder, which she casually whisked away with a wave of her hand. The toddler was splashing and kicking the water joyfully just in front of her. Being a very common scene in this part of Africa, there was absolutely nothing unusual about it, until the woman turned to face David's direction, and suddenly looked right at him.

David inhaled sharply, immediately falling backwards onto his rear end and dropping his telescope in the process. Adrenalin came rushing instantly through his veins as he experienced both shock and total confusion.

Nothing made sense at all.

CHAPTER SIXTEEN
Empire

"NKOSAZANA!" DAVID SHOUTED at the top of his voice as he stood up from behind the rock, "What are you doing here?"

Nkosazana jerked her head up in fright and looked towards David. The infant in her arms nearly slipped from her grasp. For a moment she looked terrified and pulled her toddler close to her.

"It is me, David Langbourne," he shouted again to calm her uncertainty. "I see you, Nkosazana."

A smile crept into her face, and her body language immediately began to relax. David started to laugh; he could not believe he had found someone he knew in the middle of the African bush. As he began to walk towards her, his laughter increased and Nkosazana, too, began to chuckle. The connection had been made and David extended his arms into the air as if to embrace the Lord for his blessing, chortling to himself. *Oh, what a glorious day*, he thought.

"I see you, Nkosazana, I see you," David repeated.

"I see you, Boss David," she smiled in return. "It has been a very long time since we have met."

"Yes," he clapped his hands with joy, "your daughter, she has grown so much since we met in Mafeking." David unintention-ally, but quite naturally, slipped into the Xhosa tradition of talking about family matters before business matters at hand. "You have another child I see."

"Yes, this one is called 'Buhle'," she beamed proudly, "it means '*Beautiful*'."

"A very good name," David complimented her and gently pinched Buhle's chubby cheek with his thumb and the knuckle of his forefinger, which prompted the cute child to smile openly.

"What about Boss Morris? Is he in good health? Does he have any children yet?"

David laughed and shook his head. "No, he has no wife yet. What of your husband, Daluxolo? Is he well?"

"He is well and he waits for you with his brother, Nguni."

That statement was music to David's ears. He was elated. He had found the men he had been seeking so hard and so long for, the odds of which were pathetic at best in this vast unexplored continent, and therefore he had found the wagons. "I have been looking for them for many months now. It is through you that I find them. My heart is very happy."

"I will take you to them. Their hearts will sing for joy to see you. They are near-near."

In a single deft movement which only African women seemed able to master, Nkosazana held her baby by one arm, before single-handedly swinging Buhle over her shoulder and onto her back and securing her snugly with a blanket that she pulled tight around her body. Nkosazana then picked up the clay pot of water and bal-anced it on her head. David meanwhile lifted her first-born and carried her on his hip as they walked off into the bush.

"You must show me the way," David stepped aside to let her in front.

"No, it is our custom that you walk ahead. I will walk behind you," Nkosazana said shyly, bowing her head, while waiting for

David to take the lead. He did not argue as it was not for him to question their cultural ways.

The walk was a mere 300 yards, and as David entered a clearing he saw Nguni and Daluxolo sitting on upturned metal buckets, engaged in a conversation with each other. His heart leapt as he recognised his two Xhosa friends, and wanted to call out to them, but just at that moment Daluxolo turned to look at the approaching figures expecting to see just his wife and children. The sight of a European holding his child caused him to stand instantly in surprise, then realising it was David, stepped back one pace in mild shock and tripped over his improvised chair. Watching his brother's reaction, Nguni snapped his head around to see what the problem was, and stared in disbelief.

"Ghaw!" Nguni hawked in surprise, staring at David with very wide eyes.

"I see you, Nguni. I see you Daluxolo," David said calmly, restraining his excitement with great difficulty, but not succeeding very well. "I have been searching for you tirelessly."

Nguni stood up and began to laugh, his perfect white teeth shining through his broad smile. "We have been waiting for you for a very long time, Boss David."

David looked about him and noticed that four wood-and-mud thatched houses, built in their traditional way, had been erected in a semi-circle around the clearing where the men sat. A place in the centre of the clearing was obviously used for cooking, since a blackened pot, some ash and half-burnt logs were all that remained in the fire pit. Holding what looked like a folded rug, a woman appeared at the entrance to one of the huts and stared at David with a look of fear on her face.

"You built yourself a place to live?" David asked curiously. Only then did it dawn on him that the wagons had been lost for almost a year.

"This is our village," Nguni beamed and walked over to meet David, clasping him by the forearm. "We welcome you."

"I see you, Boss David," Daluxolo finally found his voice, and quickly followed his brother over to David, also clasping arms, and warmly welcoming him. "Come sit, we must drink beer together."

"You make beer?" David was astounded.

"We have a small village, but we have everything we want," Daluxolo chuckled. "Come and sit with us and we will drink beer and tell you what we have done." He took his little daughter from David's arms and handed her to Nkosazana.

As they sat around the extinguished fire, sipping a calabash shell filled with traditional sour beer, Nguni and Daluxolo began the time-honoured ritual of discussing their families, the weather, and all matters that were important to them. David talked about Morris and his two younger brothers, and the Matabele uprising that had interrupted his search for them.

The Xhosa men were pleased to hear that all four Langbourne brothers were in good health and unharmed but because of their isolation, they had not even been aware of the uprising. The Xhosa brothers then took up the story from the day the oxen had died suddenly, and the fear they had experienced in believing that King Lobengula's ancestral spirits had visited their caravan. With all the drivers and herders fleeing back to their homelands, it had been left to just Nguni and Daluxolo to look after the wagons.

Torn between running back to their homeland in equal fear of the spirits, and honouring their duty to look after the wagons, the two men had decided to move well away from the dead oxen, where the spirits would not find them, but still to remain close enough to check on the wagons once per day. They therefore had walked east for about half an hour and had crossed a small river. Believing that they would be safe from the spirits on the other side of the stream, they had set up a temporary shelter where they had remained to ponder their next move.

"This river that you crossed is that the same river over there?" David questioned, pointing to the direction that he had come from.

"Yes, the very one," Daluxolo wiped some of the thick, curdled beer from his mouth with the back of his hand. He had grown a sparse beard on his chin, and some of the beer had dribbled into it. "The river is good. It flows during every season and the water is sweet."

"When all the oxen were dead, the spirits left," Nguni continued in his characteristically deep voice, "and Daluxolo chose to go to Bulawayo to find you."

"But it was the wrong decision," Daluxolo shook his head and stared at the ground. "Boss Morris was very angry for me leaving the wagons, so I came back here as fast as I could."

"No," David reached over and held his friend's shoulder firmly, "you did the right thing. It was Morris who was wrong to get angry, and I apologise for him. He gets angry very easily; it is just how he is. When people are angry, they make mistakes and his mistake, a very stupid mistake, was that he did not ask you where the wagons were."

The brothers continued in turn, telling the story of their lives since Daluxolo's return. The goats and chickens did not die from the *rinderpest,* so they nervously recovered them from the wagons and tended to the animals, erecting a protected pen for the goats, using thorny Acacia branches. They made a chicken coop in much the same way and both goats and chickens flourished. They then set about building two mud pole-and-thatch huts for themselves, and, with maize and millet grain they found in bags on some of the wagons, Nguni planted some crops. Daluxolo, meanwhile, walked back to his home village near Mafeking and collected his family, including some of his nephews and nieces and their spouses, to help with watching over the wagons, crops and livestock.

"So, you have indeed built your own village," David glanced around at the huts and patchy fields of crops thriving behind the row of dwellings. A lone chicken walked across the smooth, brown earth that made up the communal area of the village and stopped to scratch and peck at something it saw on the ground.

"At first we needed to eat the maize that was stored on the wagons, but with plenty of good water the maize we planted grew fast." Daluxolo was suddenly apologetic. "There is no maize left on your wagons, Boss, but all the other stock is still there."

"I don't mind that you ate the maize, Daluxolo!" David chuckled. "For heaven's sake, my friend, you needed to eat."

The reunion went on for another two hours, Daluxolo introducing his family members to David, and David filling them in on the news of all the fighting in Bulawayo, and his search for the wagons. Since Nguni expected David to spend the night and had made arrangements for one of the huts to be prepared for his stay, he was visibly disappointed when David was forced to explain that he was travelling with a friend who was helping him in the search, and that he needed to get back before sundown or his friend would be very worried. A pre-arranged rendezvous was a rule Abe and David had agreed never to break, since a failure to appear would indicate that the other was in trouble, and he did not want to worry his friend on that score. David rather suggested that he would return the next day with Abe and the two of them would then spend the night in the shelter of their hospitality, and this suggestion was well received.

The formalities over, David then respectfully asked if he might see the wagons.

"We will take you now," said Nguni and stood up immediately, the others all following suit. David bid Nkosazana farewell, and followed the Xhosa brothers down the footpath towards the stream. They waded through to the other side, Nguni stepping only on exposed rocks with Daluxolo treading in his footfalls. David also did the same, but – looking back at where they had stepped – he noticed that the men were not standing on soil or sand.

"I see you do not leave footprints," David commented curiously.

"Yes," Daluxolo confirmed and turned to face David. "If other people were walking down this river, we do not want them to see our footprints going this way and find the wagons."

"I see," David frowned, "and so it was that I only saw the footprints of your wife and children. I would not have found the wagons had I not seen Nkosazana, because I looked at the other bank and saw no sign of people's footprints. You did very well," David commended his friends.

Daluxolo smiled, and then said something that shook David to the core. "We also did not want to attract people, especially Lobengula's spirits, to our village. Therefore we only light our fire after the sun goes down, and before the sun comes up. When the sun is up we put water on the fire."

"There is no smoke to be seen," David said distantly, trying to understand what Daluxolo had implied.

"Yes, Boss David."

"So," David turned to look at their wet tracks leading to the water, and stared beyond at the village now hidden by the bushes, "if you have hidden yourself and the wagons so well, how did you think I would find you?" He turned to face Daluxolo and Nguni, bewilderment written all over his face. "There are no tracks or signs to be seen. I was looking for smoke from your fires, but my plan would never have worked."

"When I was in Mafeking," Daluxolo explained, still smiling, "I went to see our traditional spirit medium, and he said you would find us after the summer returned again, but it would be Nkosazana who would lead you to us. That is why I brought her with me."

David stood speechless. He didn't know if his friend was joking or being serious. He had been told that the power of the spirit mediums in the African villages was immense, yet little understood. Certainly, what had just been told to him defied all logic in his world, but he was not prepared to question or dispute what had happened on this day. It had been a year since the wagons had become lost, and it had been Nkosazana who had led him to his friends, who would now lead him in turn to the wagons that had been hidden in a spot in the bush without footprints or bush signs to guide him there.

"Come," Nguni's baritone voice boomed, "the sun is moving and you have many miles to travel to be with your friend."

After another fifteen minutes of walking through thick shrubs interspersed with thorny acacia bushes, further signs of the *rinderpest* began to emerge. All the skeletons of the dead oxen were randomly littered on the ground. Attached to their exposed ribcages, all the carcases still displayed some remnants of their sun-hardened hide and hair, streaked with the bleached excrement from several vultures, while the empty eye sockets in their skulls continued to plead for mercy. Since a feeling of unease still pervaded the area and the air smelt terrible, all three men had good cause to become jittery.

The shape of a wagon with its tarpaulin cover began to appear as they approached what had once been a clearing in the bush. The vegetation had grown prolifically during that year, and, indeed, the wagons were very well concealed. As they reached the first wagon, David could easily make out many others, all arranged into a laager. He smiled to himself as he recognised the wagons, because for many weeks he had tended to them, repaired them, and cajoled them through the Transvaal bush. He knew them intimately and recognised every little scratch and dent as if he had left them only the day before.

Everything, apart from the perishable goods, seemed to be exactly where he had left them a full year previously. He wanted to dance for joy, and his heart wanted to sing. A strange sense overcame him, a sense he did not understand; it almost felt as if he had just walked into his family home, a place he belonged. It was a very deep happiness. David started to chuckle, then turning to face his smiling friends, he shook their hands in the traditional way, thanking them profusely for their loyalty and concern for his family.

*

Abe waded over to the large round boulder that dammed the trickling stream, and which had caused the pool to form. The water was clear and he could easily see the debris and rocks that formed the bottom of the pond.

In his right hand he held his mustard-yellow, enamel plate with the blue decorative line that marked the rim, the same plate off which he had eaten his evening meal for almost two months. Taking a deep breath, he gently slipped below the surface of the water and placed the plate on the floor of the pool, close to his side. Then he firmly gripped a rock the size of a horse's head, strained hard, lifted it carefully, and swivelled it to the left, before depositing it roughly, while he listened to the dull thuds of its collision with the nearby boulders. Only then did Abe surface to take a breath.

Over the next hour, he removed all the rocks and waterlogged stumps, sticks and decayed leaves from the immediate area. The process very quickly stirred up filth and muck, and for the most part he found himself working with his eyes closed, using his sense of touch only. The water was more than murky, it was black. When Abe reached soft dirt he prodded around with his bare feet, and, satisfied with the results of his preparation, waded back to the slope of the cave and hauled himself out to soak up the warmth of the sun's rays for a short time.

Feeling a little more energised, Abe slipped back into the water and faced the large boulder once more. Taking a deep breath he dipped under the surface again and grovelled for his plate. He couldn't remember exactly where he had put it, and began to get very annoyed with himself. In frustration, he stopped diving for it, placed his hands on the boulder, and began feeling around for the dish with his bare right foot. After only a moment he touched it, and heard the dull scrape of metal on rock. Keeping his foot on the plate he gently dipped under the water and retrieved it, and although a very slight smile caught the corners of his mouth, he was annoyed with the lapse of concentration that could have halted his plans before they had really begun.

Taking another deep breath, he dipped back under the water and pushed the edge of his plate into the now exposed soft mud and very carefully shovelled as much of the mud onto the plate as he could manage. Surfacing ever so gently, he shook the water droplets from his eyes, and then, turning his back to the rock face and facing the sunlight, he began lightly to pan away at the black mud, just as a typical gold digger would have done, gently allowing the insignificant light dirt to be washed away. When there was almost nothing left in his plate he stopped, and very carefully poked about in the settlings, looking for the elusive gold.

Abe's heart sank; nothing could be seen, but for a few, small stones and some grit.

Undaunted, Abe kept at it, digging deeper and sifting with quiet patience through the draff within the plate, before throwing the worthless earth aside back into the water. After a while, Abe took a break to lie on the rock and soak up the welcome warmth provided by the brilliant African sun. He looked up at the sky and estimated that he had about two hours left before a shadow would steal his warmth and light, so, without wasting any more time, he reluctantly slid back into the water to resume his panning for gold.

Abe had dug a hole about two feet deep by this stage, and each time he surfaced with his plate full of mud, silt gently filled the cavity he had created. It was somewhat annoying, because he wanted to get deeper, but with a patience born of necessity, he methodically continued in panning off his dirt and studying the bottom of the makeshift pan.

Suddenly, a small sparkle flashed up at him from the bottom of the plate.

Staring intently at the golden speck, Abe waded over to the far side of the pond where the clean water softly cascaded into the pool, and carefully allowed the clear water to wash over the enamelware. And there it was: the unmistakable speck of a piece of pure gold.

Abe's spirits soared and he let out a shout of joy that echoed off the granite walls of the pond, before he carefully removed the speck and ran it between his wrinkled, water-logged thumb and forefinger, gingerly feeling the ever-so-slight lump of gold.

Wading back to the cave floor, he realised that he had not thought to bring anything within which to put any gold that he might find. He had been disappointed so many times before in his life that gold had been the last thing he had expected to find on this trip. Retrieving a piece of lichen from the rock floor, he gently placed the speck on it, then hurried back to the muddy hole he had created.

He was not going to stop panning until the sun was low in the sky.

*

David rode at a leisurely pace into their campsite as he had plenty of time to spare. As he crossed the stream for the last time before he reached Abe, he noticed the water had turned murky, and smiled to himself, knowing that Abe had been hard at work in the pond up ahead. Arriving at the campsite, he saw Abe's horse tethered in the open, grazing calmly on the dry grass, indicating that his friend had finished panning and had brought his horse out of the protection of the thick bush that surrounded the secret oasis. David realised that the vegetation was so dense in that area simply because the elevated water in the pond fed the earth in the immediate vicinity.

As David rounded a thicket of bushes he saw Abe hunched over the fire, fanning the flames to life. He tried hard to contain his excitement about what the day had brought him as he wanted to surprise Abe with the good news when they were comfortably seated at the fire. Abe looked up at David, and acknowledged his arrival with a polite nod, which David returned in the same manner. He dismounted, tied his horse to a bush, and casually strode over to Abe who was now enveloped in white smoke.

"Any success?" David asked nonchalantly.

"Hmm...," Abe hummed, as if searching for an answer, "actually, I did manage to find a little gold." He looked up and winked, smiling slightly.

"You did?" David exclaimed. "That's wonderful!"

"First time ever for me, actually," Abe put the blackened kettle on the fire.

"So," David encouraged, briefly forgetting the news he wanted to share with his friend, "how much did you find?"

"Oh, some. Here, have a look for yourself."

Abe reached into his trouser pocket and pulled out a small cloth purse that was tied closed with a piece of string. He fumbled with the knot and opened the bag slightly, passing it to David.

"Careful now," Abe cautioned.

David held the purse and immediately noticed it carried some weight. "This is heavy," he commented, testing the weight by lifting the bag up and down a couple of times. He looked into the purse and saw a small pile of gold granules. "There seems to be a fair amount in here, Abe!" He stole an excited look at the one-time prospector.

"No, not really a fair amount, David," Abe looked concerned, then suddenly his face erupted into the biggest smile ever. "Actually, it's a very *large* amount, probably about five to six hundred pounds' worth!"

David began to laugh and when Abe joined in, David couldn't help but bombard Abe with questions, while Abe was unable further to contain his excitement. His face was bursting now with expression, as he spoke animatedly with his arms and hands and gesticulating wildly, telling David of how he had moved all the surface debris and rocks, and, how – after digging about two feet into the soft mud – he had started coming up with granules of gold at every spin of his pan.

Abe couldn't help grinning from ear to ear. "I'll bet this is the most lucrative gold deposit ever found in this country!" he exclaimed.

"You need to peg this site and register your claim as soon as you get back, my friend," David said, equally excited.

"Let's claim it together, you and me, partners," Abe laughed. "After all, it was you who found the pond and the cave."

"Thanks, Abe, but you keep the claim; I'm not in the business of mining, and – in any event – I also found my gold mine today."

"No, no, no. I insist," Abe put his hand up in protest, "if it wasn't for you, I would never have…."

Abe stopped in mid-sentence and stared at David disbelievingly. He cocked his head and studied the broad smile on David's face. Even his eyes were smiling.

"I… er… I beg your pardon, but what did you just say?"

"You heard me right. I found the wagons, together with Nguni, and Daluxolo. They and the wagons are all safe. They've even built a small village, with chickens and huts and all."

"Where?" Abe asked incredulously. He wasn't sure if David was joking.

"Just down the river. Remember that woman we saw through the telescope? It was Nkosazana. Their village is just to the left of the river, and the wagons are about half a mile to the right."

"Nkosazana? The Xhosa woman who worked for you? Who made the best shortbread in the world?"

"The very one," David nodded with a wink and a smile, "Daluxolo's wife. The wagons are well hidden, and the bush has already covered all tracks. Even when the men go to check on the wagons, they cover their footprints, so they're totally concealed."

Abe thought this over as David handed back the small bag of gold granules. He opened the container again just to feast his eyes on the golden glitter; it made him smile. "So," Abe looked up at David, "if they have a village there, why didn't we see the smoke trail?"

"Very good question. They are very superstitious, as you know, and they thought the *rinderpest* was the work of evil spirits, so they only light their fires under the cover of darkness in order not to attract the spirits, and – of course – to prevent the Matabele from finding them. It was really very clever of them. Had someone found them, there would still be no trace of where the wagons are hidden."

"Has it occurred to you that our system of tracking smoke columns would never have worked for us? Has it occurred to you that when they concealed themselves from not only spirits and Matabele, or whatever else might come along, they would have concealed themselves from us, too?"

"Yes," David said simply.

"And had you not gone back to check on that woman, we would have passed by and never found the wagons?"

"Yes."

"What on earth made you go back?"

David shook his head and looked at Abe sideways. "Very strange, actually. I was thinking about that a lot during the ride back here. It was something you said when you looked at Nkosazana through the telescope. You spoke about her walking very tall and proud when she left the river."

"Yes, she did. I remember saying that."

"Well, it somehow reminded me of how Nkosazana used to walk - tall and gracefully, like she was royalty. You know that 'Nkosazana' means 'Little Princess' in Xhosa?"

"Yes, I knew that, but it didn't mean anything to me," Abe admitted.

"I think that's what got me curious last night. What you said reminded me of her, and somehow something was playing on my mind. I never expected to see her, but when I did, I got such a fright I fell right on my butt! Also, I think that, in the back of my mind, I was wondering why - although there were people by the river - we had seen no smoke to indicate the presence of a village there. That was another thing that bothered me, but without my really understanding why."

"Well," Abe grinned, "the odds were that we should never have found them. Apart from them being lost out here somewhere, they were totally hidden as well. It was meant to be, wasn't it?"

"Yes, it was, actually; but they knew I was coming."

"How so?" Abe looked startled.

"Daluxolo saw a spirit medium when he returned to collect Nkosazana and some of his relatives, and the medium said Nkosazana would bring me to them after one year."

Abe was silent for a moment, but then spoke softly. "There is a lot to be said about the African spirit mediums. They double as doctors, and their potions are very powerful. They can cast magic spells and can foresee the future. They drive out evil spirits and bring rain. I don't understand it, but I must say I am very wary of them, to the point of being scared. I have seen too much to disbelieve it all as a hoax. If the medium said Nkosazana would bring you to the men, then it would happen. You will more than likely find that what the medium said is the reason Daluxolo brought her back to the wagons in the first place."

"He said as much," David replied, feeling a little nervous and uncomfortable with the conversation.

"I'm surprised he said as much," Abe said flatly, "but don't ask him any more about it as it would be disrespectful, and, in any case, you found what you were looking for."

David felt a shiver run down his back. "Come on, Abe," he said, quickly changing the subject, "let's have another look at that gold before it gets dark!"

"I still want you to be an equal partner in this claim," Abe insisted, handing the small bag of gold over to David again. "If it wasn't for you, I would never have found it."

"No," David shook his head, smiling comfortably at his friend. "No, if it wasn't for you, and what you said about Nkosazana that made me go back to have another look, I would never have found the men or the wagons. They would be lost forever, of that I am certain. The wagons belong to me, the gold belongs to you. Let's just agree that we have both helped each other out. Fair's fair; all is equal."

Abe pondered over what David said for a moment. "Alright, my friend," he nodded slowly, "I will accept that."

David reached over the fire, extending his hand to Abe in a handshake. "Agreed?" he asked.

Abe reached over and shook David's hand firmly.

"Agreed."

*

When they turned back to the topic of the Langbourne wagons, it was the logistics of getting them back to Bulawayo that dogged the conversation, especially as David would have had to use mules instead of oxen, and that they would generally need three mules to one ox, such was the strength of an ox.

A third matter that was discussed around the dying flames of the fire, in hushed tones, even though there was no possibility of anyone hearing them, was how they would hide the location of the cave and pool, as well as the wagons, within their map. It would have to be coded so that, if the map ever fell into unscrupulous hands, the location of their respective treasures would remain a secret.

Using a little imagination, the two decided to chart their journey many miles off to the east, indicating that they had not been anywhere near the area. Then, carefully identifying the area where the cave was located, they folded the map for the first time, rather than rolling it as a scroll, and used the convergence of two creases in the folds to mark the spot. Just to the side of the intersected creases David drew the imprint of a leopard's footprint, and wrote the words, "Leopard sighting" beside it, before rolling it up again and placing it in its scabbard. It was understood between them, anyhow, that they would never need a map to find their way back.

It was a strange thing about the African bush: once someone had become familiar with an area, or had traversed it several times, they would tend to remember landmarks and points of interest over hundreds of miles in much the same way as a homing pigeon mysteriously finds its way home.

"Tomorrow we spend the night in the village," David mumbled as he curled up in his blanket, "it is expected of us. They will slaughter a goat to celebrate our arrival and share their homemade beer. It will be a good feast, trust me."

"Suits me fine, David," Abe muttered from his side of the glowing embers. "Do you think Nkosazana will have baked some shortbread for us?" he joked.

"Hah!" David let a laugh escape, "no chance of that, Abe, sorry. They will ask you why you stirred up the water and made their stream dirty. Just tell them you were prospecting and apologise for hurting the river."

"Will do," Abe agreed. "Did I really stir up the sediment that much?"

"Oh yes," he chuckled softly. "You must have gone insane when you found your first lot of gold. The water is *black* with dirt for miles downstream. I wish I was there to watch you. The sediment in the pool will have settled by the morning, but Nkosazana will still see traces of your efforts. Sleep well Abe, and well done on your find."

Abe grunted something unintelligible, and within minutes the men were sound asleep. It had been a day to remember, and a time that the two of them would talk and laugh about till the end of their days.

CHAPTER SEVENTEEN
Business

FOR DAVID AND Abe the final straight home to Bulawayo was long and weary. The heat of the African summer was upon them and the rains were yet to arrive. When David had estimated that they were about a day and a half out of town, he had decided to start before sunrise and had pushed through until darkness had fallen. He knew that water would be a problem for a full day's hike, but Bulawayo was tantalisingly close, and he was determined to go home. They had ridden hard on the last few days so that, not only were the men fatigued, but also the horses. Abe did not complain, because he was equally anxious to see his lovely wife again, to let her know that he was not just in good health, but a rich man, too, with the potential to become even richer.

When the signs of human civilisation began to appear, the horses seemed to understand that their destination was near, and their previously sombre moods began subtly to improve, their ears pushing forward as their gait quickened. After the sun had dipped below the horizon, a very welcome puff of cooler air gently brushed the men on their cheeks, and they smiled at each other, knowing that it would be only a few minutes more before they would be walking their horses down Main Street.

As they reached Sharon's dress shop, illuminated by the faint glow of candlelight, Abe halted his horse and nodded a farewell to David, who responded in kind. After so long in the bush together, words were seldom necessary. When David turned into a deserted Abercorn Street, it exuded an aura of peace, the occasional candle-lit glimmer from a few shop windows adding to the sense of calm.

Since the Langbourne Brothers warehouse had no glass windows at all, the building seemed to be in total darkness. Instinctively, David went around to the service lane at the back of the buildings on Abercorn Street, knowing that the back door to the warehouse would be the easiest access point. He needed to tend to his horse for the night, but wasn't sure where the horse might be stabled, but for now he was going to greet his family. He dismounted in the small courtyard at the back of their premises and noticed the small, rusted-iron trough that they used to bathe in, a simple idea from Harry that allowed them to use the warehouse both as a home and a business.

Inserting the wide-necked cork that was lying at the bottom of the trough into the drain, he began to fill it with water for his mount to drink, and the sound caught someone's attention inside the warehouse. David heard a chair scraping along the floor, before one of the big double doors opened slightly and Louis poked his head outside, blinking a few times to adjust to the darkness.

"David!" he exclaimed excitedly. This was immediately followed by more scraping sounds as his other two brothers leapt to their feet and crowded the doorway.

"You're back!'

"Welcome!

"We were worried about you!"

With all the excitement, David could hardly get a word in, but he felt quite delighted to be welcomed so heartily.

Morris took his brother by the shoulder, guiding him into the shop, and gently pushing the younger siblings aside to make room. "Come in, come in," he beamed. "Are you alright? I was very concerned about you, but you look well, although you might need a haircut. Just look at that beard!"

Since Morris kept on babbling in excitement, it was Harry who sped to the crux of the business. "Did you find the wagons?" he asked.

David threw his hands up in the air, trying to calm everyone down. "Yes, yes, and yes. Yes to everything!"

Morris, however, still needed to put his anxiety to rest. "Do you mean to say that you found the wagons?"

"Yes, I found the wagons."

"Thank the Lord God Almighty for that," Morris sighed, and then smiled.

"It's been almost two months," Louis added.

"More than two months," Harry corrected. "Are you hungry? Do you need some dinner?"

"Tell us about the wagons," Morris insisted.

When the hubbub had subsided, David calmly related everything he could remember about his search and his ultimate discovery of Nkosazana, Daluxolo, and Nguni, and the wagons of course. His brothers were excited beyond words, and the storytelling went on well into the night. David was pleased to hear that, while he had been away, their business had been brisk, which meant that their stock levels were running critically low. Their discussion turned immediately to how they might recover the wagons and to the various options they had at their disposal. They finally agreed, however, that they would not make a decision until Morris was able to meet with Major Seward and to see whether the BSAC could help with the loan of the mules. Morris felt that, with all the shortages in Matabeleland, the BSAC would be only too pleased to assist, if they knew that their efforts would help to bring in those goods so desperately needed by the local population.

"Alright, enough of the wagons," said David, wanting to

change the subject. "Tell me what I have missed while I have been in the bush."

Morris leaned back in his chair, "Quite a bit, actually," he replied. "Mr Rhodes has had three indabas with the Matabele chiefs, and they have agreed on peace. Unfortunately, with all the BSAC military down here because of this war, the Mashona in the north have taken up the Matabele cause and started a similar war up there, so a lot of BSAC men have left for Mashonaland. This country really is in a bad state of affairs, but for now, because the Matabele have agreed to peace, we have seen the levels of confidence rising and the settlers are beginning to build and to re-invest in this part of the country."

"That's good, I suppose; good for us, that is."

"Yes. The bad news comes from further north, around Fort Salisbury, and all the surrounding districts, but that won't affect us. Oh, and I've heard from Father."

"Wonderful!" David exclaimed. "Good news, I hope."

"Well, not really," Morris sighed, a frown crossing his brow. Louis and Harry started to chuckle softly.

""What's wrong?" David asked quickly, stealing a confused glance at his younger brothers.

"Well, we have another half-brother," Morris sounded unimpressed as Louis and Harry chuckled louder.

"Really?" David sat straight and scratched his head. "Father and Aunt Helena had another child? What's his name?"

"Erin. He was born about six or seven months ago."

"Looks like we might have to expand Langbourne Brothers," David joked.

"No," Morris disagreed curtly, "they are not brothers, they are half-brothers, and our business, Langbourne *Brothers*, is exactly that, for the brothers; you, me, Louis and Harry," Morris looked at his brothers sternly. "Mother only had four sons, and the business will remain in the ownership of us four, and no one else."

"What about our half brothers?" Harry enquired.

"Hmm…." Morris pondered, "they can work for us; we will employ them, so that they won't go hungry – I have no problem with that – but they cannot become shareholders in our business."

David expressed his concern. "That's a bit tough, don't you think?"

"No," was Morris' simple answer. "I didn't create this business for them. They didn't have to deal with all the hardships we endured. No" he stated with finality.

David locked his fingers behind his head and rocked back in his chair, as an uncomfortable silence fell around the table.

"Alright,' David said finally, "I have one more piece of news I need to discuss with the family before we go to bed." He paused to look carefully at each of his brothers, making sure that his statement had made an impact on them, which it certainly did. "I discovered a fairly large pond of water, about the size of our building, hidden in a very thick pocket of bush. I was not the first one to find it, but it seems that I might have been the first to visit the pool in many hundreds of years, possibly thousands of years."

"How could you tell?" Louis interrupted.

"There was a cave on one side, not a deep cave, but it had ancient paintings on the wall and roof. It truly was a secret place. Anyhow," David unlocked his fingers and leaned forward in his seat, "I left Abe to prospect there while I went to check on that woman who turned out to be Nkosazana, and he found gold."

"Well done!" Morris clapped his hands together. "About time."

"He found a lot of gold."

A deathly hush enveloped the young family once again, as the brothers exchanged glances with one another, but Morris' curiosity immediately began to eat at him.

"How much, David? Tell us!" he blurted out.

David leant back in his chair again, locking his fingers behind his head as he had done before. "This has to remain a total secret. I need your word of honour that you will not say anything at all outside of us brothers."

Their father, Jacob, had taught them that an assurance was something to respect, a promise was never to be broken, but a word of honour was far more important than the other two combined; it was total and ultimate, not ever to be used lightly. Never in any of the brothers' lives had they been asked to give their word of honour, and now their own brother was demanding it of them. It was a big occasion.

Once David received their verbal honour, he continued. "In one day he panned about five hundred pounds in value out of the pool."

"Good grief!" Morris was shocked at this amount.

"He has pegged the site and Abe will register his claim tomorrow. He wanted me to have a half share in the claim because it was me that he found the pond, but I declined. He's not getting a share of our wagons and he helped me find them. In fact, if it wasn't for something he said about Nkosazana those wagons would never have been found. So I turned him down; fair is fair. This is why I am telling you, and I hope you agree."

"Of course," Morris smiled. "That was the right decision, I agree, and I thank you for telling us. It would have been nice to have a share in a profitable gold mine, but we are not prospectors or miners, we are traders, and *this* is our gold mine," he gestured widely at the shop around them. "Tomorrow the hard work begins, because we have an empire to build."

*

Leaving the younger brothers in charge of the shop the following morning, Morris and David walked down to Sharon Kaufman's place of work; firstly, so that Morris could personally thank Abe for his dedication to the finding of the wagons; and secondly, for David to get a haircut from Sharon. Although he had shaved his beard off, two months of neglect in the bush had let his unruly hair run wild, and this did not match well with his business suit.

After David's haircut, all three men walked down to the BSAC offices to register Abe's claim, and to meet with Major Seward. Registering the claim was easy, virtually a formality. Abe named his claim "Nkosazana Mine", after the elegant woman who had led both him and David to their fortunes. With the paperwork clutched firmly in Abe's hands, the men made their way to see Major Seward who, as always, made time for them.

"Good morning Morris, morning David," he greeted them, bounding round from his desk and shaking the brother's hands, "and Abe Kaufman, good to see you, too. How is your dear wife, Sharon?"

"Greetings Major, and thank you, she is well," Abe smiled, shaking the jovial man's hand.

"Sit, sit, sit!" Major Seward repeated quickly as he pointed to some empty chairs. "I've just received a pot of fresh tea, will you have some?"

Despite the heat, the three men agreed to join him in a cup and promptly took their seats, allowing the major to pour some of the hot liquid into porcelain teacups, all the while chatting idly and joking about trivial matters. Once the major took his seat, though, Morris got straight down to business.

"Mr Seward," he addressed the major by his civilian name, something he would usually only do in their own company, "we need to take you into our confidence, because we need your help."

"I'll certainly help if I can Morris, you know that," Major Seward looked at him seriously, deep furrows creasing his brow.

"Over a year ago, I took a very big risk - an exceptionally big risk. I felt that with the first rebellion over and the Matabele soundly defeated by the BSAC, Bulawayo would experience a business and population explosion."

"Indeed we all thought that," Seward agreed, nodding, but still frowning.

"David and I went south and procured a large amount of stock, a *very* large amount of stock. We bought basic necessities, as well as extravagant and exotic goods from the Far East. The cost was prohibitive, but I used all the means at my disposal to procure this shipment, and I borrowed heavily from everyone I could."

"Well, business must be good for you," the major smiled, reaching for his cup, "you must have sold it all as I popped my head into your store last week and it was rather empty."

"Well that's the problem," Morris continued as Seward sipped the hot tea noisily. "The stock never arrived."

Seward swallowed hard, his eyes darting quickly from Morris to David and Abe, before placing his teacup down carefully. "What do you mean, never arrived?"

David took over, sounding very forlorn. "We got caught by the *rinderpest* and all our oxen died on the way here, so we lost the wagons somewhere between the Limpopo and here."

"Lost?"

"Yes, lost," Morris looked at his shoes and shook his head in regret. "It was my fault. When our man arrived here to tell me what had happened, I lost my temper and sent him back to the wagons forthwith, forgetting to ask him where the wagons were."

David quickly took the attention away from Morris' error of judgement. "I went looking for them," he said, "but, when I came back here for a re-supply, the second Matabele war broke out, and that suspended any efforts to find them. Abe and I, however, have been out in the bush for the last two months and have now located them. They have been lost for over a year, but they are still completely intact, minus the oxen, of course."

"Well done," Seward complimented David and Abe. "So, how can I help you then?"

Morris shifted nervously in his chair. "We need mules to bring the wagons back here," he replied. "We can't afford to buy a team of mules because we are as broke as the next man, so we want to hire as many mules as possible to pull the wagons here as quickly as possible."

"You want to hire some of ours?" Seward asked cautiously.

"Yes, not only do I need to hire them urgently, I cannot pay you for them until the wagons arrive and I can sell some of the stock. The way I see it," Morris continued quickly, to avoid the major throwing any further questions at him, "Bulawayo is very short of commodities, including food and money itself. Now, we don't have any food on our wagons, that is a fact, but we have household goods and a lot of luxury items, such as exotic carpets from the Far East. I appreciate that right now we need basic food items, but our household items will help to lift the morale of this settlement, which as you know, is hurting from the recent war."

The major rocked back in his chair and pondered Morris' explanation. He was not sure if he really agreed with his argument, but it did have some merit. He looked over at David's expectant face, and cast a glance at Abe's deadpan expression.

"How many mules are you looking for? Half a dozen? A dozen? You know even mules are in short supply, don't you?"

"Hundreds, actually," Morris replied without a pause.

Seward's eyes darted rapidly between the men, a look of confusion clouding his face. His eyes turned into slits, "How many wagons are out there?"

"Thirty, sir," David answered calmly.

Seward leaned forward quickly, his chin almost touching his desk. "Thirty!" he hissed in shock.

"That's what I'm trying to tell you," Morris sat tall in his seat and adjusted his tie slightly. "We risked everything in this endeavour, believing things were going to go very well here. The coach line was in town, the telegraph line had connected us to cities and towns to the south, and we will soon have a rail connection, too." Morris shrugged. "Things have to come right for this town, so I took a huge gamble. But we were subjected to problems beyond our control, and beyond what any sane person would have imagined. David nearly died in quicksand, and then he fell ill to some mysterious sickness. The *rinderpest* struck, all our men fled believing evil spirits had descended on them, and then the good doctor took your military force down to the Transvaal Republic, allowing the Matabele to rise up again."

The major looked to the heavens for support. "Don't talk to me about Jameson!" he sighed.

"Now that we have found the wagons," David calmly continued, "we have a chance to bring a massive amount of stock into Bulawayo, which will surely improve the lot of the people here to some degree. And it will allow us to pull ourselves out of the dire financial situation we find ourselves in, a situation caused by no fault of our own."

Seward stood up and walked to the window behind his desk, staring out at the empty, dusty street, lined with neatly planted young trees. He stood silently in his deep-blue military tunic, his hands clasped behind his back, his three visitors sitting as still as possible. David stole a glance at Morris, who looked very concerned, but still risked raising an eyebrow at David. He did not know what the major was thinking.

"You have thirty wagons out there?" he asked again, turning on his heel to face the trio.

"Yes sir," David replied as Morris and Abe simply nodded in agreement.

"You Langbournes are crazy. Stark raving mad, I'd say. Whatever possessed you to bring thirty wagons up here all at once, and on your own?"

Morris and David simply shrugged, and Abe just smiled, he knew these brothers had a determination and courage that even the fiercest of the lions in Africa would admire.

"I would agree that the community is very miserable right now," Seward continued, "but there is a strong underlying sense of progress among the people here. To bring in enough wagons to fill ten trading stores would be a powerful show of determination. Give me one week to get every mule I can muster from the outlying districts, I'll probably be able to gather about three hundred of the beasts. I'll also supply you with five armed soldiers to protect your wagons on their journey. You depart from here at first light next Tuesday."

"With three hundred mules we would need two or three trips to recover the wagons…." Morris began.

Seward cut him off. "Don't push too far, Mr Langbourne. I don't want to know what or how or why, just get your wagons into Bulawayo as quickly as possible. You have 30 days. Any losses of our mules will be for your account. Understood?"

Morris' face was a picture as he tried to digest what he had been told. He could never really read the man's facial features and wasn't too sure whether Seward was being serious or not, because a period of thirty days would test the limits. Nevertheless, Morris nodded carefully at him. "Understood, sir," he said quietly.

At this point, the major ended the meeting abruptly. "Get going," he snapped.

The three men immediately stood up and thanked the major profusely, before leaving in somewhat of a hurry.

Major Seward walked out of his office and turned to an orderly who was stationed at a desk in the corridor. "Lieutenant, send a message to all the outposts in the district. I require every available donkey in the area within one week. I'll need them for thirty days."

"Yes sir," the Lieutenant obeyed without hesitation or question.

The major returned to the window in his office and stood silently with his hands behind his back once more as he watched the two young Langbourne brothers and their older, gangly friend walk down the street, talking and laughing between themselves.

"Mad buggers," Seward said quietly, shaking his head and chuckling quietly to himself, "mad, mad buggers."

CHAPTER EIGHTEEN
Traditions

AT PRECISELY FIVE o'clock every evening, Harry would signal the close of trade for the day. Every evening he would walk to the front of the shop and unhook his daily suit jacket from a wooden hanger, before slipping it on and straightening out the creases. After dusting off some imaginary specks of dust from his shoulders and lapels, he would step over to the door, bring himself up to his full height, lock his hands behind his back, and bellow at the top of his voice: "Time please, ladies and gentlemen!"

Those customers still remaining in the shop would respectfully finalise their transaction and leave, Harry nodding his appreciation for their custom with a broad smile and bidding them a good evening as they left. If a customer chose to dawdle and took too much time to depart, Harry would consult his wristwatch with exaggerated disdain, and, at exactly five minutes past five o'clock, he would shout even more loudly, dragging out the last syllable, "THE DOORS ARE NOW CLOS-I-I-ING!!!" and begin shutting the door.

Because of the lack of glass in the windows, this had the effect of dimming the interior of the building quite considerably, thus speeding up the wayward customer's departure. Still standing to attention by the front exit, Harry would open the door graciously to allow the customer to depart, again with his nod of gratitude, but somehow he had managed to perfect a sarcastic smile, which they could not mistake for anything else. Harry, in fact, was quite capable of mastering a sarcastic air about him which he used constantly to his advantage when it suited him, much to the annoyance of David, the humour of Louis, and the indifference of Morris. Although they were brothers, their characters could not have been more diverse.

Harry's closing ceremony had become more than a routine, it had become a tradition, and one that was known among many of Bulawayo's community. On one occasion, a mother brought her child into the store at closing time, simply to witness this classic end-of-day ritual.

When the last of the customers left, Harry would lock the door, bang on it twice with his fist, then shout to his brothers, "Thank you, Gentlemen!" as they finished up their various chores. Without fail, the salutation never failed to bring a smile to Morris, David and Louis, and Harry knew that. The day was therefore never considered complete without the performance of Harry's closing ceremony.

It had taken nine very long weeks to bring their thirty wagons into Bulawayo, the 30-day deadline having been totally ignored by both Morris and Major Seward. The quantity of mules which the BSAC administration had provided had been enough to create five teams at a time, so when David coordinated the recovery exercise together with Nguni, Daluxolo, and some Matabele herders, they had begun a relay of five wagons each, spaced one week apart. This meant that the five wagons would arrive in town once a week, during which time Louis and Harry would unpack the wagons as fast as possible, and Morris, who never forgot a price, set about coding the goods into their Black Rhino code. It was a

14-hour exercise for them, because – no sooner had the stock been sorted and coded – then the next wagonload would arrive, and the process would begin again. And to make matters worse, Morris insisted the shop remain open for trade during normal working hours.

Cracks started to show in the small family unit as tempers began to flare at the slightest incident. After only three weeks, the boys experienced a particularly tough day. It was the kind of hot, dry, and unrelenting summer day that Matabeleland would so often use to delight the population. With sweat stinging Harry's eyes, his hands slippery with grime, and Louis standing directly below, Harry dropped a container off the side of the wagon before Louis had been ready to receive it, catching his brother heavily on his chest, which had caused him to fumble the box and let it fall, crashing to the floor. The muffled sound of broken glass instantly escaped the confines of the container.

"Harry!" Louis scolded instantly, rubbing his chest vigorously, "wait for me to put one box down first, for Pete's sake! Now look what you have done," he waved irritably at the box on the floor.

"It slipped. I'm sorry."

"It's smashed."

"It's not my fault," Harry objected, "Don't blame me."

"You could have killed me if you had dropped it on my head. It hurts like hell," Louis was rubbing his chest with both hands now.

"It's not heavy; it's not going to kill you. Don't be such a cry-baby."

"Don't you call me a cry-baby, you idiot!"

"Hey!" Morris exploded from the warehouse door, "Stop this nonsense! What's going on here?"

"Harry threw a box at me and nearly killed me."

"Talk rubbish! It slipped. I said I'm sorry."

"What's the number on the box?" Morris demanded, uninterested in whether or not Louis was hurt.

Louis bent down and turned the carton on its side exposing

a hand-written code, while a tinkle of glass was heard dimly from inside. "G15," Louis mumbled angrily.

"Oh, lovely," Morris sarcastically looked at the heavens, "'G' stands for glass, and 'Box 15' is a set of twelve wine goblets for £1.20p each. You can bet they are all smashed. Who's going to pay for this now? I have a mind to deduct it from your wages."

Harry stood tall on top of the wagon and put his hands on his hips. "What wages?" he demanded. "You have never paid us a penny since we've been here!"

"*When* we make some money, *then* you will be paid; we have discussed this already," Morris shot at his brother. "Now, you have taken a week to unload three wagons, and still have two wagons to go, with five more arriving tomorrow, so you boys are getting very behind. Stop arguing and shake a leg!"

"We could use some help, Morris," Louis sounded dejected, "or we need to tell David to slow down. The wagons are coming at us too fast."

"How can I pay for help if I can't pay you? I'm busy in there signing up wagon traders, loading their purchases, serving customers, coding stock, and keeping the books," Morris flashed an angry glare at his siblings. "You want to swop with me?" he paused very briefly. "No, I thought not. We've only had three weeks of these wagons, and have at least another six weeks to go, so stop griping. Now hurry up, and don't ruin any more of our stock!" Morris spat, then turned on his heel and stormed inside again, a very dark and threatening cloud hanging over his head.

Louis and Harry stood in silence, looking at the open door that their older brother had just vanished through. Louis shrugged, and, without another word, the boys continued to work.

There were many such days, but with each cool start to the morning, tempers were calm and enthusiasm was high. On some days, the boys' moods would remain cheerful; on others, they would degenerate into tiffs that hampered their progress. For nine long weeks they worked day and night, some nights only managing four or five hours of sleep. But they all knew it was for the family, and they never faltered.

David came into town a day ahead of the last lot of wagons, and immediately set about helping his brothers where he could. When the final wagon had been unloaded, it was well after eight o'clock at night. Louis carried the last box into the warehouse, proudly announcing that he held in his arms the very last of all the boxes. David and Morris, who were desperately trying to keep up with the flow of stock moving into the shop, paused, and gave a symbolic round of applause.

Only a minute behind him, Harry walked in, covered in dirt and sweat and his shirt torn on his right shoulder. He, too, received a round of applause from his siblings. Smiling, he took hold of the large iron handles of the wooden rear door of the warehouse and began to pull it shut.

"Doors close-i-i-ing," he sang out joyfully, and slammed the solid door shut with a loud bang. Then, as if testing that it was firmly locked in place, he thumped it twice with his clenched fist, and turned to face this three brothers. "Thank you, Gentlemen!" he called out, signalling the end of nine weeks' worth of sheer hard work. The Langbourne brothers burst into laughter, and, prompted by Morris, shook hands with one another in congratulations for a job well done.

And so it was that Harry began a tradition of signalling the end of a hard day's work.

*

One late afternoon in November of 1897, Morris extracted himself from his gloomy office and walked onto the warehouse floor. He didn't smile as he looked at the shelves and tables bursting with all their valuable stock. His mind was racing, overflowing with numbers, business strategies, contingencies and possibilities. David and Harry were busy straightening merchandise that customers had shifted, and Louis was graciously seeing three important-looking women out of the front door with their newly acquired purchases. No sooner had they exited the building, two other groups of customers entered, one lot being quickly greeted and attended by Louis again, with Harry rapidly approaching the others and caring to their custom.

Morris looked at his wristwatch and frowned. It had stopped as he had forgotten to wind it up that morning and it irritated him. "David," Morris called softly to his brother, jerking his head slightly to summons him.

David carefully put down the Eastern European lead-crystal brandy decanter he was dusting and walked over to Morris. "You look concerned," he ventured.

"Actually, no, not concerned at all. I was reviewing our accounts and our financial situation is in much better shape than I had imagined."

"Well, that's good to know," David smiled.

"Are you aware that with the chronic shortages this war created, we are about the only store in the country that has any stock to sell?"

"Yes, I know," David grinned. "We seem to have a reputation. Just today we had three customers who arrived from Fort Salisbury to buy from us. It's pretty dire up there. Even cash is in short supply."

"Well, here's the interesting thing," Morris ran his fingers through his hair and glanced around to make sure no one was in earshot. "Losing the wagons for a year has, oddly enough, worked very much in our favour. While we were busy looking for them, our competitors ran dry of stock, and prices around us went sky high. Now that we have found them, no one has stock, and we have 30 wagon loads of goods that we bought at very reduced prices more that 18 months ago."

"Which we are selling at current market prices," David interjected.

"Which are ridiculously high."

"So our profits must be very good."

Morris lowered his voice and stole another quick glance

about the shop. "I wouldn't say 'good', I think the word *obscene* is more appropriate."

David let a short laugh burst out, before quickly checking himself. "But our prices are no higher than the next man. In fact, I thought our prices were rather keen."

"Indeed they are, and that's another reason people are flocking in here. I project that within 6 months from now we will have paid off our debts in their entirety, and have made a healthy profit, enough to recoup the losses we incurred through both these Matabele rebellions."

David shook his head in amazement. What Morris was telling him was outstanding. "So," David paused as he now scanned the building for eavesdroppers, "what you are saying is that Langbourne Brothers, here in Bulawayo, is more profitable than our cigarette business ever was in Port Elizabeth?"

"Precisely!" Morris almost hissed.

David suddenly became pensive and a gentle frown crossed his forehead. "We would not be in this position today had not been for the total and unconditional loyalty of Nguni and Daluxolo for our family. You do know that?"

"Yes, I do." Morris looked humbled. "I have thought about that often; it even keeps me awake some nights. I don't know how we could ever reciprocate or thank them enough for what they did. One cannot put a price on loyalty, and this needs to be a lesson we must never forget."

"We must make a point of telling our children and grandchildren this story so that these two men are never forgotten.

"I agree," Morris said, nodding his head and looking towards the front door of the shop as the silhouettes of two gentlemen entered. The gangly gent who didn't remove his tacky felt hat was obviously Abe Kaufman, and the other, he correctly assumed, was Phil Innes, so Morris raised his hand to catch their attention and call them over.

"Something else," Morris whispered quickly as he took David

by the shoulder and began to walk towards the front of the shop to greet his friends, "the first £75 000 profit we make belongs to you and me, thereafter we will share equally with our brothers. I want to recover what we made in Port Elizabeth first. After all, it was the money you and I made, and risked, that got us to this point."

David nodded that he understood, but felt there might be some resistance from Louis and Harry to this scheme, however he also knew that they would not dare question their elder brother and mentor.

"Abe, Phil, so good to see you," Morris smiled and extended a warm handshake in their direction. Standing in the middle of their large warehouse, and almost swamped by all manner of exotic merchandise, the four men exchanged pleasantries.

"We are going down to the Charter Hotel to meet Herbert Bachmayer for a drink and a meal," Abe offered, then quickly removed his hat looking somewhat embarrassed. "We'd like to ask if you and your brothers would care to join us?"

"Delighted!" David didn't hesitate to accept the invitation.

"How's business, Phil?" Morris never wasted any time turning the conversation to important matters. "And the goldfields, Abe, still productive?" he continued in his usual manner of blasting out questions before any answers were forthcoming.

Phil quickly raised a hand to slow Morris' barrage down. "Indeed, business is booming, as is yours, it seems."

"Could be better, could be better," Morris shrugged in feigned resignation.

Suddenly a subtle but distinct click caught David's ear. It was Harry using a secret signal to catch his brother's attention. David acknowledged him, stole a glance at his wristwatch and then nodded his approval at Harry. "It's closing time," David stated.

"Oh! You have to watch this, Abe," Phil exclaimed excitedly, grabbing his slender friend by the shoulders and turning him to face the entrance to the warehouse. "He does this every evening!"

"What?" Abe was suddenly confused.

"Watch and see!"

As was his custom, Harry strode over to the doors, pulled on his jacket and pompously dusted off the shoulders and lapels, before clasping his hands behind his back, puffing out his chest and loudly bellowed: "Time please, ladies and gentlemen!"

"Good grief!" Abe wanted to laugh, but controlled himself. "I assume we have to vacate quick-as-sticks."

"No," David smiled, "stay a while, it gets better."

"When are you going to put glass in your windows, Morris?" Phil frowned with concern. "When Harry closes those doors it must get frightfully dark in here."

"Almost pitch black, yes. But we can't afford panes of glass yet," Morris lied. "Hideously expensive you know."

"You'll get more customers in here if the public could see into your shop, and see what stock you have, you know that, don't you?" Phil pressed.

"Our type of business doesn't need potential customers to see our merchandise. Our reputation and word of mouth do us proud," he defended.

Abe turned slightly and looked down at Morris. "There's a retail shop on Fife Street," he said slowly, "just around the corner from Sharon's dress shop. It became available for rent this morning. Apparently the rate is very acceptable, and almost the entire shop front is glass. The previous tenant is a friend of Sharon's. I can put in a good word for you if you like."

Morris suddenly looked at David, cocking one eyebrow. David shrugged slightly, and a very indiscernible smile caught the corners of his mouth. They held that stare for just long enough to understand exactly what the other was thinking, before Morris broke off their brotherly telepathic conversation, and quickly looked up at Abe.

"What a splendid suggestion, Abe!" he beamed. "Indeed, please do make an introduction for us."

Suddenly Harry's voice boomed across the warehouse. "THE DOORS ARE NOW CLOS-I-I-ING!!!" and with that he swung the heavy doors shut with a resounding boom, plunging the entire building into almost total darkness. Then, from within the depths of the silence, Harry clenched his fist and heavily pounded the wooden door twice.

"Thank you… Gentlemen!" he sang out to his brothers at the top of his voice.

A new and exciting era of Langbourne Brothers was about to begin.

MINUTES OF AN EXTRAORDINARY GENERAL MEETING

OF LANGBOURNE BROTHERS

Held at Langbourne Brothers, Abercorn Street, Bulawayo, Rhodesia.

On 8th June 1898 at 5:20pm

Present:

M Langbourne (Chairman)

D Langbourne (Secretary)

L Langbourne (Treasurer)

H Langbourne (Member)

Chairman's Address:

The Chairman welcomed those present to the meeting and expressed his gratitude for the help with the business.

ML confirmed that all debts to the business had been settled.

With the advent of international telegraph wires, and the arrival of a railway line, the company was ready to expand internationally.

The new retail store on Fife Street was performing exceptionally well under LL's management, and he was heartily congratulated.

HL to proceed to Johannesburg and command Langbourne Coetzee. DL to oversee Jbh and both Byo stores. DL tasked to reward Nguni and Daluxolo for their loyalty.

Dividend:

The first dividend of the business was unanimously approved and distributed equally between ML and DL.

Shareholders:

LL and HL invited to become equal shareholders of Langbourne Bros. They accepted and were warmly welcomed by ML & DL. Future dividends to be shared equally between ML, DL, LL and HL.

All matters were unanimously agreed upon.

There being no further business, the meeting closed at 5:26pm with a vote of thanks to the Chair.

Signed:

Secretary   Chairman/Treasurer

Acknowledgements

I'M VERY LUCKY to have a mentor in the form of Cindy Kramer in Cape Town. Not only does she give me the confidence that a new author desperately needs; she has a way of telling me where I am going wrong in such a manner that I can't help but agree with her at every turn. I am truly indebted to her.

I'd like to thank my editor, Mike Kantey in South Africa, who took on my manuscript with such enthusiasm and encouragement. I also thank Steve Landau and Nancy Wiseman in the USA for proof reading the final manuscript and for their valuable guidance. I once again thank and recognise John S Landau in the USA for openly sharing his memories of the Langbourne family, particularly of Morris, before their story was lost in the haze of history.

My deepest gratitude is extended to three people who came to my rescue whilst researching hotels in Bulawayo in the 1890s. Denise Taylor, Nick Baalbergen and Lewis Walter. In particular I'd like to thank Lewis Walter for sending me a copy of his 'Matabele Times and Mining Journal' (1894), and for giving me permission to place a copy of it on my website.

I would especially like to acknowledge the support and constant encouragement from a lovely woman called Sharon, who became my wife just before this book was released.

And to my readers, I truly hope you enjoyed this story as much as I enjoyed telling it.

Alan

ABOUT THE AUTHOR

Alan Landau *was born in Salisbury, Rhodesia (now Harare, Zimbabwe) in 1959. In 1978 he joined the British South Africa Police (formally the BSAC). At that time Rhodesia was entangled in a civil war that ended in 1980. After serving in the new Zimbabwe Republic Police for a short time, Alan retired to enter the commercial world.*

Alan worked in Zimbabwe's widely known tobacco industry for five years before joining his father and ultimately taking over the family business when his father retired to the UK. Later on, Alan was involved in the travel, tourism, hotel, property, financial, and retail sectors. His service to his community took the form of Rotary International with a committed focus on the Rotary Youth Exchange Program.

Having migrated to Brisbane, Australia, in 2001, Alan bought a franchise in the retail sector, which he successfully ran with his late wife and two children. In 2012 he sold the business and went into semi-retirement. He now pursues his hobbies of writing, travelling, wildlife safaris and ornithology with his wife, Sharon.

More about the author can be found as follows:
Web: www.landaubooks.com
Twitter: @landaubooks
Facebook: www.facebook.com/landaubooks
Instagram: landaubooks